Squirrel Haus

Squirrel Haus

Dustin Hellberg

ROUNDFIRE BOOKS

Winchester, UK
Washington, USA

First published by Roundfire Books, 2014
Roundfire Books is an imprint of John Hunt Publishing Ltd., Laurel House, Station Approach, Alresford, Hants, SO24 9JH, UK
office1@jhpbooks.net
www.johnhuntpublishing.com
www.roundfire-books.com

For distributor details and how to order please visit the 'Ordering' section on our website.

ISBN: 978 1 78279 026 6

A CIP catalogue record for this book is available from the British Library.

Design: Stuart Davies

Cover photograph copyright: Dustin Hellberg

Cover design: Yanyun Chen

Printed and bound by CPI Group (UK) Ltd, Croydon, CR0 4YY

For Brad Dacy and for Hillary Brown.

Says the day, I shall assemble you from the dust, and tell me what you believe, because you will have to say it quickly. No, really, I'm all ears it says. I shall assemble the dust from you, it says. Your skin recounted, noumenal, and again it says, and probably means it, but won't say exactly what it means. Nothing touches nothing if you look close enough, it says, just look at your shoddy housekeeping. It then asks about your motivations, to which you have no reply. Look close, it says: All is valence rejecting valence. All a'walk on an electric hum. Why tread lightly, it says. Some further assembly seems very required, it says. Go forth, it says, and find your debt. It says, I shall assemble debt from you, in your footfalls, and have you counted them because I have, it says. You have two billion four hundred thousand seconds on average, it says. Where are you, it says. Says and says. Self-consciousness is a bitch, now say something new, it says. It says all of this, and then says it all again as in its saying it says, and it says, and is, in the saying, only what it says.

sunt lacrimae rerum et mentem mortalia tangunt
Publius Vergilius Maro

Well, Art is Art, isn't it? Still, on the other hand,
water is water. And east is east and west is west
and if you take cranberries and stew them
like applesauce they taste much more like prunes
than rhubarb does. Now you tell me what you know.
Groucho Marx

Now remember, when things look bad
and it looks like you're not gonna make it,
then you gotta get mean. I mean plumb,
mad-dog mean. 'Cause if you lose your
head and you give up then you neither live
nor win. That's just the way it is.
Josey Wales

January

Mythos

The beauty, and the city mired in it,
lost in weeks old January snow, wears
its shadows like scrimshaw, ornate
in chiaroscuro. Narrow sidewalk,
marred by, packed by others' progress.

Because this seems to matter now.
Like the muddawbers' spent nest I cocooned
in my hand. It fell from above the portico
as I shut the door, and I turned my palm

down and returned it to the snow. As not a thing
religious, not political, but chimerical,
like a name, as glad a telling
of someone else's heaven, not to be the last.

***Soundtrack*:**

Townes van Zandt, *No Lonesome Tune*
The Pogues, *Fiesta*
Hank Williams III, *5 Shots of Whiskey*
Cat Power, *Metal Heart*
Wu Tang Clan, *Triumph*
R.L. Burnside, *The Criminal Inside Me*

I'll tell you what I don't know, and some of what I do: I stood in front of 933 Daniel Street, under some branches, tiny cobwebs interlaced in the needles belonging to the scrubby pine, the tree low-slung and untended, in the front yard which belonged to the house which belonged to the landlord who would be by later today to collect the rental deposit, almost all the money I had. Nothing much belonged to me. I rattled my pack of American Spirits, checking the contents by weight and measure, like a trench-bound infantryman checking ammo in a magazine. A year of dearth. No, years of dearth, and only two calloused hands by which to judge it, and, judging by the looseness of the material inside the shaken pack, only eight cigarettes. Just those small tools with which to measure and weigh the heft of my debits and credits, twenty-six years and change, which was not much more than I had in my wallet past the initial deposit money. Season of counting and recounting, making lists, lists of future vacations to take and places to live, and fine clothes to buy, lists of things that sounded good to eat, all meaning augmented and spun in the tangle of time and change, like words unmoored. Etymological season, and names less and less themselves with every mention. A season without vowels except what I chose to speak. I checked my watch. High noon, almost. January 20th, 2003.

Griffin rolled up with a wave in a weather-beaten Dakota, pumping his fist to "Going Back to Cali," tinny bass from cheap speakers. The truck looked rumpled, as if rolled repeatedly and slowly down a grassy embankment. He put it in first, the clutch slipping a little. Gears wrenched. A giant black dog was pacing in the bed, tongue out. A thick bead of saliva glinted in the weak afternoon sun. He got out, wasp-waisted and with his rugged looks, shoulders still broad like an Olympic swimmer and deeply tan. He let down the tailgate, pulled out a case of Budweiser, and walked over to where I had stood up, his smile wrapped around a cigarette, and big aviator sunglasses reflecting the world in each silvered lens. The dog followed him.

We clapped hands with violent admiration, too long, too long, and how many years, and another long hug. No hellos needed. I wrangled up my best drawl.

-Sounds like you done chose the wrong song there, Mr. Buch.

-Yeah, I wrote a new one on the way out here. I'm running running, away way, from Cali Cali, he said laughing with a little dance thrown in.

-Sun-ripened Jesus, Griffin, it is good to see you again, I said.

Griffin made the sign of the cross while lighting a second smoke and handed me a beer.

-I know, he said. Iowa. Can you believe it? I haven't even set foot in this state in five years.

-Wasn't there a bench warrant out for you here?

He nodded, sipping from the can between the two cigarettes.

-Those fucking cops, so they get me with a ticket for underage drinking a day before my birthday.

-I know, I remember. What time was it again when they got you? I asked.

Griffin shook his head, eyes rolling, Twenty-three minutes till I was twenty-one. Cop wouldn't let me off. Just like Cinderella.

-So, how was California? I asked. You never sent me a postcard.

-I never had any idea where you were living, he said.

The giant dog nuzzled my hand and bit at the air.

-Pickle wants to say hello, Griffin said.

I was formally introduced to the dog, Pickle. Half rott, half mastiff. He had the broad, thick body of a rott, and with the mixed breeding, stood hip high. At least a hundred and forty pounds. He slobbered incessantly. I patted him on the head roughly, tussling his thick coat, which brought on another round of joyful slobber and a shake of his jowls which flung the excess slaver. Griffin told me he got Pickle from the pound in Placerville, and the first night he had him, Pickle had growled at Griffin's girlfriend, so he took a table leg and gave the dog a blunt-trauma lobotomy. After a few whacks, Pickle never again snapped at anyone except addicts, *loadies* Griffin called them, and people in uniforms. He'd chosen the name because that was the only thing the dog seemed to respond to. Pickle later chewed the table leg in half.

-So, can we go inside? Griffin asked.

I twirled the keys on my finger. The old tenants gave me the keys already, I said.

I gave Pickle another pat to the head, and we three went inside. The front door opened to the kitchen, large enough to accommodate a dining set. To the right was the living room, which led to one of the bedrooms. Straight through the kitchen and up a single stair was a narrow hallway, with a bathroom on the left, the anterior bedroom just behind, up one more step, and a closet on the right. The back bedroom accessed the back door and the cellar stairs. We opened fresh beers in the kitchen, shaking our heads at the weird crossroads-gravity of time and place and plot.

-So tell me about the swimming pools and movie stars, I said. You see any celebrities or any crazy poolside drug parties?

-I got flipped off by Michael Keaton one time because my car stalled at an intersection and he got around me in his Porsche, but that was about as much celebrity contact as I had, he said. I would describe the rest of my experience as dead broke in a very hot place.

-Yeah? Broke under a hot tin roof? I said.

Griffin nodded

-Coachella Valley has about 367 days of sun a year, he said, and I saw it get up to 128 one day. Lucky for me, most of the plumbing work I did was indoors. Toward the end, Pickle and I were living in unfinished houses for months after I got kicked out.

-Layna kicked you out?

-Yeah, he looked down at Pickle for a moment. You still

writing?

-Not a lot. Not much since grad school. But there's at least one good thing I just realized.

-What's that? he asked.

-You haven't used the word hella once.

-Yeah, well you haven't tried quoting some poignant pretty poem yet, college boy.

-Let's make a deal, valley boy, I said. You can't use the word hella, and I won't recite you any poems. Deal?

He rubbed his chin and pulled at long imaginary hairs of wisdom.

-Poetry gets you laid, though, he said.

-Deal?

-Deal, he said. First you get the poems, theen you get the power, theen you get the weemen.

Griffin stubbed out his cigarette and giggled. Hella lotta women, he said. So, why did you run away from Utah? Mormons oppressing the white man out there?

-You might say that Mormonia was the extent of my Manifest Destiny, I said.

Griffin rolled his eyes. I'm serious, he said. There has to be some reason.

-I don't know. I had two teaching jobs. Was living with this girl. Was about to get married. Probably about to get a real college job. I just left. I just put the ring I'd gotten her on the counter, packed all my stuff and lit out.

I paused to light a cigarette, and handed one to him. He lit it, and looked at me, You think we can smoke in here?

-I certainly don't think it will hurt the décor.

-Got her a ring and everything, huh, he said. What happened, she have an abortion or something? You cheat on her?

-Things were good, I said. She loved me. But it was all generically happy, but it was like I was living someone else's life. Her apartment, her lease, her yard. I don't know. Does a man need a reason to destroy himself, Griffin?

Griffin ruffled Pickle's head, Nope, he said. I know I never have. We're men of action, he said with a tone and a smile, raising his fist in the air. And we cannot be shackled by the womanflesh.

We cracked more beers and walked the house. Each room and partition received a name to mark it as ours. The back bedroom was *The Dais*. The other bedroom dubbed *Waterworld*, its walls and floor a filmy blue. I had offered *Costner's Farrago*, which was roundly rejected as too highbrow. The pisser and kitchen respectively were left as the *Pisser* and *Kitchen*. No need to elaborate on everything. The living room became the *Harem* because of the utterly random arched doorway leading into it. Not a rounded arch, but pointed, the inverted, bastard offspring of a U and a V, though the craftsmanship wasn't bad, which made it seem at odds with the flophouse feng shui that years of landlord disrepair had wrought, the house's frankensteined assemblage of bits of other houses. Mismatched countertops, jerry-rigged toilet, doors that didn't fit their frames and wouldn't shut.

-This place would drive your brother crazy, Griffin said. How is Zeke?

-He's good. Got a baby now. His carpentry company is starting to take off. How's your brother?

-Kell's good. Out in Arizona fighting fires. He might come visit at some point.

-It would be great to see him, I said. But I think we should fix the place up before we have too many guests over.

The place was, like most low-cost rentals, a shabby fractal. The closer you zoomed in anywhere, the more the decrepit pall revealed itself. Cracked and discolored slats on the venetian blinds, holes in one wall covered over by last year's calendar, a hole in the screen door, a few of the windows wouldn't open. The previous tenants had paid the rent through January, I explained to Griffin, and had been anxious to move 'somewhere a little closer' to the downtown area. I thought nothing of their desires or motives, but they had struck me as perhaps a little too eager to please, too eager to get out. But we wouldn't pay rent until February, and would have a phone until then, too. I chalked it up to the kindness of strangers, Midwesternly hospitality. The apartment was in rough shape, but it was better than sleeping in my van under a mound of down comforters and loose clothing scattered like leaves, or bouncing around town from couch to couch, girl to ex-girlfriend, stealing scraps of food. Griffin uttered his words loud, and slow, shaking his head, What . A. Shithole.

The kitchen carpet was two large sections that joined in a ratty seam in the middle of the room, half blue and half brown Berber, faded the color of deep bruises. Griffin picked at the seam with the toe of his boot. A four-foot section of linoleum had been tacked to the walls to act like wainscoting, running the entire length of the kitchen. The basement was wet and smelled like a soup-kitchen sponge, even in the yet-snowless January. An old-style breaker box, with the twist-out replaceable fuses, had been nailed to a support beam which stood in a large pool of water. The Bilge. How this place was legally rentable or hadn't yet immolated someone or collapsed on them, I couldn't figure out. Back up the cellar stairs, hanging on the wall, near the landing and the rear door was an abortive attempt at abstract art, and in an exquisite frame. I took the shitty painting off the wall, and we walked into the kitchen.

Adjoining the kitchen, next to the bathroom, sat a closet, moldering, the drywall pocked and swollen with moisture. I pushed at some of the material and it flaked and fell in clumps.

-Christ, look at this Heart of Darkness, I said. We're going to have to seal it off as a biohazard.

-We should get some Killz and try to block in the mold, he said. God, I have got to get some rental properties here. Can you believe they're allowed to make money off this place? It's like Bob Vila raped a slum and then aborted it on the lawn.

The problem with Heart of Darkness was simple. The foundation of the rear addition hadn't been deep enough, and now the whole tail-end of the house was ripping itself free like a rogue glacier, riding out into the rear lawn. The weak grey daylight was visible through a large crack in the rear of the closet, exposing the bricks of an old chimney, and I poked a wire hanger through it. I slid the closet door shut, and we decided it was something to take up with the landlord. He would be by soon with the lease. Griffin walked out to his truck to get some of his belongings.

We flipped a coin for the rooms. I got the Dais, and Griffin got the larger Waterworld. We took turns helping each other lug our few possessions into the house. I had a stereo on loan from my brother with a hundred CD changer, and a Playstation 2 I had forgotten to return to a Blockbuster in Utah for which they had charged my credit card, maxing it, and so straight out the White Elephant's window where I tossed it onto the wet highway when I left Salt Lake. Griffin had a TV and a VCR. I had a lot of books and stacks of CDs. His parents had given him various pots and pans and cutlery. I had a nice steak knife and some unmatched chopsticks and a bowl. Neither of us had any furniture except sleeping bags and thin blankets, so we piled those in the living room and Pickle promptly nestled there, licking his front paws. There were a number of folding chairs in the basement, and we set them in the Harem, plugged in the TV and stereo, ran all the cables from connection to connection, wire to wire. Griffin put on a Rolling Stones CD and set about unpacking in Waterworld.

Boxes were dumped and their contents spread, photos shared and commented on. Griffin had a nice Walther PPK 9mm, and we decided to go shooting soon. I shuffled back toward my room to see if I had any random bullets among my trifles. I could hear Pickle sniffing and whimpering in the bathroom, scratching his nails on the linoleum. I went in to see what the rumpus was. His nose was pointed at the bathtub, his paws working furtively at the caulking along the floor. I calmed his insistent whining and listened at the tub. There was a scuffle, and scratching underneath the floor. I could hear animals scurrying, tiny claws at work, a nervousness below. I walked outside to examine the exterior. Below the bathroom window on the side of the house, about three feet up from the foundation, was a small hole chewed through the pulpy wood siding. I couldn't see into it, and even when I brought back a flashlight and pulled loose some of the rotting wood, peering into the cavity, nothing visible down into the house, the smell there of wet wood and animals. Rats, I guessed, maybe mice. I heard some chittering and saw the flash of a bushy tail. I walked back inside and tried to speak over the music, It would seem we've got ourselves a Squirrel House. Hey, Griffin! Squirrel Haus!

He hadn't heard me. He was still in his new room, throwing clothes on the floor. Books, some old pictures of us in high school, a wooden shoe, little treasures that moor the dispossessed to places and people past, all coming out of his boxes. He walked into the kitchen with another box, unloading some utensils, a hunting knife, a miniature leather riding crop. Then he held up a framed picture, summarily walked to the sink, lifted it and smashed it twice into the basin in a ceremonious fashion, tone sarcastic.

-The bitch that ruined my life.

The frame came down a final time.

-Don't worry, he said. I'll clean up the glass before the landlord gets here, he said and gave me a reassuring nod as he poured in some lighter fluid followed by a match. It whooshed aflame and burned down.

-I'm not worried, I said. We'll just tell him your glass eye fell into the sink, I said. What happened? Between you and her.

-Same old shit you hear in any country song on work radio. Too much time around me, yet never enough. She got sick of living in a shitty apartment, working a shitty job, having a shitty boyfriend. Wanted more. Wanted babies. Wanted me to not drink so much. Wanted the pretty, pretty moon, too.

-You guys were together for five years, right?

Griffin looked in the sink and nodded at the smoldering mess. Almost six, he said.

-You didn't want to get married?

-I was going to, he said. She talked about it a lot, but you know how it is, you never want to get married when you're poor, but without a decent job you can't make any money, and bills and gas and rent and smokes and beer. Same old wheel of misfortune. You know how it is. I was going to ask her, though.

-She wouldn't wait? Where's she now?

-Living in San Francisco with her mother, he said. I talked to her before I came back here. She said she might come out and visit. I don't know. Seriously, D, when is the last time we even saw each other?

-No idea, I shrugged. But I'm definitely going to buy one of those Chicken Soup books and get my life on track.

Griffin walked outside, swept his hand at the passing clouds and celestial spheres beyond, as if about to make a proclamation to a crowd of medieval peasants.

-Yeah, that's a good idea, he said through the door. I am going to take up astrology and reading tea leaves, set up a 900-number psychic hotline.

-What do you see in my future?

-Are you an organ donor?

I joined him outside.

-I hate recycling, I said.

-Let's get some patchouli and crystals downtown. We'll have a séance.

We laughed, hoisting the cans together.

-Wonder Twin powers, activate.

-Touché.

-Touché.

Downing them, we cracked more beers, musing on the myriad these and those along the years apart. We talked family and gossip and the weather, and went back inside.

-It's kind of weird, isn't it? he said, that we haven't talked in what, five or six years, but here we are. And living together.

-Plenty of time to catch up.

-At least we won't have to repeat stories back and forth, he said.

-Touché. Oh, I said, what do you want to do about the squirrels in the wall?

Griffin fiddled in the sink, suddenly wagging his hand, a trickle of blood on his finger.

-Goddamn glass. Squirrels in the wall. Is that some sort of metaphor? I thought we talked about this poetry shit.

-They're nesting in the wall cavity and below the tub. Pickle bird-dogged them. We are living in a literal Squirrel Haus, complete with nature's own glory hole.

I made sure to spell haus again. The bathroom was quiet, and we stomped the linoleum. We walked outside and checked the exterior wall. Griffin poked at the rotten wood smudging a droplet of blood on the orangey siding.

-Can we scare them out and tack a board over the hole? he asked.

-Probably, or maybe some wire screen stapled over it. They might chew through the wood again. I mean, this is some prime real estate for rodents. That's all we need is a case of the Hanta Virus.

-Hanta comes from mice. Squirrel Haus. I love it. Hey, check this out, he said and gestured toward the front of the house.

He walked me back into his room and pulled a small wooden placard from one of his few boxes. On it, a squirrel was standing on its hind legs, engraved with skill, and the creature had been painted a bright red. The animal was holding an acorn in its front paws and the grooves of the rendering had been scorched black into the wood. Griffin nodded at the plaque.

-How's that for prophetic? I got this from my uncle who died a month ago. That's where I got all those pots and pans.

-Mom's brother or dad's? I asked.

-Dad's.

-Fuck, I'm sorry. Were you close to him?

-Not really, but he was a nice enough guy. But are you ready for the big surprise?

He grinned widely, and again told me to follow him. We walked to his truck, and in the bed he lifted a blue tarp, revealing a treasure I hadn't seen in years. It was the stuffed head of Diomedes the Deer. Griffin had procured it at a garage sale for ten dollars while we were in high school, and Diomedes had traded hands from friend to friend several times. Griffin explained that he had gotten it back from Brom, who'd had it from Saul, and Jeremy before him, and that from Noel, when Griffin had lost it in a card game to another friend, Kermit. The giant circle of possession now finally come around.

-Holy hell, I said. I assumed he'd ascended back to his home on Olympus.

-When Brom found out I was moving back he told me he had a little surprise waiting. I swung by his place when I got to Iowa, and there he was. Free of charge.

-Brom had it? That cocksucker never told me about it. I tried calling him a few days ago, but couldn't get a hold of him. Is he still doing the paramedic thing?

-Yup, Griffin continued. The guy's like Cage in *Bringing Out the Dead*. He gives a whole new meaning to the word danger pay.

-Danger pay?

-Paid for putting the people he's helping in danger.

I carried Diomedes inside, a trophy of earlier days, and harbinger. His fur was ripping loose in a few places near the mounting board, and one ear had been chewed off, but overall, he was in fine condition considering his age, and who'd had him over the years. His rack was mostly intact, with just one of his eight points broken off, but that was the way of a wandering warrior. Battle scars standard. I got my toolbox from the White Elephant and busied myself gluing the seams of fur back down against the wood and wire frame underneath.

-Who the hell gave him that name? I asked.

-Diomedes? No clue. Someone just started calling him that when I was living in that apartment by the Mississippi.

-That place over the bar?

Griffin handed me a stapler.

-Yeah, that place above The Blues Shop, he said.

-He's in pretty good shape considering who's had him.

-Diomedes the Godslayer, Griffin nodded. We'll mount him outside above the door for all to see and marvel at. The neighbors will leave gifts of myrrh and virgin's blood at our door for fear of his divine retribution or some bullshit. Hell, maybe they'll leave some virgins while they're at it. You're sure you didn't give him that name? It sounds like you.

-I'm pretty sure, I said. It's hard to say with the mind-fugue we went through in high school.

There was a divot in the deer's lip and Griffin worked his smoldering cigarette into the hole, and flipped the cherry into the sink. We fixed a screw into his left hoof and mounted a spent beer can there. We would have to find some longer wood screws and build a brace to hold the weight above the door, especially in the half-rotted siding. We drove to the hardware store a few blocks away and bought long wood screws, staples for Griffin's hammer tack, some plastic sheeting, and procured some scrap plywood from a guy in the lumber department who said to take whatever we wanted from the discards. A pretty girl in a blue smock stood smoking outside in the small lumberyard, her blonde hair sifting in the cool air. She looked at us, and I smiled. She dropped her smoke and went back inside.

When we returned home, we decided to put away the tools for a while. Griffin was sick of tools, and the reminders of labor. We pocketed a few beers and walked down the street to the park, a block away, and threw around his faded, red Discraft, enjoying the relatively good weather. Griffin remarked how odd it was to be throwing a Frisbee in January. Pickle watched, panting, head tracking the flight of the disc back and forth. The landlord would be by at some point, so we trekked back to the apartment. Along the way, I saw something lying in the gutter, matted and squat like a flattened raccoon. I stopped and turned the mass over with a stick. No dead animal, but a real fur bombardier hat, too dirty to wear, but not too dirty a helm, I figured, for Diomedes.

Back at 933 again, I brushed the dirt and leaves and offal from the hat into the yard. Griffin found some flat white primer in the basement and some brushes and brought the deer head outside on the stoop. He painted a 9 and two 3's on the mounting board below Diomedes' neck. A thin white line dribbled down from the 9 and onto the cement steps.

-Oh, shit, I almost forgot, he said.

Griffin handed me a wad of bills, half for the deposit. $250. I didn't count it.

-Christ, thanks. I need to get a job, pronto. That deposit cleaned me out. This is all the money I've got.

-It's all I've got too, old friend, he said.

He laughed loudly and walked inside, procuring another beer from the fridge.

-What do you want to do about the squirrels? Smoke them out?

-We could get some shaved rubber and light it on fire, and put it in the hole.

-That's all we need is a tire fire in our first week. I was thinking we keep them. Like mascots. We can train them to dance and play pinochle, take them down to the Pedmall and entertain the hippies.

He hooted some circus music and took a long drag of his cigarette.

-We'll just take it up with the landlord, I said.

-You know, D, Squirrel Haus is pretty appropriate a name. I've seen shopping cart tents in better shape than this down on Skid Row in LA.

Once the homefront trenches were secured and our few belongings unpacked, we checked the time and decided that we could risk a brief supply run. We put Pickle in the basement, and locked the door. It was strange to lock my own door. It had been years. Griffin drove us to the supermarket and we bought some essentials. Three cases of beer, vitamins, steak, carrots, a small potted fig tree, and two cartons of American Spirits. Griffin constantly made comments on the prices of this item and that in comparison to California. Elle had done most of the shopping in Utah, so I couldn't have offered a running commentary on the skyrocketing costs of asparagus or condoms.

We returned and set the case of beer between us on the little cement stoop, reveling in having, finally, a refuge, a place to come home to. A while later, a blue Dodge 3000 pulled up in front of the house. There was a lawnmower in the back, and some orange cones. I gestured with my can at the truck.

-Maybe this is the landlord. He said he'd be by around 4:30. At least he's punctual.

The thing that half stepped, half fell out of the truck looked barely human. The truck's suspension kicked, the leaf springs creaking, as he finally shifted his weight out of the cab to his feet, standing fully erect with obvious difficulty. He was around six and half feet tall, and must have weighed close to 400 pounds. His upper body was disproportionally monstrous compared to his legs, like a wrecking ball balanced on two unicycles. As if some Great Hand had grabbed his lower half and squeezed the contents like a toothpaste tube, forcing everything up into his massive torso. Under his breath Griffin muttered to me.

-Holy shit, look at that fat bastard. Like a Nordic Andre the Giant.

-Bit by a radioactive hippo, I said.

The Fat Bastard waddled over to us, his knees shot from having to move that great bulk around year after year, and I could tell by the slightly side-shifted posture that his back must be just as bad. He was out of breath by the time his forty-foot journey was over. Short rachitic wheezes as if his lungs were full of pulp. I looked at his hands, baseball mitts with the web and lashes all cut loose. Bear paws. His thin, long, blonde-grey mane of hair blowing, and his equally colored beard jutting. It was warm, but only warm for January, and this beast was wearing just a button-up shirt with the top three buttons unfastened, sweating in the thirty-eight degree weather. He kept pushing his large wire-rimmed glasses that were big, even for Kim Jung Il, back up the bridge of his wet nose. Griffin was holding Pickle by his collar. Pickle didn't like this huge man, and the dog had his tongue set half-back in his mouth and a low growl caught in his throat.

-Hey, boys, you must be the new tenants. Keep a hand on that dog, right? Wheeze wheeze.

-He doesn't bite, Griffin said.

Griffin shook with Fat Bastard, his hand disappearing into the mammoth paw. The same with mine.

-Yessir, I'm Griffin and this is Dunham. And this beast is Pickle.

-I'm Dan O'Finn. I manage the place. I manage about 200 units in the area. Wheeze wheeze. Griffin and Dunham. Sounds like a law firm.

-200 units? Must keep you busy, Griffin said.

-Lot of driving, lot of paperwork. I spend way too much time in the truck. No time to exercise, and the paperwork will make you nuts. Wheeze. The company who owns the properties is out in Arizona. Wheeze wheeze.

Though he'd had a moment to catch his breath from, well, walking, he seemed perpetually about to topple over in a wave of vertiginous breathlessness. We walked inside.

-Well, let's take a look at the place. You already met the former tenants?

-Yeah, I met them yesterday. They gave me the keys. There was only the one set, though, do you have another, I asked.

-I've only got my set. You can get another set made at the hardware store. Wheeze

-If we make a new set, can we take it out of the rent, Griffin chimed.

He ignored the question. He was looking at Diomedes sitting on the kitchen counter.

-You boys hunters, too?

-No, we're pacifists. That's a family heirloom. In Griffin's family for generations. It's from the Civil War.

-Yes, Griffin cut in, it belonged to my great-great Uncle Beauregard.

-Hm, yeah, Fat Bastard shrugged. It looks pretty beat up.

We walked around the place and did the rental dance. Fat Bastard tried hard to gloss over the Heart of Darkness, saying that he tried every gosh darned thing there was to do. I offered to fix it for him for a reduction in the first month's rent, to which he agreed after I rattled off enough carpentry and construction vocabulary, and informed him that Griffin was a certified journeyman plumber. I also said that if we weren't able to fix it, we would be calling him. He asked whether we had lived around Iowa City before. I told him I was moving back from Texas, and Griffin was back from shrimping in Alaska. Griffin said we were going to write a memoir about our experiences called *Tears for Steers* or else *Two if by Shrimp* and we needed a quiet place to write. Fat Bastard said Iowa City was full of writers. He laughed a little croaking laugh, and then started coughing. He turned to me.

-Did you go to school here? Cough wheeze.

-No, Texas, I lied. I studied accounting.

-I almost had a scholarship there. Wheeze wheeze. For wrestling, but I went here.

-You wrestled for Iowa? Griffin asked.

-Yeah, I made nationals back in '73. Wheeze.

-Back in the Days of Gable, eh? What weight class?

- Wheeze. I was heavyweight. You ever wrestle? he asked me, looking me up and down, eyes amplified in the giant lenses.

-Not me. Boxing's my thing. Griffin, you wrestled, right?

Griffin set in to a story about trying to become a pro-wrestler in California, saying he had been jettisoned from a semi-pro league because he refused to take a dive and had to flee the retribution of the wrestling cartel. Fat Bastard blinked at the story and then looked at the burnt remains of the picture frame in the sink. I tried to segue into other avenues of talk. I didn't want him to think we were crazy, inveterate liars, at least not until we signed the lease.

-Yeah, we're Iowa boys, I said, moving back to write a memoir. Just need a good place to settle down in.

-Well, the place isn't the greatest, but it'll do. Anymore, cheap rentals are hard to find. This is one of the cheapest I've got. Wheeze wheeze.

-You've got cheaper places? Griffin asked.

-Why? Wheeze. Are you interested?

-No, no. This is fine, he said. But there are some squirrels living in the wall. We're not sure what to do about them.

-Well, try something and if it doesn't work let me know. Wheeze. Oh, before I forget to mention it, someone will be moving in upstairs in a few weeks. She just signed her lease, but needs to pack her stuff at the halfway house and so on. Wheeze.

-She? She a looker? I inquired. What did she do to land in a halfway house?

Fat Bastard shook his head smiling, trying to breathe.

-I have to admit, she's damn good-looking for forty or so. Black lady. I don't know why she's at a halfway house. Not my business. Section 8, government rent. Wheeze wheeze. Steady check.

-That's good to hear, Griffin said. It's always nice to have good-looking women above you. I like them dark-skinned.

Fat Bastard was writing something in a notebook, and slid it into his shirt pocket. I looked down at the carpet. Fat Bastard had tracked in a daub of white paint, fallen from Diomedes' mounting board. I took a step to my left, trying to draw his view. The giant looked at me.

-Not me. Nothing against blacks, but not my thing, he said.

-Some of my best friends are attractive, Griffin said. You married, Dan? Any kids?

-Yeah, twenty-two years, and got two kids. A girl and a boy. Thirteen and fifteen. Pains in the ass. You know how teens are, he shook his head. Wheeze.

-Who's older?

He didn't answer, scratching his mark on the various lease copies, and sliding them across the counter toward us. We signed ours. He was looking at his watch and his cell phone rang. He rifled the device from his shirt pocket, barely able to cram his fingers in. Listening, he pulled out a notebook and wrote something down, and was shaking his head, muttering and wheezing and sweating, and he replaced the booklet. A great sloth titan with spindle legs, he dialed and put the phone to his ear. He slouched his ponderous gait toward the door and pointed at Pickle.

-Something came up and I have to go. Oh, by the way, that dog, you can't have it in the house. He'll have to stay outside.

Fat Bastard made his way across the yard, muttering into the phone about a lawyer and a court date, got in his truck and drove off. He waved without looking at us. His truck loped down the block, the cab leaning noticeably to the left, and rounded the corner. Griffin put Pickle inside. I looked at the lease, the first time my name had been on any official document in years, aside from the odd speeding ticket and the adjunct payroll checks I'd exchange at the Quick Money cashing place, standing in line in my cheap tie between the Navajos in their flannel and the teen mothers holding bawling infants. It was quiet outside, no cars, and the wind swept some leaves along the concrete. We sat down on the stoop reviewing the document. I handed Griffin a beer.

-Holy Christ, I thought he was going to have a heart attack.

-Fibrillatin' Dan O'Finn, he said and laughed. It would make a good pro-wrestling name.

-Imagine Brom's skinny ass having to give him mouth to mouth. You'd have to trampoline on his chest to get his heart pumping.

Griffin handed over the lease to me.

-Hey, look at this. We didn't initial the part here about the house being in satisfactory condition. Fat Bastard forgot about it on our copy. Did you initial on his?

I shook my head.

-I don't think so.

-Good, he said.

-And we can work off the next month's rent just repairing the place. I bet we could get out of the whole month's rent. We might not have to pay until March.

Griffin touched the side of his nose, then pointed at me.

-Hell, he said, the shape this place is in, we could live in it for a year and keep fixing it up. No rent. Now I can finally afford to get Pickle a Valentine's Day present.

Pickle, hearing his name, was whining at the door and thrust his giant maw through the hole in the screen, working it through until his head emerged like a mounted animal on a wall, panting.

Griffin grabbed Pickle's jowls, pulling them out and shaking his massive dog head. Pickle grunted, and affectionately coated everything with drool, head protruding in slapstick gimmickry.

-That's what you get, you dumb mutt. Go on, pull your head out, Griffin said with a teasing tone.

Pickle was panicking now, especially since we weren't helping him extricate his huge head. With a nervous heave back he pulled into the screen, his ruff a piled mass at his neck. He yelped. It was the old kind of screen, steel mesh, with long stilettos of wire at the frayed edges of the hole. He yelped again and bound forward, ripping the hinge plates loose from the soft wood of the doorframe. I caught the door as it fell, Pickle's head still stuck. Griffin ripped gingerly at the screen, pulling it wide enough for Pickle to escape. I leaned the door against the house. The dog happily nudged Griffin's thigh with his nose, shaking his black frame which shuddered and trammeled like a wild boar. Griffin happily smacked him across the head and ruffled Pickle's ears.

-You dumb dog. We've been here a few hours and you've already wrecked the place. Repent for what you've done.

Pickle licked his hand and Griffin took the wet drool, made the sign of the cross and touched his thumb to Pickle's head.

-In nomine Pickli, et filii, et spiritus sancti, he intoned.

-It's no problem, I said. We can add it to our list of repairs for Fat Bastard. We'll tell him the goshdarndest thing happened. The screen door just fell off. We came home and there it was.

-God willed it so, Griffin said with a nod, and it was good.

-When's the last time your folks dragged you to church? I asked.

-The spirit is strong in them, he said, but I haven't gone for ten years or so.

-Amen, said I.

-Last time I went in high school, my mom started speaking in tongues. That was it for me.

He aped the babble, and we laughed and drank, and smoke

and talked. We were roommates now, and there would be plenty to do in the coming days. Plenty of new tongues in which to do commerce and to speak the Word. We knew that it would be important to revel in the downtime, before the onus of jobs, debt, rent and responsibility would settle back down on our heads, before the cur-packs of creditors caught our scent and hunted us down like scared, woodland animals fleeing bugle and blood-hound and bullets. We plugged in a cordless phone I had and called all the numbers we could think of.

Griffin and I talked that night about ways to make money that wouldn't require the ruination of spines and knees. The need for jobs was looming now, and talk was the only alleviation to the gathering realization. We were going to invest in a copper beer vat, and we drummed up names of our future *Squirrelen Haeuse Brauerei*: Commie Red Ale, White Man's Burden Pale Ale, Bubonic Stout, Old Swill Pilsner. We drew the labels and set up our marketing strategies. We would brew it in the Bilge to get that authentic monkish taste of mold and gangrene, and make a mascot of Diomedes to capture that essential fifteen to eighteen male and female high-school dropout river-rat demographic. Another idea was to sell drugs. We wouldn't need marketing. We'd just sell it to friends and friends of friends. We had plenty of acquaintances in the trade with connections, and Iowa City was not known much for turf wars or drive-bys. We put the idea off. No use setting ourselves up to go to jail yet. I would go to the library soon and check the internet for jobs.

The weather turned sharper the next few days, in accordance with the season, cold and dry. Overcast. The windows frosted opaque against the opaque heavens. We set about fixing the place, and it was in great need of attention, starved for repair by the typical greedy jackal-landlords that populate college towns and prey on the weak and the students and the poor alike. We made several trips to the hardware store and I managed to catch the eye of the young blonde whom I had seen smoking outside. She was working the check-out, and her line was the fullest, so we took another, but I caught her intentionally not looking at me, at least twice.

We set to the Heart of Darkness with expanding foam, silicon sealant, some Killz, and sheets of plastic, hoping it would at least stop any leaks and the persistent draft that issued. We kept all our receipts to show Fat Bastard. We drove around the next day, finding the various household articles left on curbs. Near-wrecked lawn chairs, a ratty recliner that we decided against taking, a coffee table missing one of its glass panes, a smaller wooden table. The house was slowly looking more house-like. We named the fig tree Figworth. Figworth, esq.

Misha stopped by the next day, bringing little handmade soaps, individually wrapped and ribboned. She shook her head when I explained the necessity of Figworth, Esquire. She told me I should be more careful with my money, just like she had back in grad school. I would never be able to convince her of Figworth's morale-boosting powers. Griffin made her laugh with a story about us from high school. She declined our rum and beer proffering, saying that she had a law review article to work on that evening. There was a strange finality in her eyes that day, and when she hugged me goodbye her hips held stiffly away from mine. A letting go. Finally. I felt it in my heart, even where it swam out there in the black Oort. She left, and I wondered whether I would ever see her again. I resigned myself against the thought, and opened a beer, walked into the bathroom and washed my hands with the nice soap.

-What's the story with her? Griffin called from the kitchen.

I walked out, toweling my hand on my shirt, and leaned on the jamb near Heart of Darkness.

-She's the one I left to go to Utah to live with the ballerina.

-Then why on earth is she still talking to you? Griffin said. You got some golden cock in your drawers there?

-I don't know. I don't deserve it, her kindness, I said. Maybe I'm just some charitable tax write-off.

-You think women would put up with you if you weren't so pretty? Griffin said, holding his fingers to his cheeks.

-What's that supposed to mean?

-It means you're pretty, pretty boy, he said with a smile. I don't mean it in a bad way.

The squirrels in the bathroom started a little row, scratching and clawing at the walls and the tub. I stomped on the floor and kicked the tub. There was more scratching and commotion as they fled their home, and I ran outside and put my ear to the Glory Hole, listening for any traces of baby squirrels, entirely uncertain whether they made noise. I slapped the house, heard nothing, and with a clean conscience, I nailed on a piece of a cabinet door I'd found in the basement. We jabbered at one another that afternoon as we put the screen door back on with long wood screws, but the door wouldn't close right. I chiseled out the rot wood and screwed in pieces of plywood where the hinges would go, and reaffixed the door.

I called my brother and he asked whether we would be home in an hour. I told him to bring a ladder so we could hang Diomedes. He drove up later, and walked the ladder over to the house. It was obvious he needed to get out of the house, away from the baby, away from the woman. I told him I would rent the ladder in exchange for beer. He told me he would take that offer. My brother was overwhelmed with Life, and could only sneak a few hits from a joint in his basement once in a while. His only refuge was that, and working. He was a father now, trying to run a remodeling business, paying for his girlfriend's college, paying and paying.

Zeke, marveling at the decrepit state of the house, laughed through his beard at the squirrel problem. He helped us frame up a little brace above the door, driving the long wood screws with a cordless drill. I handed Diomedes the Godslayer up to him, and balanced with one foot on the loose handrail and one foot next him on the ladder, to help hold the deer in place while his 18-volt Dewalt sunk screw after screw, mounting the deer to the siding. He got out his torpedo level and made sure it was plumb. With Diomedes in place and the work done, we went inside and talked for an hour about his daughter, Isis, fatherhood and work. He grabbed a beer for the road and said he had to get back home.

Semi-bored and antsy, we set about to create the first work of Squirrel Haus art. I got my oils and brushes from my toolbox, and Griffin retrieved the skin magazines. In antithesis to Misha's soap gift, Griffin's cousin had given him a traveling set of smut, passed from friend to friend for years. Several magazines and some VHS tapes. We tried to watch one called *Fuckfest Olympians,* which consisted of a boxing ring with three couples in it, all dressed in togas. There was a small crowd around them, men who looked like unemployed truckstop attendants, cheering on the action, bedecked in togas too, and sweat-stained baseball hats. We got about two minutes into it, watching a guy thrust at a permed blonde's open maw with the crowd cheering *Fuck her face, Fuck her face.* Griffin got up, ejected the tape and smashed it over his knee, laughing.

-Jesus Christ. Can you believe our friends have been jerking off to this shit for this long? That's not porn, it's tragedy. Pornogedy. There you go, college boy. I just invented a new literary genre.

The magazines were all of the lower variety. *Hoopla. Gamut. Dee-lite.* One was simply page after stapled page of various women pissing into storm drains in public places, palm trees lining the sunny streets in the pictures while the women struck garish poses, bright red lips puffy with collagen. I threw the magazine at Griffin.

-Is that all California is? Women running around pissing in

gutters? Where's the story? Where's the love?

-Pretty much, he said. No one would bat an eye out there. That's par for the course.

I shook my head.

-Let's paint. This place needs some class.

We took the horrid abstract painting into the basement and removed the frame from the canvas. We cut out various pictures from the skin mags, and glued them to the wooden frame. Pictures of women pissing, leathery women in black riding chaps, glass dildos thrust hither and thither, monstrous cocks. After an hour of cutting and pasting, we had our motif. We set in to the canvas with the paints and brushes, doodling at first. I lit a cigarette. I was very tempted to ask Griffin more about Layna, but opted against it. He'd talk in time.

Griffin waved a brush at the canvas.

-So, what should it be? I was thinking of something with the Iowa mascot on it. You know, school spirit. We have to blend in, he said.

-How about we do each other's portraits dressed in a Herky costume?

I went upstairs and found a pizza coupon touting the football season, bedecked in Black and Gold, with the Iowa mascot on it. I put in a CD Griffin's brother had given him, some solo album by Keith Richards. I took the flier downstairs. We had to make certain to get our subject just right.

The painting ended in a different direction. We painted the savage-looking hawk-mascot in the upper right corner, teeth bared, a scowl of contempt and lusty eyes. The mascot's pants were down, as were his shorts, his gigantic member exposed and issuing forth a torrent of golden coins, cascading in a small arc down and left, across the celestial blue-grey background we kept from the original painting. The coins rained and piled on the sketch of a woman at the bottom left. It was hard to paint her face mid-orgasm, hard to get the curl of lip and Klimty vertigo of the eyes exactly right, so I roughed in a plague doctor's mask on her, but the rest of her writhed.

I tried to use my gold-colored paint sparingly to make it last, but after four hours of work, the tube was gone. So were most of the other colors. Griffin was painting some hairs on the anthropomorphic hawk's inner thigh, and tiny cross-hatching for depth. We worked until two in the morning, giddy with beer and turpentine fumes down in the Bilge. I dropped a brush into the cleaning can.

-Zeus and Daphne, I said. Perfect for football season.

-A rape a day keeps the football team at play, he said. Let's call it, *Go Hawks!!*

-*Go Hawks!!*, it is. Me likey.

I took a lecturing tone of voice.

-In this painting, the Masculine Gaze, in this case personified by college athletics, is in fact an ironic decentering which entitles the Feminine Personhood to realign its aporeia through a deconstructed alter-hyper-alterity, thus forming a non-binary pair of oppositional semiotic relations, representing the ongoing paradoxes of our time, etc. It is in fact the non-personhood of personhood that addresses us here through the rhetoric of non-spatial ululations, etc. The representation of a form which forms the form of the sense of the Politics of the Body of the Artifact of the Form that is trapped in the No-Now duality of failed masculinity, etc.

Griffin held up his hands in protest and flicked his smoke at me.

-Etc. indeed, he said. Shut it, pretty boy. Is that all they teach you in college?

-Quite a bit of it, yes, I said. That and how to rack up student loans.

We laughed and Griffin lit another.

-In my hood in Californiaese, they'd castrate you for talking like that, he said with a smile. How long will this take to dry?

-I don't know. Day or so. The gold takes a long time.

-We should start an art gallery. Squirrel Haus Galleries, LLC.

I nodded in consent.

-I'll phone our lawyer tomorrow morning, get the paperwork going. Isn't your cousin a lawyer?

-Mark? He passed the bar in Kansas, but not in Iowa yet, Griffin said.

-How has he been?

-Good. Living in KC with his missus. They just bought a new house.

-Lucky him. All I've got is a Squirrel Haus.

Griffin shook his head.

-We, he said. All we've got. When I get a house of my own, I'm going to carve myself on the door, make it out of a big piece of oak. I'll be there on the door, and I'll get an elephant tusk for my cock and use it for the door knocker. There won't be a doorbell. You want to get in, you have to use the knocker.

-I'll just throw a brick through your window then, I said and looked at my watch. Christ, man, I need to go to bed. I'm fucked up from these fumes and I think I'm drunk.

-Me too. I've got to look for a job tomorrow.

-Yeah, so do I. Back in the mines for us.

Griffin rolled baleful eyes.

-Don't forget to bring a canary.

-That's what the squirrels are for, I said.

I lay down on my sleeping bag, a sweatshirt for a pillow. Sleep wafted over exhausted eyes. I'd keep my eyes open around town for a discarded mattress or two. Sleep.

Scratching. Then more. Like teeth being filed in frenetic bursts. I half opened my eyes. The sounds issued from the bathroom and the wall and floor like a tendon splitting.

-Pickle, I said. Knock it off.

The noise continued, furtive and desperate, fingernails on tin sheeting. I propped myself on an elbow and got up. Pickle was sniffing at the bathroom door. I shuffled half-awake back into my room and grabbed a bottle from a box and walked outside. Sky sifting grey in the chill. My feet bare and unfeeling. There was a new hole in the cabinet door I'd nailed up. I poured in a glug from the bottle and stoppered the escape with a rag. There was a thrashing and a choking, hissing and then quiet. I capped the bottle and went back to my sleeping bag.

When the sun found me, I gauzily remembered what had happened. I looked over at the half-empty bottle of chlordecone. The room had a faint tinge of gasoline, industrial solvents. I'd forgotten that I even had the bottle. I stared at it, piecing my actions together.

-Shit, I said and got up.

Griffin had made coffee, and poured me some.

-You smell something? he said. Smells odd in here.

-Maybe we're just acclimating to the real stink of the place now.

I went outside and checked the hole, the fumes strong. The squirrels now in their big sleep. I took a shower and poured a libation of bleach on the bathroom floor and in the tub to further mask the odor, past the coffee and cigarette smoke in the kitchen. I had to figure out what to do about the bodies before they went to rot. No time for remorse just yet.

I walked the block over to the Solace Grove Funeral Parlor. The parking lot was empty except for two cars in the employee slots. Two tiny bells on the door announced my entrance, and a woman came around the corner, dressed in dark blue. Everything about her seemed torsional and tense. Her face was taut and pretty as if she had duct tape pinned behind her ears.

-Hello, may I help you?

-I've got a slightly odd question for you this morning, ma'am, but would it be possible to purchase some formaldehyde from you? I would ask my friend's father who runs a funeral home where I'm from south of here, but I think I'll need it sooner, and it's a three-hour drive.

-What would you possibly need formaldehyde for?

That was indeed the question. I would have to think about this. I smiled at her question, trying to look upstanding as much as possible. Don't slouch, shoulders back. She'd assume that I wanted it to lace some pot, I reasoned. How could I explain my situation without seeming depraved and addled... *Yes, well, we had an infestation of vermin in our run-down house because as far as I can tell, our landlord is a shifty, crooked sonofabitch, so I dumped a dose of illegal pesticide into the exterior wall where they were nesting. I was only half awake and not fully cognizant of what I was doing, you see, and while I eradicated the problem, I neglected to realize that it will soon be spring and their bodies will not likely mummify, so I was hoping to get some more carcinogenic chemicals from your fine establishment to pour down there, too, in the hopes that I can counteract one mistake with a slightly less bungled one, preempting any olfactory offense, likely doubly poisoning me and my good friend in the process.* No, I thought, that would be the wrong tack and heading.

-Just general embalming. You know, bugs and snakes and stuff. I was a biology major in Utah and...

She cut directly in to my spiel.

-I'm sorry, sir, but we're a funeral home, not a shopping center. Why in Heaven's name would you even come here to ask such a question?

Her tone of voice was only slightly judgmental, and I knew she would not budge on this issue. She looked at me, and I kept my eyes up, straight into hers.

-I understand, ma'am, that's okay. I had a small project go awry. Of squirrels and men, you know. I usually buy in bulk anyway. I'm sorry to bother you. Have a good morning.

She watched me quizzically, not saying anything as I smiled

and backed away. The little bells sang me out of the building, and I walked home. What would I do with those bodies lying in state? I got my keys and drove to the hardware store to get some lime. I parked and walked through the automatic doors, asking a blue-frocked kid where I might find a bag of lime. He thought I meant fruit and informed me, through a yawn, that the supermarket was a few blocks away. He scratched the back of his head. His name tag said Gary. I told Gary that I needed to speak to his manager. The manager shook his head when I told him that incompetence of this order should not be tolerated in such a fine establishment as Nagel's, and could he please direct me toward the lime. Gary was a nice kid, but, the manager confided, a little slow on the uptake, if I knew what he meant. I told him it takes all kinds, and thanked him.

They didn't have quicklime, only hydrated lime, so I hefted a twenty-pound bag on my shoulder. The shift manager, when I queried him on the effects, had no idea whether it would work on a decomposing body and looked repeatedly at his watch. If nothing else, I figured, we could just rip some of the siding off the house and dump in some concrete, like Hoffa. The squirrels were too deep inside to exhume. The cute blonde stood sentinel at the register, and there was no one in her check-out line. At the counter, I queried her.

-Do you think that hydrated lime will work as well as quicklime on a decomposing body?

-What kind of body are you dealing with? she said with a half-smile.

Her name tag said Roxanne. She had kohl-dark makeup thickly lining the rims around her eyes, and a set of skull-and-crossbones earrings and two matching bands on her fingers. 9:32 AM and saucy.

-The kind in need of lime, I said.

She smiled drily and silently gave me my change, her eyes staring flatly into mine. I smiled back at her.

-My name's Dunham Goldberg. I just moved back to Iowa to train. I'm a boxer.

-So?

-Do you like the sweet science?

-The what?

-Boxing, the sweet science. Too bad. I'll show you some moves sometime, if you want. Slip the jab.

-Do I get to punch you?

-I'd have it no other way, I said.

I told her my address, and picked up the sack of lime, thanked her, and wrote my name and address on the receipt.

-933 Daniels! Stop by some time! Dunham! Ask for it by name.

I walked quickly toward the automatic door. It didn't slide open and I ran full tilt into it, and took a step back, waving my hand at the lens above. I could hear Roxanne laugh behind me, so I turned and gave a sweeping bow, turned again and left. Back at Squirrel Haus, I found a two-liter wide-mouth soda bottle in the basement and cut the top off to use as a funnel. I went outside, jammed the funnel in, and I coaxed all twenty pounds of lime into the cavity. Poor little things, I thought, I really didn't want to kill them, but they gave me no choice. You cannot rouse a working man from sleep and expect clemency. I was overcome with a weird sadness, a definite sense of the strange futility of life, that intangible and prepossessing ceremony of participation and promise, oaths spoken the color of bone. Hadn't I tried to barricade them out for their own good? Hadn't I tried to save them the trouble of dying? It wasn't really my fault, though, I reasoned. This was nothing more than the evolutionary realpolitik of the animal kingdom. Sleep well in your run-down sepulchre, and the Great Oak Tree in the Sky, I thought, pouring the remainder into the hole.

I had a smoke, wondering about the toxic mess I'd made with a banned pesticide. I'd had the bottle for years, and never really thought I'd use it. It was just for show, and now half of it was seeping into the ground and walls right next to my room.

-God, you're an idiot, I said out loud.

I opened the front door and something dropped from the eaves, onto Diomedes and into the dry grass. It was a mud-dawber's nest, about the size of a golf ball, empty. I walked to the backyard, stood for a moment, and tossed it underhand into the slim tree-line between our yard and the opposing house's.

Walking through the door, I heard Griffin calling from the bathroom, inquiring about toilet paper. The shopping list on the refrigerator currently said only 'food' and 'fig tree for Figworth?' and 'beer'. We had forgotten toilet paper on our supply run, and our dwindling supply of restaurant napkins had finally run out. I ripped the first twenty pages from the phone book and slid them under the door.

-It'll have to do, I said.

-Thanks, he said. Here go the emergency numbers. Beggars and all that.

-Don't worry. I've got them memorized.

He was crinkling the paper, trying to soften the pages, laughing a little.

-Take that city comptroller, his voice from behind the door.

I threw a shoe at the door to tense him up. He threw something back with a clump.

-Goddammit, he said. I'm trying to exercise my civic duty in here.

-Let your fingers do the walking.

-Fuck off, he laughed.

-Those squirrels are dead, I said.

-Yeah, he called back. How'd you manage that?

Crinkling of paper, then his voice again.

-What the fuck is that smell, napalm?

February

Walking Back from a Nude
Beach in Italy

No crude bid, I hope, to ponder the answer
to the merest question formed when, squat,
you pissed in the train tunnel, no chance for
privacy as I snapped the joking photo. And what

then of the bitumen tide that beats boulders
into rhetorical granules, deep in sea-pockets,
or that near-invisible hunch of your shoulders
when tired and pressed you paused in that socket

of dark stones which suddenly, coldly flashed
with surprising fury, like a phoenix or anvil
blasting sparks? No…simply two people, cached
and alone in one moment's glimmer, who strolled

below the mountain's lazarine starkness,
while around them wheeled in startled flight
an ancient machinery of light and darkness,
and another of darkness and light.

Soundtrack

The Pixies, *Bird Dream of Olympus Mons*
Notorious B.I.G., *Shit Done Changed*
The Ten Commandments, *Hell Machine*
The Pogues, *The Sickbed of Cuchulain*
Lenny Bruce, *War Criminals*
Led Zeppelin, *In the Light*

The house smelled of chlordecone for a week, but not of squirrels. They were with us in name only. I spent the week sleeping in the living room. It was nauseating to use the bathroom, and we did so only in short, controlled bursts, wearing a biohazard mask that Griffin had from work. He was more pissed after I finally told him about the pesticide.

-I still don't get why you did it, he said.

-I told you, I was half awake. I didn't even realize what I'd done till later.

-It's not like they were hurting anyone, he said.

-Whatever, friend of the earth. You want me to get you PETA membership for Christmas?

-You're sick, D, he said and shook his head. I'd expect more from the educated.

This went on all week, back and forth, while we worked on fixing the house, especially the Heart of Darkness, which was still leaking on days when the winter snow shaded off to rain, a large puddle forming in front of the bathroom and running down the single stair into the kitchen. I did the calculations and between labor and materials, we had almost covered February's rent in the first few days of the month. I had spent nearly six hours alone blackjacking the shingles on the roof around the defunct chimney, but it didn't help. Squirrel Haus was rotting, and its wounds were leaking, the foundation was being reclaimed by the earth. I called Fat Bastard about the work for rent ratio, and he said to send him an invoice, but that next month he would need cash, but we could take our materials cost out. I figured a construction job would be the most readily available source of income. I had just spent the week in training for it.

With the rent mostly out of mind, we spent a few days driving around town, looking for various job sites, hoping to get on with a crew. Griffin could find work easily, being a licensed plumber, but I had only framed houses in grad school, and done some odd jobs for my brother and his small remodeling company. Zeke was now subcontracting, and offered me some pick up work until I found something more regular, and so I worked with him for a week in a new subdivision in North Liberty. Zeke expected that everyone be as good a carpenter as him. He took issue with a piece of trim that I'd nailed a bit crooked, and I walked off the job. Brothers are like that. I made sure he cut me a check before I left, scribbling the amount in a barely legible, angry hand. He was trying to help me, and I felt bad as I drove away. He really didn't need my help.

I drove to the check-cashing place, and stopped at the cigarette shop next door. The Smoke Shoppe. I bought two packs of Nat Shermans and a case of beer, and drove home. I stopped randomly at the offices of Stearns' Construction, just down the street from Squirrel Haus, on a whim, to see whether they had any work. The secretary said that they were looking for framers on a new housing complex. I would be hired on at $10 an hour if I had my own tools, which I did or could borrow, and I would start the next day. I drove home and Pickle greeted me at the door.

-What? You didn't cook anything, you worthless mutt. I want a divorce. You can have the house and the kids. I just want my freedom.

He slobbered and pranced in the kitchen. Griffin got home about 20 minutes after me. He had found a job, effortlessly, the day before with a plumbing company, and had started today. He was now a sort of strange, tanned oddity in the midwinter wastes of Iowa, too weird a combination for Midwesterners who rose at 3:45 AM dutifully every morning, to drink their incessant cups of weak Folgers and eat greasy eggs with buttered toast, work all day and go to bed at 9:00. Men whose lives were defined by their jobs, for whom the whole history of the human race could be divided and reduced ever down into its bedrock essence of daily labor. Work, God, Work, Coffee, Work.

Griffin recounted his day, setting his bag of tools down with a groan long-practiced over the years, and fished a beer from the case. One of his coworkers was a cop. Angel, about five years older than us. He had married the owner's daughter and worked with them part time, morning till mid-afternoon, then putting on his uniform for some second shift protecting and serving. He was half-Mexican, half-Caucasian. The crew was okay, gruff and Midwesternly, Griffin explained, opening another beer, but he was in a double bind since neither the owner nor Angel would put up with him smoking pot. There weren't any drug tests, but the crew was decidedly anti-drugs, and the owner had told him such point blank, making several comments about California this and Liberals that. Griffin would have to be totally discreet about it. I told him that he wasn't exactly someone known for discretion. He smiled back, and bowed deeply.

-I'll be like the marijuana ninja. No one will ever find me, Dunham-san.

He jumped up and clicked his heels and took a karate stance. I took a horse stance, chopping at the air.

-I don't know how you guys can smoke pot and work, I said. I'd be worthless.

-Numbness makes the world go round, Griffin said. Reality is too mind-numbing otherwise.

-I've got to start tomorrow at 7:00 for Stearns.

-You quit with Zeke? he asked, fishing a joint from his cigarette pack.

-For this project. It's all trim carpentry. I'm shit at it. You know how he gets when things aren't perfect.

-He's under a lot of stress, you know. Worst part of my day, he said pulling long on the joint. Listening to modern country music.

-Make nice with Angel so we'll have an amigo on the force. A get-out-of-jail-free card.

-Already working on it, brother. I'll cozy up to El Jefe and get him on our side, Griffin smiled.

I nodded knowingly.

-Bueno.

-So you're going to stick with the construction thing? he asked. In this weather? I thought you went to college to escape this shit.

-It's an easy bet for a job, I said. Anything else and I'd have to apply, fill out forms, wait, do interviews. We've got rent coming up. Besides, Iowa City is full of people who come and never leave. There's no way I could land anything decent right away. I'll be standing next to the philosophers in the unemployment line. I can't afford to wait.

-Did you put your college stuff on the application at Stearns?

-And get hassled for being a bed-wetting college boy? Fuck no. I get enough flak from you, I said and Griffin smiled his little smile.

A beat up, tan Mercury had pulled into Squirrel Haus' driveway, and the thin gravel crunched. We looked outside. The car was loaded with half-opened boxes. The woman who stepped out was wearing a puffed purple coat, and had swept back, straightened hair. Her skin was lighter, and smooth, small freckles like a dark diadem stood out near her hairline. Her face looked regal, high cheekbones and live eyes like an Ethiopian princess, but she bore the drawn features of a mending addict. Hollowed cheeks and dark circles on the eyelids contrasting with her copper skin. She dropped her cigarette onto the ground, twisting it out with her foot, and lit another. I stared out the window.

-Must be the neighbor Fat Bastard told us about.

-She is pretty hot. How old do you think she is? Griffin asked.

-Forty maybe. Fresh from the halfway house.

-I'm not sure this place is a step up from a halfway house, he noted.

We set our beers down, put on our coats and went outside, Griffin introducing us with his hand extended.

-Hello, there. You moving in? We live down below. I'm Griffin, and this is Dunham.

-Oh, hello, there. I'm Michelle.

-Pleasure to meet you.

-What great names. They fake? Sounds like TV names.

Her laugh was raspy and staccato.

-No, ma'am. Our parents just had good taste, Griffin said.

-How long you boys live here?

-Just a few weeks. Not long, I said. Do you need any help with your stuff?

-Well, two strong young men like yourselves. Sure, she smiled.

She walked around to the back door and we carried her boxes upstairs, filled mostly with clothes. Almost entirely bedclothes as I could see, and everything inside smelled strongly of stale cigarette smoke. She had a slight accent, southern maybe, though I couldn't tell which region, and Fat Bastard had been right. She was very attractive. Dirty attractive, sensuous in the hip and eyes that hung in yours a half second longer than normal. She was rifling through one of the boxes, chainsmoking cigarettes and stubbing them out in the sink.

-How's your apartment? she asked.

-Run down, but the neighborhood is nice and quiet. Your place is in much better shape than ours.

-I'm just glad to be out of that damned halfway house. Ah, those damned meetings and everyone with their problems. Me, I like to get down, you know. I can hold my shit, though. It's the weak that's always wantin'.

She rolled her head, and laughed. She had a gold incisor, and was missing one of her rear molars. Her apartment was much smaller than ours, with a central living room and small bedroom. I didn't smell any of the pesticide. We lugged her remaining boxes of gowns and frilly things up the stairs. She turned to me, offering a Kool, which I declined.

-I can't tell you how grateful I am for all your help. I got a bad back. On disability right now till it heals, but I get some good pills, so if you boys need anything, you know what I mean, you just let me know. Okay?

-Sure thing, I said. By the way, do you know if Fat, well, O'Finn is coming by at all? For the lease or anything? If so we'd have to take down the deer head.

-No, I already signed it at his office, she said. He's a big man, ain't he. Why you all put that deer up there anyway? You tryin to scare off the ladies?

-We thought it would look funny up there. Distinctive.

-A deer head? You boys are somethin' else, handsome too. If I was twenty years younger.

-Well, thank you, ma'am, Griffin said.

-Don't you go callin me ma'am and makin me feel old.

-Yes ma'am, Griffin said with a wink and Michelle laughed again.

She rummaged in one of her boxes and took out the head of a Barbie doll, the black version, and rubbed its afro with her thumb. Griffin made a face, and she smiled at us.

-Had it since I was a girl. Keeps me calm for some reason. Say, can I use your phone, if you've got one?

-Sure, I said. We've got to switch names on the account soon, but the line is still working.

-You mind bringing it up here? she asked, rubbing her back. I got this bad back, like I said.

Griffin shrugged.

-Uh, yeah. Okay.

We went downstairs, I got the phone, and brought it up. She took it and immediately started dialing numbers and walked to the bedroom, plumes of smoke and breath rolling into the air, the bodiless plastic head stared intently at me from the table. We debriefed in our kitchen.

-Christ, she seems like handful. I thought I smoked a lot, Griffin said.

-Yeah, she's got a weird vibe. Did you see the Barbie head? Hell the only thing she carried upstairs were her fucking cigarettes.

-Bad back, you know. There is something about her, now that you mention it. She's attractive, but there's just something off.

His face coiled in mock pain, Griffin bent over and held his back.

-Besides, I've seen these disability types before. There's a million in California. Ooh, my toes hurt, I can't work. Ohh, I've got a toothache. Ooh, I'm ugly and no one likes me, and I'm depressed so give me a check and some free drugs.

-I'd think the president has set a good example, I said. Look how far the retarded can get.

-No shit, he said. The only color that matters anymore is green.

I craned my neck to look out the window.

-Is she still on the fucking phone?

Michelle came back, a half an hour later, banging on the screen door with the phone.

-It's dead.

-It's been off the charger all day, Griffin said, taking the phone from her through the screen. He put it back on the wall mount. Pickle made a low rumble and Michelle squeaked.

-Why didn't you warn me you had a dog?

-He won't bite, Griffin said. He's a love dog.

-Black people afraid of dogs, you know, she said, holding the screen door shut.

Griffin looked at her through the screen and pushed Pickle away into the kitchen.

-I got a doctor friend, she continued, said it was evolution why black people are afraid of dogs and can't swim.

-I'd never heard that theory, I said. Maybe Darwin said something about it.

-Maybe, she said.

She stuck her hand through the tear in the screen door and dropped some pills onto the floor.

-There you go. Thanks again, baby. Sorry about the battery.

-Yeah, no problem, Griffin said. What are these? Uppers? Downers?

She paused to light another Kool and peered around him at Pickle.

-Percocet. Good shit. My doctor friend writes me a scrip for 200 a month. Every month. I couldn't have them at the halfway house, but I ain't living there anymore.

-Thanks.

She waved with her fingers, a cigarette there, and walked away. Griffin shut the front door, and popped one of the Percocet, and put one in his jacket pocket, and gave the other two to me.

-Our tax dollars hard at work, I said. There's no way she pays for this stuff.

-Hell, at least with her you see a return on your taxes. Little pills, pittle pills. Not like we get health care. We should save these for when we need them.

-Yeah, I said. I'm on the Walk it Off, Pussy insurance plan.

Griffin washed down his pill and a half and wiped his hand across his mouth.

-What do you think she was in the halfway house for?

-Who knows? Dealing. Burglary. Arson. Pope peddling.

-The poor, poor pope, Griffin said. Can't the white man get any justice in this crazy world?

-Not for little white men like us, I said. Is it okay if I turn up the heat a little? I think I'll have another pill. I've got a serious life pain right now.

Starting work for Stearns the next day was standard construction fare. Show up, brief introductions, jump in, work, smoke, lunch, listen to a ton of bullshit stories, smoke, work, remain cold and uncomfortable all day, smoke, go home. The only problem was the weather had turned bad, and I didn't have much cold-weather gear. The wind picked up, and a dry massless snow blew through it. I didn't even have any longjohns. I had stupidly given away all the winter gear when I shoved off for Utah. I drove over to my brother's house after work the first day and borrowed some Carhartt bibs and an old jacket. He looked tired. The baby was up all night, and so was he, working 10 or 12 hour days in order to cover the medical costs, insurance, mortgage, gas, his girlfriend's college tuition, the payments on her car. I had never liked his girlfriend. She never liked me. In Utah, when Zeke had called me to say Kate was pregnant I told him congratulations, hung up the phone and threw my beer bottle into the street. There was something you could see in her eyes. They weren't keen with intelligence, but dry and patient like an ancient spider's, staring down from some arch of stone.

The next day after work I decided to call the phone company while we still could. I had promised the previous tenants that I'd set up phone service as soon as possible, but the phone still worked. We needed communication. There possibly were only a few days left on the old account before the tenants or the phone company shut it off, and neither Griffin nor I had a credit card.

I came home, got a beer in me, and looked up the number for Quest, the local provider, in the bathroom phonebook. I needed to use Griffin's name. I probably owed Quest 20 dollars from years ago, which would have amassed fines and fees and ballooned into an unpayable sum. Better to use his name. He hadn't lived in Iowa for years. He had written his social security number on a piece of paper and stabbed it to the wall with a screwdriver that morning.

I called the phone company, and routed myself through the

fog of prompts, until finally it was ringing for a human being. Remember, I told myself, what would Griffin do?

-Hello, this is Jeff with Quest, how can I assist you today?

-Hello, Jeff, my name is Griffin Buch, and I had called you guys about three or four days ago, hoping to switch over the service in my new apartment.

-Hold on, let me check our records here and see what I can find. No, I'm sorry, but I don't see here that any call has been made to our offices. What's the address?

-Yes, well, I am sure that I did. 933 Daniel. I called on Groundhog's Day. I remember it well because it reminds me of the movie. Did you like that movie?

-Movie, sir?

-Groundhog Day. Bill Murray. It's a classic. Bill Murray?

-I'm sorry, sir, I haven't seen it.

-You should check it out. You sound like the kind of guy who would dig it.

-Uh, yes, thank you. Well, as I was saying, the report was not logged in our system, and I deeply regret any inconvenience that…

-Do you know who I am?

-Who you are, well, no, sir, not personally, I…

-Well, that's how it should be. No one is supposed to know where I am, or who, or what I'm doing. I've got nothing against the Midwest, trust me, but I just got back into the country.

-I don't know, uh, anything about the state of your…

-My partner and I just got back from an assignment in Afghanistan. We work with National Geographic. I write, he takes pictures. We absolutely have to have this phone set up in my name, or else I won't be able to call my editor. We're lucky to be alive. Do you have any idea what's going on over there, Jeff?

-Well, sir, I enjoy reading National Geographic. I have a subscription, and…

-Yes, well, this is a governmental thing, too. You don't waltz in and out of a war zone without attracting some attention. I need this number changed soon, otherwise I can't call my editor and then my story's blown. We were embedded with the Bedouins for six months to break this story. My skin is still blue from the sheets I had to wear. I kind of look like a Smurf right now, thus the low profile. I can't say too much on this line since it's not secure. Once my editor knows it's me, he can arrange to have the line protected. This is Patriot Act territory, Jeff. It's getting tricky, and like it or not, they're taking our rights, one by one.

He didn't sound dumb, and the Bedouin thing might have been too much. The Sahara is a far cry from Afghanistan, but it's hard to contend with someone when they talk like a blunderbuss.

-Well, sir, I didn't know that the Bedouins... I'm not sure if Quest can protect a line like that. We're a private company, sir. What you're talking about is the federal government. It's a private line that you have.

I lit a smoke and took a nervous tone, as if someone might be listening in.

-They're migratory, the Bedouins. Good people, Jeff, like you and me. Anyway, if the federal government gets wind of the information we have, it's over. This could be a national scandal, or at least bring some real light on the entire military industrial complex. I can't go back to jail. I was arrested once already over there and had to bribe my way out with a pair of boots and the five hundred dollars I had in them. The first amendment doesn't hold up too well in Afghanistan. People are dying.

-Sir, I...

-We must have this phone line set up, in my name, or else everything is fucked, if you'll please pardon my language, but this is my life's work, and I know I'm just some stranger to you, but I really need your help, Jeff.

-Well, sir, I....

-Jeff, look, I'm talking basic human rights here. Those people are dying and it's because of the military complex. The NRA. Halliburton. There's absolutely no oversight. They fly around and shoot camels, villages. Camels, Jeff. It's all the same. It's like 'Nam. Napalm on the elephants. I know that you can't do much, Jeff, and anything you could do to get this order up and running would be great. Look, I know it sounds weird, but once I get my new number to my editor we've got machines that'll encrypt the conversation on both ends and I can get my writing done. Jeff, this is life-and-death stuff, what's happening in that country, and America deserves to know about it. What do you think John Pilger would do? The internet's not secure, Jeff. The phone is the only way.

-Mr. Buch, I will talk to my manager and personally make sure that your order is expedited. I am terribly sorry that we have caused you any inconvenience. I was a journalism major in college, too. Pilger's a hero of mine.

-Good, Jeff, good. Keep fighting the good fight, Jeff. I can't divulge too much information on this line, and please keep the matter hush-hush with your manager, but we can beat them, Jeff. We can win. A true patriot is the one who asks the hard questions. Thanks so much. You've really helped me out a lot here. I'll be sure to mention you in the article. What's your family name?

-Winterbottom. Jeff Winterbottom. Thank you and have a good day, Mr. Buch.

-You too, Mr. Winterbottom. You too.

I hung the phone on the wall. I felt good. That had been almost too easy. I had some beers, read a few chapters of Herodotus, and watched *Conan the Barbarian*. The next afternoon after work, the phone was dead and as I was cursing Jeff Winterbottom's goofy name and his whore mother for spawning and raising such a twisted brood, when I noticed a telephone service truck pull up out front. I walked out with an extra beer to greet the helmeted man. He was exceedingly friendly. I thanked him, offered him a beer, which he declined, and I went inside.

The days went, workweek to work's end. The only redeeming part about employment with Stearns was getting paid every Friday. I went to Fast Cash and exchanged my paycheck, and picked up a case and a carton of smokes. Buy in bulk, I reasoned, for the economy. There was a message on the machine from Noel. He said he'd be back in town in a few days. That night another friend called, asking for directions, and stopped by an hour later. It was Wim, just back from Oregon, and many years between sightings. He walked in and hugged me, his big grin and big frame enveloping. He brought out some beer from a sack and we swapped recent histories.

He had been living out in some commune there, he said, and ran afoul of the law when the place was busted for meth manufacture. Authorities had no hard evidence on most of the people, so they let them all go with express orders to stay the hell out of Oregon for good. He was strangely vague on details about the commune. He was staying with his parents out in the country in the southern part of the state, and when he heard that Griffin and I were in town he decided to drive up to Iowa City. He told me a little about Oregon and I told him about Utah. Griffin was out running an errand, and when he returned, we three got very drunk that night and snorted a bit of the meth that Wim procured from a baggy in his sock. The hot blasts of the drug through the nostril and bloodstream, like inhaling gun powder, wound us up till four in the morning, reanimating bodies ground down by hard labor.

Saturday we all slept in, and I made coffee around ten. We had a couch now, Big Red, another piece of the floating friends' hand-me-down-and-hand-me-arounds. Wim was snoring on the couch and I sat down on him, balancing my cup to not spill on my robe. I nestled on Wim's back.

-Good morning, you dirty hippy. This is not a commune, and you're expected to sing for your supper, and caw for your coffee. No such thing as a free lunch. Right, Pickle? See? Pickle the

Pinko-Eater agrees with me.

Wim squirmed under me, and Pickle licked his hand.

-Fuck, I ain't no hippy. Get off me.

-No, but you're the offspring of hippies. Monkey see.

He pushed me off and I held the coffee cup under his face where it hung off the side of Big Red. The steam rose and he grimaced.

-Want some? I said.

-God, leave me alone. Ten more minutes.

I heard Griffin giggle in his room, and he said, I'll take some coffee if he won't.

-There's plenty for all. The Squirrel Haus Commune Cornucopia. Drink, eat and be merry for tomorrow we work.

It was Saturday, but I did a little work on the house just to have an excuse to go back to Nagel's for some odd materials and flirt with Roxanne. She had started to laugh at my jokes, looking down when she grinned. I lingered at the register after she gave me my change. At Squirrel Haus, Wim helped me patch some of the siding on the back of the house, and I bought him some beer. He asked if I wanted to buy some more meth from him. He was coming back up next weekend to sell some pot to Griffin, and could bring some other goodies along too. We agreed on an amount and price. He also told me that he could help us steal cable from the house next door if we wanted. I had met our neighbor a few days prior when I was retrieving a pack of smokes from the White Elephant. She poked her head out of her tidy house and waved me over. I introduced myself and Griffin, and listed our bona fides. Her name was Dorothy Somethingorother, 83, long widowed, a tough old woman. I told Dorothy that if she ever needed any help with anything at all, to just give us a call. I wrote down our number. All the neighbors seemed nice, but had an edgy insularity. Except Dorothy. I told Wim I'd think about the cable purloining, and gave a wave as he puttered off in his car and turned right onto Kirkwood. No use burning another bridge just yet, I mused. Keep the neighbors on our side.

The Sunday Sabbath disappeared with a poof, and it was again time for work. Monday morning. I met Griffin as he was about to leave, bundled for the cold. He apologized for not making another pot of coffee and swept out the door. A wall of cold rushed in and dissipated. I made some coffee. I had almost sixty minutes before I'd have to leave. I stood in the poorly lit kitchen and patted Pickle's big head.

-Why don't you pull your weight around here, huh? Get a damned job. Make some coffee next time.

Pickle slobbered and panted happily. I read some more Herodotus, and ten minutes before I had to leave I ran out and started the van, turning the heaters on high. It was humid, and cold, but luckily no wind. Probably five or ten below. It would snow today.

At the job site the big, propane-powered tube heater was already running inside the half-finished three-story monstrosity of a building, and apartment complex to be. Men huddled around the heater, stamping their boots in the cold, hammers jiggling from their tool belts.

The owner pulled up in his giant Ford 3500 diesel dually. The crowd at the heater scattered, and we all settled in to various tasks. The $9 guys were busy picking up trash and kicking loose the scrap wood where it lay frozen to the ground, hauling everything slowly over to the windows, chucking the foot-long pieces of wood one by one down into the dumpster. I framed in the heating and cooling ductwork with the $10 and up guys. Later I helped lift one of the large, exterior walls on the third floor. It was an easy morning full of small chores, and around 10:00 a dry snow began falling, settling on the deck and sifting here to there and back.

At lunch, everyone moved back to the second floor, the tube

heater was barely warming the place. My hands and toes ached with the thaw in them. The boss was telling stories about his son, the foreman, who had been a pro football player for a year or so. His son, also, never around. Evidently, the boss went on, his son been insulted one night at a bar by some nigger wrestler, and had dragged that nigger out into the pedestrian area in downtown Iowa City and proceeded to beat the shit out of him. Reading the faces of the other men, he had told it many times, I guessed. I thought about accidentally dropping my hammer on the boss's head later in the day, but figured employment was better than justice for the time being.

No one on the crew really talked much, even when gathered for warmth on break around the blast-tube heater. Just the boss who talked, and talked, and yelled, and muttered. He was especially hard on the only non-white guy in the crew, a middle-aged Mexican with a handlebar moustache. Luis was his name. The boss would walk up to where Luis was sweeping and point and yell, and say *comprende* and *si* and *goddam immigrants*, and storm off to his truck which he left running all day. Luis would go back to sweeping and scrapping out, whistling a tuneless song.

Another day, I was tacking down the roof sheeting with some tenpenny nails. The roof was already half on, the third floor below closing up. The boss was yelling at someone and I poked my head over to see what the hubbub was. One $10 guy, a moose of a manchild named Greg was stuck at the top of the ladder we used to get on the roof. All he had to do was get a hand on the roof, take a step up on the perpendicular fire-blocking between the wall studs, and pull himself up. He blubbered, saying that he was afraid of heights and had lied on his application and really wanted down, openly weeping. Everyone was laughing at him and shaking their hips as if about to fall, aping his fear. The boss was livid, and called him a sissy faggot, and told him to get on the roof or get off the site. Greg was fifteen feet up in the air, and the ladder wobbled violently. I walked over and looked down at him, offering my hand. I wouldn't be able to pull him up since he outweighed me by a hundred pounds, but I thought it might encourage him.

The ladder rattled, and he did reach his hand up, but the bottom of the ladder had worked itself out from the vibrations, and its angle combined with Greg's weight kicked it out and he fell straight down. I had seen a guy nearly cut his hand off with a circular saw, saw another guy slide off a roof on a piece of loose OSB, but I hadn't yet seen a crying man fall off a ladder. He hit the ground squarely on his feet, stood there a moment, uttered a wail and fell over. Someone drove him to the hospital. He blew out his knee, we learned later, and would be out on workman's comp for a while. Greg became a running joke for the rest of the time I worked for Stearns, and anyone balanced on a top plate, or on the roof, would swish his hips around, crying, and everyone would laugh. I had to admit, it was pretty funny, the first hundred times or so.

Wim came up the next Friday, brought along some special party favors, and I called in sick to work. I got a little too tweaked with him that afternoon, and we spent much of our time throwing my chef's knife at a piece of plywood we set up in the living room, a human form spray-painted on, and the occasional errant throw lodging in the wall behind. When I went to grab more beer I noticed a message on the machine. We hadn't heard the phone for the music. It was Noel saying he'd be back in a few days. Griffin came in the door with a waft of cold air and Pickle plodded out to greet him. He rubbed the dog's head with his glove still on.

-You feed him yet? he asked.

-Earlier, around noon.

-You didn't go to work today? Griffin asked.

-We've been practicing for the circus all afternoon, Wim said, and tossed the knife again at the plywood.

Griffin grabbed a beer and took a few turns, walking after every throw to wrench the knife free from wood or wall. Wim got some 16-penny nails and we tried throwing those but one ricocheted and broke the window, so we went back to the knife. Griffin ran a seam of duct-tape over the crack.

-We should have a party later this month, Wim said. A Squirrel Haus Jamboree. The Thrilla in the Squilla.

-Perfect fucking idea, Griffin said, rubbing his hands. We can make up fliers and hand them out downtown. We'll see if Pete and his band want to play.

-What's his new band's name?

Wim scratched his head, saying, I think it's Perpendicular Jesus now. I don't know, I haven't talked to him in a long while. If you guys have a party, you should get a keg and charge a few bucks for cups.

-That is something to look forward to indeed, Griffin nodded. Fun for all. We should get one of those dancing air clowns they use at car lots. Or a trained bear.

-How about a couple of those Shriners' cars?

Doffing an imaginary hat, Wim smiled.

-I'd be happy with just the fez, he said.

-What exactly is a Shriner? Griffin asked.

-They're the ones, Wim said, who sell the Gideons their Bibles.

I drudged in the cold the next two weeks, laboring and hammering, smoking a lot of cigarettes to feign the idea of warmth. The crew was given overtime to try to button up the project by deadline, and I got a little bonus on my check when it was all completed. I'd helped my brother a few weekends, too, and had a nice, tidy sum already. Enough for next month's rent, enough for a little bit of fun. I decided to quit Stearns. It seemed like a good enough time to quit, and it was cold outside. I had had enough of the constant griping racism too. Griffin's crew wasn't hiring for labor, but I knew something would come along, and put out a few resumes for office jobs, editing, reporting. I would be careful with my finances, and stretch them. I looked at Figworth in the living room.

-Your mail-order bride will have to wait, my friend.

Figworth said nothing, so I gave him some water, and filled Pickle's bowl, too.

An envelope from the phone company arrived a few days later. Christ, I thought, they're billing us before the month is even out? I was about to throw it in the trash, but decided to look just to see how deep our tally had already extended into the red. I looked with disbelief at the total owed. It said, Credit $300. Oh, that word, credit. A boon and a bane depending on its context. I read it a few more times to be sure. Boon. A credit of $300. Herr Winterbottom had come through after all. We wouldn't have to pay for the phone all year long so long as we used calling cards for long distance. I couldn't believe the good luck we were having. The heathen gods were smiling upon us, for once, thanks to the pull of *National Geographic*. Who didn't like that magazine, I wondered, with the nice photos and native girls' breasts to boot?

Friday, a few hours after work, Michelle came down and was knocking on our door again. I figured she needed to use the phone again. Sometimes she'd lay a pill or two on us, and sometimes not. There had been a lot of traffic in and out of Michelle's apartment since she'd moved in, various men, usually older. They all stomped the ceiling, and talked in loud voices. Griffin muttered that he was going to start charging her to use the phone. Saturday, she knocked on the door and I answered. She needed our help upstairs.

-Isn't there someone up there who can help you? Griffin asked.

-Scuba Hank can't fit up in the hole, she said. He got too big a belly.

-Fit in what hole? I asked.

-Something's dead up there, she said, and we don't know what.

We followed her up the narrow stairwell. Her place stank of death, like a sickly-sweet lozenge on the tongue.

We walked the apartment, trying to locate the source. The guy, Hank, shirtless, followed us around with a scuba mask dangling from his neck, his tuberous gut, glowing in the fluorescent light, slick like a shaved seal. I stuck my head through the attic access, balancing on two plastic milk crates. There was definitely something dead up there. It was cold outside, so Michelle had her heat cranked well into the 80s, which would keep the attic warm enough to allow decomposition, at least if whatever died was nesting in the insulation. I put the lid back down, saying that something had died up there. Michelle begged me to get it out, and said she'd give me a handful of pills in return.

I went downstairs and got my Petzl headlamp, the gas mask, a bandana for my mouth, and went back up. I asked for some Vicks and she had the Walgreen knockoff kind, so I rubbed it under my nose. I pulled myself up into the hole, and shimmied onto the joists, casting the light around me, trying to notice anything out of place. The attic was tight, with the loose blow-in cellulose insulation everywhere. I couldn't wear the headlamp and the gasmask, so I dropped back through the hole and dropped the mask to Griffin.

-Not going to work with this thing on, I said.

-You can wear my scuba mask, Scuba Hank said.

I raised myself back in, trying to locate the source. The stench became stronger as I neared the defunct chimney that ran up through the attic next to The Heart of Darkness.

I sunk to a precarious knee for slope of the roof. Griffin poked his head through the honey hole, wincing in the beam of light when I turned.

-See anything? he asked, laughing. Scuba Hank wants to know.

-No, but it fucking reeks over here by the chimney. Can you get me a plastic bag or something? I should have brought gloves. See if you've got some surgical gloves in your med kit.

While he got the bag I was picking the insulation gingerly out of the recess, knees balanced on the inch-wide joists. I had to cram my head further down where the roof line met the wall below. The soffit was wide open to the attic where the old house had been joined to the sinking addition in the rear, letting in the cold. Shoddy fucking construction, I thought. I was practically on my stomach, peering down into the dark. Whatever it was, it was definitely right there. The smell was horrid. I cleared out another handful of insulation and spotted a bit of grey fur and a foreleg where the old and new sections of the house met, in a little shelf-like area, next to the chimney. Shit, I thought, it can't be.

Griffin's head popped up through the hole.

-Getcha bags here! No luck on the gloves, though. All we've got are some sandwich bags and some winter gloves. Did you find it?

I scuffled back on the joists in order to turn my head to speak.

-I'm going to need a coat hanger too. You won't believe this.

-Believe what?

He called down to Michelle for a coat hanger, and then bent it into a hook. He hopped up into the attic with the bag and tool.

-God, it stinks up here, he said.

-You should get a whiff from my angle.

-I'm good from here. God, that stinks, he said and put on his gas mask.

He handed me the wire, and I worked it into the soffit, nudging the corpse back a little so I could get a better view of it.

-It's a squirrel, I said.

-From downstairs? Did one of them escape?

-This one didn't. Maybe it crawled up through the wall or something and then died up here.

-No one escapes their fate in la Casa de Squirrels.

He giggled again. I reconfigured the hook into a sharper angle. I only had a small space through which to see the animal, and would have to work mostly blind. Some of the cellulose had gotten under the bandana and I spit it out. I shuttled further into the crevice to get a better grip on the squirrel. Griffin lit a cigarette behind me.

-How does that insulation taste? he asked.

-Only a bit better than this fucking squirrel smells.

I reached my hand further toward the hole and pushed the squirrel's body back against the wood. Out of sight, I had to work blind, by touch and guess. I felt the hook end press up into something soft and tried to jerk the wire into the body, but it wouldn't sink in. I readjusted several times, breathing death and insulation, trying to aim the tool into the soft underbelly. My shoulder was cramping a little, and my left leg almost slipped off the joist when I shifted my body for a better angle, legs perpendicular to the joists. Michelle had handed up a flashlight and Griffin shone it at my hands.

-You're my hero, D.

He giggled a little. I rested my arm for a second and stretched it back in toward the cavity, turning my head to the side so I could press my body a little further into the angle. I fished around with the hanger to test for head and tail, gauging where the stomach might be. I hooked and could feel the resistance of flesh.

-I think I got it. Get the bag ready.

There was a hiss and the cramped air around my head went rank with methane. I gagged. Griffin groaned behind me. The squirrel bounced on the end of the wire hanger as I slithered my way back along the joists until I had room to rise to my knees.

-Fuck, take it. Take it, I said.

Griffin held out the plastic grocery bag at arm's length, stooping down. I lifted the little carcass into the bag and he twisted it shut around the wire. It looked like a flat black balloon. His face contorted, his neck rolling away from the decomposing beast.

-Holy hell, that's foul.

Griffin dropped through the hole, and I handed down the bag with the length of wire hanger, careful not to disturb the contents. I followed him down. Michelle was spraying a cloud of air freshener all over the apartment, and Scuba Hank put on his mask and muttered. She thanked us three times, and dropped a large number of Percocet into Griffin's hand. Outside, I shook loose the remaining insulation that I could and Griffin walked the bag out to the trash can near the curb. Inside, I washed my hands vigorously, and opened a beer to wash out the acrid taste of death.

-I hope that's the last of them, I said. I am not doing this again. I've got that fucking cellulose all over me and all I can taste is dead squirrel.

-You still smell like it a little. You smell of death. Death, he moaned and tittered in his high-pitch laugh. I rubbed my jeans in protest of the odor.

-Seriously, though, how did that thing get up there? I said. Do you think it's one of the original squirrels? It would have to chew its way up through the fire-blocking in the walls from down below.

-Maybe there's no fire-blocking, Griffin offered. I wouldn't be surprised.

Griffin twiddled his fingers in front of him, like playing a piano.

-Maybe it's a zombie. Spooooky squirrel zombies.

-Did you see that guy? I said. Scuba Hank.

-What the hell is going on up there? he said.

-No idea, he said. Look at it positively: at least she didn't ask to use the phone.

-You just made my day, Griffin. Always fucking sunnyside up for you.

We went inside and strategized and worked out a list of chores and an itinerary. Tomorrow was Saturday, Judgment Party Day, and we had lots of things to get ready. I took a shower to wash the death smell off, and for once the faint pesticide smell was by contrast welcome.

Horizontal Jesus had agreed to play and would be by in the afternoon to set up, which was nice of them because they had some local clout and could have charged if they wanted. We called friends, and told them to spread the word. We had two kegs ordered through a friend of Noel's who worked at Dirty John's Grocery. We had already run copies of our fliers at Zephyr. Each flier was a whole page showing a squirrel, crucified, a beer in one paw, a crown of thorns, a cigarette hanging from its mouth. Its eyes stared directly out at the viewer, angry. It read, *Horizontal Jesus Playing Saturday Night At The Squirrel Haus. 933 Daniel Street. 7:30. WWSJD? Look for Diomedes the Deer. Judgment Day. So it is written, so it shall be done.* We had plastered many of them downtown, and handed out the other 200 by setting several stacks on cars and letting the wind do the work.

Saturday morning, Griffin and I walked around the entire block, telling the neighbors about the party so there would be no angry calls to the police, leaving fliers in doors and mailboxes. We invited everyone, regardless. Most politely declined, which was fine with me. It had snowed in the night and slow clumps like loose down fell throughout the morning. I hoped it wouldn't deter people from coming.

Around noon, I knocked on Dorothy's door and waited for her to potter over across her thick orange rug. I explained to her that we'd be having a party that night, and there would be music, but it would be done by 8:30 or 9:00, and if it was too loud to please call and tell us and we would be quiet. I wrote out my number in nice, large and legible digits. She told me she was half deaf anyway, and to have fun, and she'd give us an earful if we made too much racket. I told her that I would be shoveling her sidewalk, stoop and rear walkway to say thanks for putting up with the noise, and there was nothing she could do about it. She was the kind of woman to insist that she could do everything by herself, proud and defiant. I asked if she had any rock salt. She pointed me out toward the backyard, and said to look in the green bin by the garage door. I shoveled the whole of it in fifteen minutes, and then proceeded to salt the paths. It felt good in the still, cold air of the afternoon amid the flakes that fell straight down. Bracing, bluey. I shoveled the sidewalk in front of her house, and she watched me from the window for about a minute and waved. I waved back, and smiled.

I shoveled our sidewalk and walk, too, borrowing a little of her salt. It wasn't too cold, so the salt would keep the snow melted well into the night. I finished up and replaced the shovel and Dorothy's bag into the green bin. Snow had piled high on Diomedes and his winter hat. His cigarette still hung from his mouth, and the white pile on his head looked almost like a crown. I gave a little bow as I walked below him. Inside, grabbed a beer and sat down. Wim and Griffin were picking up the kegs in Griffin's truck. Pete's band would be by in a few hours. I took a Percocet and sat down on Big Red, soaking in the bright quiet that sifted finely through the blinds, and I blew smoke high into the air enjoying the repose.

Griffin and Wim pulled up twenty minutes later. I helped lug the kegs around back to keep them cool. Through our friend we had managed to avoid paying the deposit, so were able to afford an extra case of good beer for our troubles. Inside we hoisted bottles of Flying Dog in the kitchen, celebrating everything, why not, why not. Griffin had glanced at something outside. He grabbed my arm, pointing through the front window.

-Holy shit, look outside!

There on the freshly scooped sidewalk lay a quivering form, a blue jay, on its back, jerking and seizing. Griffin grabbed some surgical gloves from the kitchen drawer and ran outside. I followed closely behind him. The bird was shaking, convulsing. Good grief, I thought, was the entire property toxic? He picked it up, carefully, and brought it inside. Wim held the door. Pickle was excited to have another animal in the house, and his tail thumped the floor where he sat.

Griffin set the blue bird on the kitchen counter and we gathered around it. It was dead now. Its spasmodic movements had ceased, and its wings drew in to its sides half-cocked, like a shuttered Japanese fan. Wim leaned in.

-Try mouth to mouth.

-You've got to be fucking kidding me, I said. Zombie squirrels and now a suicidal blue jay on our front lawn? What's next? A mountain lion in the basement? A tiger in the toilet bowl?

-No. It'll be a yeti, Griffin said. Just watch. Or a chupacabra.

-Why do you guys have a giant box of surgical gloves in the kitchen? Wim asked.

-Griffin didn't tell you about my encounter with the zombie squirrel?

I ran him through the story about the attic, while Griffin pushed on the bird's chest with his forefinger, trying to revive it with CPR. Wim looked puzzled.

-What do you think killed it? he asked.

-What, the squirrel?

-No, the blue jay. You think it was poisoned by the pesticide?

-I don't know, I said. The cold? Broken heart? The economy?

-Good thing I'm not superstitious, Griffin added. I mean, it died right on the sidewalk.

-What are the fucking odds? Wim added.

We decided to put it in the freezer and keep it for later. Griffin didn't feel angry about this animal's death because no one had harmed it. It died on our property, he reasoned, and now it was ours. We could paint it, or have it stuffed as a companion for Diomedes. I wrapped the dead bird in a giant black plastic bag and laid it in the freezer door's shelf.

Pete and his band showed up around 4:00. We helped haul in the speakers and gear from their cargo van. I thanked Pete for playing for free.

-It's nothing. The band always gets laid.

-Well, don't look at me, I said. Is that true?

-What? he asked and whisked his bangs out of his eyes with his hand.

-That the band always gets laid.

-Sometimes, he nodded. You expecting a lot of chicks tonight?

-I don't know what I'm expecting. I just hope people show up. Put Squirrel Haus on the map.

-Horizontal Jesus, at your service, Pete said.

He gave me a priest's benediction with his right hand, and touched my forehead.

-Go in pussy, my son.

By 6:00 there were around 20 people, and an hour later the number had tripled. I collected money and handed out cups. With the snow, most of the people had walked, but the small street was lined with cars. I called Ezekiel, but he was too busy with work and the baby to make it. He'd stop by tomorrow. Kermit and his girlfriend were there. Noel showed up, freshly back from his trip to parts unknown, with Amy, his longtime flame, a young elementary school teacher who liked her nipples bit so hard, he confided one night, that it made his jaw ache. Noel was selling some of his many wares to the community inside, and once in a while he'd motion me into a corner or a room and we'd sniff some blow from keys and talk, catching up on the past year's doings and dones.

I smiled and chatted a bit with the crowd, then stepped outside for some air and a cigarette. Saul, an old friend, pulled up in his new Range Rover, parking against the grain of traffic. He stepped out and threw a giant wad of wet paper towels at me which slapped the house and stuck.

-Hadoken, he bellowed and laughed.

-Jesus, what was that?

-I spilled a bunch of beer on the passenger seat. Just paper towels.

-That's a nice ride, I said. You pull another scam with your insurance company?

-Sure did, he said. You know it's my mutant ability.

His always foul-smelling pit bull got out, limping in its slow, menacing gait. I lit a cigarette and waved.

-Cleanliness is next to dogliness, I said. Don't bring him inside. He might start a fight with Pickle.

-No problem, Saul said. I'll just let him run around. He won't go far.

Saul went inside. The first few tuning chords were played. The bass responded. Microphones were checked. I looked around the block. The lights of other lives played warmly at the windows down the street. I exhaled deeply, watching the breath expand and dissipate in the dark, the warmth and light of my own cohort at my back. I went back inside, talked a lot. I was telling one guy the squirrel story and he said the reason the squirrels loved the house was because we were all nuts. He repeated the word several times, chuckling to himself. *Nuts, nuts...*

Horizontal Jesus played through their set. I went outside and checked the volume. It didn't seem too loud. They were a hilarious band. Mostly instrumental, loud buttrock thrash music. They even played a song dedicated to Griffin's brother's motorcycle, Hell Machine. It was too crowded upstairs, so I went into the basement for some elbow room, chatting with a girl I hadn't seen since the undergrad days of yore. She'd stayed, got married and divorced, trapped in the gentle gravity of the Great Pillow of Iowa City. We caught up and she gave me her number. The band finished playing an hour later, and the house filled with cheers and applause. Pete's voice came through the mic.

-Applesauce!! Thanks!

I returned upstairs to the fiesta. The Pogues were playing on the CD changer, loudly but not so that you had to yell to talk. The perfect volume. Griffin was sitting in the living room underneath *Go Hawks!!*, talking animatedly, pointing at it in explanation. Wim was smoking some pot with Noel's girl, smiling his wide grin. Things were good. There was a knock on the screen door. It was Michelle and two acquaintances. She came in, smiling an addled smile, eyes shiny and loose. She had heard the music upstairs and wanted to see what was up. In the wake of the Revenge of the Squirrels I had forgotten to invite her, but ushered the three in. She didn't seem afraid of Pickle now, though we had sequestered him in Griffin's room, in case he got edgy with all the people. One of Michelle's friends was a large, blubbery guy who called himself Bubba, wearing a Rastafarian hat. The other man's name was Hank, edgy, and lacking the inebriate sociability of his friends. Hank had a vibe to him, something troubled in his eyes. Perhaps too nervous. He wouldn't look at anyone directly, but rather at the cheek, or at his hands, then finger an ebony scar that ran from his sternum to his left ear. He informed me that he was a security guard at the mall downtown.

But I handed them cups, on the house, and bowed a neighborly bow. Bubba was a janitor Michelle knew from the halfway house. He had gotten out the week before and while his words spoke of staying clean, his red-rimmed eyes and incessant, low chuckling said different. Hank was diabetic, and drank down his first beer in one draught. I pumped the keg for him as he refilled the cup. I wanted to know about the scar, but he said he didn't want to talk about it. He would divulge in time.

Someone poked me in the kidney, more than a festive jab. I turned and was looking down at a pretty yet unmistakably underage face. She was smiling broadly, her eyes semi-waxen, semi-ablaze, sirenically smoldering in her cherubic visage.

-Hi. I'm high.

She laughed at her joke. I minced a smile.

-You certainly are. How old are you?

-I'm 18, she said.

A slightly taller girl pushed up next to her, with the same come-hither, dilated eyes. Her jabbering made me uncomfortable. I wasn't sure why they were here. It pitched me a little, in the saddle.

-No she's not. She's 16 like me. I'm Claire. We've been watching you. What's your name? We took some mushrooms. Do you want some? We got some and...

-No, but thank you very much, I said. My name is Othello. Please excuse me for a minute. I'll be right back.

I finished pouring myself a beer from the keg. They were saying Othello over and over, laughing to each other. Holy Jesus, I thought, who the hell brought these albatrosses here? At least they weren't on ecstasy. Mushrooms we could handle. I found Griffin in his room, rolling a joint.

-Did you notice those 15-year-old vixens out there?

-Yeah, they wanted a joint, he said, so I'm rolling one for them if they promise to stay off my cock. I don't need any half-wit jailbait getting me arrested.

-What are you rolling that with?

-Bible pages, he said. It's only about half weed. The rest is tobacco.

-You using my copy, I asked.

-No, it's some Gideon one I found in my truck.

-Who brought those girls anyway, I asked. Did Wim invite them? How long have they been here?

-No idea. They probably just saw one of the fliers.

-Yeah, I forgot about that potential. Tell them they need to get out. Never come back.

Griffin licked shut the second joint.

-Kids these days, he said. No respect for their elders, dagnabbit. With their rock and roll music and teenage pregnancy.

-Make sure anyone smoking dope is in the basement, I said. I don't want to make this easy if someone calls the cops. One whiff and they'll send in SWAT.

-Who'll call them? Griffin said. The music's over. We told all the neighbors. Hell, we invited them.

-Who knows. Just in case. So long as they leave after that joint.

-It might be fun. Come on, how many parties did we crash when were kids?

-Maybe something about not wanting to go down for accessory to statutory rape, I said. I don't know most of the people here, and that Brat Pack is making me jumpy.

Griffin giggled.

-Yeah, the naughty little Brat Pack, he said with a smile. Is your brother coming tonight?

-Nope. He might stop by tomorrow. Baby time tonight. Kate has her classes so he's watching Isis.

-It's good that he's being responsible.

I shook my head slightly.

-Does he have a choice? I asked.

-Bummer, though. Hey, my brother's going to be in town next month. Smokejumping season is over. He'll be in Iowa for a month or two. He's got some art he wants to show us. He called me earlier.

-I'm looking forward to it.

-Besides, Griffin said, the worst you'd get is contributing to the delinquency of a minor.

-What?

-For letting those kids get drunk here. At most it would be

like a week in jail or a fine.

-I don't want to get a fine or spend a week in jail, I said.

-I know, he said, peering closely at the freshly rolled joint in its page. Like the good book says, 'Do not let Hezekiah mislead you by saying something something something.' Think about it.

-Ask not what Moses can do for you.

-How long before Wim puts on his whiskey mittens, Griffin asked with a smile.

-His what?

-Oh, you'll see.

I smiled and shook my head, and went out into the living room. I overheard Wim ask one of the 16-year-olds whether she'd like to see a frozen blue jay. I walked over and told the girls again to leave, but the slightly more sober one pleaded with me to let them stay. No tomfoolery. What they did outside and off the property was their own business. They promised and their eyes tuned in and out to roil of the drugs in their blood. Wim stood behind them, a wry smile smooth across his face. I pointed at him, wagged my finger.

The party went on, pleasantly, and the kegs were soon tapped. Beer runs were made down the block, but it was of no use. The moment a case was introduced, it was descended upon and ravaged. People started frittering their precious ichor away in pockets or bags. I had hidden a spare case outside the back door, near the basement stairs under a pizza box.

An hour later, I was in my room, chatting up a girl whose name I'd forgotten the moment she told me. She looked Middle Eastern with dark, lusty eyes the color of her hair, ravendown. An aspiring undergrad writer. I was discussing art this and poetry that, working the casuistry angle hard. It seemed to be slowly winning her over. No forced laughter, no sidelong glances. I was trying to tell her a joke I'd heard on a Townes van Zandt record about a drunk guy who reports his car stolen to a cop. The cop asks him where the last place he saw his car was, and the drunk guy says, 'At the end of this key,' to which the cop informs the man that his fly is down, and the drunk says, 'Dammit, they got my girl too.' She smiled and wet her lips.

-Stop that, I said.

-Stop what?

-Distracting me, I said.

-How?

-Your incalculable cuteness.

-You'd prefer I was ugly?

-I'd prefer to get to know you better.

Someone came in, flirtus interruptus, and said that the cops were at the door. Griffin was talking to them. I had seen Griffin about thirty minutes ago, and he was already past the stage of intoxication where talking to the Law was a good idea, having tossed back eight or nine whiskey cokes and any number of beers. He was tiptoeing the smart/smart-assed line, if I judged right. If cops were here, they needed to have no idea what was happening inside, and if they were given berth, Squirrel Haus would quickly become our Titanic, Hindenberg, and Jonestown all rolled into one. Contributing to the delinquency of a minor, maybe implied consent, possession of controlled substances, hell, kidnapping if the cop was creative. I tried to compose myself, and checked my watch. 11:34.

I excused myself to the sultry-eyed girl, saying I'd be back in a moment. Griffin was at the door. I looked in the Harem, making sure no one was harassing the 15-year-olds. They were sitting on the floor, pointing at *Go Hawks!!* and laughing again. Christ, I thought, I have to get them the fuck out of here. Griffin was swaying gently at the entrance, vaguely unintelligible, but still innocuous enough that the cop couldn't justify breaking the door down and macing the room. Not yet anyway. I walked up to the door and put my hand on Griffin's shoulder. He was telling the police that if they really wanted to see a party they should travel to Mexico, and that down there it's pronounced socCER, not SOCcer. He dropped Angel's name, saying they were coworkers. He turned to me and gave me a wink. The cop was looking at him, and then to me, eyes bright with impatience. His partner stood behind him by four or five feet, his breath slow in the cold air. He kept looking up Diomedes, hanging above the door. I half patted, half pushed Griffin back inside.

-I've got it from here, I said.

-Sure thing, D, garble garble garble...

He went back inside, smiling wide, and I heard his laughter mingle with the Brat Pack's. I leaned out, careful to keep my beer in my left hand, out of sight, blocking as much of the scene inside with my body. No use looking guilty by association.

-Hello, officer, I also live here. He's my roommate. What can I do for you?

-He's pretty drunk. Is he okay? Did he drive here? He said he didn't have ID.

-No, he lives here with me, like I said. Why do you need see my ID anyway? Officer…?

-Welsh. There was a noise complaint at this address.

Weird, I thought. Same last name as Misha. Why hadn't she shown up? Welsh's partner was trying to peer in through the blinds.

-Really? For what? For this address?

-It says in my report, '933 Daniels. The place with a deer on the house.' A neighbor said the music was too loud. I'm not sure the deer is legal to have outside here.

-We had music maybe three hours ago, but stopped around 8:30 so we wouldn't disturb the neighbors. Are you sure it was a neighbor? I went and told everyone in the area that we'd have music, and no one seemed to mind. We were very careful about that. We haven't been living here long and we don't want anyone around here to have a bad opinion.

-Well that's the call that came in. Would you mind if I had a look inside?

At this request, I set my beer down, and stepped outside. Keeping the door open was further invitation in the cop-brain.

-There's nothing going on in here. Just a bunch of old friends getting together.

-So I can come inside?

-Well, there's no point. It's quiet and the music's not too loud. We try to be good neighbors. We shovel everyone's walk when there's snow. Everything's under control, and we're doing nothing wrong.

-Why don't you want me to come inside? Is there something you don't want me to see? Drugs or underage drinking?

He sniffed at the cold air and smacked his lips.

-You know everyone that's inside right now? he continued. I mean, if there's nothing wrong in there, then why not let me make sure?

He employed the normal cop ruse. I knew to be polite, but firm.

-Well, sir, I know everyone here, and they're all my age, and there are no drugs, and honestly, under the Fourth Amendment, you've got no probable cause just because of a noise complaint that happened two hours ago from an anonymous neighbor, or a source you won't disclose. It's quiet now, and we're minding our own business. No one's passed out in the yard, there's no fighting. We're all old friends here. All is well and right with the world, sir.

The mention of the Constitution had irked him visibly. I could see his eyes narrow when I'd juked his questions. His mouth narrowed, tightening into a sarcastic grin, thin with malice, when I said the word Fourth followed by Amendment. He glared at me for a moment, his eyes making small circles in their sockets. He had no reason to come in. Constable Welsh leaned into his shoulder radio. A sharp set of words issued as he glowered at me.

-Yeah, that's negative at 933 Daniels.

He took a step toward me, pointing into my chest.

-You'd better keep a close eye on your friend in there, the drunk one. If he steps foot outside I'll arrest him. That goes for anyone else.

I decided not to press him on private property issues or entrapment, and decided to just enjoy my narrow victory.

-Will do, sir. I'm an attentive host, and a respectful neighbor. I'm just trying to get by like anyone, and I certainly don't want any problems tonight, especially with the law. I know you're just doing your job, and I respect that. Have a good, safe night.

I allowed a hint of smugness to enter my voice. Just the tiniest, haughty glaze of it, like sweet honey brushed on a suckling pig turning over a spit of hot coals. As he walked briskly back to his car, his cop shoulders were tight, his elbows back and arms raised out, as if his armpits were lined with steel wool. His partner followed, glancing up at Diomedes one last time before returning to the car which sped off and turned the corner at the end of the block without braking, the tires slipping in the snow and the rear went wide.

I figured that he might stake our place out once he cooled off, sniping the drunks as they departed. We had been warned, and I had a gaggle of utterly arrestable offenses milling around the house. Time was, as Jesus said, of the essence. So in that brief window, I had to act fast. People pestered me with questions about the cops, and were they going to raid the place, and I said no, so let's not give them a reason to. I finally found Wim making out with one of the jailbait girls on my bed amid the stack of coats, his hand up her shirt.

-We have to get these kids out of here, I said. Stat. That cop was fucking pissed.

He looked up at me, a naughty grin on his face.

-Oh, hello, Othello, Wim grinned. The girls were asking about you, and I was just telling her some details about how you killed your wife. What was her name?

The girl pushed his hand out of her shirt.

-Did you really kill your wife?

-Sure, yeah, I said. What do you think O.J. stands for? Othello Judas. Seriously, though, it's time for you kids to kick rocks. Wim, take your whiskey mittens off.

Wim looked at her wistfully, with giant blue eyes.

-Sorry, sweet thing. Playtime's over.

-We're not kids, she said, adjusting her bra. I lost my virginity when I was thirteen.

I herded the Brat Pack out the backdoor and we trudged in the snow, through the adjoining neighbor's yard to a street parallel to ours, harshly whispering to keep quiet. I pointed generally downtown, and bid them a-fucking-dieu. They looked like they'd be okay. One of them asked me to show them where The Vine was, and I pointed again and told them they'd have to have fake IDs to get in anyway. By the time I got back, the raven-haired girl had left, and many of the others had taken the cops' visit as a bad omen, and were shuffling out which was fine by me. I checked the basement, just in case she was down there getting high, but no one was there except some fat hippy with thinning hair and dreadlocks, passed out in a lawn chair. We were down to 15 people.

Griffin was in afterburner mode by this time, talking loudly and swinging a can of beer around, manic and gleeful, challenging the room to persuade their parents to say anything negative about the Kennedy presidency. The place had thinned by two thirds, and so we put on some Keith Richards, and I relaxed. The main jailable offense had been dodged, and I could finally settle into the evening. Wim was disappointed, but he had gotten the girl's number. Dig your own grave, I thought. He congratulated me on handling the cops, speeding through his sentences, a bit tweaked, eyes unblinking.

-Great fucking job with the heat, man.

-Crush your enemies, I said, see them driven before you, and hear the lamentation of their women. It's just how I roll with the 5/0.

-And James Earl Jones is your father, Griffin said with a whoop and another pull at his beer.

I looped a white towel on my head, trying to do my best John Paul. I crossed my hand in front of my face, a benediction. All were sanctified in Squirrel Haus, the Isle of the Blessed. Pope abuse be damned.

-He is everyone's father. Amen.

1:12. The party waning, and Griffin painting someone's portrait on a canvas tacked to the wall. Paint dribbled down the plaster. Wim was still up, talking to a girl I didn't know. The music was low, and a few people were trying to pump beer from the dead kegs with esoteric party tricks that they kept swearing back and forth would work. A knock rattled the screen door. Pickle barked stentoriously.

-Shit, are the fucking cops back?

I opened the door to find gothy Roxanne from the hardware store, and hello, and hello, and you saw one of the fliers, and no, Pickle never bites cute girls, he is an ambassador of love, and yes, she would take me up on some of that rum I had offered and I poured her a cup, and oh what a party she had missed, and she told me her stories, and I told her some of mine, and the next morning, legs twined, she told me that she was 17 but almost 18, asking if she could come over again. I left the bed and threw up a thin hacking bile. I could smell chlordecone vaguely in the bathroom, barely perceptible at the base of the tub. I went back, and asked her with all the gentleness and charm I could muster to please leave. She had already dressed anyway and smiled and gave me a receding kiss that brushed across my cheek, and left. She understood, understood something, and I didn't. She left and I lit a cigarette. Griffin shuffled out with a moan, and took a smoke, rubbing his eyes.

-Looks like you had the golden touch last night, brother, he said with a smile. She finally came around.

-Yeah. Everything I touch turns to shit. King Fucking Minus.

I got a dog-hair drink from the fridge. There was a message on the machine from my brother. He needed help framing an addition. $12 an hour.

March

Orfeo e Euridice

A love and a death for his abandoned imagination:
her piled hair, the back of the neck, an ear, then soft profile.

One calls to the apparition with a fast-fading smile.
In the corner of whose eye there is no recognition.

Soundtrack:
Rage Against the Machine, *Voice of the Voiceless*
Beck, *Motherfucker*
Digital Underground, *Humpty Dance*
The Pogues, *Turkish Song of the Damned*
Bonnie Prince Billy, *West Palm Beach*
Geto Boys, *Fuck a War*

In March the War began, Xtian versus Moslem, an oil war, 'Merica and Aye-rack, the Great War of Bush's Imperialistic Push, though no one ever said any of this in the big papers, or anything at all with any conviction. Koppell and other anchors and crews of cameras rolled across the deserts in fatigues, and tape came back of night-time explosions in Baghdad and there was talk of quick victory. The War was not a surprise. Bush had been given the green light the year before, and Colin Powell had been in the papers last month, holding a vial of anthrax. We had no TV channels at Squirrel Haus because we needed an antenna, so we could only glean what we could from newspapers, or friends' televisions, or the radio. It was absurd. Reporters reporting only what the military reported to them. Shock and Awe.

A war had begun at Squirrel Haus, too, of growing size and complexity. Michelle had been there for about two or three weeks, and already there had been a huge increase in the amount of traffic, coming and going, from her tiny apartment. Most of the men were much older, and a few looked well-to-do. Scuba Hank would show up carrying a gym bag. An older man, wearing a threadbare t-shirt with two cans of pork and beans printed on the front, covered by a ratty, unzipped poncho, knocked on the door one day. It was a Saturday. His shirt read, *Two a Day!* He looked like Santa Claus, long yellow fingernails, and dark spectacles. Santa grinned at me, scratching in his yellow beard, licking his lips. He seemed moist, like he'd been dipped in a vat of bodily secretions.

-Michelle here?

-Wrong apartment, I said, holding Pickle by the collar.

He licked the front of his teeth.

-Where is she?

He poked his head toward the door, sniffing, and Pickle sniffed back.

-Upstairs. She doesn't live here. Her door's around back. Don't knock on my door again.

-You're a kind one, he said. Smells like a parable in there.

-I'm serious. I don't care what you're doing up there, but I don't want people associating me with it, or me with you.

-Meh, he said, handing me a business card. It said *Pork and Dreams*. A pig sat in a bathtub rubbing its back with a brush, one little hoof raised. No name on the card. Just a number.

He turned and waved his hand dismissively at me, as if I had said something silly. I shut the door. Griffin laughed in the living room when he saw the man pass by the window, going around to Michelle's door.

-Jolly old Saint Nick has fallen on hard times, he laughed.

-Look at this card, I said, handing it over.

-What the hell is this? he said laughing. Jesus, what is goin on up there?

-Pork and dreams, my friend.

Griffin laughed and looked at the card again.

-What the hell does this even mean? We have to call it.

He dialed the number, long distance, and a woman answered.

-Hello?

-Yes, ma'am, I was hoping to get in on your pork and dreams. I think this opportunity sounds right up my alley.

-Excuse me? Who is this?

-Griffin Buch. Who else would it be? Now, let's get down to brass taxes. How much to buy in? Ground floor. I've got the pork, and I've got the dream. What's it gonna take to make this happen?

He held the phone out and stifled a laugh and then put it back to his ear.

-She hung up on me. Can you believe that?

-What do you want to do tonight? I asked. I'm in the mood for a burger. Want to go to George's?

-Greasy food and greasy beer, and greasy wenches to serve it. Sounds like a decent Saturday. I'll call ze boys and see if they're down.

Michelle came by ten minutes later, asking to use the phone.

-You know, please tell your visitors not to knock on our door. It makes Pickle edgy, I said.

-Oh, I will, baby. I will.

After she was done with the phone, she handed over a few pills, and Griffin and I walked the twenty minutes in the brisk air to the Pedmall and over to George's Bar. I hadn't been there since I returned to Iowa City. I missed the tight booths and tight pint glasses of the place. And the greasy food. And there was a waitress, a skinny girl named Steffani, with high cheekbones and a tender, lukewarm smile the color of milk. What interested me about her were her shoulders. Their angle and the way the muscles tensed around them, the shoulder blades pointing up and out from her spine, angular and jutting. I asked her whether she used to be in ballet. She said she had. She asked me how I knew. I explained it was obvious from her shoulders. I asked for her phone number, which she wrote on a napkin. We left her a larger tip than average when we left, and I told her I'd call her the next day. I thought about maybe calling Elle that night, but Griffin said it was a bad idea. No use drumming up the desert ghosts, he said.

Sunday we spent painting, talking of war and women. We moved the canvases to the kitchen and put down plastic sheets. Five bodies that we counted came in and out of Michelle's place. Santa was back, and a new face we hadn't yet seen. A doughy kid with sagging, pasty cheeks. He was inside for five minutes, his heavy footfalls up and down her staircase. That night we went to bed around midnight, punctuating a quiet, uneventful weekend.

There was a pounding at Michelle's door late that night and heavy eyelids drew up from over my eyes. The beating at the rear heavy and insistent. Michelle's door was right next to Griffin's and my bedrooms. I sat straight up in bed. Shit, I thought, I forgot to call Stacey. The knocking harrowed the still in the house.

-Michelle! Michelle? Please. Please can't you just sell me some more…

The voice was alternating, yelling then crying, loudly, and continued desperately throughout the knocking, begging to be let in, to be sold to. My hunch had been right, though this event was new. Over and over. I heard Griffin yell through his window, which faced Michelle's door.

-Shut the fuck up!

-Michelle! Please…

I got up, as did Griffin and Pickle. We met in the kitchen. I was pulling on pants and a shirt, and Griffin threw on the light. He was shirtless. We stuck on our boots without lacing them. I put Pickle on a chain so we could use him as leverage and get rid of the bawling junkie. We went around back. Pickle was agitated and edgy because we were, and he took his cue perfectly, issuing a low bark the moment we rounded the corner.

The fat kid was back. He froze, mid knock, at the sight and sounds of Pickle and us, shirtless, and redrum in our eyes. I gave Pickle some slack and he jerked against the rope, pulling me bodily. I gave Pickle some more and he smacked his maw at the kid.

-Get the fuck out of here, I said, or else I'll turn him loose.

-I… I'm here to see Michelle.

-It's three-thirty in the fucking morning. People live around here and are sleeping. Get the fuck out of here, Griffin spoke low. Show some respect for people who work, you loadie fuck.

Griffin's light illuminated the backyard scene through the blinds. The junkie's eyes widened with decisions. He could leave and not get his drugs, or stay and run the risk that we were actually going to loose a giant dog on him. His brain wrestled with it, his jaw working small circles, the body's need for his fix, and the very real bodily threat in front of him. Three full seconds passed.

-Okay, I'm going, the kid said. I'm going.

I pulled Pickle back to give the junkie some room. Griffin gave him a push toward the sidewalk.

-If you ever fucking come here and wake us up again, Griffin said, you're not going to like the results. You're lucky we don't call the cops. Do this shit again and I'll kick your fucking teeth in.

The kid hustled away into the night. None of the neighbors' lights had come on, but I was sure they watched through their windows. His crying disappeared into the dark. We went inside. Griffin rubbed Pickle's head.

-This is fucking bullshit.

-I'm going to thrash the next junkie who comes by, I said. I've got to work tomorrow.

-Christ, man, he said, the neighbors are going to start calling the cops. They already did when we had the party, and we told everyone on the block about it. What are they going to do if junkies are running up and down the street all fucking night crying and screaming?

-I don't know, but it has to stop. We look guilty by association.

Griffin laughed, low, and unamused.

-I've got to be up in an hour, he said. Goddammit. Wee Weepy Loadie, coming up the stairs.

-Heh. See you.

-Night.

I fell into a half-sleep, and lay there, my brain unwilling to cease its grindings. I could hear movement out in the house, coffee bubbling, and knew that it was almost time to get up, so I did. Griffin and I didn't speak of the junkie. There was only work to think about, a fact to stare down, and then accept. We had some coffee and talked instead about the War, then Griffin went to work. I called my brother's cell phone and he said he'd be by around 7:00. I had nearly an hour and a half, so I went through the classifieds, looking for any jobs of interest. I refilled the coffee pot and dumped the fresh brew into a thermos, just before my brother arrived. Isis had slept through the night. He looked rested for the first time in a while.

The house that my brother and I would be framing was actually an addition off the back of a house owned by a local shiatsu masseuse named Tyrell Froth. Froth lived on the north end of town, five blocks from Misha's place near the cemetery. Zeke had gotten the referral from a guy called Special K, but whose real name was Something Something Kellog. Everyone called him Special K because everyone else did. Zeke picked me up, and we chatted in the kitchen briefly. Zeke refilled his travel mug, and we drove over to meet the new client.

We pulled up to Froth's house, a sprawling monstrosity of a dwelling, with a wide yard that ran behind to a gulley full of leafless trees. I finished my coffee and flicked the cigarette out the window. Misha told me she had gone here a number of times. I lit another smoke.

-Crikey, I said, will you look at this place?

-Yeah, Zeke said. I've driven by it a million times and always wondered who lived here. Turns out it's a massage school.

-Do they give the proverbial happy ending?

-We can ask. Maybe they'll give us a rate. Wait till you get a load of this guy.

-Pork and dreams, I said and Zeke gave me a weird look.

-By the way, he said, don't litter in my clients' yards.

Ezekiel knocked on the door, and some figures the shape of blurs shifted inside behind the frosted glass. A younger guy, rotund, named Kyle answered the door and invited us in, and pushed a button on the house intercom system, announcing our arrival. He served us weak coffee with cinnamon in it. Who the fuck puts cinnamon in their coffee, I thought, drinking it to be polite. Froth came down the stairs and introduced himself to me, shaking hands. He looked like Falcore the Dragon, a sallow face with ropey cheeks, and a huge moustache that bristled off his lip, sweeping out to the sides. Falcore, or a mutated Goose Gossage. The theme from *The Neverending Story* played in my head.

My brother had already drawn up some floorplans and elevations for the addition, and was going over them with Froth, spreading the designs out on the kitchen counter. I chatted with Kyle, and stepped outside for a smoke. He joined me. I dumped the rest of the cinnamon-infused liquid into the snow, and set the cup on the front porch. I walked around the house to get a sense of its size. It was a huge, stately place with columns, and in the back a triple-level deck with stairs that run from the ground to the third floor. I lit my cigarette and stood in the chill. The sun hadn't quite crested the trees that lined the gulley.

-Fucking cinnamon in coffee, I said.

Kyle smiled and shook his head.

-No kidding. He does it every morning. Cinnamon.

-Every morning?

-Yes, he said. I'm a student here. Learning massage therapy.

-You live here? I asked.

-Yes, with the other students, Kyle said. Froth has his clinic, his school and home all in one. —You got a light? he asked, taking another smoke out.

-Here you go, I said, handing over the lighter. How big is the house?

-It's like 6000 square feet, he said.

-How much does he charge you for rent?

-It's market price, he said. I did some research. My room has wooden floors.

-Do you all do massages?

-Yeah, but since I'm still a student, I don't get paid yet, but I can keep any tips.

We all four walked two blocks over to the coming job site. Zeke and I spitballed some ideas about the addition's foundation and how we'd get a cement truck back behind the house to pour it. It was a single-level dwelling with a walkout basement that opened into a large, green backyard that ran toward the same gulley adjoining Froth's. It seemed a shame to me to chew up such a lovely, open space with a bed and breakfast. Bed and breakfast? Where did this guy think he lived, the Swiss Alps? A waste of money. I said that we could maybe get a pump truck to move the cement behind the house. Or we would just rent a skidloader. Froth fretted about costs and he and Zeke went inside to hash out details. Everyone wants a happy ending. There was nothing for me to do, so I walked over to Misha's and knocked on her door, but she wasn't home. I walked back to my brother's truck and waited.

Zeke emerged from inside, and told me to test the ground with a post-hole digger. The first foot was easy, pliant enough. The second foot down was hard with the long cold of the season, sealed tight with frost. The metal nose rang off of the hard earth. I bounced it a few times off the frost.

-Man, this stuff's as hard as that shale we hit out in Colorado with the cabin's foundation.

-Yeah, Zeke said.

-Do you want to try and make it back out there this summer?

Zeke looked around and thought for a moment.

-Colorado? Oh yeah. I've got enough money saved that we can probably frame the house and put a roof on it. I was thinking of a sky blue metal roof.

-How are you saving money? I asked. Christ, you've got real bills, a family. All I've got are student loans I don't pay.

-You ever going to pay those back?

-When I get a real job, I said.

-You have a real job, he said flatly.

-You know what I mean.

We rented a skidloader with a big bore Archimedes-screw attachment to do a pier foundation for the addition. It was my job to stand with a garden hose and pump water into the hole to try and melt the frost so we could get through it while Zeke ran the machine. It bucked and lifted as the screw struck the frost-bitten earth, the full weight of the Bobcat bearing and the tremor in the ground as the steel bit spun. Zeke sunk the bit into the earth, spinning up mounds of dark soil that littered the snow around the twisting steel, the machine stuttering and jolting as he drove the loader arms down, lifting the front tires to give it the full weight. I sprayed water in and shoveled the slop. This process was repeated over and over until he finally broke through into the unfrozen dirt below, churning up heaps of it which I shoveled to the side.

It was a long, muddy, cold day. My feet ached from standing in one place, and I envied Zeke in the heated cab, working the controls deftly. He offered to switch places with me, but, I figured, it was his company, so I might as well let him have the fun parts. By the week's end we had dug the sixteen holes, down four feet each. Even if the ground froze solid, it wouldn't heave the addition's foundation. Quite unlike Squirrel Haus.

Wim's Datsun pickup pulled up in front of the house that night around 8:00. I was watching out the window at the snowfall mindlessly admiring its beauty, heavy and without a break in the white. He got out and ran across the lawn, flapping his arms to knock off the downy snow. He came in without knocking. Pickle looked up from in the living room, and went back to sleep with a grunt.

-Hola. You got a beer? Roads are getting bad.

-In the fridge where they always are, senor. You been at your parents?

-No, with a friend.

-Anyone I know?

-Probably not. Where's Griffin?

-At his cousin's, I think. Not sure, I said.

-Oh, I've got a good idea tonight, since it's snowing so much. It'll be perfect cover.

-Cover for what?

-No, we steal the cable from your neighbor, he said. It'll be nice and dark, and no one will be wandering around, and if we fuck it up, she'll just think that the weather knocked out the line.

-I don't know the first thing about stealing cable.

-Don't worry. It's as easy as white-collar crime.

Wim went to his truck and brought back a long line of insulated wire. We ran it from the living room, through the kitchen, and out the bathroom window which faced the neighbor's house, dropping the coiled excess out into the snow. Dorothy's living room light was on, and the rest of the house lay dark. Wim threw the wire up around an electrical line that ran from the top of Squirrel Haus, and then looped it again.

-That way it'll look like part of the main line, he informed me.

We went through the backyard, around the fence, and trekked up behind Dorothy's. Wim had loaded his coat with pliers and other tools, and was jumpy from whatever he had in his bloodstream. I had given him my headlamp. He scrambled onto the roof by way of a shed that housed a lawnmower, the snow crunching, and he walked gingerly up the low pitch of the roofline. I threw up the wire. The little lamp was muted in the flakefall, and disappeared above my head as Wim pulled the excess back toward him. I stood in Dorothy's yard, warily eyeful for any movement inside. She had no motion lights around her house. I thought I would suggest installing one for her, for safety. The wire tensed and relaxed, and finally, after ten minutes, was yanked up and disappeared into the weather.

Wim came to the edge and dropped the tools to me, and then leaped off, rolling into the yard. We hurried out of Dorothy's yard around the fence. Inside, Wim drew the wire taut from the bathroom, and we duct-taped it along the wall then across the kitchen floor. He went back out to his truck and retrieved a plastic box, returned, and spliced the many colored wires from the line to the box, finally plugging the assembly into the TV's UHF receptor.

-Basic cable, at your service, he beamed.

-Where in the hell did you learn how to do that?

-Dude, I lived in a commune for six months, he said. You learn some useful things there. Some guy who used to work for the cable company showed me. I showed him how to fell trees. I can make soap, too.

-I should learn to counterfeit money. Do they teach that there?

-That's Commune 101, brother.

-So long as you don't start making patchouli in our bathtub, I said.

I didn't bother asking him to show me how to rig the cable. I liked the mystical nature of the operation, and wiring things, besides, gave me a headache. By the time Griffin got home at 10:00 we were watching the news on CNN, and we got most of the basic cable channels, as far up as the TV's dial went around, to 20. Wim left an hour later to visit a friend. He threw a joint to Griffin on his way out the door. Griffin lit his gift and puffed thoughtfully.

-He wouldn't say which friend he's staying with, he mused. You think he's got a girl he doesn't want us to know about? he said, puffing at the thing.

-Have you ever known him to keep secrets?

-I can't believe we have cable, he said.

-Yeah, he was like a pro, I said. He had the whole thing rigged and done in half an hour. It was pretty incredible.

The phone rang, and I answered it. A voice I hadn't heard in a long time.

-Dunham? Why haven't you called?

-Haley? Holy shit, I thought you were in Toronto.

-I've been back a month. Didn't you get my email?

-I haven't checked my email since January. Where are you staying?

-At Monk's, she said. How have you been? When did you get back to Iowa?

-Two months ago, I said. I'm good. I mean, I'm well.

-Do you want to meet tomorrow? I ran into Misha downtown and she said you were back, and gave me your number.

-Misha, I said. Christ, how did that go?

The voice paused for a moment. Haley spoke again.

-She was polite. As usual. Still hates me, though, and understandably. I could tell. Do you guys talk much?

-Not for a couple of weeks, I said. Yeah, I'll swing by Monk's tomorrow. Is he still at the same place?

-Yeah. I'll see you tomorrow.

-You too. See you then. Can't wait.

I hung the phone on the receiver in the kitchen. I had forgotten to ask for Monk's number. Griffin was reading the back of a box of breaded chicken filets, putting the frozen chunks into the oven, talking to Pickle who sat there, slobbering.

-Why can't you find any food anymore without high fructose corn syrup, Pickle? Who was that, D?

-My friend Haley. She's been in Toronto. I haven't talked to her for ages.

-Do I know her?

-No. I've known her since undergrad. Last I heard from her, she was staying in Toronto with some rich guy, shooting smack and living some weird fantasy life.

Griffin turned from his reading.

-What like *Eyes Wide Shut*? Is she a loadie?

-No idea, I said. She spiraled hard after her marriage went bust. Christ, she could've been a Rhodes Scholar.

-How'd that happen?

-What, I said.

-What messed up her marriage? Griffin asked.

-A lot of things. You might say I was part of it.

-Oh, do tell, Griffin said, and put down the box of chicken.

-I knew her husband. He was my teacher when he was in grad school and I was an undergrad here. We were friends for years, but he was kind of a schmuck to her, and she was unhappy being with him. He wasn't a bad guy, just that she said they got married too early. Anyway, she and I got to be really good friends over the years, and she started cheating on him with another guy, Monk. It's a long story.

-So how did you ruin her marriage?

-Well, I slept with her.

-While she was married?

-Once, I said. We were all loaded on opium.

Griffin smiled at me, eyes rimmed with mirth, and incredulous.

-You don't have to bullshit me, he said. Just once?

-Yes.

-While she was married to your friend?

-Yeah, and I feel like shit about it, I said.

-Never knew you for the guilty type, he said.

-Neither did I.

I lit a cigarette and opened a fresh beer, sat there quiet.

-Let's watch the news, Griffin said. Baghdad ought to cheer you up. I've got to get up early tomorrow.

-Me too.

I stopped at Monk's the next day after work. He was still working on his Ph.D. and still smoking crippling amounts of weed. Haley looked ragged as I hugged her, bones in her like a whisk. She had lost a lot of weight, and had eyes rubbed bright to desperation. We drank some Beam on ice, her favorite. She was going to visit her parents in Texas in a few days, and then head back to Toronto. Evidently, the guy she was staying with there was independently wealthy, some trust-funder, and had unlimited access to drugs and fun. She invited Monk and me to come up sometime, and said that we'd like the guy, Conrad, an Oxford dropout. She went on about the houses, and parties, and drugs and the weird women that circulated between, perpetual debutantes and all of it like a masquerade of group showers and orgies, insulated by a high wall of family money. I said that Toronto was pretty low on my list of places to visit, but I'd keep it in mind. Besides, I thought, it's not every day that you can freeload on the back of some rich asshole. Haley said she would be back to Iowa City next month. We had a few more glasses, and I said I had to leave. I got Monk's new phone number, and gave him my address. He said he'd come by when I mentioned we had a pot hookup. I walked home in the semidusk, each footfall in the thin, new snow like a voice hushing the stars themselves, and I thought about as little as I could.

The next day Zeke and I set the posts in the ground, and used the skidloader to move the cement into each hole. I learned the various hand signals to give orders to the driver who sat in the cab, watching from his mirror. The next day after the inspectors again came by and made sure there was enough cement for each pier and signed a piece of paper. We ran the floor joists and the OSB for the floors, all anchored firmly to the original house with steel bolts that held the rim board fast. We were out of the mud. We set about dismantling the old house's rear, removing the siding, and setting the stage for the bout of coming construction. It was easy, but tedious work. I let my brother do all the thinking. It was his company. Later, I called Ballet Steffani, the waitress, and made plans for the coming Saturday and the rest of the week was work.

Wim brought over three girls to Squirrel Haus Friday afternoon. One of the girls he knew from Oregon. They were artsy girls with patent leather converse shoes and fishnets like they only shopped in the Hot Topic bargain bins. One, Clarice, was heavier, with a nose ring and the knee-jerk sarcasm that fat girls have. We five quipped and chatted, and played some video games, and drank. Wim did his two-handed trick. He could roll a perfect joint with one hand while driving, and two simultaneously if his hands were free. He could probably roll them underwater blindfolded. I was jealous. My rolled cigarettes looked like I'd wrapped toilet paper around a deformed cockroach.

Griffin was out cashing his check and running errands. He'd forgotten his license at home that morning, and had to drive home, pick it up, then drive again to Fast Cash. He had been rejected for a bank account days before. Evidently his credit was almost as bad as mine. 355 is a good batting average in baseball, Wim joked to the company.

But I liked having the girls there. Their laughter rinsed away some of the flophouse veneer and made me feel a little less like a carnival barker amid the whirr and rush of Michelle's seedy patrons. The girls were sassy, and had known each other since grade school in Iowa City. Design majors, except for Wim's old commune buddy, Atiya. Her name meant gift in Arabic, she made a point of clarifying. She was a hairdresser, and had her nipples pierced, she said. I jokingly told her to prove it, and she did. Left breast. I winced at the little ring that looped through her dark, erect nipple.

-Holy hell, didn't that hurt?

-Unbelievably, but it goes away pretty quickly. I dated a guy who had his cock pierced.

-Sounds penetrating, Wim said.

-He had to pee sitting down because it would shoot in two directions.

-How would you get through airport security, one of the girls asked. Did it set off the metal detectors?

Wim laughed, and put his hand on Atiya's knee.

-Anyone else got anything interesting pierced? he asked.

Clarice leaned forward on Big Red.

-Yeah. I got my ass pierced. I've got door knockers running through each cheek.

-Ding dong, Wim said, rapping at an imagined door.

-Okay, no one make any backdoor jokes, please, Clarice said.

-What about you, Laney?

Laney shook her head, smiling. She was the quieter one of the three. Griffin got home with a case of beer, and we all drank at Squirrel Haus until 7:00. They thought that *Go Hawks!!* was hilarious. I told them we should collaborate some time. We then walked downtown and hit a few of the cheap bars. Clarice, Griffin and Wim were smoking pot in one place and they told us to leave, so we went to the Foxhead and tried to shoot some pool, but the old men that played there religiously every night beat us soundly, so we quit. One guy who had been there since I was an undergrad and always wore the same faded flannel shirt ran the table off the break. He looked like a Viking, with a long grey beard and the pool table his little felt vassalage and the quarters stacked on the table's rim in tribute.

Later that night, Wim and Atiya slipped off to parts unknown, leaving us with the other two girls. We walked home in the snow. Laney was leaning on Griffin, holding his arm. We had plenty of beer left at the house, and went straight back. It was only midnight, so we each took a Percocet and watched a movie. Then Griffin and Laney went into his room. I could hear her laughing, the only time that night I'd heard much more than a peep from her. The warmth of the drug was doing its slow bodily wave, and Clarice put her feet up on my lap, stretching out on Big Red.

-Can I see your ID, I asked.

-Why?

-I want to make sure you're not seventeen. I only count ten toes here.

She laughed.

-Take it on faith, she said, and grabbed my hand.

We pottered off toward the Dais, and so I kissed her and she cuddled close, and eventually some stuff happened and it was fun. She had a swastika tattooed on the small of her back, rolling and looped across the doughy folds, right angles buckled and warped as if a living illustration of a space-time curvature. I wasn't prejudiced. Hell, free speech and all, everyone has a right to festoon themselves with idiocies of all stripe and creed, I thought. The world is a cold place some nights and upon the terra is only the human warp of assortment and death.

Over coffee and a half pack of cigarettes the next morning, Clarice told me about some friends of hers that sold pills and various things if we ever wanted more than Michelle's Percocet, and since Noel primarily sold coke and weed, and Wim usually only had meth, it seemed like a good idea to diversify our portfolio. Griffin and Laney hadn't come out of his room yet, so Clarice and I talked in the kitchen. She gave me the guy's number and said to mention her name. I thanked her, saying I'd let her know if anything came of it. She had to get to work, and didn't live too far away. I gave her a ride. When I came back, the house was awake, and I offered Laney a ride, too. She didn't live close. After I got back, I realized that no one had made a single *Silence of the Lambs* joke. Not even a mention of fava beans.

Saturday night Griffin stayed over at Laney's, and Ballet Steffani came over with a bottle of raspberry-flavored vodka and Scrabble. She said she had never been beaten. She pulled heavily from the bottle, and chainsmoked menthols. She confided later that she was anorexic, but she didn't need to tell me. Her skinniness was past normal, and her hair was thinning, showing the scalp on the back of her head. She said she liked the paintings we were working on, and she said she painted too. She took a Percocet and washed it down with more vodka. I beat her at

Scrabble soundly, and eventually we were in bed together. I pulled off her panties, finding a crude tattoo on her pelvis. It looked like a five-year-old had drawn a cat's head with a dull crayon on a plastered wall, the lines irregular and wobbly. The cat, clutching a rose in its teeth, looked anorexic too. It was the worst tattoo I had ever seen. I asked her about it, and she told me she had it done in Mexico when she was fifteen. I kept my aesthetic sensibilities to myself. Later, I was kissing her thigh and noticed that she had stopped moving. I looked up. She was asleep. Passed out from the liberal pulls of vodka and the pills. I sighed.

-Shit.

I got out of bed and pulled on some surf shorts and a sweater, wondering why the media couldn't objectify women in a healthier fashion. I looked down at the tattoo. I'd have to remember to ask her why she was in Mexico when she was 15. I pulled the blanket over her, got a beer, and fell asleep on the couch after finishing *The Last Dragon*. When I woke up the next day, she was gone, and had left her Scrabble board and the near-empty bottle of vodka. I couldn't stop thinking about how crude the tattoo was, the kitten with its round head and ears like glommed-on triangles, the porcine nose and the whiskers like lightning bolts. So she dropped her drawers at 15 in Mexico and chose that? It sounded like it would be a good story.

The following Monday Griffin beat me home as usual. We decided to call Clarice's friend, get some speed and work on a painting together. I dialed the number. It rang three times.

-Yeah?

-Hi, I'm Dunham. I'm friends with Clarice.

-Yeah?

-She said you can get things. Fun things.

-Yeah.

-She gave me your number.

-Yeah? How do you know Clarice?

-Through a buddy of mine. Friend of a friend. Clarice has an interesting tattoo on the small of her back.

-Yeah.

-So is it cool if me and my buddy swing by?

-Yeah.

-What's your address?

He gave it to me, and I wrote it on my hand.

-Cool. See you in an hour.

-Yeah.

We decided to bike over, for exercise, still in our work clothes and boots. The weather had turned, and the streets were wet with the melted ice and melting snow. The guy lived on the other side of town, and we made the ride in a little over twenty minutes, blowing through several stoplights, lawns and back alleys. By the time we got there, our hands were numb and our legs soaked. We cursed our rash decision toward health.

We found their place with relative difficulty. Few of the houses along the block were numbered, and the whole neighborhood had a downtrodden look to it, all the houses wretched and waterlogged, the paint sagging on each. We stopped after a few blocks and consorted. Griffin rocked his bike back and forth.

-I don't think the neighborhood coven enforces much around here, he said.

-You mean a covenant?

-Yeah, whatever, he said. I feel like I need a malaria shot.

-Or a rickets booster.

Toodling his bike back and forth, Griffin looked down the street.

-Or a rockin' pneumonia inoculation.

-What's the address again? I asked.

We rode up and down several blocks, triangulating the odd and even numbers, and finally located the house, a squat single-story hut the color of dry margarine and faded magazine covers.

The upstairs looked abandoned and the windows were grimed, filmy. There were two mailboxes, one stuffed with adverts and 'Resident'-addressed envelopes. The other mailbox read simply '416 1/2 BACK'.

We walked down the basement steps, cluttered with leaves and cigarettes, and knocked. A guy with a Mohawk that faded off into a mullet answered the door. A dog-collar tattoo festooned his neck, and he spoke in quick bursts. A throwback punkrocker in the body of a twenty-three-year-old. He was missing a front tooth, and had a slight lisp whistling from the gap in his face. He looked at us neither warily nor with interest. A swastika tattooed on his right hand where he leaned on the jamb.

-Yeah?

-We called earlier, about getting some things. We're friends with Clarice.

-How do you know Clarice again?

-Friend of a friend, I said. I pointed at my back. Her tattoo.

-Yeah, okay. Right. Come on in.

Their basement place was dark and cramped, a low-rent affair and standard-issue punk rock domicile. There was a veneer of trash and a spoilt smell to the place, a layer of vague mildewey dampness floating on the chill, like a minor chord of Heart of Darkness, plus a hint of catshit. There were a myriad fist-sized holes punched in the drywall. Everything was narrow. Griffin whispered to me.

-Mullethawk!

We walked down the hallway, trying not to giggle, toward the kitchenette. One doorless room on the left had some band equipment in it. The kitchen was separated from a cramped living room, covered in swastikas and Nazi posters. A younger couple were making out on a ratty couch, illuminated by a TV screen, and two other shaved-headed types sat there in the dark watching them. There was nearly no volume, just sucking sounds. The couple turned toward the kitchen for a moment, took us all in, and went back to each other's faces. Riefenstahl's *Triumph of the Spirit* played on the TV.

-So whaddya guys want? Speed? Pills? I got some meth, too. Pretty good. Snortable. Or just throw it on a foil.

I settled against a corner, looking toward the TV. Flags and waving babies. I turned to Mullethawk where he stood near what I assumed to be his room, piles of bedclothes and junk visible.

-Nothing supercharged. Ritalin or Adderall would be good. We're health conscious.

He nodded in consent, and ambled off toward the rear of the apartment.

-Yeah, I'm with you on that. I'm vegan, he said.

Griffin was staring at something in the kitchen from where he leaned on the counter. Mullethawk was muttering behind us from the gloom. The neckers necked and the sucking sounds continued. Griffin whispered and gestured.

-Look at that.

On top of the refrigerator sat a plaster figurine of a bear, gaily colored. Its arms were a bright, florescent yellow, and its body was hot pink, with light blue legs. It was twisting slightly, as if caught mid-dance, reminiscent of a Buddha. It had a weird kind of smile set in the yellow head that might make a child cry, and dead eyes that bugged maniacally outward and stared straight out above its trance-like smile. On its forehead a swastika was carved deeply, embossed with bright red paint in the grooves of the symbol. Griffin moved toward the fridge.

-Keep an eye out.

I glanced at the couple in the living room, still making out with a syrupy, practiced enthusiasm. He unzipped his backpack, slowly, and lifted the figurine in a quick rendition of Indiana Jones, slipping it quickly into the bag. The couple on the couch hadn't budged from each other's coagulants, and Mullethawk was still rummaging in his room. Griffin closed the bag and handed it to me. The figure was heavy, solid plaster. I shouldered the bag and we moved away from the scene of the crime.

Mullethawk came back with a cigar box.

-Man, I thought I'd lost this, he said. So what did you want?

-We've already got some Percocet, I said, so we were hoping to get something to lift our spirits. I'll take some weed if you've got anything good.

-Nothing decent right now. Just schwag. Got some Adderall if that'll do. Ran out of Ritalin.

-How much, Griffin asked.

-Five per pill. I'll give you twenty for a hundred-five. I mean, twenty-five for a hundred.

-How about a hundred and five for twenty, Griffin joked.

-Huh?

-No, I'm just fucking with you. Twenty-five for a hundred sounds perfect.

-Sure you don't want any meth? I've got some coke, too. Decent stuff.

-Nah, no thanks, I said. Coke is for the rich man. You guys have a cat?

-Cat? Mullethawk said with comtempt. I fucking hate cats.

He poured a heap of blue pills onto the counter from an aspirin bottle. For a moment, I would have sworn he looked directly at the fridge where the figurine had been. He counted out the allotted number, and pulled the plastic from the bottom of his cigarette pack, slid in the pills and sealed it with a lighter. The couple on the couch were no longer in their throes, and had turned around, watching the transaction. The guy had a shaved head, and the girl had dark hair, combed flat across her forehead and spiking from the sides like a hedgehog. Behind them on the TV, rows of Nazis were marching along.

We handed Mullethawk five 20s, said thanks, and walked toward the door, the backpack heavy with the strange idol. As I was about to turn the knob, a voice sounded behind us.

-Hey!

I turned, ready to fend off a blitzkrieg. The hall was narrow, giving us an advantage like Thermopylae. Mullethawk just waved at us.

-If you guys want to trade any of that Percocet, let me know. I'll do an even trade, pill for pill. Just keep it up in the ear.

-Ear? Griffin asked.

-Yeah, Mullethawk replied, circling his finger in the air. Up in the ear.

-Will do, mein Freund. Auf wiedersehen, Griffin said and opened the door.

We sped away in the chill of dusk, giggling. Not stopping until we were home, panting and wet from the wet roads and exertion. I set the bag down, removing our purloined treasure, and Griffin handed me a blue pill.

-Can you believe those Nazi fucks?

-They were making out to Nazi propaganda films, I said. Genocide: nature's aphrodisiac.

-Look at this Nazibear, Griffin said and hoisted the idol from the bag laughing. Complete with Hitler moustache and everything.

Griffin held the plaster doll and shook it in the air, then held it in front of his face.

-We liberated you from the Nazis, you fucker. You will give up your bigoted ways or else. Where is the Nazi gold? Wo ist das?

Griffin placed Nazibear on the counter and rummaged in the drawer, procuring the Bowie knife, and scraped some of the plaster from the bear's undercarriage. He dabbed the powder with his finger and spit it out.

-Nope. Plaster.

Griffin placed a bill over one of the Adderall and crushed it with the figurine's base. He inhaled the blue with a whoosh through the five and held out the rolled paper.

-Want some?

-Sure. Crushed and powdered Smurf.

-Your name sounds Smurfish.

-I think it sounds Smurfy.

-We should have told those Nazi fucks that you're Jewish.

-Why?

-I don't know. It would be funny.

-I'm not Jewish, though.

-But you are Smurfish, Griffin said.

We crushed another pill and braffed it. I was blowing blue and bright green snot from my nose all night and would for the rest of the week. Where were the warning labels against that? I should get a lawyer, I thought. We painted until 1:00 that night, smoking heavily, finally stopping when we realized we had to work the next day. At least tomorrow's Friday, we agreed, and went each to our restless sleep.

I had noticed a swelling under Griffin's chin several weeks before, on his left side, up near the jaw. Over the weeks it had become larger and larger until one night he could barely talk. He'd always had these growing up. Tiny cysts that formed under the skin. A benign form of cancer, he'd told me. It caused him a lot of pain, and I didn't usually notice them, but he had a lot of scars on his neck and back where they had been removed surgically. He bore it, though, with a stoic grimness. Like a soldier who lost a limb. Life got on. No use crying about it. He came up to me when he got home from work.

-Man, he said. I need you to cut this thing out.

-Why don't you ask your mom? I have a degree in fucking poetry, not surgery.

-I need this thing out now. It's fucking killing me. It's pressing on my throat and tongue. If I could see it, I'd cut it out. I did them on my shoulders. I can't see this one well enough.

-I'm not sure I can, I said. I can maybe do stitches, but this?

-I can't cut it out. Not on my neck.

-Not even a mirror, I asked? I mean, I don't want to hurt you.

-It's not going to kill me.

-I only play a doctor with girls, Griff.

Griffin swilled from his can.

-Now you'll have the chance to play real doctor. Really impress some chicks. Come on, I've got everything you need in my kit.

-I'll need a drink or two first, I said.

-Me too. You can huff some of that pesticide, knock your jitters right out.

He explained with obvious pain, working his jaw, that if I would just cut down to it, that he could pop it out. He didn't feel comfortable cutting his own neck in a mirror next to the artery. I took a Percocet for my nerves, and gave him two. I passed him a bottle of rye. He took a deep quaff sucking the air between his teeth against the venom squirts, and passed me back the bottle. I did the same. I took another Percocet, washed down with half a can of beer. He had a nice med kit, from his mom, and I got out cotton balls, rubbing alcohol, the scalpel handle and a couple of the individual blades. An hour and a half later, I was ready for my new role as sawbones. I washed my hands and put on the gloves.

-Which scalpel size do I need to use?

-Any of them will work, Doctor.

-Doctor, it's time to prep the patient.

-Doctor, he nodded with confidence.

-Doctor.

We tied Pickle up outside so he wouldn't get antsy with the knives and blood. Griffin lay on his back in the kitchen with a towel under his head, and I took a seat beside him, Indian-style, but shifted to my knees for better balance. He wiped down his neck with rubbing alcohol, saying it would be cooler to use the whiskey, but we decided against it. I took a Sharpie and drew a dotted line over the bulged skin. I took another slug of the rye, for courage, and Griffin sat up, took a long draw, and I went to work. I set my right pinky on his jaw, drawing the scalpel tenderly across the line. Biting on wooden spoon, Griffin winced when I made the first real cut, and a thin, watery line of blood ran down from the incision. I pulled the skin, spreading it taut with my thumb and forefinger. His neck muscles bulged, pulse thumping. I moved his chin back slightly for a better angle and better light. I held the instrument like I'd hold a paint brush. He spoke through his teeth.

-Come on, hucker. Cuh ih. He removed the spoon. Cut the fucking thing.

I drew the blade a second time into the reddening tissue. With each pass the skin would part a little, white and pulpy, then fill red and flow. I figured that after five beers, two Percocets and a healthy bracing of whiskey, I wasn't in any shape to be hurrying along with a razor. I dabbed away the blood that flowed thin and steady from the widening incision. I had closed a wound on my arm once with fishing line and a needle in Colorado, but had never played surgeon.

The subcutaneous flesh split more easily with each pass of the razor, and a tiny hole appeared in the middle of the cut, a dark mass emerging from the rent flesh. I sliced gingerly at the sides, nicking at the edges of the wound with the blade. I could feel Griffin's legs tremor softly. I made another pass with the instrument and brought the cut a full two inches under the jaw.

-I'm almost there. I can see it. One more cut.

I pulled the scalpel a little more and the skin, tight from the pressure of the cyst. I flipped the scalpel around in my hand, and got the bottle of isopropyl alcohol.

-Hold on, I said. This is going to hurt like a bitch.

I poured a small stream just above the wound which came out red on the other side. He stiffened at it, wincing through a groan.

The cut itself wasn't bleeding as much as I thought it would, but the alcohol thinned the blood and it pulsed out. I daubed at the wound with a cotton ball and gave Griffin some latex gloves.

-The rest is yours, Doctor.

He didn't say anything. His eyes were nervous, edge of feral. He reached up, and pinched at the cyst with his left hand, and with his right he dug and picked at his neck. His eyes now in a thousand yard stare. There was a sound, like a tiny foot pulled from mud, and he doubled in pain. A gush of blood spurt from between his fingers onto the floor and towel. I bent down to help but he pushed me back, and a moment later he tossed the cyst or tumor or whatever, onto the floor with a plop. His eyes were watering, and his jaw tight. I gave him wad after wad of gauze, each quickly turning a bright red.

-Here, I said. Here.

He held the gauze at his neck, and lifted his hand so that I could pour a bevy of isopropyl into the wound. He hummed in pain, breath panting, and his hands shook when not clamped to staunch the blood. I did the rinse two more times, then he dried the area with more gauze. He lay back down, in a different spot on the floor, and I held the skin back together on his neck while he winced. The skin was loose, but not flapping, and I applied seven butterfly bandaids, then a patch of gauze over the whole thing, taping it under his chin and to his neck to hold the viscera underneath. I looked at my watch. The whole thing from cut to swaddled had taken eight minutes.

He took the isopropyl bottle and the rye bottle, and went to his room. I went outside and let Pickle in. He sniffed at the blood. I poured the last third of the rubbing alcohol on the floor, and rubbed at it with a clean section of the bloodied towel, and set the med kit and items on the counter. I didn't see the cyst. The stain was not coming out of the tan Berber, and it looked like someone very tiny had given birth and lost a lot of blood.

An hour later, Griffin came out and looked at the stain on the kitchen carpet. He spoke stiffly, and slowly. The last of the rye was gone and he set the bottle on the counter next to the pile of steel and bloody gauze.

-Christ, that bled like a stuck pig.

-I hope I did it okay, I said. Something that deep might get infected.

-I've got antibiotics, he said. Besides, I'm on the Walk It Off, Pussy, insurance plan.

I laughed.

-What's the co-pay?

Griffin put his finger lightly to the bandage again and smiled with pain.

-Co-pay is no-pay, dok, he said.

-Let me know if you need any dental work done. After this, I'm up for anything, I said.

-Yeah, I was thinking I could use a gold tooth. Like Michelle.

-Are you sure it feels okay?

Griffin nodded and touched at the bandage.

-You did great, he said. Thanks.

-We'll keep an eye on it. Watch for infections.

-Yeah. Christ, my head hurts.

He got two beers from the fridge, and handed one to me.

-Doctor.

-Doctor.

He held his palm against the bandage for a while.

-Fuck, he said. I think I'm going to have to take a day off from work tomorrow. Thanks for helping with that.

-Anything, Griff.

-How big was the cyst? he asked.

-The thing is, I don't know where it went. I tossed it on the floor and it's not there now. I think Pickle ate it.

Griffin laughed, winced through the smile and gave the dog a rough pat on his giant head.

-You dumb dog, he said. I was going to donate that to science fiction.

The workweek came and went, cold and damp, and the next weekend we were out with Noel and Brom, marching around downtown in the March spring. Wim was at his parents' land helping clear branches, fallen with the weight of the wet, heavy snow. We four visited a few of the nicer bars to ogle the girls and flirt. We sidled into Quinton's around 10:30 because they had good deals, and were usually stocked with the floozy, frat-chaser types. We were settled in a booth, idle and smoking, catching up with Noel and Brom. The place wasn't too crowded.

A guy sitting in the booth next to us, with a polo shirt and pretty hair, turned around leaning over the divider and asked me, across Brom and Noel, for a cigarette.

-No problem, I said, but you have to tell me a funny story. It's my only rule.

He got out of the booth, and walked over, standing at my right.

-Come on, dude. I'll buy one off of you, he said and took out his wallet.

-Go buy a pack then, dude, I said. Sorry, that's my rule. Just one funny story. What's the big deal?

The guy puffed his chest a little, as if to load up on charm.

-Why won't you just give me one? What's your big deal?

-Why won't you either buy your own pack or tell a funny story? I said. They sell smokes at the bar.

His jaw flexed and he turned to the bar where I was pointing, shaking his head. He returned to his booth. Brom smiled and leaned forward, speaking lowly.

-I was about to give him one, Brom said, but I wanted to see how far you'd push him.

-Push him? Fuck him. He can't just buy a pack? Christ, it's just one funny story for one cigarette. They are American Spirits after all, not those cheapjack Camels you smoke, Brom.

-How long have you been doing that? Griffin asked.

-What, the story thing? I said. The smokes cost me money. What does a funny story cost to tell? Sometimes you get a good one.

-You never ask us for stories when we bum, Noel said.

-You boys, I said, tapping off the long ash for effect, are hilarious enough as you are.

Noel put his elbows on the table.

-These guys behind me are talking about how they should kick your ass.

Griffin rolled his eyes. I smiled at Noel and Brom.

-Really? Fuck them. Let them try. After I beat his head a little, maybe he'll end up with a funny story after all.

I scooted over a little so the befratted booth would have a clear look at my face. I smiled, very warmly and politely, and shook the pack of smokes in the air. Not a snide hint on my face. One of polo guy's boothmates saw me. I made sure our eyes met, and I smiled some more. A very polite grin. He looked confused and moved his head out of my line of sight.

We ordered another round, and Noel eavesdropped on the other table's snippets and bluster. Griffin lit a cigarette and blew the smoke in their direction.

-Remember what happened to Kildere?

-Yep, some frat fucks like this kicked all of this teeth in, Noel nodded.

-He was in the hospital for weeks with reconstructive surgery, Griffin went on. He even knew the name of their frat because they were wearing the shirts, but the cops wouldn't do a fucking thing.

-I know. Eye for a tooth?

Noel pushed forward from his listening post.

-Don't get in a fight here, he said. I'm still on probation. I can't get in trouble. Besides, it's not like it was these guys who did that to Kildere.

-They all look the same to me, Griffin said.

-Noel, you sell drugs, Brom said. Lots of them. Why are you worried about probation?

Noel shook his head.

-It's not like I'm clocking on a street corner. I've still got another year left.

-How much pot did they stop you with again? I asked.

-Like five pounds, Noel said. It cost me ten grand in lawyers just to get four years of probation. My lawyer had me dress up in my army uniform so the judge might be lenient.

-But it worked, Wim said and flicked ash into the tray. Didn't special forces count for anything?

-I'd say the ten grand worked a lot harder than my service record.

-Lawyers, guns and money. Too bad we've got none of them, Brom said.

-I've got a gun.

-You know what I mean, Griffin.

We decided to leave before any hostilities flared up. The waitress brought our bill, and we left our stack of fives and ones on the table with a nice tip in assorted coins. I didn't put my coat on. As we passed by the booth I heard someone mutter *Assholes*. Without turning, I put up my left hand with the *droit juste* extended. Fuck you.

I could hear them get up behind me, and a small scuffle with Brom ensued. I could hear Brom talking in his staccato bursts. Noel kept moving toward the door. I didn't blame him. I winked at him and turned around. Polo guy pushed Brom as he tried to offer a Camel. Brom pushed him back. I blew some smoke out and took a drag from my cigarette in cinematic fashion.

-Come on guys, I said. No need to get stupid.

The guy threw his arms out in a questioning manner, the old you-wanna-piece-of-this stance. He moved toward me, repeating the movement.

-Why? he said. You want some of this? Huh? You want a piece of this?

I laughed and he pushed me. Shit, I thought, the guy was strong. He had protein shake and creatine muscles. Ham Arms, like blocks of processed meat, and big all the same. He looked back at his friends and pushed me again.

-Look, I said, anyone with an IQ over pi should know this is stupid. You want to start a fight over a cigarette?

He mouthed the word pi. He pushed me again.

-This isn't a fucking tickling contest, I said.

I flicked my smoke in his face.

-There's your fucking cigarette.

His hands went wild at his face and the cherry burst gleefully all about. I grabbed his shirt and brought my left elbow in a tight arc into his cheek. Bone on bone. I pushed him off, and he staggered back. Griffin darted past me, joining the fray. He punched Green Polo Guy square in the face before he had a chance to react, and he stumbled back into Ironic Pink Polo Guy who had just stood up. Green Polo Guy fell back, holding his nose, which instantly ran red. Griffin's gauzed jaw was seeping, too.

Ironic Pink Polo Guy then punched Brom in the head with a chopping shot, and Brom grabbed his shirt and they scrabbled at each other. I turned toward Ham Arms. He turned toward me with a soot mark on his cheek. He took another step, and his jab got me in the nose. I circled to his left and his second punch went wide, and he lurched forward. I brought a hard right hook into his temple, and grabbed his hair and began uppercutting. His jaw slammed against skull, an ovation of loud clicking amid the din. Something hit me in the back of the head, and my vision went opaque. I let him go, and a bottle rattled on the floor.

Green Polo Guy was still wrestling with Brom, and Griffin slid behind him, putting him in a full nelson. Griffin slammed the guy's face into a table, then threw him onto the floor. One of the crew, tall, with a ball-brush patch of hair above his chin, hadn't moved at all, and when I raised my eyes to him, he put his hands up and shook his head, looking at this three friends. I looked up at the bar. The bartender was on the phone. I hadn't seen Ironic Pink go down. Ham Arms punched me in the side of the face and I returned.

-Shit, we have to get out of here, Griffin said. They're calling the cops.

We skedaddled. Noel had been outside the door, watching through the glass. We'd scratch Quinton's off of our social tableau for a while. There were other venues. We hustled into the dark. Noel's bright yellow puffy coat was too big a risk out in the open. My head was still throbbing from the bottle, and there was blood in my nose. We took seats at a booth in the Deadwood, ordered some beer. I wetted a napkin and ran the tissue in and out of my nose. Griffin ordered a vodka for his wound, and another for himself. He procured some gauze and tape from his pocket, poured the vodka on the wound, and let it dry in the smoke-thick room. I checked the incision with a lighter. The butterfly bandaids were still fastened and no spread of red through the skin. Griffin pushed at the wound. A thin line of blood stemming. We replaced the dressing and spent the rest of the night happy with our crusade against the fascist-hearted and storyless brutes of the world.

The remodeling project was going smoothly, now that Zeke and I were well out of the mud. The week sped by. Within three weeks of starting the bed and breakfast we had nearly the entire frame up, and the roof on. The design was similar to what we would do with our cabin that summer. A great wall full of windows would face west to catch the setting sun, and the second floor would open out, with a steel railing at the edge, to the cathedral ceiling of the main room. Two bedrooms would occupy the upper floor. We thought it good that we had the chance to do a trial run here, with someone else's money, to prepare for any bumps that might occur in Colorado with our cabin.

It rained lightly on Saturday, clearing much of the remaining snow that had drifted and piled in the backyard. The thawing brought out more and more junk, slow trash materializing, and now with the drizzle, the rust heaps rose like sogged flowers as their white shells shrank. It was all there when we moved in, the pile of old bikes, yard's corners with ruined lawn furniture, middens of dirty milk crates, all of which went under the shrill white cocoon and so under the memorial fog of work and wassail. I stared at the mess from the back window, and decided to do some spring cleaning. Griffin found me pulling on my raincoat and wanted to help. I handed him a pair of leather gloves. We set to task on the Gordian mess of steel and springs and wires, wrenching free what we could.

-Who the hell lived here before, Sanford and son? I said.

Griffin pried loose a bike chassis from another.

-If it's gonna be that kind of party, I'm gonna stick my dick in the mashed potatoes, he said.

-Moreland, I said. Fucking hilarious.

-It's not Redd Foxx?

-Nope. Mantan Moreland, I said. Now, if you'll excuse me, I have to go fuck the chicken.

We worked in the rain for four hours, stomped the frail grass to mud around the yard, and later we backed up Griffin's truck and loaded all the junk into the bed, then drove it over to Oak Grove Park. There were several sets of train tracks there, and a small access road that led down past a set of couches and chairs and a three-legged table that the homeless used sometimes. We unloaded all the bric-a-brac at the hobo campsite.

-Maybe they can sell the steel to the scrapyard, Griffin said.

-Or assemble the bikes and start a bike gang. Santa's Hobos.

-Dingaling, he said, holding out his hand. Can you spare several linear feet of copper pipe, brother?

We were still giggling when we got home about hobos wheeling around Iowa City on bikes, with baseball cards in their spokes and little baskets full of cans, one hand on their handlebars and the other on a chain whip, dragging lengths of copper wire and pipe behind them. There was a message on the machine from Layna, and Griffin held the machine up to his ear. I couldn't hear what she said very well. He deleted the message and took the phone and went to his room. He came out an hour later, an odd smile playing on his lips. I had started *The Outlaw Josey Wales*.

-Layna's going to visit in May.

-Really, I said. Visit visit?

-I don't know, he said. Seemed like she might want to get back together if I can just get my shit together. She said she missed me.

-So she's talking about moving here? I followed him into the kitchen where he hung the phone on the wall and stood, looking confused, nodding his head slowly.

-Seems so. Maybe. I don't know, he said. I don't know.

-Good news, brother, good news. Endeavor to persevere.

Griffin nodded solemnly again.

-Time to clean up my act, he said, opening the fridge for a beer.

-Any royal oats you need to fuck out of you? I asked with a smile.

-No. I can't lie to her, he said. I never have, and it's not time to start.

-Well, I said, you can't slip into the same woman twice.

-What does that mean? He turned to me from the fridge.

-Hell if I know, I said, and we talked of the better things to come.

Griffin brought home a urinal from work the next Monday. His crew had been hired by the city and were running pipe for a new school. Someone had ordered the wrong fixture so the crew had thrown a brand new, perfectly good urinal into the dumpster. Griffin fished it out and brought it home.

-Christ, he said, it's fucking ridiculous the amount of waste in a city job. No wonder they can't fund the schools right. They throw away all the money before they even get the desks in the rooms.

-Is our children learning?

He laughed.

-You wouldn't believe the overhead, too. If something doesn't fit, something isn't exactly right, they just throw it away. It's unbelievable.

-You know, why don't they install urinals in every home bathroom, too?

-I know, he said. It's hard enough to piss straight after sex.

-I should write a poem about it.

-Check this out, he said, changing the subject. The news said that Geraldo Rivera is being kicked out of Iraq because he gave away troop positions.

-Maybe they'll send him to a military court and shave his moustache. Twenty years in the brig for treasonous facial hair, I suggested.

-You know who also works for Fox now? Oliver Fucking North.

-Ollie North? Wow. Who's next? Liddy? A holograph of Nixon?

We talked about installing the urinal in the bathroom, but after a summary examination of the network of pipes in the basement, Griffin decided it would require far more work than would be worth it. Besides, it would be a hard sell to Fat Bastard to knock off another month's rent for the effort. We wrote the name 'Duchamp' on the edge of the urinal bowl in black enamel paint, and mounted it on the wall in the kitchen, higher up than normal in case some guest at a future party were to get the wrong idea in an addle-headed state and fill it with his micturitions. The house was in bad enough shape without someone pissing all over our art. The urinal added a personal touch to the kitchen. Maybe we could put a plant in it. The mismatched kitchen carpet was calico now, stains of color and stains of paint and blood creeping in like bruises.

I heard the phone ring in Griffin's room and he walked in and answered. I heard some talking which grew more excited and pitched. Two minutes later he came out, the phone in his left hand, laughing.

-Was that Layna again? I asked.

-No. Are you ready for this? Patman just got out of prison in Arizona. He's heading for Iowa City.

-Patman? Fuck, I said. I haven't seen that crazy bastard in years. How's he getting here?

-Knowing him, hitchhiking or stealing a car. You know his feelings about going Greyhound.

-Crikey, I said. You didn't give him our address, did you?

April

History

I would ask
you to explain

the moments of
bare declension and

lilting isolation but
I have only

one vocabulary called
poverty and four

dried bodies two
bees two wasps

collected today from
my window sills

and this story
because I've time

to speak of
industry and rest

Soundtrack:

Led Zeppelin, *When the Levee Breaks*
R.L. Burnside, *Shake 'em on Down*
The Hollies, *Long Cool Woman*
John Lee Hooker, *House Rent Boogie*
Nick Cave, *Papa Won't Leave You, Henry*
Blind Lemon Jefferson, *Gallows Pole*

It was raining daily now, unceasing in variations of light and heavy, knocking the chill from the corners of the season, and the clouds swung open like casements with a patch or two of direct light and then back together again. Friends came by in their raincoats and under umbrellas, and drank and talked and parted, and at night during the week sometimes we would paint together or they would call out ideas and Griffin and I would try our best to draw what the others saw in their heads. The Heart of Darkness spewed forth its rancid offerings, and the kitchen carpet soggy at each step, so we patched and repatched and bagged and laid out plastic by the ream. The kitchen was filling with canvases, too, some paintings tacked loosely to the walls and others stacked and leaning, sitting on bricks to keep them out of the water. Haley was back and she and Monk came by a few nights, and played cover songs, or their own stuff. He on guitar, her singing. She had a beautiful voice, a smoky tremolo like a whiskey aether, and she swayed unsteady as she sang, this or that substance addling the equilibrium. I wanted to talk to her, convince her to seek some sort of help, but the Walk-It-Off-Pussy insurance doesn't cover lapse and relapse and triple lapse. You can't force anyone to stop when they don't want to. Interventions are for suckers, she'd always said. But she was cleaner now in Iowa City, and some color had returned to her cheeks, thanks to Monk.

I began carving a bow from some extra materials left over from the remodeling project. I had a piece of oak, nice grain that ran like a map of the wind, but I would need a piece of poplar from the hardware store. It took me a while to find a decent piece, sifting the many boards stacked in the lumberyard. Too many knots through the grain. I found one, and ended up the line next to Roxanne's cash register. She smiled at me, more a grin of formality, a victory and some weird prize with no actual kindness, the cheshire flouting of something. But what? I smiled back, lip extending more up than out, and grabbed my receipt from the cashier and went home.

During the days Griffin and I would work our respective jobs, come home, and work on our projects, whatever came to mind to make. Griffin was doing the arrows, fletcher's apprentice, sanding thin shafts from straight branches collected at random points along our drives or perambulations. He then dried them over a barbeque his cousin Cyril had given us, in the backyard under a tarp hung from the trees at the property line as the rain ratta-tatted on the thick cotton duck. I whittled and sanded the bow, adding some red finish to give the wood flavor. I had bought some hemp twine and braided a seven-foot length from three strands, then sanded the bow some more. A few evenings later in the kitchen, Griffin fletched on three feathers to each arrow, securing them to the shafts with fishing line and super glue. The gash in his throat had healed. I cut notches in the ends of the bow for the hemp line, tying one end securely. I bent the length across my thigh while Griffin tied the other end. It had a good pull, smooth, hand back to shoulder. I dabbed some more glue on the handle, wrapping some twine around it, and then more twine where the shorter oak ended. It made a nice flexing noise when the bow was drawn, clenched and taut.

We put on ponchos and took the bow into the backyard. Griffin had lacquered the arrows and charred their ends so they wouldn't shatter on impact with a trash can or car door. We nailed a four-by-four sheet of plywood to the back of Squirrel Haus, and then nailed a couch cushion to that. Michelle poked her head out her window and watched us. We'd painted three concentric circles of diminishing size on the cushion, and a white dot for the center. We shot arrows that thumped on the wet cushion until we couldn't see in the dusk, and went inside, the happy huntsmen. Spring filled our lungs and the trees like tuning forks ahum in the grey air and little buds on them the season's autobiography each. The thawing earth smelled rich, fecund, a little of death, decayed leaves turned to loam under the blanket of snow, now released to remind the living of metaphors and transience and such. Work was good and life steadied. The junkies visiting Michelle's apartment came and went but quietly now. Griffin had to chase only one away, at 3 AM, brandishing a tire iron and the loadie running away down the block, crying from fear and his jones. Michelle still regularly asked to use the phone, and would stand in the front yard talking, with an umbrella. Griffin wanted his own bow, so we started that. I was writing a lot of poetry, too.

The Heart of Darkness bled its rust-colored water every day, and every effort we made to staunch the flow was futile. Like shooting a cannon at a jungle. I pulled two breadbags over my feet and walked in the kitchen to call Fat Bastard. I told him the place was beyond our expertise, and something would have to be done. He said the rent was due by the fifth, and somethingsomethingsomething. We ended up sandbagging the closet with bags from Griffin's truck, since the snow was gone and he no longer needed them for traction. The water flowed down the rotting drywall like down a cave's flowstones, glistening and pulsing with movement, under the several sheets of plastic we'd lain up. There was nothing we could do about it. You cannot wrassle with nature. The Bilge had an inch of standing water in it, and smelled of mold, taste in the nose like licking an old postage stamp. We would have to figure something out. I sent off the rent for the month.

On Monday, the second week of April, my brother handed me an envelope.

-Here is your tax information.

-You're not filing me? I'm an employee, aren't I?

-Well, you're subcontracting from me technically, he said. I report paying you, and you have to report what you made. Business is business.

-Don't you have to have insurance to be a subcontractor, like if I get hurt?

-Subs only have to insure themselves, so just don't get hurt. I can't afford the extra payments. I'm putting away the extra for Colorado, for the cabin.

-Okay. What's the IRS designation?

-1099, he said. You'll have to file receipts and all that stuff if you want to avoid paying.

-Receipts? I don't need no stinking receipts. I never save them. You get most of the ones I don't throw away.

-I know. I do have them if you want them.

-I don't think I make enough for the IRS to chase me down.

-Don't underestimate them, he said.

-Maybe someday they'll wise up and stop giving all the rich people breaks. Bush wasted all of Clinton's surplus on those $300 checks we got last year. I never even got mine. Poof. Gone.

-Well, politics aside, you should file that, he said, pointing at the forms.

-What did you buy with your $300?

-A muffler.

-Did you keep the receipt?

-Duh, he said.

Let the tax man come, I thought, nothing taken from nothing leaves nothing anyway.

The remodel was moving along at a feverish pace. Ezekiel had learned the brunt of his carpentry from a lapsed Amish guy named Little Paul. He was short, with thick hands like an Eskimo, and was strong in a showy, workman way. I had worked with their crew in grad school, for the extra money, and learned what I could. Little Paul was not a member of the Amish community any longer, but still had the work ethic of a Mennonite bull ox doped to the gills with speed. Ezekiel had adopted the same pace and unrelenting drive.

We now had the addition fully sheeted and tyvekked. We had

rolled the tar paper on the roof the previous week, on a day when the rain stopped and the sun was out and the wind loved the earth and trees, drying the roof. Froth would hire the electrician, and we would do the wood floor, and the siding, too. Zeke offered the plumbing work to Griffin as a sub, but he said he couldn't do it on the weekends. He'd have no time to relax. He was making good enough money with his crew, but would ask around. We finished his bow, and some more arrows over the next few days after work, and had regular archery contests in the backyard into the dusk. The strangers coming and going from Michelle's gave us strange looks when we greeted them as Junkie, or, Hey Loadie. We had a deer's head mounted on the front of the house and were often in the backyard now, arrows zipping from homemade bows, and dark looks for the junkies that moved to and fro. We wanted a precedent set that we would give no quarter when it came to Squirrel Haus and our peace and quiet, unless we were the ones wrecking it.

That Saturday, I finally went to the library to check my email. There were a few important ones, and a lot of stuff that would make my penis larger. No one had complained thus far about it. I printed off some tax forms, and paid for the pages at the counter. I couldn't check out books because I owed the library fifty bucks. But I could still use the computers. I had plenty of books at home anyway.

I got home and Wim was there, talking with Griffin about his bow in the backyard. We agreed to make him one too, if he bought the materials. He'd been flashing a lot of money lately, and we just assumed he'd cashed in one of his several trust funds. He invariably brought over designer-type beer and always had a steady diet of drugs at the ready, so there was no real point asking. We took turns shooting the cushion on the house.

-Do either of you know anything about filling out a 1099

form? I asked, pulling them from my back pocket.

Wim turned.

-What's that?

-Subcontracting form. Evidently I'm a sub to Ezekiel.

Griffin waved his hand through the air.

-I haven't done my taxes in years, he said. Don't bother.

Wim smiled.

-I've never done my taxes, he said. No need.

-You just know how to steal cable?

-And how to hire an accountant, he said smiling.

I took the papers and documents inside, and got beers from the kitchen. I traded a can for the bow.

-When's the last time you paid taxes, Griff?

-I haven't ever made enough for the government to care. It would be a complete waste to try and find me, let alone audit me. Let's get down to brass taxes here. You can't squeeze blood from an empty wallet.

Griffin loosed a shaft which thumped dull against the cushion and fell into the grass.

-Besides, he continued, I'll just get an accountant. Hire one from in front of Home Depot.

-Oh, bother, Wim said, I seem to have dropped my monocle into my cosmopolitan. Jeeves, Wim snapped his finger at me. Procure me another martini, and on the double, there. And a wheelbarrow of gold. Dunham, fetch me a glass of shampahn, the 1972.

I bowed deeply, arm circling before me.

-Bully for you, suh. Coming right up, chop chop, suh. By the way, Wim, can I borrow forty nickels for a box of wine? I'm talking about the 2003 vintage.

Wim dug in his pocket and threw a handful of change at me, acknowledging the reference.

-No, old sport, bully for you. For your trouble.

I picked up the change, laughing, retrieving every coin, and looked at Wim.

-Where the hell have you been disappearing to these days, Wim?

He smiled coyly and handed us each a designer beer.

-A gentleman never asks, and a lady never tells.

Griffin shook his head.

-Wim, you're neither a lady nor a gentleman.

Smiles again from Wim.

-Can I borrow that bottle of pesticide? he asked.

I squinted at him in the last rattle of sunlight.

-The squirrel juice? What do you need that for?

-I might have a rodent problem.

-Sure, I said. What are friends for?

That night Wim and Griffin went downtown, and I stopped by Monk's place. Haley was out with some guy. Monk was showing signs of wear, the caretaker role playing hell with his eyes and heart. We sat down in his living room and he offered me his bong, which I declined.

-You're looking worse for the wear, Monk.

-Friends like these, he said, and took a long rolling pull from the tube.

-Between us, how is she?

-You know, he said, it's not that she's doing poorly at the moment. That's relatively good, but only relative. I'm talking about how she used to be.

-I remember.

-I mean, she was brilliant, Monk went on. Then all that noise transpired with her marriage, and then with her and me.

-I was in the mix, too.

-I guess I just feel responsible, he said and drew again from the smoke-filled tube, and spoke exhaling. One moment it's all back to school this, straight and narrow, and in the next breath she's on the phone with that asshole in Toronto and he's flying her back first class.

-You want me to talk to her? I said. Not that it will somehow supersede what you could say or do.

-I don't know, he shook his head. How do you make someone want to live?

-I don't know, Monk. Read Nietzsche. Work carpentry. Do too much acid?

He didn't respond.

-She's not going to change if she doesn't want to, I said.

-Let's go for a drink, he said. I'm sick of sitting here and looking baleful.

We joined Wim and Griffin at the Foxhead. Griffin wanted to go see whether Laney was at home and he dropped some money on the table and departed. The rest of us stayed, and watched Longbeard the Poolslayer rack up his wins and stroke his long Viking beard. I watched the balls fall, listening to a whiny alt-band on the juke. The balls caromed, and whacked, and in their little vectors they went around and fell in holes and were lifted out that darkness again and again to be placed into their plastic geometry.

Wim and I took off. Monk was nodding off in the booth, so we walked him home and wished him a good night. The rain had stopped, and water dripped now from the trees, so we walked in the streets. Wim and I got home and watched the news. Evidently poor people with darker skin than ours were dying the world over. But mostly breaking news about celebrity sightings and other chatter. An hour later, there was an odd hum, off through the air, drifting in the open windows along the night's street. I went and opened the blinds.

-What's that noise?

I heard a scuffling gait coming down the sidewalk, loud, but far away. It got closer, but the street was dark and I couldn't see far. Then I heard the noise again. A kazoo. Rossini's *Barber of*

Seville. Griffin came into sight, in front of the house, joined at the shoulder with another figure. Griffin was tooting the kazoo in staccato bursts between bouts of laughter. He was very drunk. Noticeably.

We were introduced with flourishing hands, and a kazoo rendition of *Thus Spake,* to Major Tom. Griffin played the Bowie song, just in case we'd missed the reference. Major Tom was a scruffy-looking homeless guy whom Griffin met in the Hobo Jungle where we had dumped the bikes and other junk from the yard the month before. Major Tom was holding a nearly empty bottle of cheap-label rotgut, and the brown fluid dripped from the tangled grey wires that stuck from his lip and chin, giving the menagerie a sheen. He pulled off his weather-stained poncho, wet and shaggy-dogged. He wouldn't let Pickle get near him, and his hand moved toward something in his pocket when Pickle moved. Griffin beamed and handed Major Tom a can.

-Don't mind Pickle, he said. He's too damn lazy to hurt anyone.

-How did you guys meet? I asked, watching Major Tom dump the pile of clothes on him into a pile on the floor.

-I was taking the shortcut through the Hobo Jungle, Griffin started in. No offense Major Tom, and he was sitting at a fire.

-Right on. And?

-I took a seat and didn't have a harmonica so I played a kazoo tune, and we got to talking.

-So you brought him to Squirrel Haus?

-That's what you call this place? Major Tom said through sucking teeth after a hard pull at his bottle.

Griffin pointed toward the bathroom, trying to sound serious.

-Yeah, he said, Dunham there agent-oranged a family of squirrels.

Major Tom took another pull and mashed his brows.

-What's with the deer head, then? You guys hunters, or just weird?

-Both, Major Tom, Griffin said. Major Tom is a fucking vet. Vietnam. Tell them some of your stories.

-I don't much feel like retellin' them, the hoary man said and swigged his dregs.

-You told me, Griffin elbowed him. Come on, man, there's plenty of party left in you.

-What do you want to know, bub? he said, jabbing his finger at me. I got an upper-case heart and a lower-case life. No family. No kids. Happy?

I got him a towel. He smelled sour, like spoiled linoleum. He rifled through a tattered duffel bag under his disrobed poncho. The kitchen carpet was dry enough from our sandbags and my shopvac work a few days prior, so we took seats there. He took a seat in the corner, and borrowed cigarette after cigarette from Wim, not from me. Wim rolled a joint and passed it between them. I was offered a hit out of politeness, and as usual declined. Griffin started in again.

-No, I'm serious. This guy was in the Shit. He was telling me all about getting caught a clearing in the jungle and the Vietcong were blasting his platoon. Hairy shit.

I gestured at Major Tom.

-Are you a major? Is your name Tom?

Major Tom shook his head, his cheeks red in patches, big-pored, purply nose. He fixed his eyes on me, deep folds of skin encircled them.

-No. He said that, not me.

-My grandfather got shot in Korea, I said.

Major Tom sniffled and hit the joint, both speaking and inhaling.

-Did he die?

-No, I said. Lucky for me. He was 17.

-Hm. Lucky him.

-My second cousin was a tunnel rat in Vietnam, too, I said. Maybe he was my third. I don't know.

-That so.

Major Tom wouldn't join in the chatter, quiet, with a yes or a no or a hm-hm in answer to all queries. I asked him if he wanted to paint, or do a collaboration. Griffin leapt up off the kitchen floor.

-That's a great fucking idea. Major Tom, you tell me what to paint, and we'll paint it. It will be like art therapy. Some people pay a shitload of money for this stuff.

Major Tom shifted nervously, and said no, and his hand went back to his bag. Griffin sat back down, dejected, and played Chopin's *Death March* on the kazoo. Ten minutes later Major Tom was snoring in a corner. I got a round of beers for everyone, and set one in front of him. I looked at Griffin, teetering at the waist on steadier legs. He took the kazoo from his mouth.

-I like what he said. Upper-case heart and a lower-case life.

-Everyone's worth a bit of poetic wisdom, I said.

Wim pointed at the instrument.

-Where did you get that?

-The kazoo? Griffin said. I have no idea.

We stayed up late, and Griffin roused Major Tom who said less and less, only moving his head with small jerks as answers, slipping in and out of sleep. He fell asleep again in the corner with the empty bottle in his hand. Confidence in the kindness of strangers just strange enough to defuse worry. I threw a blanket on him, his hand jerking suddenly toward his breast pocket. He refused a pillow. I told him yawningly there were some chips and food around the kitchen if he was hungry. He hadn't asked us for anything the whole time, except cigarettes.

Wim slept on Big Red, and Griffin stumbled to bed and fell down, exhausted, leaving his door open. I brushed my teeth, yelled 'It's 3:23, and no Vietcong ever called me nigger' into the house, locked my door, and knocked off, promising I'd cut off more than a finger if they ever brought the draft back. To hell with a finger. I had more.

-Fuck!!

My eyes opened, smeary and heavy with sleep. I sat up, and Griffin's voice bellowed again through the house.

-Fuck!! That motherfucking cocksucker.

I limped out to the kitchen. My knee hurt from something. Major Tom was not in the kitchen, and the blanket we'd given him was folded neatly on the floor. Wim was sitting up on Big Red with a towel wrapped around his head, eyes like innocent rhinestones peering through in the clear morning. I walked into Griffin's room .

-Did you see me put any money on my bed last night? he asked, flipping bedsheets from the floor. Or on the counter? Anywhere?

-Huh? No, I said. I don't think so. I saw you go to bed is all.

-That fucking asshole.

-What? Wim asked.

-Major Tom. He ripped me off. I'm sure I had almost fifty dollars last night. I thought I stuck it on my bed, or on the desk.

He pointed at the cinderblock and plywood desk. There was nothing on it except a plate with some marijuana seeds on it, and some loose change.

-You sure you had it, Wim asked. Maybe you spent it.

-No, I'd fucking swear I had it right here. Did you hear him leave?

-No, I said. I was dead in the water. Wim?

-Nothing at all. Dead to the world.

-Well where the fuck is my money?

-Let's look around the house and go check the Hobo Jungle.

We poked around Griffin's room, checking under the bed and in his various pockets. We found nothing and walked at double step toward the woods by the train tracks. There was no one there. Just a spoilt fire, wheelless shopping cart and other bric-a-brac, and some of the bike parts we'd dumped. I half suspected that Griffin had just spent his money, imagining that he still had it by night's end because it's always better to imagine money's presence than the absence. I had done that many times. Plenty of money imagined and plenty more to lose.

Monday morning I drove the White Elephant over to the job site. There was a rusted pickup in the driveway, next to my brother's, with the faded sign of a long-defunct catering company on the side. Sweet Eats it said and the words there like shadows in full sunlight. I parked in the street and walked around the back of the house. My brother was talking to a guy, skinny, with a stoop to his spine and closely cut but kinky black hair. When he laughed he bent at the knees.

I introduced myself and shook his hand. He said a bunch of things in a hurtling gait, and I understood none of it. Thick Creole accent, and when I asked him something in French, he bent at the knees, laughing. His French was as undecipherable.

-Hooah, det dah su pro fransay. Noom lah wee tah dowmb Loosana. Jwase, nie ta. Ha dey yuh sai dee ah pahr lai fransay? Hoo. [My heavens, that is some proper French you have spoken. Quite unlike the dialect spoken in my home region in Louisiana. My Christian name is Joseph. It is a pleasure to make your acquaintance. If I may posit an inquiry, how have you come into such Francophonic adequacy?]

-I dated a French girl in high school and another in college, I said.

-De so' loukah, hain non on em old kriol. Hoo. Sho la gem sum dah ejikay tay. Collguh, fusho. Hoo. [Yes, the women of France are rather fetching, however they cannot compare in the slightest to the fairer sex from my region in Louisiana. I would rather enjoy pitching woo to a matriculated woman, though. Hoo.]

He rolled at the knees again. Zeke cut in saying that Joseph was the electrician Froth had hired. Joseph rented another house around town that Froth owned, and was here working off some back rent. Joseph pottered off talking to himself. He was around thirty, I wagered, and seemed a good-natured sort. He spent the morning laughing to himself, all around the jobsite, hoo hoo hoo. The building inspectors came by that afternoon to check the framing. There were no problems.

The next day Ezekiel's voice called from around the front of the construction site.

-Dunham, look at this!

I slipped my hammer into its hook on my belt and walked to the front of the house in the garage. Zeke was holding a business card. He handed it over to me, laughing. *Long in the Saddle Video. J. Froth. Director and Producer.* There was a silhouette of a cowboy in a duster, holding some rope on the card. The card's stock was quite nice. I handed it back and he turned the card over in his hands.

-Is that what I think it is? I found it here on the ground.

-Long in the saddle? It has to be porn, I said. What else could it be?

-Maybe theme porn. You know, cowboys and Indians.

-You could call one *Bury my Cock in Wounded Knee.* Poke-her-haunches is a lonely housewife, living in her teepee. Her husband is away declaring war on the white man, and the pemmican delivery guy comes by one day.

-Then the drums start in.

Zeke nodded.

-*Wounded Knee*? Yeah, he said.

-What about *The Battle of Little Big Porn*?

-Nah, too easy, he said. Starring General Longdong Custard, and Cumosabe.

-Geronimo!

-Shouldn't that be Geroniho, he said.

I shook my head derisively.

-Let's not get offensive, now.

We swapped offensive titles for days, and plots and names, laughing. It was hard to keep a straight face when Froth would come by to check our progress. He smoked thick, expensive cigars, was a porn-directing masseuse building a bed and breakfast, and looked like an evil version of Falcor. It was too perfect. Whenever he walked off, Zeke or I started singing the song from *Neverending Story*, fa la la la la. It was good to see my brother smile.

Joseph's head popped up one day from where he was stooped, running wiring in the bathroom.

-Ya bi laun heah nuh du wee. Wah so droh? Wah so fawn? [You have both been distractedly amused this past week, laughing. Might I inquire as to the genesis of your droll mirth-making?]

We explained the joke, showing him the card. Joseph told us that he'd known Froth for years, and had once bought an RV from him, thinking he could fix it up and live in it. He said he had found a backpack full of dildos inside. He walked us the two blocks back to Froth's giant house and into the basement, entering through the walk-in door, where Froth kept his tools. In the adjoining hallway, under the stairs were several large boxes, full of bondage porn from the past three decades. His knees rolled, and he couldn't stop laughing. Neither could we. The magazines were old, grainy photos in each.

Back at the job site, Joseph also told us that the whole house was wired with surveillance equipment. He'd seen it all in a room which Froth kept locked, but one day the door was slightly ajar and Joseph had peeked inside. Monitors and speakers and VCRs. He asked to see the card again, chuckling.

-Does he tape inside when people are getting massage treatments? I asked. They have to get undressed before and after.

-Hoo, dem ah ain sai. [As per your query, I am uncertain.]

-Fuck, was he taping us looking through those boxes? Zeke said.

-Nah, deah on saif parm haw, unnerm stayah. [Fear not, my friends, he does not use surveillance equipment under the stairs. It remains one of the few secure areas in the house, away from prying eyes.]

-We'll have to start calling him Sinister Money.

-Ya connay dem Spel K? Hoo, I go bo un dai, wah ahs worrnn fuh dyeh, tray ennweh, sa ah gon trew deh devees, trew e ehn, das o Spel K gin ih tah suhma bel dahm. Hoo hoo. [Do you recall our mutual acquaintance Kellog, whose sobriquet is Special K? One day I was overcome with ennui whilst in Froth's general employment working around his maison. As I was perusing his DVD collection, I happened across some of his private collection, which contained, lo and behold, Kellog, making passionate love to an anonymous belle dame. Hoo.]

Joseph laughed again, and made the international sex sign with his fingers, hooing, his face cracked in smile.

-Hoo. Spel K, Spel K. Gawdam. Hoo hoo.

I would have to call Misha and warn her.

Sinister Money stopped by with regularity now that the interior projects had started up, and he could get a feel for the layout and size of the house. Every visit would send Joseph into a fit of laughter, and my brother had a hard time talking to Froth without smiling. Especially when I would stand behind Froth and drive my hips, back and forth, swinging a lasso, mouthing *Special K, Special K,* my hammer's handle swinging back and forth from my belt. After Froth would leave Ezekiel made us promise to not fuck around anymore, but he could never say it with a straight face.

We had set the windows and doors, and were at work on the siding while Joseph ran the myriad wires and light fixtures inside. A plumbing crew arrived we didn't know. Froth had hired them without consulting Zeke. The inside of the project was expansive, though, and when Froth would bring by his friends or clients, they would speak in low tones of admiration. I heard him tell one friend that he had designed the house himself, while he chomped on a fat cigar. I told Zeke later that day.

-He said he designed the place himself, I said.

Zeke threw his hammer to the floor.

-That greasy motherfucker.

-He'll get his, I argued. This project is costing him what, a hundred and twenty thousand? For a fucking bed and breakfast in Iowa City? He'll go broke trying to cover the mortgage. There's no way this place turns a profit in Iowa City.

-But that costs me potential work. If someone came here and liked the place, and they knew I designed it, they might want to hire me. You know.

-Is defamation a tax write off, I said.

-Ask Sinister Money, CPA, Zeke said.

-Fucking Sinister Money.

At home there was a message from Misha saying she needed help moving, and no one she knew had a truck. I called her back.

-Why? I asked. You can't fit your stuff into your friends' Saabs?

-Don't be an asshole, Dunham. Can you help or not?

-Of course. Why are you moving?

-I found a new place, she said. This was just a month to month. I took it after you, uh, moved.

-I see. When do you need to be out of there?

-Next weekend. Can you help?

-Most certainly.

-Great. I can buy you lunch or something after.

-That's bully.

-Huh, she said.

-Nothing. I'll give you a call in the next few days.

-Look, I really appreciate this, she said.

-It's nothing. By the way, don't get any more massages from

that school by your house. Or, well, your soon to be old house.

-The clinic? Why not?

-I'll tell you later. It's a long story.

-Why not just tell me now, she asked. I've got an appointment there in a few days.

-He's sinister. Trust me. You'll be ready this Saturday by eleven or so?

-Wait, tell me more about that guy.

-I'll tell you the story this Saturday.

I asked Griffin if I could borrow his truck the next weekend, and he consented, saying his parents would be coming up, to visit, so he wouldn't need it. I tacked a note to the wall next to *Go Hawks!!* reading *Take down before G's parents arrive.*

-When does your brother get here, Griff?

-A couple of weeks, he said. He's coming in and staying with my parents, then heading up to IC. He has to be back in Arizona before fire season starts. He's way more tolerant of their sermons and brimstone bullshit than I am.

-Yeah, I said. Zeke's the same. He can deal with it somehow. So Kell's a bona fide smoke jumper now?

-Yeah, Griffin said. He's got some stories to tell. It's a crazy line of work.

-I can't wait to see him again. It's been years.

Work, week, and work went by at the bed and breakfast. We had tied the siding of the addition into the existing house's as best we could. They wouldn't match exactly, but with a coat of paint, it wouldn't be too noticeable. We were also given the roof, which would take another week, and then the wood floors inside. I asked my brother whether he wanted to help Misha move that weekend. He said why not. Any excuse to get out of the house. Isis was well, but things with Kate weren't. He mentioned the words post and partum in a voice that belied a deeper issue. I left it alone, and knew he'd talk when he wanted to.

Griffin's parents showed up Saturday around 9:00. Griffin and I were up, having coffee and Zeke showed up, too. When Thom and Linda showed up I ran over to *Go Hawks!!* and threw a blanket over it. A work in progress, we could claim, and it cannot be seen until it's completed. I hadn't seen Griffin's parents in ages. We passed an hour of pleasantly distant conversation, his mother fingered the crucifix on her neck as her eyes drifted over the contents of the house, paintings covered on the walls, and an arrow through another painting that Griffin had lobbed there a few days ago as performance art, Diomedes upon entry and a blue jay in the freezer, tales of dead squirrels in the walls, and a toxic pesticide, and the whole flophouse mélange requiring strained filial apology, but so long resigned had his mother been that she could no better counsel her son than the Good Lord could or would in His way and mercy, a sentiment echoing the same general bent from my parents. I loved them, but I'd had about enough Jesus for three, maybe four lifetimes.

During a lull in the conversation I called Misha before the less polite questions issued from Griffin's parents. Misha had finally packed all of her things. I remembered moving in with her some years back. She was sentimental about every rock, stone, or scrap of paper, broken vintage telephone, ribbon, phone book from college, middle school, boarding pass and receipt from foreign trips. She could throw nothing away. I hoped there wouldn't be too many boxes to haul. My brother and I excused ourselves and left Griffin and parents, and drove over toward Misha's. With my brother's truck, we wouldn't need Griffin's.

Misha was outside when we each pulled up. She waved and returned to moving some of the smaller items into her car. We waved and parked. Walking toward the house, Zeke turned to me.

-Be honest, he said. Did you slash her tires that one time?

-No.

He smiled.

-You can tell me if you did. I don't care.

-I really didn't.

-Really?

-No one believes me anyway.

His eyebrow raised, and he cocked his head at a funny angle and pulled at his beard, drumming a deep octave.

-Oh. Really? I believe you.

-Fuck you, I said. It was my car. She was borrowing it. Why would I slash my own tires?

-Maybe if you didn't act so crazy all the time people would be inclined to trust you more.

-Yeah, well, I guess I'm fortune's fucking fool.

-Well, you got the last part of that right.

-Seriously, I said. Do I really act that crazy?

He looked at me for a moment.

We moved the assortment of boxes and furniture from her apartment into the two trucks. It took two trips, lugging all the pieces of a life I used to belong to out and to another place, wondering whether she'd been with anyone, knowing that I shouldn't be jealous, but knowing that I couldn't not be. I resigned myself against such thoughts on the second trip, and we were done in five hours. Misha thanked us, always directing the praise at Zeke. He was especially charming around others' girlfriends. They talked about Isis and Zeke produced several pictures from his wallet, and Misha promised to babysit once in a while, if she had time.

She ordered from Flabbo Bros. Pizza. We had a beer, and Misha had lemonade, busying herself with opening boxes and putting things in their places, excited at the contents of each box as if she'd never seen them before. Her new place was airy and bright with April's sun. There was no rain in the next days' forecast. The pizza came, and she handed me a twenty. I walked down and back up the stairs. I set the box on the counter, and opened it. All of the toppings had slid off the pizza, and lined the sides of the cardboard, integument piled beneath another beneath another.

-What the fuck? Zeke said. Did you drop the damn thing? I'm starving.

-I didn't drop it, I said.

Zeke called Flabbo's on his cell phone. He began calm.

-Yeah, hello. We just got a pizza delivered and all the toppings fell off the pizza. I think your delivery driver must have dropped it. It's no big deal, but we're going to need another one.

I could hear a voice through the phone, tinny, go on about something. Zeke threw his phone into the couch and directly started putting on his boots. He nodded at me.

-Put your boots on.

-What did they say? Misha asked.

-That motherfucker said the pizza was delivered flat and called me a lying asshole, Zeke said.

-What? said me.

Misha looked up from the box of pictures she was rifling through. She was familiar with these outbursts from me, but not from Zeke. I put my boots on. She picked at one of the pieces.

-Well, maybe we can salvage part of this.

Zeke told her no. I turned to my brother.

-He really called you an asshole?

-Verbatim.

We drove over to Flabbo's with the pizza in Griffin's truck. Zeke was too conscientious as a business owner to risk the potential publicity. The place was near Squirrel Haus, a block down from Iowa City's two porn stores. In the parking lot, Zeke turned his shirt inside out to hide the logo, and we walked in. I recognized the guy behind the counter from the delivery, his belly unmistakably huge. There was one customer in the place, eating a slice and listening to a Walkman. The delivery guy was evidently the only one working that day, busy at the ovens, the phone, and the driving. Stomach protruded over his belt, and his shirt clung to him for the sweat. He recognized me, and took a defensive posture with a long wooden pizza paddle.

-What do you want? he said.

Zeke dropped the box onto the counter.

-I'd like my money back. And an apology from your delivery driver and the guy I spoke to on the phone.

-I am the driver, the guy said, and I delivered the pizza flat. What happened after that is your problem, not mine.

-What do you mean flat, Zeke continued. You haven't seen the pizza, but you know what's wrong with it.

-I didn't say what was wrong with it. You did.

-So, I spoke to you on the phone, too? Zeke said. Do you think it's good business etiquette to call your customers assholes?

-I never said that.

-So you're calling me a liar?

Zeke flipped open the box on the counter. I stood behind him, trying to look menacing with my arms crossed, but couldn't stop snickering.

-How do you explain this? Zeke pointed to the box.

-You must have dropped it, the man said. It was fine when I brought it.

-So now you're calling me and my brother a liar, I said.

-I didn't say anything, the man said and ran his forearm across his head. Just get out of here before I call the cops.

-Call the fucking cops, you prick, Zeke said, voice rising. We haven't done anything except come to complain about a shitty employee and shittier customer service and your shitty product.

-Oh, yeah, look at you, tough guy. You've got a real big dick, don't you?

-Yes I do, and what's better, I can actually see mine, Zeke said. What kind of way is this to run a business?

The phallic reference seemed to wound the guy and his eyes

narrowed. My brother looked back at me to shake his head, and I saw Flabbo snake his left hand under the counter for something, holding his arm stiff and to his side. He edged near the flop-down door of the counter, dividing the kitchen from the eatery, and slammed it home while he raised his other fist toward Zeke. I saw a little canister in his grip.

-He's got mace. Don't you dare mace him, I said.

Ezekiel stepped and flashed out his right, slapping the bottom of the can, and it flew from Flabbo's grip, rattling back into the kitchen. Zeke threw the counter lid back and nearly went after the guy, but instead, put up his hands like an old bareknuckle boxer you might see in a photo wearing a singlet and a handlebar moustache.

-Queensbury Rules, he said.

Zeke smiled back at me where I stood with my arms crossed, and rolling his fists in an old-timey fashion he turned back to Flabbo. Flabbo grabbed a large butcher's knife, also behind the counter, his hand shaking as he brandished it, and its shape shone gleamy. Something moved in my periphery. The sole customer was edging toward the door.

-Don't come any closer, Flabbo whined.

-The customer's always right, I said.

Flabbo held out the knife, shaking, and told us to stay back. Zeke looked at me, not believing it either. His eyes wild and shunting, Flabbo picked up the phone and dialed. The bells on the door tinkled, and the customer was out through the parking lot, jogging away and looking back over his shoulder. His slice of pizza half-eaten on the table. Flabbo's words raced.

-Yeah? 911? I'm here at Flabbo's and these guys are all over me. I don't know how long I can hold out.

-Are you fucking kidding me? Zeke said.

He turned his blubbery cheek into the receiver, voice high and wailing.

-They're coming right at me!

My brother laughed and picked up the pizza box and hurled it past the counter, past Flabbo. It made a beautiful slow-motion arc through the kitchen behind, flying past the oven, the toppingless slices pulling apart with the furtive motion of the hurl, one landing in a sink, another glancing off a hanging ladle, some falling to the floor, and one slice slapping the wall on the far end of the restaurant, another slapped the wall, leaving a print of reddish grease along the tile.

-You can keep your pizza, you degenerate puke, Zeke said.

The man was frozen, the knife still wobbly in his hands. We went outside and I gave Zeke a cigarette.

-Can you believe that guy? he said. Holy hell.

-Some people aren't cut out for the service industry.

-They're coming right at me, Zeke said.

-I don't know how long I can hold out.

We laughed for ten minutes.

Two cruisers pulled up with little thumps of their tires as they entered the lot, while we leaned against the truck, idly smoking and laughing about the pizza slice stuck to the wall and Flabbo's squeal. One officer jumped out with his hand on his weapon, and the other went directly inside in the same manner. We put our hands up, still laughing, and held out our IDs.

Everyone's story was taken. The two officers conferred outside, by the restaurant door. They were smiling, and pointing inside. A different cop came over to us, head shaved, and skin the color of burnt sienna. He tried to take a serious tone when he spoke, but his voice cracked a little.

-So, I need to get this straight, the cop said. You guys didn't go behind the counter at all?

-No, sir, Zeke began. He insulted me over the phone after he botched the delivery, and we came down here to rectify the situation, peacefully of course. I'm a business owner. I have a reputation to uphold. That guy in there is stressed out, I'm sure.

I totally sympathize. I work hard, too, but there was no need to threaten bodily harm. He was brandishing a knife, and he lied to you guys on the phone. Isn't that a crime?

-Well, the cop said, when the call came in to us from dispatch, they made it sound like there was a robbery going on.

-Robbery? Zeke said. The only robbery here was our lunch. We've been ordering from Flabbo Bros. for years. It's our favorite.

-Well, no one here is going to be pressing charges. There's no crime. The best I can do is get your money back for the pizza.

-That would be great, sir. We would appreciate that. Thank you, sir.

I could see Flabbo watching us smile with the cop inside from behind the glass door, his hands and belly flat against the pane. We were given our money back, and got some sandwiches elsewhere, then drove back over to Misha's. She wasn't surprised at the story, and laughed at the guy's call to 911. We ate lunch, and said our goodbyes. As we drove back to Squirrel Haus I wondered aloud whether her move had been symbolic, like a breakup-haircut, but Zeke didn't think so. He said she looked like she had just moved on, not just moved. We returned to Squirrel Haus and my brother recounted the story to Griffin. His parents had left already. He handed us each a beer from a sack in the kitchen.

-Coldbeer?

-Don't mind if I do, said Zeke.

-Goldberg Bros. versus Flabbo Bros, Griffin said after a long draught. Classic.

-I haven't been that close to trouble in a long time, Zeke said. It feels good once in a while to let loose.

Griffin shook his can of beer and opened it with a knowing smile, spraying the liquid all over the counter.

-Pressure, my friend. Pressure requires release.

-Exactly, Zeke said and took another drink.

We had an archery contest and kept no score. Everyone got a trophy of foaming aluminum. Our aim was getting better, and we passed the afternoon dregs peacefully until Ezekiel had to get home. I gave him a thanks and a wave as he drove off, and took the bow from Griffin, alternating shots between sentences.

-When exactly should we expect Patman?

-I don't know, Griffin said. He goes here and there they say.

-And what exactly was he in jail for this time? I asked.

-Best I can tell, Griffin continued, he got caught selling pot to an undercover cop out in Idaho, or something like that. He had somehow cozied up to some rich people there, and was on a yacht, tried to sell to someone, and then got popped. I heard this all through the grapevine.

I let an arrow fly. Almost a bully.

-Christ, I haven't seen the guy in something like five years. About as long as you.

-Well, Griffin said, he's been in jail for the past two, so put on your fun hat when he gets here because he's going to want to rage against the machine.

-Was he in state or county?

-County, then state. The real Mordor.

Shaking my head, I sipped my beer.

-I'd gladly take no jail at all, I said. I'm too pretty to go to jail.

-You and me both. Patman, though. Well. Maybe he's Patdawg, now.

-With 'thug life' tattooed across his stomach. Or 'drug life'.

Griffin laughed and lit a smoke.

-Better than 'smug life'. Remember that time he threw a dry ice bomb into Wal-Mart?

-Yeah, charged with terrorism, I said. He couldn't get a passport after that.

-Back when terrorism actually meant something.

-He'd be blackbagged and adios these days.

-Brassest of taxes, Griffin nodded and made the sign of the

devil. Are you ready to rock, Guantanamo?

Work: Zeke and I set into the flooring. Froth wanted cherry for the floors. An expensive choice, but lovely wood to work with, dark, and fine grained, and we made an intricate design alternating the cherry with pale walnut at the entrance and on the landing. Joseph was finished with the electrical work, and hadn't been by for a few days. The flooring was easy work, and we got through it quickly, the living room too, and up the stairs to the second floor, which would be carpeted. We ran a sander lightly over the areas of the wood to remove any rough joinery. We then put down a coat of clear lacquer.

That night Haley called and wanted to spend some time at Squirrel Haus. She and Monk had gotten in a fight about her drug intake, and she told me she needed a place to crash for a few days. I told her sure. No problem. She cajoled Monk, calling him too boring on her end of the phone, but I countered and reminded her how much he cared about her. She got angry, hung up, and came over, angry, scattering a handful of pills on the counter. We talked about Monk and her marriage.

-I just think you're being hard on Monk, I said.

-Dunham, we're not all good guys like you.

-I'm not a good guy at all, I said. I tend to fuck up everything good in my life.

-Fucked up, Dunham? Look at me. I'm a total fuck up.

She was unsteady, hips jerking slightly to the sides in small angles. Heroin? I looked her in the eyes.

-No, you're not. You need to stop going to Toronto and hanging out with that guy.

-Don't you start in with that crap. Same as Monk. What, are you jealous? she asked and downed a random pill. She went quiet for a moment.

-You were the first, you know, she said.

-First what?

-First time I cheated. I told you it was Monk before you, but you were first.

-That was a long time ago, Haley.

-You were good friends with…

She paused. I took a drink.

-Robert, I said, flat in tone.

The mention of the ex-husband's name stiffened her, and she poured a liberal glass of whiskey.

-Something changed in me after the divorce, she said. I don't know. Like I don't care if I live or die.

-You can't blame yourself the rest of your life. You can't blame yourself for life in general. You know that.

-He will. For the rest of his life.

She pointed off in the imaginary direction of her ex. I took a deep breath.

-So what? I said. You're not married to him anymore. Look, I'm not really good at counseling, but I'm here in case you need anything. I know it sounds stupid to say, but…

-You're right, she said. It does sound stupid. We're friends, right?

-Of course.

She was quiet, alternating with long quaffs, then quiet again. She started a silent bout of tears and weeping and her shoulders shook till finally her chin buckled and the facade fell. I took hold of her shoulder and hugged her in the small kitchen with its small light until her small shoulders stopped.

-And you love me, right? she asked with a wipe of her nose.

-Of course, I said. We fucked up, yes, but you can't destroy yourself over a mistake.

-Robert's getting remarried, she said and finished the glass.

-I heard from Monk. Is that why you're upset?

She poured a full glass and pointed her finger at me.

-Why don't you want to be with me? Why not me? You don't love me?

Her voice hit a quiver and the eyes welled again. I gave her a hug and she spilled the whiskey on my back where her hands joined.

-I don't love you like that. Not like that, Haley. You know what I mean. You're living with Monk. And that guy in Toronto. That's never what we were.

-So what are we then? she asked. I'm not living with anyone, and I'm not some fucking piece of property to be passed around.

-Haley, neither Monk or me thinks that. You know that. You're just pissed and drunk right now.

-But I love you.

-Not like that, I said. Because I don't want to ruin our friendship with it.

-What about my feelings? I have them, you know.

-You're just mad at Monk. You know it wouldn't work with us. You don't love me like that and you never did. We're friends, kiddo. Doppelgangers.

-Just another friendly demiurge? she asked with a dark sarcasm and she turned toward the counter and rifled the pills. You really want to round down to the commonest clichéd denominator?

-What do you want me to say? The embodiment of the Platonic Ideal? I'm fresh out of togas and laurel wreaths, I said.

She smiled weakly.

-We've got whiskey at least. She quaffed half her glass in a go.

-And you've got that guy in Toronto. Conrad?

She registered the joke, but looked away and back, minor chords of rage in her almond eyes, and she spoke in a voice like rough jade.

-What does that have to do with anything? she said. It's not like I'm whoring myself out to him.

-I'm just saying. You spoke of love a moment ago. I'm trying to put things in context.

-What context are you proposing? she asked.

-We're just worried. It's getting out of control.

-Who the fuck are you to talk about control? We? You and Monk? He can't even finish his dissertation. And you, you're right, you're a consummate fuck up, she said, poking my chest.

-Maybe so. But can we please sheathe the claws for a moment.

-What, you want me to go to rehab like Monk said? Go back on meds? Be brain dead again?

-I'm not judging.

-What? she pleaded with eyes lit. You want me to do electroshock again?

Memories there of losing memories showed in her face, her little mouth set firm and tears tracked their way dark again down her face through mascara.

-Haley, you know what I'm saying.

-But you're just saying, she said. Always saying. Always saying.

Griffin came in the door, looked at us, turned hard right with a case of beer under his arm, and went straight into the Harem and turned the TV on loud.

-Deus ex machina, she said, laughed and finished the glass.

-Haley, I know I'm not a very dependable person. And we can argue all night. I care too much about you. Besides, I'm not clear of Misha, and the ballerina. And everything's all a mess. Maybe you and I would have worked out in another life.

She took a deep drink, nodded, and smiled.

-I know. In another life. Always another life. Someone else and far away.

-Maybe, I said. But not in this one.

-Dunham?

-Yeah?

-Thanks.

She wobbled a little, took some pills from the counter and gave me one.

-Now, let's talk about something fun. Quote me some Larkin.

And she laughed a little, and went and sat on Griffin's lap.

Haley stayed the next couple of days, and migrated from Big Red into my room, slowly, like a wary animal. I saw it coming, and something in me didn't care, or regarded it all as an accident, something I wasn't in control of. I thought about Monk. He was a friend, too. We were all friends. I'd watch her slink in those nights, and fall into bed, hair mussed thereafter, and I thought of Robert and her, how they'd joined me and Misha on our ridiculous trip to Italy that we couldn't afford, just a few years back, and we all stayed up late, pooling every lira for as much table wine as we could, and it felt like something in a book about people on the edge of great things, something we'd all write about in memoirs, and then, Haley'd straddle me or fall over, interrupting the memory, and I'd run a finger over the side of her face, an irresolute sadness in me, a tiny thing I couldn't bear to acknowledge, and so I'd put my face and lips to hers to stopper the thoughts of all the loss and all the faceless voices of deeds and promises and lies spoken on this earth, tremulous little bandwidths hurtling out into the void, toward alien ears in these our frail, human frequencies, frequencies we barely understand even in these our own tongues.

A few nights later I was in bed with her, exhausted from my exertions. There was a commotion in the kitchen, and my bedroom door flew open. I instinctively shot up, naked, in a defensive stance, wobbly on the mattress with a head full of sleep and rum. It was Noel.

-Whoa, you just get out of a cold shower? he laughed.

-Huh?

Noel laughed again.

-Put on some clothes, he said. We have to do some cocaine and buy a Playstation.

-I already have one. Jesus, what time is it? I asked, trying to slap myself awake.

-Around three, he said. Here, get dressed.

He turned, shaking a giant baggie, and then began fiddling around in the kitchen cabinets talking to himself. I put on some clothes and walked out into the light. He had dumped a large white pile into a Pyrex casserole pan on the kitchen counter and was rolling a five into a straw.

-Pickle didn't bark at you? I said. He gets nervous around people on drugs. Even me sometimes.

-Not a peep. Where's Griffin?

-I don't know, I said through a yawn. He's not in his room?

-No. Just Pickle.

He bent over snorting straight from the pile in mechanical fashion. There was so much powder that cutting it into lines was impossible. Pickle was in the kitchen now, plodding around and looking at me for reassurance. Always ready for action. I patted his head, and so did Noel, and I took the blowhole. It was good stuff. Barely a hint of ether or cutting agents, and I bent in and stood, rubbing my nose.

-A bump like a snowhill.

-Huh?

-Nothing, I said. Big white pile. Why are you buying a Playstation? Why now?

-Why are you inhaling cocaine? Because it's there. I need to upgrade my life.

-Just borrow mine, I said. I never play it.

-I need my own, he said.

I saluted.

-Yassir. Let's pimp your life at three in the morning.

Haley moved around in the Dais, and was dressed now, our talk having roused her. She shambled up and I handed her the rolled bill. Our heads dipped to the lines several times each till we were good and epoxied, and then we loaded into Noel's Subaru and drove the deserted streets toward the highway. He explained in a rush that his girlfriend, Amy, had left him, this time for good. I shook my head.

-How do you know it's for good? I said. You guys break up all the time.

-This time she took the ferrets. It's serious, Noel said. I fucking hated those things anyway. They stink. They're not charming like Riki-tiki-tavi.

Haley's voice from the backseat.

-He was a mongoose.

-Tomato, tomato, Noel said. You crack wise again, Haley, and I'll pull this car over.

She leaned in.

-And I'll hammer your ploughshares into swords, beeyatch.

Noel laughed.

-You coming on to me? I'm single now, you know.

She cuffed him in the back of the head, chuckling. When we got to Wal-Mart we squirted a healthy dose of nasal spray in us each, and did several heavily-loaded keys before going in, scuffling from the back end of the parking lot toward the glaring effluence. The bright florescence inside was unnerving, and made everyone look ashen, false. Noel raced through the store, wheeling on the back of a shopping cart. Haley and I followed at a leisurely pace, jabbering about consumerism. She had been a Marxist as an undergrad, but was now unsure whether the prevailing ethos of insular individuality wasn't a more fitting model for how the world works. I rubbed my numbed nose.

-You going full Rand on me, I said.

-Marx was too idealistic, she said. I need something more in tune with now.

-There's always Jerry Falwell. Or Pat Robertson, I said.

We located Noel in the electronics section where he was tossing game after game into his cart. He asked the section cashier to unlock the case and get him a Playstation 2. He paid for it all with cash in various denominations, laying out the stacks of ones and fives and tens, and ironing them flat with his palm, sniffling from his red nose. We left the store and went back to Noel's. His place was half-empty, and little pock marks lay sunk in the carpet where his girlfriend had taken various pieces of furniture. We did a lot of coke and played video games all night, and were still playing well past the grey of dawn. At 11:00 Noel finally passed out and Haley called Monk for a ride. She went back home with him, and he dropped me off at Squirrel Haus.

That night Griffin and I went to the Deadwood, and later to Gabe's Bar, the local punkrock and live music dive, because Griffin said Laney might be there and he wanted to get laid. He wouldn't talk about his girl in California, so I assumed he'd tell me when he wanted. We sat outside in the beer garden, sipping the cheap swill from the plastic cups they gave the free-range patrons, the muted drone from a shitty local band intoning dully inside. The place stank of piss and sweat, and the beer was cheap. I thought Noel might drop by, too. My head was still cloudy from the cocaine the night before, so I told Griffin I wanted a peaceful night.

We didn't see Laney or Noel, but we did see Clarice. She was with Mullethawk and some skinhead types, looking like hooligans straight from a Klan rally, tight jeans tucked into their combat boots. Mullethawk drew a beeline for us.

-You fuckers.

-Huh?

-You fucking thieves. I know you stole the beer.

-Beer?

-Bear, asshole, another guy said. From on his fridge.

His friends had assembled, five in all, lightning bolts and other regalia tattooed on necks and arms and hands. I laughed and finished my cup.

-Come on, guys. Why would we steal a bear? Or a beer. Sit

down. Have a bear, I said smiling.

-Are you ready for this? the larger one said.

-Ready for what?

-Stand up, he said, and pushed my shoulder. I poured some more beer from the sweaty plastic receptacle.

-Fuck you, you racists, I said. Go home and blow each other, you Nazi fucks.

The larger one moved toward our table. Clarice said something to him. Had she seen Nazibear at our house at some point? Had she been over before or after we stole it? Was there a mole in our organization? I looked over to her where she stood behind several of the assembled figures.

-What the fuck, Clarice? Griffin said. Was Dunham that bad in bed?

The Enforcer looked from me to Clarice, a weird look in his eyes.

-You cheated on me with this prick, he said.

He took a place at my right, standing above me. I poured myself some more beer from the plastic pitcher. He pushed my shoulder as I tried to take a drink, spilling the semi-warm liquid on my shirt.

-I tried to show her a good time, I said smiling. You people. You people are just so hard to please.

He pushed me again, spilling more beer on my shirt. I looked down and back up.

- Oy vay, my bubbe gave me this. From the old country.

Griffin stood up and set his cup down.

-Okay, Hitler Youth, this is ridiculous.

The Enforcer leaned down to me.

-Stand up, faggot.

I tried to channel my best Rodney Dangerfield, and pointed at the HH emblem on his shirt.

-So if I buy a shirt like that do I get a free bowl of soup?

He pushed me again.

-Stand up.

Rodney again, and I adjusted my collar.

-Pork and dreams, cocksucker.

I dashed the beer in his face and brought my forearm into his groin from where I was sitting, standing up in the same motion, partially lifting him, planted my left foot and dug my elbow into his throat. Griffin winged the half-full pitcher at Mullethawk's chest, exploding the beer on everyone around. I grabbed the guy's head, pulling down, and kneed him several times in the face until he fell down. Griffin had bumrushed the other three, the furtive momentum catching them off guard, and he clotheslined one, knocking him onto the concrete. Mullethawk hit me on the ear, leaving a wetness there from the beer all over him. Griffin kicked one guy in the knee, and laid him out with a nice right cross, then kicked the other skinhead, who was still on the ground, a few times for good measure.

I ran Mullethawk by the shoulders back into the brick wall of the building. He said he knew where we lived. I told him to stop by for a bear, anytime, then he punched me and split my lip, so I headbutted him, then jerked him forward and down by his leather jacket, into a wooden table. We ran out of the beer garden into the alley, turned right toward the police station. No one would suspect that. We darted across the street, past the cop shop, and down toward Noel's. We slowed to a walk once we were under the cover of darkness some blocks away, and I lit a cigarette for me and another for Griffin. I rolled the smoke's butt over the cut on my lip.

-Dude, I said, don't kick someone when they're on the ground.

-Why not? It's not polite? Not Queensbury Rules?

-No, you can go to jail for attempted murder, I said.

-How could it be attempted murder on a pack of Nazi assholes? he asked. Oh, that's right. The police are in league with them probably.

He turned around and yelled down the street.

-Go back to fucking hell, you fascist fuckers.

He turned back to me with a laugh.

-Seriously, he said. What the hell is wrong with some people? It's just a plaster bear.

-Gimme back my beer. Bear? No, beer. You know, Griff, they have their constitutional rights to be douchebags.

Griffin pulled hard at the cigarette.

-I know. I'm not a fascist, D. Land of the free, right.

We stopped instead at Monk's because it was closer and we had just assaulted five people, so we needed to be off the streets for a while. Haley was there and called me into the kitchen. She dabbed a wet rag at my lip and explained to me that she was going to stay with Monk again, that they had made up, and that she'd also be leaving for Toronto in a few days. Griffin and Monk got very high, and Haley was very flirty with me, but I smiled it off. Haley caught me in the kitchen later and asked why I was ignoring her, that it wasn't like she and Monk were actually dating, that this was a trial period. I tried explaining that I had at least a few principles, and that if she was living with Monk, then nothing could happen between us. She understood, and didn't protest further, but her eyes did.

Griffin and I took off an hour later, bought some beer from a convenience store, and got home around 1:00. We came in through the neighbor's yard and surveyed the street for police cars, or a truckload of angry skinheads, but the street was empty except the usual vehicles. No lights were on in Michelle's apartment. I turned on the kitchen light, the single low-watt bulb, and set the beer on the counter, and gave Pickle's head a scratch. I spun around with my beer in hand with a little Michael Jackson flourish and cry. Then I noticed something. In the Harem, near the stereo, lay a dark form. I looked at Griffin.

-Who the fuck is that? Did you invite anyone over?

-I didn't invite anyone over, he said.

We peered into the gloom from the kitchen. A heap of breathing clothes, snoring, and a small gravestone rested at the head against the wall. I smacked Pickle's head for letting someone in the house. The degenerates and tricks that Michelle had been bringing into the neighborhood had put us on edge, especially since the front door wouldn't lock. Griffin had forgotten his keys a few days ago and kicked in the door while drunk, splintering the doorjamb. Pickle had been our only line of defense against junkies like this breaking in and stealing what few possessions we had, or loading up and passing out on our floor, and now he had failed in his charge. Was it Major Tom? How had he gotten past Pickle? I couldn't see there in the dark.

-Some goddamned guard dog you turned out to be, Griffin said.

I drank down half the beer and turned toward Griffin.

-See, now you brought the whole nest of them in like roaches and fruitflies, I said. They'll pass this around their fucking hobo camp that there's some flophouse up on Daniels where anyone can sleep and shit and piss and shoot up. Stop bringing home strays, you and your bleeding heart, Griff.

-Yeah, it doesn't pay to be nice to people, he said and finished his can.

I strode over to the mound in the dimness, and rolled the form's shoulder with my bootheel. It roused a bit, and turned toward me. I wound up my leg for my best Pele impersonation, and sunk the boot into the shape's ribs. The figure doubled and started coughing.

-Goal, motherfucker! Who the fuck do you think you are, you fucking trash! Do you think we're running a charity for scumsuckers and bottomfeeders? Get the fuck out!

I kicked again and a voice rose from the floor.

-What the fuck, man!?

The shape sprang up and an arm shot under my groin, and I was hoisted in a fireman's carry and slammed on the ground.

Griffin switched on the light and I lay in the Harem, air concussed from lungs.

-Patman, I managed to say.

-Is that any way to treat a guest, man? I called you guys earlier to let you know I was coming, man.

Griffin laughed, and Patman helped me to my feet. He rubbed his chest and ribs.

-I never knew you were so violent, man. I got you guys a housewarming gift, too, man, he said, pointing to the gravestone.

-Where did you get that? Griffin asked.

-Someone's grave, man. Where else would I get it? K-Mart? Graves-R-Us, man?

Griffin brought us beers and we sat on Big Red and told Patman about the skinheads and showed him Nazibear, and told him about Michelle upstairs and all the guys and junkies coming over, saying I thought someone had broken in. He said he understood and waved it off. He sat the gravestone on the kitchen counter. The name and date in the worn limestone worn past name and date.

-Why the hell would anyone want to break in here anyway? Patman said. I was afraid to even let the air touch my cock when I took a piss. This place is worse than prison, man.

May

Finding the marks

a friend made
in the book I
loaned her. In-
vasion a partial
love, meaning
tender participant.

Words are never
simple nor twice
the same. Each
has a name, ab-
solute in aftermath,

adding through both
tongues, for who'd
believe mine, or
the nearest rhyme?

Soundtrack

The Pogues, *Summer in Siam*
John Lee Hooker, *The Waterfront*
Richard Pryor, *Bicentennial Nigger*
Harry Nilsson, *Jump into the Fire*
Rage Against the Machine, *Sleep now in the Fire*
Geto Boys, *My Mind is Playin' Tricks on Me*

My brother and I had worked ourselves out of work at Froth's. There was nothing left for us to do on the remodel for at least a few weeks, until the drywall crew and painters finished their respective jobs. Ezekiel called Little Paul, asking if they needed any help. Little Paul agreed. They were building a big rental property north of Iowa City, right off the highway, and could use a few more able hands.

Most of the crew was still the same as when I had worked with them back in grad school. Donnie had a new baby girl. Big Joey still complained about his back, tossing his thin sandy hair around. Cutman Ricky was still selling his low-grade cocaine on the side, stepped on so many times with baby laxatives it was practically unsnortable, gummy and reeking of ether. Hence, the Cutman. Diminutives and diminutives of diminutives the common currency on nearly every construction site. On my first morning back I was snapping lines on the second floor with Donnie. I pulled the chalk tine tight and gave it a pop while he held the other end. I looked up.

-Whatever happened to Crazy Eddie? I asked.

-You mean old Charlie Manson? The guy got arrested for raping his daughter, Donnie said. He got her pregnant.

-Jesus Christ, his own daughter? I knew the guy was fucked up, but that's something completely else. Remember that thermos he had, filled with his patented bathtub gin?

Donnie smiled.

-That fucker'd drink it all day, he said. You ever try it?

-Once, I said. Lucky I didn't go blind. His fucking daughter? Really?

-Yeah, he said, really.

-How long is he in for?

Donnie shook his head.

-No idea. Hopefully forever. Sick fuck.

-What are they going to do about the baby? I asked.

-No idea, he said. I forgot that about you. You always ask so many goddamn questions.

We worked a breakneck pace, and Paulie was happy to have the extra help, and the only respite aside from lunch was to stand still for a moment and fish a cigarette out of your bags and light it. Or to tune the radio if the station was fuzzy. There was a constant war of attrition between the Country Boys and the Classic Rock Boys about the radio. The factions were split evenly, and at random points in the day, someone would sneak to the radio and flip the station, and the offended cabal would whoop and holler, and stage their own little coup when Little Paul wasn't watching. Every day like this amid the toil. I switched the radio one day to NPR. *Fresh Air* was on. The chirpiness went on a full twenty seconds before Little Paul walked across the worksite, grabbed the radio and threw it out of the third-story window, cursing that the next goddamned person who fucked with the radio was getting their boots nailed to the deck because if you want to stand still at least then you'll have a godamned reason. We laughed at that one for weeks.

Thursday afternoon, we had finished for the day, and Ezekiel, Donnie, Paulie and I all sat in Paulie's big red Dodge crewcab, basking in the A/C. I was in back with my brother, and I was telling stories about Utah, and Donnie and Zeke were swapping baby tips. Donnie's wife called his cell phone, and he nodded at his phone several times, and tossed it in the console between the seats. Little Paul gave him a friendly push.

-Damn, Little Paul said, she's got you by the short and curlies, son.

-Bullshit, Donnie said. You know I don't take orders from no woman.

Paulie turned back toward us, laughing.

-He's probably got little girls' underwear on right now. All pretty in pink.

-Fuck off. I just like the lace, Donnie said. It makes me feel pretty.

We laughed.

-Shit, he continued, when I get home tonight, I'm gonna do her in the ass. You know, rub her butt down with canola oil. The low calorie stuff. I'm a health nut. Only unsaturated oil when I get in that ass. I don't want her to get all fat.

He mimed the motion and the application of the canola oil, popping the lid off the imaginary bottle, gyrating in the front seat. We all laughed, lit cigarettes. Little Paul noted that olive oil was low in saturated fat, too. Donnie lit a cigarette, laughing, put the lighter back on the dash, then applied more of the phantasmagoric oil replete with various sound effects. Everyone laughed again. Donnie looked down at his phone. His eyes narrowed and widened. He hadn't flipped it shut. It had been on the whole time. He picked it up, gently placing it to his ear.

-Hello?

A sound issued, a torrent of noise and epithets, rolling like Zeus' own thunder. He flipped the phone shut after a full minute of his wife's cursing and put it in his shirt pocket. His eyes wide and his jaw masticated the air, no sound.

-Paul, he said. I'm staying with you for a while. I'm a dead man if I go home.

-Jesus, Donnie, Paulie chortled trying to get the words out for his laughter, she's going to put you in the hospital like her last boyfriend. That sumbitch was six-two. You need to hit the supermarket and stock up on your canola oil, too. And gauze because she's going to stomp a mudhole in your ass.

Paulie was fully doubled over on the steering wheel, convulsing and gasping, his forearms causing the horn to beep in little bursts with his spasms. I was crying with laughter, and Donnie sat there shaking his head. Zeke tried to make a joke, whether Donnie preferred his olive oil extra virgin, but couldn't speak except for the word extra and then could barely make it through virgin. Another round of breathless peals ricocheted inside the truck. Donnie leaned toward the window and blew out some smoke.

-Fuck you guys.

I had a message at home from an old friend from grad school who was coming through the Midwest with her boyfriend. Patman was off visiting people around town, crashing couch to couch. My friend lived in New Jersey and was taking her beau home to Illinois, and would swing through Iowa City to see me. The warming weather and clear skies seemed to bring together the confluence of friends, and Squirrel Haus was now nightly visited by familiar faces from around town, and around the country. All roads led there, it seemed. Griffin's brother would be through that weekend too. There. Michelle had evidently gotten a phone because she had stopped coming down and asking to use it whenever we got home from work.

Sarai and the beau, Mike, arrived Friday night, driving a newer Volvo. We did the rounds through her haunts of old, showing Mike the sweep of the city. He was a professional motocross rider, and showed off a slew of scars on his arms and legs from wrecks and collisions. I showed him mine where I'd been stabbed in the back during a fight in Colorado, and another on my hand where it had caught on a guy's teeth. The night passed peacefully, and I gave them my bed, sleeping on the floor in the Harem. The next morning while we were talking over coffee, there was a roar from the street. Griffin's younger brother Kell, fresh back in town, braked his motorcycle and shut off the engine. He took his gear from the bike, came inside and hugged everyone, even Sarai and Mike. Wim came by that night, bringing his bag of goodies, designer beers and some rawhide for Pickle to chew. Pickle's head swiveled the whole time, the rawhide hanging from his jaw, excited at the reverie and talk, drooling and begging for a scrap or two. And sleep came easy to everyone.

We spent Saturday barbequing, painting, having round robins with the bows, drinking Sierra Nevada to commemorate the event. Kell started the coals with a drip torch on which he had written *Phlogiston*. He had strapped it to the side of his motorcycle, Hell Machine, 1700 Vulcan, esq. Kell had grown a special forces beard, as he called it, and it sprang bushily from his face around his constant smile, as he stood above the fire. Sarai and Mike told stories from Jersey, and Kell from his days of fighting fires in Arizona. Griffin and I talked about The Squirrel Haus Day Massacre and Fat Bastard. The evening shaded off into the low cicada drone, early for the season, susurrations across the pleasant yard where the breeze flowed through the little spring buds on the trees and everything felt suspended in a light the color of aether and honey, and time felt a thing so salubrious that you could almost taste it when a breath lifted it to mouth.

At late dusk, some mosquitoes came out en masse, and we decided to go inside. We went downtown later, and had beers at the Deadwood. I flirted with the waitress and she eventually gave me her number, her ballpoint chewing up the soggy napkin. Sarai and Mike would have to leave the next day to visit some more family of hers in Illinois, but would be back through town in a week. Griffin told them they were welcome anytime. We went home early, and talked late. When some of Wim's party favors came out and had been passed around, Mike said he could get liquid acid. Everyone was interested. Mike promised he'd send some back upon their return to Jersey. Acid was safe through the post. Drug dogs couldn't detect it. Kell and Griffin started a new painting, a take on Ingres' *Oedipus*.

Sarai and Mike's Volvo shot off the next morning, and Griffin and Kell and I decided to get breakfast. We drove down in the White Elephant, with Kell in the back. I had taken the seats out long ago, and forgot where I put them. It was Sunday, and a local evangelical church was downtown protesting and handing out fliers against the Emma Goldman Clinic and Planned Parenthood. There were close to eighty zealots there, and we tried to press through the crowd. An elderly woman handed me a piece of paper.

-Here you go, dear, she said. You should come to the rally next Saturday.

-Why would I care what a woman does with her own body? I asked.

-It's against God's law, she said. We're all of us born into sin.

-Where does it say 'Thou Shalt Not Commit Abortions' in the Bible, Griffin asked.

-It says 'Thou shalt not kill.'

-No, I said. It actually says 'Thou shalt not commit murder'. There's a difference.

-Abortion is murder, she replied.

-We all know Jesus was murdered by the Jews, Kell said, turning to me with a smile.

-What do you have against Jews? I said to Kell. My last name's Goldberg. I'm Jewish. Did I kill Jesus?

Kell shoved me with a wink.

-You yids need to read the Gospel of B.A. Baracus, he said. Verse 4, chapter 20: I pity the fool who crucify Jesus.

I pushed him back, and he knocked into a woman holding a picture of a foetus in a trash can.

-You anti-Semite, I yelled. Next you'll be talking about stolen bears.

The woman shoved back against Kell and he in turn careened into another person, and the throng seethed like a mosh pit, elbows and arms and people striking out with their placards to gain some space to breathe. I saw the old woman disappear under the mass with her handful of little fliers. Someone struck me in the back of the head, and Kell finally pulled me out by my collar with a huge grin in his beard.

-Free Mumia, he yelled. To the mountaintop.

Jesus Christ, I thought, the errant crusaders running amok. We pushed through the edges of the throng and someone was on a megaphone calling for order for the love of God. We sauntered over to the restaurant and passed a pleasant ersatz mountain-style breakfast of steak, eggs and beer, making plans to go camping the next weekend on their parents' land.

Griffin took the next two days off to spend time with his brother, and Ezekiel and I worked with Little Paul. Donnie was still staying with him, terrified to go home. He said he'd tried to call his wife once, and she started in yelling again, so he hung up. While we were at lunch, someone slipped a bottle of canola oil into his toolbags, some pink underwear, a condom and a note that read, *Lover not a fighter* in frilly script.

I got home around 4:30 on Tuesday, bringing a sack of food and beer into the kitchen. There was a thunking against the house, and I went around the back where Kell, Griffin and Patman were shooting arrows. Patman was loading an arrow, and Griffin was beaming.

-Afternoon, gents, I said and waved.

Patman pointed the bow at me, drew, and let an arrow go, whacking the house a foot wide of me.

-What the fuck, Patman? I said.

I ran at him and tackled him before he could get another arrow notched. We tussled in the yard until we were out of breath and we helped each other to our feet, laughing. He took his shirt off and wiped the dirt from his face.

-I wasn't going to hit you, man.

-Did you get those new tats in jail, Kell asked.

-Most of them, yeah. I made friends with an Apache doing time for murder, man. He had the whole rig, so I'd just trade him smokes for tats, man.

He had a bunch of new tattoos, his name in cursive on his neck, and the words *Puss* and *Cock* on the knuckles of each hand, because he said he was better with the girls with the left, and the boys with his right. Already quite drunk, a pile of Icehouse Light cans sat on the ground in the grass, and he tossed another onto the heap. His eyes had a weird distance in them. Prison had changed him. I poked my finger at his huge bicep.

-Holy hell, Pat, what do they feed you in there.

-Liver, veggies and little boys, man.

-Three-course meal, Griffin said. I'd rather not know what you had for dessert.

We quizzed Patman on the ins and outs of his prison stay. He said he'd been doing gardening in Idaho, somehow, for a rich country club set, and they'd invited him out to help cater a yacht party, and he got busted trying to sell pot to an off-duty cop who Patman said was hitting on him. I thought it odd that he'd do so much time until he added the detail that it had been a pound of weed he'd been caught with. His sentence had originally been five years, but he got out in just over two. He told us that his second day in, awaiting transfer in a country jail, that the guy next to him in line was jumped by two vatos and stabbed to death. It was unsettling to see his eyes as he described it. He had always more of the hippy sensibility. Now he had undergone the transformation from Patman to Patdawg. Hippy to Rippy.

I worked the week near Cedar Rapids with Ezekiel and Little Paul and the crew, and every day when I came home, Patman would be sitting on Big Red, watching *Conan the Barbarian* or *Conan the Destroyer*, drinking Icehouse tallboys. He would watch for twenty minutes, then do fifty pushups and fifty situps. Old prison habits, he explained. One afternoon I interrupted him and Haley on the couch. She was half-naked, and jumped up from the couch, breasts out, startled. Patman didn't seem troubled. He only pointed to the kitchen, and took a sip of Icehouse.

-There's a message for you, man. I almost erased it by

accident. You gotta show me how to work that machine, man.

Haley had her shirt on now and came into the kitchen. She was smiling. I was not.

-I stopped by to see if you were here, and he and I got to talking. And suddenly we were, you know.

I stopped her.

-I'm not pissed. I know the room is called the Harem, but that's just not something I want to come home to.

I motioned her toward my room out of Patman's earshot, and she stuffed more completely herself into her shirt and joined me where I stood. She took my arm, and her voice quavered.

-Dunham, I don't know what I'm doing.

-With Patman?

-With everything, she said.

A tear balled in her eye, at the corner.

-I feel like I've given up more than I ever had. Like I lost more than I had, she said. It's not even a zero sum game now.

She hugged me and tottered. I helped her sit down on the bed.

-Are you okay? I asked.

-I'm fine. I took a few pills an hour ago.

-What did you take?

-Just 100 milligrams.

-Of what?

-Morphine, she said. I'm fine.

-I find you rolling around on the couch with Patman when I get home from work? What's fine about that?

Her voice shifted, accusatorial.

-Look, it just happened, she said turning her face fully to mine. Are you jealous?

Her eyes settled on my eyes with intent. I met her gaze and shook my head.

-I'm fucking concerned, Haley. He was in prison for two odd years. God knows what he did in there, whether he picked up some STD. You want to double down on that?

-Look, she said, I don't think we would have done anything. I'm just a little high right now. It was just fun making out. When's the last time you just made out with someone on a couch?

-The way he checks to see if he has an STD is to call someone he fucked seven or eight months ago, man or woman, and ask about their health. And he's not making collect calls to the prison from my phone.

-I told you we weren't going to do anything, she said and her head bobbed.

-Haley, why don't you just sleep it off here in my room.

-Will you stay and talk to me?

-Yes, I said.

-Dunham?

-That's me.

Her head came up again, eyes staring at me, welling again and charybdine, eyes deep in their bright brown, rich almond the hue of a deeper season. A tear humbled her cheek and then another.

-I don't know what to do, she said again. I don't know where I'm going. I feel like my proverbial boots are strapless.

-I know. I know. We'll get you some new boots soon enough. Maybe a strap on, too.

-Strap on?

-I'm trying to be funny.

-That wasn't funny.

-I'm sorry, I said.

-No. I think I need to sleep. I think I'll feel better.

We talked a bit more. Her words turning to mush, slowing and noticeable, slurred and more and more scattered. She had plans to return to Iowa permanently and start work again on her doctorate. 100 milligrams was nothing, she said, but her face told the contrast, and her dark-rimmed eyes drooped and fell. She drifted off. I thought of the stories she used to tell me about growing up in Oklahoma, flat sprawl of grass the horizon out, making Iowa look like Nepal, and I pictured her standing out in the sudden spring rush of the post-rain flowers, her a little girl and prior to the welt and run of regrets that stalk down the sane and stalemated everyone once past that edge of adulthood. I slid out of bed not to disturb her. Patman was standing at the door when I opened it, holding Griffin's PPK.

-That's kind of rude, I mean, I can hear you guys talking about me, man. Hey, do you know if he's got any bullets for this?

The message that Patman had almost erased was from Nina, an ex-girlfriend from the undergrad days who was visiting friends in town. She had emailed me a month ago, and I had given her my new address and phone number if she ever made it back to Iowa City. I called the number she left. She had driven in from Indiana yesterday and was staying with Jon and Frank, a gay couple, old communal friends I hadn't seen around town since I'd been back. She had just broken up with her fiancé, and needed to get out of her apartment while he packed his things and vamoosed, so she wanted to visit the Great Pillow for a while and get some distance.

I met Nina at Joe's Bar the next day when I finished work. We hugged with a fond embrace, and ordered a pitcher of their finest afternoon-priced swill. We sat in a booth and talked, told stories, her lovely Jewish profile bobbing to the jukebox selections. Jon and Frank were doing great, and had just moved, allowing her a guest bedroom in their new house, she informed me. It had a breakfast nook, too. We played pool and I was roundly defeated six games to two.

She was telling me about Peasant Legs, the fiancé, and his boring job and boring life and boring tastes and the boring sex. He sold insurance, loved *Friends*, had cankles, and played fantasy football. I told her about Elle, and she smacked me on the side of the head saying I must be retarded to leave someone like that. I agreed. We were approached by a midget who wanted to play pool. He asked us very politely in Spanish, and I said sure. His name, he explained, was Milario and he washed dishes at Cancun's in Coralville, a town over. He was from Guatemala, lived in a cramped apartment with eight other men, and had no friends here in el norte. He pulled out a gigantic roll of bills, flipping through twenties and tens to find a single, and got some quarters from the vending machine. Christ, I thought, that's a lot of money.

Milario was a hell-on-stunted-wheels genius at pool. He had to angle his cue over his head like a Spartan warrior in order to make his shots. Ball after ball after ball. Uncanny how good he was, since he could barely see over the lip of the pool table. And like a little phalanx, again and again the cue thrust out. He ran the table once, and in four games against him Nina and I managed to sink only five balls total. Milario paid for each game and played mostly in silence, downing glass after glass of beer, nearly a pitcher per game, each going quicker than the previous. He paid for every game and every beer we drank.

He bought two more pitchers for us and sat down on a bench against the wall. He was trying to pour a beer from the pitcher, but it ran off onto the floor, his glass wobbling in the air a full foot away. He began laughing, watching the beer spill to the wooden floor below, and then he began to cry. He told me about his loneliness and his family at home, his two little girls, his job and how hard it was to be apart from them. He wiped his eyes with his stubby fingers and tried to pour himself some more beer, but he missed his glass again with the remainder of the pitcher. This made him smile. I told him how good he was at pool, and that he shouldn't spend all his money on strangers and that I was very glad to have him as a friend, encouraging him, *Eres un tiburon, mi amigo!* No one, I tried to explain to him in broken Spanish, deserves to play pool and drink beer, friendless and alone, in a place as cold and unforgiving as Bush's America. We bid him adieu after another pitcher and Nina bent over and gave him a hug.

Nina stopped by Squirrel Haus with me to see the paintings and ended up staying the night. I was groggy the next day at work, but sallied on, ignoring the pain in my head, back, elbow, kidneys, left foot, mind, and right foot. That night I told Patman there'd be no sex with anyone on the couch, which he seemed to interpret as open season on Griffin's bed or mine, which required further clarification. He offered me an Icehouse as a condolence, but I said I didn't want one. He hadn't much luck panhandling downtown that day. I suggested learning an instrument and tossed Griffin's kazoo over to him. He played the Star Spangled Banner. I could sense Patman's roots sinking deeper into Squirrel Haus, into Big Red. He asked me if I had any loose change I could loan him.

Thursday night Griffin got a call from Layna, which he took in his room. Wim and I were working on making giant papier-mâché heads of George Bush and Herbert Hoover and Calvin Coolidge. Our plan was to ride around on our bikes and dispense justice the old-fashioned way, by ruining the countryside. A friend of Wim's had given us the materials. Wim was coming and going less frequently, but the increment was so small no one really noticed. Wim was gluing on Coolidge's hair, a crown of grass and weeds.

-We'll clean up this one-horse town, he said.

-We'll call our gang *Wolftown*.

Wim nodded, approving.

-Ready for the mean streets of Iowa City.

-At least with Hoover we're showing some Iowa pride, Wim noted.

- Heah in Iowa ain't nuttin happens ceptin cow tippin and sistuh fuckin, I drawled.

-Ye ain't mention the tractor pulls neether.

-Tractors? Where you grow up, boy? The Big City? So, Wim, I

said.

-Yeah?

-Where exactly have you been lately? You got some girl we don't know about?

-What do you mean?

He was dodging the question so I knew there'd be no straight answer.

-Nothing. Just been busy.

We painted the heads the next night. Wim came down with a cold, so he couldn't join us. Kell borrowed a bike from his cousin, and later Kell and Griffin and I were stopped twice and questioned by the police while we were riding around downtown with the giant presidential heads on, but we were infracting no law, so we were let go. We traded the heads to a guy at the Deadwood for a round of drinks and all was right with the world: barter and trade and sundries to exchange long into the night.

I chatted up a girl reading *The Hobbit* in one of the booths. She bartended at a place I never visited, and like so many bartenders, was a painting major. I called her Pocahontas, and she thought it was funny. She looked vaguely Indian, though was of straight Irish stock. Back at her house, she showed me her art, and I nodded and mmhmmed, and then she showed me the rest of her. She wore granny panties that rode up over the sharp edge of her hip, and was very loud in bed.

On the way home from Pocahontas' the next morning I stopped at the library to check my email, and found a series of legalistically composed missives from a debt-collection agency with sharp remarks about payments and schedules. I deleted them and left. I stopped for a cup of coffee and noticed a large group gathered down the street. Milling around with signs and hosannas rising through the air, the Xtians were harassing the people coming and going from the Planned Parenthood building again. Some were yelling, waving Bibles in their righteous hands. There were more of them than last week. I walked closer, sitting across the street on the low wall of a parking lot, smoking. Jesus X, I thought, why doesn't anyone ever picket in front of a church? I finished my coffee and walked home.

Griffin and Kell were tapping nails into our latest project. A friend had given us a small wooden table a few weeks before, bedecked with cute, woodland creatures. I bought two boxes of sixteen penny nails, and Griffin and I spent a few odd hours every night hammering nail after nail an inch into the wood. We grouped the nails closely together so that the collected mass of their heads formed a new bristling table top, like a flat-top hedgehog. It had taken the entire two boxes. We decided not to go camping that weekend, but rather to finish up loose ends, the projects and paintings and poems. Sarai had called and left a message that night saying that she and Mike wouldn't be able to make it back through Iowa City. She thanked me for the hospitality and told me to be on the lookout for a package next week.

Kell and Griffin had just finished up the last of the hammering on the table and we decided to give it a more special finish. We brushed on a mixture of lacquer, linseed oil and resin to form a seal over the lid of nails, using a hair drier to speed the drying process. We then boxed off the table top with plywood and poured in a quarter inch of floor leveler, and hung the drier from a nail in the ceiling, pointing at the table. We shot some arrows waiting for the liquid to set a bit, and an hour later poured in a half gallon of clear acrylic sealer and again the drier. Kell handed around a bottle of Old Still rye whiskey that came by the liter. Cheapest by volume.

The next day it was mostly dry, several layers of color and thickness like a sedimentary rock. We spread on several coats of polyurethane and more lacquer. The tabletop was flat at least, and we drove nails into the side, the sixteen pennies jutting out at all angles. We called it *Hellraiser*. In all, we had put a total of 32 man hours into it.

We were watching the news that night, dragging heavily from another bottle of Old Still. The incessant news. They talked, and they talked, and they talked. Baghdad was on fire constantly, and I half expected to see the guy from *Mad Max* cruise out on his motorcycle during the news footage with his assless chaps and catamite in tow, screaming, and with his feathers dangling and face paint, microphone in hand, ready to fuck up some Truth. Koppel in a flak jacket trying to cover the news old school, embedded with some troops. Geraldo persona non grata in the TV circus. Reporters living and sleeping with the troops. Fox News, and the interviews with the warhawks and Cheney sound bites maddening. Griffin shut the TV off, and put on some music.

-What's next? Is Fox going to get a Ouija board and summon Nixon's ghost for the supernatural scoop?

-We could pow-wow with Reagan, too, if we had one, Kell said.

-The Gipper will know how to get us out of this fucking quagmire, said Griffin.

-We should have a séance, man.

-And risk The Kissinger of Death. No fucking way, Griffin said. This place is bad enough without his ghost lurking around.

-I don't think he's dead yet, I said.

-No, maybe not, Griffin said, but he should be.

After more bevvying, we decided that a séance was the only logical answer. We sanded the back of a piece of plywood, drew on some letters. We each cut our arms and bled on some money, tacking it to Hellraiser. We poured libations from the bottle onto the board and muttered curses and spells, and wrapped our heads in foil. I made mine into Viking horns. Patman made a phallus codpiece instead, citing some wiccan exgirlfriend of his. Griffin tried to play some scary kazoo music, but nothing out of the kazoo sounded scary. The spirits were not talking that night.

After two minutes of nothing much, interspersed with pulls from the bottle, Patman informed us we had to light the Soothsayer on fire just in case there were any lesser demons lurking around in the pressed wood and glue of the board. Squirrel Haus' halls already ran with the ghosts of zombie squirrels, he said. Kell got his drip torch *Phlogiston* and ignited it, then took a mouthful of whiskey and spat a fireball at the board which ignited the lacquer and varnish and acrylic and oil on the table's top instead. Griffin ran to his room and got a wooden box with an older-style Skil Saw in it, and then an extension cord from the kitchen. He then ran the saw through the flames, knocking the Soothsayer to the floor. Kell picked it up and tossed it back on Hellraiser. *Turkish Song of the Damned* on the stereo. Chunks of the flaming tabletop fell to the carpet and we stomped them out into flat piles of mushy resin.

The remaining table was completely engulfed in flames, and the smoke was getting pretty bad, so in deference to the safety drills we learned in school, we took a knee where the air was tolerably more breathable. It made a wonderful cacophony, the music and the high whine of the saw running, shearing down through the wood into the metal nails below, casting sparks and debris. Deafening and furious and free. I leaned to the window to get some air, opened it wider. A neighbor with her dog was staring at the scene from the sidewalk. I waved to her. She put her head down and continued down the walk.

A friend called from Chicago and I told him I couldn't talk too long because my Harem was on fire. He said he understood and would call back another time. Kell finally ran the burning table outside and doused with a healthy dose from the extinguisher, and the air hung in a chalky fog all down the block for ten minutes. We turned on some fans and tried to air the place out, laughing in our tin-foil crowns until the onus of sleep was heavy on our eyes. Patman disappeared the next morning and for a few days after, resurfacing the following Tuesday on Big Red where I found him after work drinking Icehouse, watching *Conan the Destroyer*. He didn't look up as I came in the door.

-Hey, man, which Conan do you think is better? I can't decide. Look at his fucking arms, man, he said and did some pushups.

Work with Paulie's crew ended. He said he would call if anything more came up. The crews at Froth's remodel were behind schedule. I flipped through a two-day-old Sunday newspaper, sitting on Big Red. Griffin was at work and Patman was not around. *Janitor wanted* read the advert. The job was at the Iowa Memorial Union, a ten-minute slashing bike ride away, the building nestled on the calm bank of the river, home to the university's student lounges and cafeterias and study areas and administrative offices. It was the only job available that wouldn't require serving food or working in an office.

I applied for the job, only filling in the high school section, and tried hard to look earnest and eager to clean up after a bunch of asshole students whom I knew, from experience, ritually thrashed the Memorial Union every weekend. I put Michelle's friend Bubba down as a reference and filled out the Equal Opportunity form, checking 'other' for my ethnicity. I got a call the next day, and went down, filled out the tax forms, and started that night.

It was a good enough job, and they allowed us to eat all the leftover personal pizzas from the cafeteria since they would throw them out anyway. I worked with an inordinate number of deposed farmers who had lost their family lands in the Big Crunch in the 80s. Not a one would bring themselves to blame Reagan. I was arguing politics my second night with the shift supervisor, Jerry. A tall man with thick hands, and a smile mediated by loss. He was showing me the various cleaning solvents in the janitor's workroom. I leaned on my mop. Jerry's monkeysuit had his name embroidered on the chest. Mine had no name.

-When did you lose your farm? I asked.

-'83, but bla bla bla Reagan, he said.

-Bla bla bla bla bla bla Reaganomics, Jerry. Let's put Reagan on the dollar, and Bush on the hundred.

Jerry leaned on his mop.

-I suppose you vote democrat? he asked. Bla bla, he said.

-Bla bla bla voting, Jerry.

He smiled a polite smile.

-Why don't you finish up here and be sure to hit the kitchen floor with the mop and the degreaser, then the bathrooms on the third floor.

-Jawohl, I said.

At home that night, Ezekiel had left a message. We'd be starting the trim work at Froth's, in about a week. He explained that he also had a bid with the city for a sidewalk repair job, and if his projected bid was the lowest, he'd get the contract. Fingers crossed, he rejoined. Things seemed to be looking up for him, which of course made me jealous and happy.

So that was it for the next week, nightshifting from nine until three in the morning. Damp mops and the closet full of chemical cleaners and solvents and loud whirring machines, the soupy gurgling of the drains, and cigarette breaks. I was always joining someone to grab a smoke, especially Barb, an Aquanet-coiffed and raspy-voiced lesbian who told hilarious raunchy stories about the good old days in the seventies when her thighs were taut and everyone was experimenting with everything and everyone. I liked Barb. When not smoking I tried to spend as much time with the Backuum as possible, a hilarious vacuum cleaner with shoulder straps and a long extension cord, resembling a rocket pack attached to a hose. I stuck the end of the Backuum on Barb's ass once. She laughed and we went and had a smoke break. Bubba had quit weeks and weeks ago, she said.

A couple of nights later we had to come in early and light little candles and place them in white paper bags lining the sidewalk outside. Some famous person I had never heard of was speaking. The sky had been dark all day with large cumulus clouds, hovering and slow to pass, and by the time I was running the bags down the walk, the wind had picked up with the coming thunderhead. It was impossible both to light the candles and keep the bags from toppling over. A few bags bent with a gust, folding the paper into the flame inside, igniting them. A flaming sidewalk that any dignitary would be proud to stride along.

Friday I was scooting around the carpeted areas, sucking up bits of paper and debris with the Backuum, and I noticed a couple pointing at me, chuckling as I passed them. I knew I looked like an idiot. He had a Rolex, and his girlfriend had fake tits. I turned off the Backuum.

-It's rude to laugh at people, I said.

-We weren't laughing at you, dude.

Sniggering and smug from them. I assented.

-I guess you were just amused because you've got it pretty good in life.

Same smug eyes from him.

-I guess so.

-That a Rolex? Submariner?

I knew it wasn't. He shook his head.

-Nah, Daytona. Graduation present.

-From college?

Smug sneer.

-High school.

-I never graduated high school. This is the only job I could get. I got three kids to feed. This is Bush's America, I said.

-I know, he said. I voted for him.

-I voted for him, too, the girl said.

I shook my head and looked him in the eyes.

-Yeah. Me too. Ain't war something.

I turned the Backuum on and finished the lobby and the nearby hallway. Down the hall out in the lobby, they were still laughing, aping my earlier movements. I put the Backuum onto the custodial service cart, full of supplies and soap and stuff. I walked off to the supply closet. I poured a spray bottle full of the industrial strength bleach we used and walked back toward the lobby to the cart, wheeling it along my rounds. As I passed them, I slowed, and took the spray bottle. I bent behind the cart where they couldn't see me. Adjusting the nozzle to stream rather than mist, I rose up and shot at the guy's shirt and pants, a good aim at five feet away. The air smelled of justice, the bottle scronching scronching with each pump I gave it. The shock of it held him immobile. Several people in the lobby gasped, and several more erupted in laughter. He looked down, and to me, and down again, and then back to me.

-What the fuck, asshole, he said, the bleach still hitting his crotch.

-Why aren't you laughing now? Someone shit in your cereal?

-I'm going to fucking kill you, he said.

-He's going to fucking kill you, the blonde said too.

-I'll trade you this backpack vacuum if you won't tell on me, I said.

-Fuck you, asshole, he said, and so did his girlfriend.

- Let's go outside. I don't want to make a mess in here. I just cleaned.

We went outside, and I held the door for him and his girlfriend. He pushed me as he passed. He took off his Rolex and handed it to the girl. His pants and shirt had gone palish yellow where I'd got him. He pushed me a little, but no punches. I didn't engage him, and eventually the blonde girl said they should just get me fired instead. He stormed back into the building, pulling her by the arm. I lit a cigarette, and loaned a smoke to a cute girl who had gathered among the onlookers. She told me a funny story and so we had a few more and talked in the idle dark. By the time I got back inside, the Backuum was gone, stolen or put away, and Jerry informed me that I was fired. I had been planning to steal the Backuum for Squirrel Haus. We needed one. Jerry told me I was lucky the guy didn't press charges because his pants were designer and bleach is a toxic substance. I said goodbye to Barb and she told me to follow her to her car. She handed me half a bottle of knockoff Southern Comfort from the trunk of her Fiero, telling me it had been fun, and gave me a kiss on the cheek. I told her I'd give her a call sometime. There were some good people in the world.

It was only eleven so I went to the Foxhead for a beer, then went home. Squirrel Haus. Dead of night. Our lights were the only ones on along the entire block, the streetlamps at either end with their greasy light around which swarmed the bugs of the night. I walked inside. Griffin was asleep, and Patman wasn't.

-Why are you home so early, man?

-I got fired.

I told him the story of getting eighty-sixed. I looked at the wall. Someone had drawn an X through our mascot.

-Who did that to *Go Hawks!!*?

Shifting on the couch, Patman queried.

-Why do you always want a job, man? And why is there a dead squirrel in your freezer?

-Dead squirrel?

-Yeah, man. It's right next to the bird.

He was right. There was a dead squirrel, frosted and frozen, lying next to the bird in the icebox.

-You didn't do this, Patman?

-Why the hell would I fuck with a dead squirrel, man? That's bad karma.

A package arrived in the mail with the Saturday post, no name or return address on it, and my name was written out simply as

Pinchy Goldboy. Kell, Griffin and Patman had gone over to Wim's to smoke some pot and see his new TV. I was alone. Noel called, to see if I was hungry. I told him maybe later, and I said I'd give him a call in a few hours, or that he should stop by later in the evening.

I opened the package. There was a brief letter, like a kidnapper's note, cut up words from the newspaper, and a single sugar cube.

[pinch][y] [for][your][mourning][coffee] [squeeze][y]

How long, I wondered, had she looked through a damned newspaper for pinch and squeeze. She was a great friend. Stay golden, indeed. She'd sent the acid like she promised.

But only one sugar cube. Dammit, I thought, I had asked for six hits. I figured that I couldn't really complain since it had been free, and she took a relative chance in mailing it to me. I had promised Griffin and Noel that I would share the bounty with them, and ancillary promises to Wim, and a very unmeaning promise to Patman, but since there was only one dose, I took it. I chewed up the hard little block, bland and tasteless sugar, and tossed down a Ritalin too. I sat on Big Red, and began reading some Dickinson, got up, had some water, waiting for the neural net to grind gears synaesthesiacally, waiting for any rattle or rustle in the house to cave in my ear's mind and mind's ear, infinitesimally recursive, like a Cartesian graph mapping a black hole. But nothing.

After thirty or forty minutes, the acid still wasn't working. Just the amphetamines. I decided that I would go for a bike ride at high velocity and at least take advantage of the upper. Maybe I would ride out the twenty miles and see my brother. A minor trek. I glanced in the newspaper at the movie listings. There was a movie playing at the dollar theater which Sarai had recommended. She'd never told me what it was about. There were still no effects from the lysergic acid diethylamide. Perhaps she hadn't put a large enough droplet onto the cube.

I rode my bike swiftly and deftly on sidewalk and lawn and street, through the pre-humid air, the evening the color of a yawn, spreading and windless and cool. I was downtown in a few minutes. I locked the bike to a bench and walked in to the Old Capital Mall. I had about ten minutes to kill, so I played some video games, and lost three matches in a row of Tekken to a twelve-year-old who stuttered when he talked trash to me, something I would never have done when I was his age. These days, kids, kids, kids and their damned rock and roll music. No respect. I threw a small handful of my remaining change, mostly nickels and pennies, at his chest and told him he should see a doctor about his fucking s-s-s-t-t-stutter, and I walked off. At the ticket booth, I paid the three dollars for a ticket and went in. The adverts and previews in the theater were thankfully ending as I sat down near the back. It was about a third full, lots of couples and a few loners like me.

The movie started, some violent things on television monitors. Then there was a monkey watching the screens. I was hoping maybe they'd get the monkey to smoke and drink and solve crimes, and suddenly, here was the acid, or there it was, or t/here and every and where, and my eyes went wide with the recognition and shock of the drug's sudden onset, peeling back my dura mater and laying bare the material beneath. My seat bottom fell out from below me so I held fast my prehensile legs, and I slumped visibly, wrestling with the armrests, and my hands could gain no purchase, slipping off like an Eskimo on a greased tightrope. Holy Christ, I thought, my brain mounting up a single clear thought in a moment of adrenaline fueled struggle, this felt bad. Had she laced it with PCP or strychnine? My jaw was locking up and… My eyes. I couldn't take my eyes from the screen. The walls of the theater were sliding, away, melting, then flowing backwards until they were walls again, but I couldn't be certain. My eyes wouldn't move. There was a monkey biting some college kids who were wearing SWEAT uniforms. SWAT.

Angkor Wat. Accents. Limey animal huggers. Puking blood. London. 28 days later. Naked guy with eyes the color of burning gasoline. Priest puking, in accent, the Eucharist. Zombies. No accents. Running zombies. Christ, they can run now? I knew I had to pay attention to the zombies, study them, but they were much too mobile, and I couldn't decide if this was real or not. I mean, was Romero notified? If I looked away for one second, God only knows what would happen, and I wasn't about to let them sneak up on me. I knew it was ridiculous, there were some fucking limber zombies up there, and I had better take them seriously, if I wanted to make it out of the movie alive. I sat and Horror multiplied and I was a tiny mote of Fear, circling in the dark, and I pulled my feet up on the seat in case there were any zombies crawling around down there.

By the time the movie was over my spine was largely seized and I might have been crying. I knew I had been muttering throughout the movie as people in my vicinity had all abandoned their seats and moved elsewhere, chiding me with loud shhh's. I let everyone in the theater leave first. This was not going to be easy. In a brief window of clarity, I braced my brain for the shock that would ensue upon leaving the dark confines of the theater.

Standing in the aisle, I stared at the luminous door to the hallway, and someone pushed past me, muttering an epithet that made me pause. I edged closer to that liminal theater door, between the land of the living and dead, but I couldn't tell which side I was on, or should I try the fire exit at the bottom of the slanting theater? My hand went from seat to bracing seat, as I climbed the carpeted ramp, the little runway lights my own personal Virgil lining the dark path, and I was at the door.

The light was shocking, grating. I poked my head out and checked both ways down the hall, keeping my head low. Empty. I took a step out into the hall and assumed my mind had broken. Had I not noticed that the hall was lined with mirrors on my way in? There was a mirror behind a mirror and a mirror behind that, flinging each other back and back, and I was caught in the middle of it. I was mortified, the infinite regress was me, and I punched at myself. I half yelled, Third man, and the green man. I needed to look down. Get my bearings. Hic sunt zombies.

The carpeting was no better than the mirrored hall. What would Bruce Lee do?

-He would be Asian, I said.

-I know that voice, my voice said.

Familiar tones, but whose. Below me seethed a complex of brown circles inside orange squares, tidal, undulations, the whole mass of it like an Escherian parachute made from a lava lamp. I felt seasick, but I felt compelled to get on my hands and knees, to get a closer look down inside the circle, because just where the hell had the Vitruvian man gotten off to? Focus. I got up off the ground and put my hand on one the walls, but gently. Just a fingertip. No use falling through and back to square one. Dramamine, I would need Dramamine from the pharmacy downstairs. I had no prescription but did I need one? I took large, lunging steps to accommodate the undulations and lolls of the carpet. High step on the crest, low for the swell. Goddammit, I thought, this carpet is not fit for a maritime excursion. Drunken Boat, drunken boat. What would Rimbaud do? *Voyelles*. After the perpetual senses, and the very long minute, I arrived at the end of the hall. The mirror trap was behind me. Charybdis crossed, but where was Scylla? I could make it out of here if I could just concentrate. Gunshots went off to my left, and I ducked for cover behind a plant.

The popcorn machine was a doomsday machine, and like Tesla's would shake this place apart. Could she see me? My eyes would be a giveaway, the eyes of the living. I crouched a little so she couldn't see me, behind a potted plant with giant jungle leaves, and I looked forward, holding the corner. Tassels and ropes blocked off most escape routes, like the slung intestines of some great beast, and its claws sharp. The glass was definitely locked, or maybe the door was locked glass. I couldn't quite be sure. Could I get out? I stepped and stepped carefully, and the carpet's tide was mostly out by now, so I could move a little more freely toward the glass. Tide at the shoreline. I motioned to the girl with my hand, and walked over, cutting ahead of some shape.

-Don't you know who Tesla Claus is? I asked.

-Excuse me, she said, putting down the bag of popcorn.

-Bruce Lee would know. He's Asian.

-Are you drunk? she asked and backed away from me.

-Hey, no cutting, something said behind me and grabbed my shoulder.

I shoved the shape and ran toward the door. I had forgotten about the zombies, and I paused at the door, staring out into the mall. A middle-aged shopper walked by me, staring at my smooshed face staring up at her. I tried to smile, but the glass distorted my pleasantry and she quickly hurried away, casting back weird glances.

The mall was very bright in the distant courtyard. I had never noticed the offensive color of musak before, either. Someone behind me asked if I was alright, but I kept my head against the glass explaining that a bodiless voice has no place asking things of the bodied. I opened the door, half sashaying in furtive momentum the ten feet to the escalator, down. I crouched on the stairs to get my bearings. The vibrating of the mechanism jostled my brain into a nervous wariness. There was a mall cop, looking at me from above, leaning on the railing across the lower food court, and he was chewing something. I knew him from somewhere. From below was visible a huge scar like a snake ascending his neck, strangling him. I clutched at my own neck, could feel the pulse thromb. I was alive. I waved to him. He stared, and I descended, clutching the rolling rail. I smiled at him, but he knew I was lying, I was certain.

Before I could reach the bottom, near the end of all stairs, where the stairs disappeared into metal teeth thrashing like a garbage can thrown in a tree chipper, I decided not to take chances at becoming pulp and did a standing broad jump. My feet like a thunderclap on the tile floor. Heels and then the hard slap of the soles. I ran the twenty feet to the doors, almost free, and pushed hard on the bar across the door to disengage the lock, but something knocked me down. I was on my back. The door had not opened. The echo of the crash reverberating through the mall and food court and second-floor bathroom where I kissed a girl one time when I was a saxophone, or sophomore. One of the two. Were we locked in? I stood up. Every face on me, their hairy eyeballs, the shiteyes, the deadeyes. I looked at the door. A sign said something about other door, use, and please. I gave a double-fisted peace sign to let them know I was friendly and leaving, and I rushed outside and pretended to talk to Griffin on a payphone there.

Seconds or minutes passed, and I took a deep breath, decided I had to move quickly. I stared for a ten-second eternity at the bike lock in a minor chord of panic and decided it would be an impossible try. The Pedmall was the shape of many shapes, non-Euclidean, and there was the shape of traffic in the street, and my own shape would have to cross this flow and into the next. I hid near the Taco Bell by the mall's exit, concealing myself in a long shadow the color of myself. I hoped, anyway. How long until they cross a human and a cuttlefish? You could put the hybrid on an American flag and they would blend right in. Like a patriot. The crossway light went green. Flee. I ran. Ran the sidewalk and across the street and ran through the Pedmall, and was careful to touch no one. A zephyr, a quicksilver surfer, stopping furtively, when necessary, to hide in a corner, or near a tree, ready to climb if necessary.

I found an alley somewhere along the scramble, from looming figure to looming figure that shambled their way down the sidewalks, and was busy hiding behind a garbage can. A cool breeze came down the space, and for a moment my head cleared with the adrenaline and wind. I had made it out of downtown. I had passed the first test, but what was coming next? I heard the night tearing and retearing itself open.

A girl walked past me on the sidewalk. It sounded like she was walking on Velcro. I put my head further down behind the trash can, trying to peer at her, leaning out toward her shoes. She was wearing cut-off corduroy shorts that ripped and swished in rhythm like an autumn crescendo of cicada song. My head was clearish. She seemed to be heading in my general direction home, so it made sense to follow her. The sound gave me something to focus on, and I knew this was a sign. One had to be sensitive to such portent.

I was cogent enough to hang back, fighting the waves of Terror and the flashes of the drug. If I startled her she might run off or find a cop. I followed the sound, trailing her by 30 feet. She walked, and I followed in rapt obedience to the sounds that issued from her legs. I discerned that she was in fact not heading in my direction, and she seemed more tense when I decided to come a little closer to get a better listen. She had slowed, the susurration from her pants like the slow rip of cloth. Had she heard me? I had been trying to walk stealthily, rounding each footfall from the heel to toe like I assume the Indians did it. But she had caught my scent, hadn't she? I accidentally cracked my knuckles out of nervousness.

She turned and looked at me. I was hunched over, like Groucho Marx, looking up at her seven feet away, my eyes wide with panic and realization. Her eyes wide. I tried to smile at her. A tear ran avalanche down my cheek and I mouthed my thoughts silently outloud, shaking and nodding my head when I agreed or disagreed with myself. She jerked to her left, bolting up the walkway to a house and began pounding on their door. Why else would she be clamoring to get inside someone's house unless she were a zombie, too. Had she seen someone more delicious inside?

Was she running from them? I shook my head for a moment, but her sudden flash had given me another healthy dose of adrenaline, and my instincts informed me it was flee not fight time. I ran up the block. The porch light of the house came on above the girl as I turned. I stopped and yelled down the block, hysteria in the voice, and laughing, for some reason.

-Don't let her in! She's going to kill you! Don't let anyone in! Call the police! They're everywhere! They're coming right at us!

I ran down the streets that had the least light until my lungs were seared, and I leaned against a tree, bent, my mind spun and foaming. I ran some more and tripped and looked up. There were myriad gravestones all around me, granite perches where below the dead were stirring. The ground bubbled and seethed with activity. I had to get to higher ground. Panicked breaths issued from my nose, and I grabbed a low tree-branch and pulled myself up, climbing in the dark until I was well out of reach of anything in the wide realm of death. Tangent after tangent of thoughts swam in my vision, and I sat there in irregular seconds until they massed into minutes or so and off into time unaware. I realized that there would be undead animals on the prowl, too, because the logic was perfect. I never messed with logic. I was shaking, and tremors ran through my arms shaking the branches I held, the thought of a red-eyed rodent clawing its way up at me too much to bear. Squirrel Revenge, and them clawing out of the Haus, stale bodies and the paper skin a'hunt, and the one waiting in the freezer. I jabbered for several minutes quite out loud. I put my hands to my head to quell the ache there, then I slipped and fell to the ground in a plop. A police car had stopped in the street below and its floodlight swung across the cemetery, enveloping me at me like a thunderbolt and I could hear the photons at work in it as the light washed over me like a slap. A cop yelled up to me. I could hear him too.

-Hey, you, stay right there.

I gave a high-pitched squeak of shock and fear, awash now

with more mind-clearing adrenaline. I ran back through the cemetery until the voices behind me faded, and through sheer luck I found a stream that cut through the graveyard's lower quadrant like a giant finger pointing home. I followed it south, stumbling in the dark, turning often to watch for zombified squirrels and I could see a pair of flashlights in the distance, still amid the graves, bobbing in the dark like unmoored, radioactive moths. You'll get what you deserve in there when the dead get out, I muttered out loud, careful not to say anything at volume. After ten minutes of wet shoes and nettles and branches scraping my face, I was out of the cemetery where the grave-littered grass opened into a quiet neighborhood and lovely flowers that glowed in the soft humming floodlights like beautiful souls. Nerves shattered by paranoia, I half jogged with my hands over my face, for anonymity I reasoned, until I came to Burlington Street's well-lit promenade. I bounded across the pavement, and finally knew my way home.

I ran at full tilt now, a blaze of adrenaline and abject dread. Griffin's gun. Tools. Bludgeons. Wood to bar the doors and windows. Everything necessary for staying among the living was back at Squirrel Haus. Nothing in, nothing out. I crossed the train bridge, finally turning on to Daniel Street. The acid was in full gear again. I could not bear to look at Diomedes' fell visage from above the door because he was saying something, admonishing me in a low voice. I crept around to the back door, but it was locked. I kicked in one of the basement windows and slid into the Bilge. I would deal with that fucking cocksucker deer later.

I crawled up the stairs into my room, and out to the dark kitchen. No one was home. Pickle looked up at me with a grunt from the living room. I put my finger to my lips and shushed him, telling him to stay low and not to panic. I crawled into Griffin's room and found his gun, and with several uncoordinated tries, managed to slide the magazine out. No bullets. I hid under his desk, rummaging in the drawers in the dark with my hand, found two rounds and loaded them, sliding in the magazine and back went the lever. I showed Pickle how the gun worked, just in case, went back to the kitchen, and grabbed my hammer from my tool belt. Patman's housewarming gravestone glowed on top of the fridge and Nazibear hummed. I didn't take my eyes from the bear. I jerked the freezer open, threw the bear and gravestone in with the frozen squirrel. I slammed the door shut and pulled the fridge down on the floor with a loud crash. I gathered my weapons and backed into the Dais.

I sat in the corner of my bedroom, with a blanket securely over my head, like a leprous beggar. I would not be seen. Time was nothing. Everything. The room sworled from white to black, through the kaleidoscope and back to nothing. I wept bitterly that my family was dead now, and I hadn't talked to them enough, hadn't spoken my feelings or expressed them despite all their pious judgment and the childhood beatings and Sunday school, and missed everyone's birthdays because I was terrible at dates and numbers. My brother dead, and my baby niece. Friends. All the babies, dead. Devoured in unspeakable ways. The scenes of mutilation and sundering of flesh ran through my eyes, and I gripped the blanket, biting it, howling at the senselessness of cruelty and all the evils of the world, spoken and not. Crazed and trembling and alone.

The fridge slammed. No, it rattled then slammed. Or maybe it slammed and then rattled. Or maybe the front door. How had they gotten free? Carnage flashing before my eyes. Someone, something, was in the house. I turned the hammer slowly in my hand to get the claw ready. There were footsteps, heavy, plodding, a real zombie, not the Hollywood type, slow and methodical. My legs ached in tension, as I took a leopard's crouch and pulled the slide on the gun.

The steps were coming toward my room, careful, controlled, and an arm pushed the door open. I was shaking my head, mouthing, No, No.

There was a form at the door, backlit, the movie poster from *The Thing*. Indescribable horrors. MacReady be merciful. The shape stood there, shapeless, Shiva-armed, a dealer of death. I jumped up, squeaked, and threw the gun. It caught the pistol mid-air. Shit, I thought, now I've armed it. I ran at the shadow howling curses. If it would speak it would need blood, and I would not sell mine cheap, nor dig the cubit hole. I hauled the hammer in the air, claw poised, readying my strike as the room's light went on and blinded me. I tripped on the blanket and fell forward, the hammer slicing into the wall and lodging in the baseboard, irretrievable, and the blankets squirmed on me. My cry hit hysterics as I expected the creature to fall on me, one bite and I was a goner, and I would join the shadow legions. I twisted inside the blanket, but it had swallowed me up, and this was how death felt, wriggling at the last moments, helpless against the grim tide with tight, difficult breaths. I struggled some more. There was a laugh, and I tried to pull the hammer free, but the head was caught behind the baseboard, and I would soon be dead anyway.

-I'm done for, I muttered. I can't hold out much longer.

-What the fuck are you doing? Are you okay?

It could speak. It spoke in tongues most familiar to me, and a voice. I decided to be honest.

-Acid, yes. I don't know.

-Jesus, you are fucked up.

I was mumbling under the blanket, rolling on my stomach from shoulder to shoulder to find the better acoustics in the blanket. Something rolled me over.

-Did you get that acid from your friends? Are you okay?

-One cubit. One cubit, I mean. That's where you put the goat blood. Otherwise the dead can't talk.

The blanket lifted, and I knew the face. It was Noel. He lifted me up to sitting, checked the gun.

-Christ, Dunham, you're messed up. You realize this thing is loaded and the safety off, right?

-Everyone's dead, I said, and almost bawled again.

He went to the kitchen, and returned with a bottle, big and glinty in backlit by the kitchen light, filled with an unctuous brown liquid, and a bag of snow in his other hand.

-Where's that Pyrex pan? he asked. You need some whiskey and blow. That'll clear you up.

-You look quite human, I said, standing and poked his cheek.

-What's this shit about goat's blood? he said.

-Bluff with a blunderbuss.

-Well, I'm glad I'm human and don't need to drink any blood.

-Goat's milk tastes like blood.

He laughed and walked back to the kitchen. A Bill Hicks CD was playing. I managed to the kitchen. Noel braffed a line from the Pyrex pan, picked up the gun and slid out the mag, replaced it, then pulled the slide to eject the remaining round which shone in the air like a whirling sun until it came down perfectly in his hand. I'd never seen anything more beautiful.

He righted the fridge back into place and fished out some beers, and half an hour at sieve and straw cut through the associative, elliptical mind fog, and I was able to string along a thought for more than two seconds at a time. Noel was laughing, at me and then at the story as I retold it the best I could. I was finally able to piece the night back together, the vague flash and glimmer of the acid still causing me to twitch, and I routinely checked at the window, standing to the side of the pane, just to be sure the world hadn't ended. You can't be too careful in an apocalypse, I told him. Noel poured more whiskey into glasses as I took another great gulp of the cocaine. He pushed the flashing answering machine button, and it said there was one message. *Saturday. 5:14 PM.*

-Hola, Pinchy, it's Sarai I forgot to tell you be careful. There's six hits in that cube. It was really great meeting your old friends. Mike says hello. Hope you guys have fun on your trip Love you. Call us soon.

Noel laughed and went to the freezer for ice.

-Dunham, why the fuck do you have a dead squirrel, Nazi Bear and a gravestone in your freezer?

-They were coming right at me, Noel. Right fucking at me.

June

Mythos

Pre-dawn now just west of the river.
A foundry in the water. Slaglight and the ash of the heavens.
It is good to have location, though it shrinks
in the light and is too soft for language
or pulse. History's the same, stands splayed

and augmented. All the dead poets of China
and the Qin emperor interred with his terracotta
army of soldiers and citizens do not swell
my little landscape an inch, throw no glaze
of morning shadow on the near-invisible willow.

These hands I accompany to work
are talking of fear, empty as they are of all
except the smell of a woman's body from last night,
and that kinship of a few dollar bills. Down
the street I can see a man light his cigarette

in the gliding aurora, below the few stars remaining
on their tall black hill resembling the small,
hand-fashioned oil lamps the superstitious villagers
used to hang at the entrances to tombs in order to frighten
away grave-robbers and sullen demons.

Soundtrack

The Notting Hillbillies, *Take this Hammer*
Townes van Zandt, *If I Needed You*
Public Enemy, *Bedlam*
Porno for Pyros, *Meija*
Nirvana, *Radio Friendly Unit Shifter*
Bushwick Bill, *Little Big Man*

Warm days gave way to the brutality of summer, the dripping of humidity. The oscillating fans in the Harem and the rooms merely moving the air like a greasy tongue, licking the bodies to a slightly less-sweaty sheen with each whirring pass. Mute Midwestern spanses of time stunted with a green flourish and air heavy as the air buckled back on itself. I collected half of the rent and mailed it, embossed with the sadness of stamps that will always carry my money away. Patman had thankfully disappeared after an incident downtown on the first day of the month. He and I had biked down to Joe's for some food. We were standing at the bar amid the din of crowd and contest, waiting for our victuals. Patman grinned at me and pointed to the pint glass next him. It belonged to a guy with his back to us, entranced with a Cub's game on TV, with his friends. Patman snuck his hand low across the bar, his eyes fixed on the group, snagged the glass and then drained it in one quaff. He then reached down, looked around the assemblage, and pissed, filling the cup, setting it back on the counter, a gargoyle's smile on his mouth. I grabbed his arm.

-What the fuck is wrong with you? I said. You want to fight your way out of here with eight guys?

-Sometimes you just have to go, man. The Cubs suck anyway.

The jibe at the baseball team caused a few heads to swivel at us. Patman smiled.

-Hey, pal, one of the guys said, what's your problem? We're just trying to watch the game.

Patman's face went tranquil, the slightest hint of a grin at the corners of his mouth.

-I just said the Cubs suck, man. So do the people that like them.

Some more patrons turned from the game toward us. Two of them stepped closer to Patman. He calmly took the pint glass he'd just filled from the counter.

-That's my beer, asshole, one of the patrons said.

Patman took a sip, smiled, and tossed the piss into the largest man's face. Then he went full dervish. He whacked the glass across another man's face and he fell. Another went sprawling back from a punch and Patman redoubled his efforts on the curled form in front of him. He grabbed the guy's shirt and pull-punched him nine or ten times until there was nothing but a mess of blood and spit at the end of his fist.

-The fucking Cubs suck, man, he said, then he darted out past the onlookers and through the door.

I went back to Squirrel Haus directly, and told Kell and Griffin the story. Kell had to leave the next day to visit family. He would leave *Phlogiston* with us, in case anything got out of hand, and said he'd be up early tomorrow. With a bow and a flourish, I explained that I would not be seeing him off. I would sleep in till seven-thirty.

I got a call from my brother. He had gotten the contract from the city Streets and Sewers Department to repair cracked or uneven sidewalk blocks around town, so he offered me a job. My brother had outrageously low-balled all the other contractors, and we learned later that he was given the job to see whether it was a hoax. We would start next week, so I had a few days of down time to try to write and paint.

Suddenly flush with the prospect of money easing me from the toil of picking the couch cushions for loose change, I drove over to the Lonely Strip Mall, with its always half-empty parking lot. I parked on the edge, away from the other cars. The airy mall was peopled with the elderly cruising around in their patented Mall Walker shoes, elbows high and sawing the air, gibbets of their skin hanging loose below the smiles and shaking with each step. In Radio Shack I was greeted by all manner of one-off toys that no kid could enjoy, the lifeless packaging and strange prices, and the million connectors and diodes and wired gizmos that filled the store. I glanced at the girl working the counter. She was pretty, in a generic Midwestern way, slightly built with a healthy dollop of flesh at her chest, cheeks that already had begun their inexorable march at gravity's behest. She gave me a minimum wage smile, and I walked the store trying to find what I wanted.

Unsuccessful after three laps, I sidled up to the counter.

-Do you sell Dictaphones here?

-Dicta what? she said, eyes blinking.

-Like a little tape recorder, but pocket-sized.

-Oh, I think we do.

She turned around and then back to me, and then pointed down at the glass case between us.

-Is that what you're looking for? she asked.

-It would seem so, I said. But, which are better, the cassette or the digital ones?

-It depends on which you prefer.

-But if you had to use one, based on your expertise from working here, which would you choose?

She blinked repeatedly at me, again.

-But I don't need one.

-But if you did, I said.

-I really don't need one, though. Why would I buy something I don't need?

I bent toward her name tag.

-It's just a hypothetical question, uh, Jesse. How long have you worked here?

-Almost two months.

-Do you like it? I asked.

Blinking.

-It's okay, she said. I get commissions on sales.

-Are you in school?

-Yeah, I study art.

-What field?

-Painting.

I managed a smile. How many art majors had I met in the past months?

-I paint a lot too. You should come over and see my work. I do a lot of collaborations. We should do a painting called Analog Versus Digital. Do you know if they make any solar-powered Dictaphones? You know, for the environment.

-The ones we sell here run on batteries, she said with assurance.

-Would you like to come over some time? Do some paintings.

-Uh, okay, she said, which surprised me. Where do you live?

-933 Daniel Street, just up from the porn shops and Flabbo's. It's right off of Kirkwood. From here you'd take a right at the funeral home just before the hill falls. I'll write it down.

I wrote down the pertinent information, bought the tape version, and some new cassettes, and left my address too on the free tape that came with the device, slid it across the counter, and then I bought some extra batteries. She said her commission percentage was higher for batteries, but she didn't know why. Suffer the mallworkers. I walked out, unsure whether she'd call me or not, but at least I had my Dictaphone. I drove over to Ezekiel's and we loaded the appropriate tools in the trailer, readying for another round of dispiriting labor. Knowing what was ahead, I intoned a silent vow as private resignation to work hard for my brother. I drove back to Squirrel Haus and had a beer, sitting, looking at the giant X through our *Go Hawks!!* mascot. The painting was hung with two knives sunk into the wall. I decided I would have to have a talk with Patman when I saw him next. No one could yet figure out where the squirrel in the freezer came from. It hadn't been Patman or Griffin.

The next night found Griffin and I drunk and up a little too late, sitting by a defunct set of railroad tracks a few blocks away from Squirrel Haus, febrile the night and all the air fraught with heat. The tracks were the tail-end of a larger set that were still used, running off with the Iron Horse, but not these upon which we sat.

We passed a bottle of wine back forth, Griffin bemoaning my good luck in having a few days off. I reminded him that idle hands don't get paid. There was a sound, small and gurgled, in the weeds near us, where we sat on the tracks pulling loose spikes from the ties, the worn buzz of the streetlamp a few yards away, and faint resinous smell of creosote lingering in weed and mote. A kitten emerged, came up to Griffin and began kneading his leg with its head. He grabbed it, his hands full around its small ribs.

-What do you want, little pussy? Christ, you look anorexic. Are you a supermodel?

-I think it wants a friend, I said.

Griffin laughed, and pointed the kitten at his nose where it nodded its maw toward him.

-We all need a friend in this shit-filled world. Should we take it home?

-It needs a name first. It'd be bad luck otherwise.

Griffin rubbed the kitten's head and made the sign of the cross.

-I dub thee Pussy Versus Pussy Franco.

-Where the hell did you get that name? I asked.

-I just thought it up, he said.

-The muse speaks. Do you think Pickle will put up with a cat?

-Pickle loves anyone that feeds him or snuggles. If you don't feed him, you'd better be a good snuggler.

He held the cat aloft, looking at it warmly.

-Are you a good snuggler Pussy Versus Pussy Franco? and he laughed.

I lit a cigarette.

-I thought Layna was coming in May. What happened? I didn't want to ask.

-She's not coming, he said.

-Why not?

-Me, I guess.

-You okay, I asked. Need to talk?

-Yup. Nope.

-Okay.

-Layna. Laney. To hell with them both, he said.

-Funny how that works, I said.

-Yeah, but not ha-ha funny. Not even close, right Pussy Franco?

Griffin walked back to Squirrel Haus with the cat in the crook of his arm, and I moseyed the three blocks to the store and grabbed some milk, cat food and smokes. Pussy Versus Pussy Franco wouldn't take any solids, but plunged its face deep into the milk, sloshing white over its fur and the carpet. It drank to satiety and lay down, stomach drawn taut. Pickle charged out of Griffin's room when he opened the door and flipped Pussy Franco over with a loving sweep of his wide tongue. Griffin smiled at me, smoke seeping out of his teeth, pointing to the toppled kitten.

-See, I told you. Pickle loves everyone.

Pickle was licking Pussy Franco, settling his bulk by the tiny kitten, now too engorged with milk to protest the bulldozing tongue. Pickle grunted, ceasing his bath duties, and lay his head by Pussy Franco with an air of satisfaction, his left eye blinking and staring down at his charge. The kitten rolled, using its last remaining strength, and settled its right paw on Pickle's snout. Pickle grunted again, and closed his eyes, deep breaths issued and rolled across the rug. And soon they were both asleep. Pickle and PvP Franco.

The days passed in idle concupiscence. I wrote nothing, and cared nothing of it. Griffin worked, and I pretended to work, reading a lot, annoyed with Pussy Franco's mewing and kneadling. He had grown strong enough to slip out the hole Pickle's head had left in the screen door, and would regularly come and go when not given proper attention. Griffin came home one afternoon that week, with typical workman's gripes, and we sat outside on the stoop where at least the breeze could pretend to cool us. A red Monte Carlo turned right onto Daniel Street, a whumping bass from its subwoofers that we had heard long off, nearing in the still, unundulating air. The car drifted down the street and pulled into the driveway, the sudden quiet engulfed the neighborhood as the stereo snapped off. Two gangsta types emerged, eyeing us with a feigned disinterest. I nodded hello, and raised my beer. One of them raised his chin, and they walked toward Michelle's door. Griffin took a long drag.

-There's some bad news right there.

They came back out a few minutes later, barely enough time to conduct business. I raised my beer again to them with feigned friendliness.

-Nice whip, I said.

-Yeah, he said.

-What did those rims cost you?

He didn't answer, brushing his hand toward us in some esoteric gesture, instead, as he got in the car. I hoisted again my flagon as their woofers began again in window rattling excess. I turned to Griffin.

-OG trouble, I said.

-Why the hell can't we just have a little PG trouble?

-Because we live in an R-rated world, my friend.

-Just don't take six hits of acid and try to fix it, he said. I still can't believe that you threw my gun at Noel.

-That's an exaggeration. He's just lucky he looked human.

-This month has been pretty calm so far, he said, but you never know when things will get X-rated.

The girl from Radio Shack called me that night. I couldn't remember her name. I told her to stop by Squirrel Haus and I'd show her how to shoot a bow, but she wanted to meet in a public place, for safety. It hurt my feelings. We met, bailed the evening out, question after question, and I went home with her. The next morning I walked back to Squirrel Haus with an indolent pace, and stopped in Java Casa for an espresso. The girl working the bar was the most beautiful woman I had ever seen, wine dark skin, seamless her skin, and her voice like dactylic hexameter, skin live with the fine sweat of work and steam. Her name-pin read Olateju. I asked her what it meant, and she said it meant immense wealth in Yoruba, and then gave me the total. I asked her on a date and she said no. I paid for my coffee and walked home rind-footed, joyless and plotless. Pickle greeted me at the door, and Griffin waved a beer at me in the kitchen.

-Where were you last night, Don Juan?

-At Radio Shack's, I said.

-Love at first purchase. Was banging you part of her commission? he said.

-Love in the time of capitalism. I just saw the most beautiful girl at Java Casa. Good fucking God, you should see her.

-What's she look like?

-Like an African goddess.

-You should ask her out, he said.

-I did. She shot me down.

-I think I could go for a cup of joe, he said with a wry smile.

-Give it the old college try.

-No, my friend, I'll give it the old GED try.

He and Pickle went for that walk, and I sat dejected on the couch thinking of her skin and smile, smoking until they got back. He held up a piece of paper with seven digits on it, and he smiled. Pickle had sealed the deal because, as it turned out, she loved dogs. We shot bows in the back for an hour.

-If she comes over, I said, I don't want to see or hear anything, you know, unseemly.

-Come on, Griffin said with a smile, I'm as seemly as they come, brother.

We decided to head downtown to the bars that night, and we ran that gamut of highs and lows. On Sunday, we rested, as per the Good Book, and sipped Bloody Marys until three in the afternoon, whiling the time with painting and nothing much but mucking up a decent canvas until the stretched cotton duck was a mottled purple of trawl marks and wasted oils. Griffin called Olateju and made a date. My brother called and said he'd pick me up in the morning. There was work afoot, which was good because I was almost out of money, and pissed secretly at Griffin's good fortunes. Work would be a decent distraction. There was a message from Wim asking about Patman's whereabouts, and a message from Patman asking the same of Wim's.

-What do you think those two are up to? Griffin asked.

-That which I don't know only makes me stronger when it comes to those two together, I said.

I tried to call Haley in Toronto, but some manservant answered and said that they were out somewhere. I called Monk, but he wasn't home.

The idea of the city concrete job was easy. A city inspector would mark certain sidewalk blocks, and give us a list, and we would remove and replace the flawed sections of sidewalk. The blocks in question were trip hazards, and the city dutifully passed the cost of the repairs to the homeowners, even though the sidewalks and the easement were civic property. The idea was easy, but concrete work was not. Spending the majority of the day bent between the degrees of 120 and 40 is no sinecure, in 100% humidity and 100 plus degrees. I had only ever worked concrete in small spurts, and only with Ezekiel, who'd learned it while employed illegally at fourteen with a bunch of roughnecks. I was going to have to remember the various steps and procedures, and quickly. Ezekiel suffered no fools. Especially me. We got our list Monday morning, and sat in the truck, and then set about cutting the blocks loose with a diamond-bladed cement saw that threw up a grey swath of dust in fine, lung-rupturing plumes. Zeke had bought the saw especially for the city job, but had neglected masks. I covered my face with a bandana, and the blade cut smooth and effortless through the concrete. Then I would sledge the block in pieces, dump them into the easement, and then line and stake two-by-fours at the edges of the cavities in the promenade. Zeke and I would drive up to each site, drop off the requisite tools, and he would drive off. It was like that for two days, until we had enough holes in the walk to order a load of concrete. We'd pour a block here and another there, the driver ever more angry that we were taking up too much truck time, calls from irate dispatchers always audible from the truck's cabin.

We then had to deal with angry homeowners who would charge from their houses at the noise of the saw screeching into the cement in front of their homes. We had no real answer why they should have to pay for the city's repairs, saying we were just doing a job, and doling out the various civic offices names and numbers whereby complaints could be lodged. The week passed in shunted silence, a slipped-disk space in the backbone of time, the heat and toil adding up to weekend's respite. Zeke asked me whether I would ever get around to visiting our parents. I said I would soon. He nodded and said he didn't believe in miracles. Griffin was hitting it off with Olateju, and they made plans to go camping that weekend on his parents' land. I made plans to go swimming at the reservoir with Brom and Noel. Ezekiel had to take Isis to the hospital for some booster shots. All was right and the undulant metronome sun and moon swept sky and time alike in predicatory arcs that cleared space for play and work alike.

Brom and Noel showed up at Squirrel Haus Saturday morning, pulling up in Brom's ragtop Wrangler. Griffin had departed for his weekend with Olateju. Brom had some mushrooms, and they'd been drinking all morning, so I drove us north toward the reservoir. We took the drugs, and they and I sat in the sun, the blind smoke of a desired piety opening over my thoughts like a mouth. Much loss this past year. All these machines and money and malls and the mercenary feel of the country, a blood-slick dreadnought that devoured its own like a spiderbrained sow chewing up its farrow. My eyes like a transom and not blinking let in the full weight of the light until it stove deep and clear in the small, crude consciousness. I would learn, through excesses of monasticism or narcissism, to love this life. I'm bound to leave this dark behind. My tragedies would only ever register in the minor keys. Minor keys for a minor, lower-case life.

We drove back, burnt of mind and body, shooting at stopsigns along the road with Brom's 9 mm. On the way, I noticed a silver stationwagon sitting near a farmhouse driveway with $150 soaped on the window. I made a note to self in the Dictaphoracle, and sped on back toward Casa de Squirrel.

That evening, Noel and Brom and I went to The Deadwood and Brom offered up a wager: if I could hold a dollar bill flush against my arm and burn a hole through it with the end of a cigarette, he would give me ten bucks. If not, I owed him five. I figured there would be an issue with heat transference when the bill was on my skin, but ten bucks is ten bucks, worth the risk of a five.

Brom helped to hold the bill against my forearm, pinching both ends with the dollar wrapped around, and I lay down the ember. I started rolling the hot ash in circles at forty-five degree angles, blowing on it, hoping that it would catch on one of the fibers and finally burn through. After two minutes or so of holding a lit cigarette to my arm, I could feel the heat in the muscle, and a nerve twitch in my neck. I pulled the cigarette off, and Brom held up the bill. Unscathed. With an air of resigned indifference, I threw five dollars on the table and stood up. My arm was throbbing.

-Well, it's been fun gents, but I've got to go see a girl about a commission.

It was only a ten-minute walk to Radio Shack's apartment, so I stopped and grabbed a few tallboys. My arm was hurting, dull pain spread, like a pinched back. At every heartbeat my right eye winced. When I got to her place, I had already finished one of the road beers. She was thankfully home and opened the door to her little cave, and she turned, sitting back on the couch in her pajamas, the shirt unbuttoned halfway, the pale curve of her breasts showing, illuminated by the blue glow of the television flooding the room.

-Hola, senorita, what are you watching?

-Nothing much.

-Sounds riveting. Want a beer?

-Sure, she said.

She took it and opened it and drank from it. She was watching *Seinfeld*. I stood in front of the TV, and showed her my arm, explaining the bet.

-How did you hold the bill and do the cigarette thing? she asked.

It took the better part of five minutes for her to understand exactly what happened. The burn by now was bubbled out, a great taut and shining blister on my arm, third, maybe even fourth degree I explained. I poked at it. She squirmed a little. I turned attention back to the blister. I rubbed its surface gently to test the contents and pressed it hard, blasting the material out the other side of the dome of skin. It splattered her face, and she recoiled as if shot. Her eyes went wide in disgust.

-What the hell are you doing?

-Oh, shit. Sorry.

I was sorry, as I hadn't meant for it to happen, but I giggled. Her face leveled, and for the first time since I'd met her, showed an honest emotion, and that of dread indignation.

-Get out, she said. Get out.

-I know. I'm sorry. I know. I'm not unfamiliar with the request.

She had not yelled. Just a monotone rejoinder whose repetition was its only insistence. She closed the door as I left. I walked up the stairs and realized I'd forgotten my beer. I stood at the window well, looking down into her blue-lit room, and threw a few wood chips at her window.

-May I have my beer at least? It's Old Milwaukee, I said. I can't let that go to waste.

She stirred, retrieving the sack and threw it up out of the window well into the lawn without a word and slid the window shut. I could see her sit back down in front of the TV, no hints of furtive gesturing, no anger. Poor Radio Shack, I mused, another commissioned cog in the great wheel of 'Merica.

I yelled thanks at her, leaning over the window well so she would be sure to see my form. She looked up at me for a moment, and then back to the glowing box full of friendly humorless images and words. I cracked a beer and moseyed toward home. The phone sat in the mailbox, dead, and I hung it on the wall. I poured a glass of bourbon and went to the freezer for ice. The squirrel was still there. Lying on its back, bone rigid next to the blue jay. The gravestone was still there too. I shut the door and put *Conan* in the VCR. I'd deal with it all tomorrow.

The week emerged, spade by spadeful of turned earth, incremental and purposed, proportioned by the small and crumbleable intentions, and dirt in human hands. The smell of lime in the concrete, acidic and grey. I set forms, cutting boards and driving stakes, the banshee cement saw and high dust in the June air, wet and smeary across everything, mixing with the powder on the skin, like a grey woad. Up and down the streets we mended the sidewalks, apertures opening and filled later with gloop that ran from the hopper and down the chute, and we, roughing the heavy liquid with a two-by-four smooth to the form, and then after with magnesium trawls to bring the cream up to the surface, scraping smooth the square, rounding the edges with another tool, and brooming the top of each block after the cement cured, drawing the shop-broom lightly for grain and traction. Grain and traction, again, and then again, street to veering street, the season hung down through branches like ganglia in a wet throat around the small sounds of our toiling bodies. My throat hoarse from smoking, from nightly incursions with the liquid cure-all, only to rise again like a salamander into the fire-brightness, the Iowa sun immolate, in which to make the small perturbations called work. And so the week passed, damp and hot, from firefall and firerise.

I was finishing a two-square section of sidewalk on Johnson Street, quiet, glad for the shade of the locust trees. Someone, voice all rumble and gruff, hailed me from the adjoining house. I looked up, and a massive form waved from the porch.

-Hey!

-Howdy, I said.

-Got yourself some work there.

-Been trying not to, I said.

The man moved his bulk off the porch, jiggling like a running bear, full of fat and meat, a Colt .45 tallboy in his hand, and he moved down the sidewalk, loosely jointed, flopping along, a swinging cadence of undulant bearing in his broad gut. He shook my hand.

-Name's Scott.

-Dunham. How're you today?

-Not bad, I suppose, he said. Wishing I had an air conditioner. Fans I got don't do much of shit. Seen you workin over here and thought I'd come and see if you was hiring.

-Yeah, I know what you mean about the air conditioning. I thought about hooking one up to the generator and hauling it around on my back.

-I seen a guy do that once, he said. Had no air in his truck, so he rigs an air conditioner to the back of his truck cab with a generator in the bed.

-Did it work?

-Sure did, he said. Till he got in a wreck and that generator come flying into the air conditioner and damn near broke his neck. Real lucky.

- How'd you get so lucky to be drinking a coldbeer at two in the afternoon, Scott?

-Ain't no luck in it, he said. They laid me off. Was working up at the hospital on a new building.

-You a doctor?

-Ha, hell no. I done most everything construction. Was doing cement walls. Forming up the foundation.

-What are they building?

-New cancer wing, he said.

-That's good. Gives me a reason to keep smoking, I said. Job security for the oncologists. Did it pay okay?

-Pretty good compared to most concrete jobs.

-I'm a bit of a novice at the whole concrete thing.

-Hell, it's like riding a bike, he said, watching a pretty blonde wheel by, slick with summer sweat and her terrycloth shorts damp.

-Well, if you know how to ride a bike, I said, watching her disappear.

-You guys hiring at all, Scott asked. Hospital will take back the layoffs in a week or so, but damned if I don't feel lazy just sitting round the house.

-I doubt it. Sorry. I'll ask my brother when he comes by, though. He runs things pretty small. Especially the paychecks, if you know what I mean.

-Yeah, I know that, he said. I'm good at it all, though, even if you guys just need some demo done. Could use some folding money to get my guitar out of the pawn.

-My brother's got an eye on buying a skidloader, so I'm not sure. Money might be tight. I'll ask him.

Scott nodded like a bobblehead.

-That'd be great. What kind of loader he buyin?

-Bobcat, I think.

-What model?

-No clue. The expensive kind?

-Can I get one of those smokes from you?

-You bet.

-Thanks. Well, I don't want to get you in trouble for jawin here with me, so I'll let you get back to it.

-Nice to meet you, Scott.

-Nice to meet you, Dunham.

- Good luck getting back on the hospital crew.

Griffin and I, desirous of a change of weekend pace, gathered some of the tribe, and we all pitched in and bought a few bottles of wine and bread, and good cheese. We sat in College Green Park, bottles in paper sacks, spreading the warm cheese with pocket knives. The sun was high, hazed, and we sat in arboreal shade. Olateju's head on Griffin's leg, Noel and a new girl with her friend, myself, and Kell, who had returned the night before, Hell Machine's twin-V battle cry ruining the Friday night quietude.

We ate the molten cheese and good bread in the park, and passed around a bottle of Merlot which disappeared too quickly, as did its companion Cabernet. The good life too good to give up, we decided to go to Café 313, a swanky wine bar downtown whose owner was a trustifarian asshole I had met once at a party in grad school. The café had a sommelier, and battery-operated corkscrews, French words on the menu that were spelled correctly, accent grave, circumflex, accent aigu. It was a place for the affluent, idly rich, upwardly mobile types who could sit and reminisce how much better the food was in New York or *Gay Pairree,* while cramming their noses into the fluted glasses, swirling the liquid inside, as if that made any difference.

The six of us went in, and were seated upstairs near the window facing the street below. The other tables were clinking glasses over expensive-looking spreads of hors d'oeuvres, buttery and variegated and rich-looking. Our waitress came over and we ordered a low-end bottle of Italian wine. She brought the bottle over, and extracted the cork with the battery-operated device. I asked her whether she had undergone OSHA approved training to handle the machinery. She smiled at me, polite and dismissive. A paid smile, but cute.

The bottles went quickly, and we ordered more. The waitress, her name tag read Nancy, apologized but that was the last bottle they had of the cheap stuff. The next bottle up was five dollars more per. I told her that the now-extinct varietal was my favorite, and that I was drinking it with my friends because I had just gotten back from Italy and wanted to share a taste of my experiences. I had been studying Italian in that region with the son of a winemaker. I rattled off a little Italian, and translated the bottle's label to establish my bona fides. Explaining that she normally would exchange the bottles, she pointed to the bar and said that the owner was here this afternoon. She would have to ask him. A minute later, the owner was at our table. He brushed his expensively disheveled hair behind his ear.

-What seems to be the trouble?

He said it flat. Not a question. He assumed we were the trouble. He pointed at the menu.

-I won't be able to exchange the bottles, he said. The prices are what they are: fair. If you can't pay an extra five dollars between six of you, then I can't be of much help.

-Well, sir, I said, it would seem to me that accommodating your customers would be priority number one, Griffin interjected. Trying to make sure that we as guests want to come back. Isn't that a preferred business model, especially in times like these when Americans have to stand together? There's a war on, you know.

-Not if the guests are cheap, the owner said.

Griffin tapped my shin with his boot under the table and nodded at me.

-Please send the waitress over, Griffin said. We're ready to order.

Nancy came back, smiling. Everything was great, I told her, smiling back, voice confident and assuring. Griffin ordered three bottles of mid-range wine, explaining that we should be celebrating my return, the prosciutto platter, large, with extra melon, and two plates of escargot to round out the extravaganza. The food came, and we drank the deep, earthy wine, so good, and a flood of real memories of Italy. I told the table about thwarting a purse-snatcher in Rome, years ago with Misha, running barefoot after the thief after my sandals fell off. I had saved some British girl's passport and was a hero for a night to a crowd of strangers. We ordered more wine, price escalating from bottle to bottle. The owner watched us from across the room as we cavorted and laughed.

The girls cantered off to the bathroom, Noel went outside for a smoke, careful to use both sets of stairs coming and going. I walked to a nearby table and asked for a wine suggestion. Olateju took pictures to record the day. I had her write a note in a generic, untraceable cursive script. My handwriting was conspicuously bad. Misha said once that my scrawl looked like stitches she'd had on her thumb once. The transcript read *'Nancy, please forgive our terrible manners, but your boss is a sadistic class-baiter, and has insulted our party to our very marrow. We would normally pay our due bill, however, we as guests feel that his Unamerican behavior has set the precedent, especially in this time of strife and war. Americans should really stick together. This tip is for you.'* I signed the note Dantes de Monte Cristo.

We ordered more wine, and more food, stacking the empty and half-empty plates on one another, telling Nancy that we wanted a visual reminder of our afternoon as Olateju snapped more photos. Nancy took our orders and then walked over to the manager and talked to him. I guessed that he had instructed her to run our orders by him, so he could ratify our consumption. He looked over at us, and I smiled and rubbed two hundred-dollar bills together.

We went through twelve bottles of wine, and eight plates of various hors d'oeuvres, and we sat there for two hours and the sun was shading off over the buildings, the sky ever more crepuscular and running rich and purpled, the color of our teeth. I looked at the owner, and met his stare, raising my glass of wine and smiling porphyrously, swirling the wine in the fluted glass, and sniffing at the contents with a refined gesture and a fluff where my non-existent cufflinks would be. He looked away and bent over to tie his shoe behind the bar. I asked Nancy for the bill, so we could sit around and finish the wine. It was four hundred and thirty-seven dollars, plus tax. None of us had ever seen a bill that high.

The girls went in various directions, to bathroom and exit, and I stood up, stretching my arms wide. Noel went downstairs, too, talking loudly with Kell about his need for a cigarette, leaving only Griffin and me. With our friends safely outside and melted into the evening crowd, Griffin and I got up. I placed the letter on the table with a hundred dollar tip for Nancy inside, amid the empty bottles and plates of half-eaten food, walked calmly to the stairs where Griffin stood, looking at an art deco print on the wall, and we ran like hell down the stairs, clomping and laughing, with Griffin in front of me. Just before I started the descent, the owner had looked up at me from across the room where he stood chatting to a young debutante in a shimmery purple dress. His eyes fixed on me, taking in my location nearer the stairs than the table, remembering, brain in its slow wheel, and then he glanced over at the table, and then back at me. I beamed as his eyes widened, his rat brain in full sprint now, realizing that our table was empty. At the bottom of the stairs, we flung the door open into the dusk, ran left, around the corner, across the street from the bookstore, and down into the adjoining dim alley. Griffin found an iron gas pipe on the side of the bank and clambered up to the top, and helped me over the edge after him. Peeking cautiously over the edge, Griffin giggled.

-Let's hope that asshole learns to be nicer to his guests, he said.

-Not if the guests are cheap, I said. Fuck that guy.

-Must be nice to have mommy and daddy's money to get by on, Griffin said. But, as Saint Biggie once sayeth, Mo' money, mo' problems.

-What would Danny Glover do? I said.

-Shoot him in the head, Griffin said with finger out. Right in the fucking forehead. His socioeconomic immunity has been revoked.

Griffin nodded and lit another smoke, pointing his forefinger toward the restaurant.

We waited an hour or so, chatting and smoking until the darkness settled in, food and wine and the warm air settling. Griffin peered over the edge, and we climbed down into the alley. We walked back to Squirrel Haus, taking roads less traveled, just to be safe. Everyone was already there and titillated. Beers were handed around. Pickle was especially pleased, and he smiled his doggy smile through his incessant drool, moving from hand to hand with a nudge of his nose in order to share in the accolades and success. Kell had been across the street from the restaurant, hiding in the Pedmall and he said the owner ran out a few seconds after us, but we had just rounded the corner and he hadn't seen us. He said the cops showed up in a few minutes. Olateju and the girls and Noel all split. The owner had stood there cursing loudly in public for a minute or two, stomping the pavement with his Italian leather loafers. I asked whether he had shaken his fist at the sky, cursing the name of Dantes Cristo, but he hadn't.

Monday found me finishing a long stretch of sidewalk with the bull float, running the long aluminum pole out across the wet mush, the float's broad flat head riding slightly on its rear edge. When I reached the end of the jointed section lengths that made up the pole, I twisted the assembly, unlocking and relocking the head into a different position in order to draw it back across the expanse, gently and steadily. I had never been too good with finishing concrete and was in no mood to put up with my brother's perfectionist standards and bilious words if I messed the job up. Steadily out, turn, and back. I was thankful that I was in the shade, and ran the bull float over several green leaves that had blown or fallen on the pad. I was at least getting better at this work. I saw Scott coming toward me. Scotty Bojangles jiggling his rubber-band limbs in my direction.

I sent out the float, making a few more passes over the concrete, drawing up the cream and the run of the sidewalk gleamed as if lacquered. I pulled the pole back in, and lifted it out into the grass, washed the aluminum head, dried my hands on my shorts, and lit a cigarette.

-Hiya, Scotty. What's up.

-Hot enough for you?

-Nope, I said. I could use a few more degrees.

He har-harred and mopped at his forehead, the long hair spackled there in the sweat and he told me the concrete looked good. I stretched my arm.

-Thanks. I hate finishing with this damn bull float. I suck at it.

-I could finish it up for ya. I used to do concrete.

-Yeah, you told me, but that's cool. Thanks anyway. If you accidentally fucked something up, then my brother'd be pissed at two people instead of just me.

-I've seen him yelling into his phone a lot. Is he always pissed and screaming?

-No, only when you work for him.

-Well, your flatwork looks passable, he said.

-Thanks. I'll tell him you said that if he starts yelling. You'll be my character reference.

-I'm quite a character, he said. Say, do you like meat?

-Meat?

-Yeah.

-What did you do, kidnap a cow?

-Har har. My friend got me a ton of free beef. I got some in the house and can't eat all of it. I figured you could use some. I don't want it to go bad.

-How much for how much? I asked.

-Hell, free. I ain't paid for it. It'd be wrong to charge for it.

-Let me finish up here a moment, I said, and I'll come back and check it out.

Scott stayed with me as I ran the float a few more times over the concrete, listening to his stories about work. When I was done, after hearing Scott's palavering screed about all things Work, he helped me clean the cement from the other tools. I wouldn't be able to broom and edge the pad for another fifteen minutes, so I put up some caution tape between the barricades. I didn't want some hippy college prick to run his unicycle into the concrete distracted by his training for the next Burning Man and ruin a whole day's labor, I said, and had to explain Burning Man. I walked the half block with Scotty Bojangles back to his house.

He opened the screen door and we went inside. Stifling heat. No cross breeze. Air thick with motes stirring in the slanting sunlight, a faint residue of cigarette smoke and body odor hung in the room with any number of unspooled flycatcher strips. Scott turned the ceiling fan on high and the flycatchers swayed like tassels.

-Come and have a look at this, he said.

We walked through the cluttered living room toward the kitchen. There were boots and cans and bric-a-brac all over the floor. Scott stood by the sink, opening a large plastic bag. It occupied one basin, a pool of lifeless dishwater sitting greasy and grey in the other.

-My friend was walking downtown the other day, he said, and that Chinese restaurant down on Clinton has an alley behind it, and left its back door open. He just walked right in and took a bag of meat from their freezer. Just walked right in and took it. Here ya go.

He scooped a large portion of the thawed, sweaty meat with his sweaty paw into a small Hefty garbage bag and handed it to me. Who was I to refuse the free stolen meat of a relative stranger. We chatted for a bit about the weather and, of course, some more about work, and the weather. He started work again in a few days, he explained, but if we ever needed someone to demo a sidewalk or reduce a driveway to rubble we should give him a call. He was still trying to get his Washburn out of hock, and needed money before it was turned out to the public. He walked with me back to the drying cement. I thanked him again, and he jiggled in his mortal dotage back to his house. I put the bag of sweaty meat in the water cooler, on top of the ice. No use getting botulism from a lack of concern about my health, I reasoned. I broomed the drying cement, and had a cigarette, and the water for the rest of the day ran out of the cooler tinged slightly red.

By Friday we were almost off of Johnson Street. Long runs of sidewalk had been replaced. Ezekiel said it was nice to drive around a city and bear witness to the places and things he had built. I didn't share the same sense of accomplishment. We were about four blocks from Scott's house, sitting in the shade, eating lunch. I had fried up the last of the frozen rancid Chinese meat that morning, sautéing it in barbecue sauce, giving the remainder to Pickle. There was a halloo from down the street. It was Scott. He was walking toward us, a prominent limp retarding his already goofy pace even further, his jangle reduced to a haltering shuffle. He got closer. Zeke's mouth hung open for a moment. Scott's leg was swollen twice its normal girth. It filled the loose soccer shorts he wore, and was crisscrossed with dark patches that looked like a henna design done in pitch.

-Holy shit, Zeke said. What's wrong with your leg?

-I got run over by a dump truck.

-What?

-At the hospital, he said. My first day back, two days ago. They braked this dumptruck with a two-by-four wedged in the wheelwell, and they needed to move it. So I was hitting it with my Estwing, and it was on a hill. The board came out and the goddamn thing done rolled back on me and ran over my leg.

-Why aren't you at the hospital?

-I was at the hospital. They told me I was lucky because the ground was muddy. My leg got pushed down into the mud, and saved it. Didn't break anything. Doctor says if I don't stay off it I'm like to lose it. Goddamn I don't want to be no welfare case.

-Shouldn't you be lying down at least? Zeke said.

-Hell, it was bad enough not working, but now I can't work, and it makes me feel so goddamn lazy.

We managed to talk Scott back on his porch, and I went to the store and bought him some beer. Scotty One Legs. We finished work and I went home, and stared at myself while cleaning up in the bathroom. There is no time to look on high and dream, except in labor's cessation, except while washing the integument of dirt from dirty hands, and in that brief respite, alone, water running brackish to drain, one can look in mirror and to the ceiling, and speak in soft tones to oneself of better days to come.

Haley called me that night. She was back from another trip to Canadialand, and when I arrived at Monk's she looked rotten, skin at eye hung and flaccid, pale, with dark spots filling her face, like high clouds' shadows across a bright valley. When she went to the bathroom, Monk told me she was in rough shape, and her feet were swollen and arms pocked. I assured him, and we made quick plans to keep her around Iowa City, and not let her jaunt off to fuck with Nanook anymore. We decided to go out for drinks.

The smarmy-eyed bartender at the Foxhead was ignoring me, washing glasses with his back to me, staring into the mirror while his hand rotated in the glass. He had a smug mouth shaped like a deflated football, and a generic Nordic handsomeness with thinning blonde hair. He looked like an ice climber or a child molester.

-Pardon me, barkeep, I said. Ahoy, Sam, will you do me a kindness?

He turned slightly, his profile to me, looking out of the corner of his eye, his little football mouth.

-Yeah?

-I'd like two whiskeys, neat, and a pitcher of PBR, please. Three glasses.

-What kind of whiskey?

-Your druthers and my others, I said.

-I'll need to see IDs for the other two glasses.

-It's Monk and Haley. They're right over there.

He looked where I pointed through the smoke, brought the drinks, and plopped them on the counter.

-Here, he said. 11 bucks.

-Thanks, and keep the change, I said.

-Wow. Eighty cents, now I can afford to pay off my student loans, he said and scooped the change from the bar.

I walked the beer and drinks over to the booth, and then the glasses. We all chatted and laughed and sweated in the weak air conditioning and sang along to *Wreck of the Edmund Fitzgerald*. An hour later, after a few more rounds, and more songs in the Wurlitzer, I was beginning to feel odd. There was a quiver in my intestine, a coiling on the pit of my stomach and loose spasms from my abdomen, like hiccups, but more violent and purposive, nerve-clenched and saliva-sprouting. I couldn't figure that I had drank enough to be sick. I excused myself and walked to the backdoor. My head felt clear, but my stomach was a tumult of noise and frothing, seething red and cramped with seizure. My mouth watered in venom-squirts as if I'd just dumped a pint of raw whiskey down.

I steadied myself on the patrons' sink, and looked at the dirty basin, the heaps of pulpy blue paper towels in the trashcan. Someone played *Wreck of the Edmund Fitzgerald* again, and it rolled its balladeering wave. Frozen Rancid Chinese Meat. Scotty One Legs. The Wreck of the Dunham Fitzgerald. Wild and roiling and violent stomach, swimming redmeat, redrum. Chippewa Revenge, served humid and sweaty. Scotty One Leg's hairy, sweaty mitts shoveling the meat into the bag, and the grey-grease dishwater and the flies in my hair.

I opened the backdoor at the Foxhead and let loose a great wind of flesh and spirits, a violent torrent of little brown and red giblets, beer backwashed, and bile that all shot straight out seven feet, over the hood of Blondie's white Mustang sitting in the employee spot. I was moved to pride. The brown river rolled down the hood, running rivulets off the sides and through the aerodynamic channels, dripping and pooling in the dirt and rocks below. My stomach seized. A second wave coming. I took a step down, and let loose in the passenger seat. Round three was mostly bile spit into the weeds. I spit a few times, and walked in the front door, bellied at the bar again. I lit a smoke to clear my palate.

-Gitchigumi, another round of beer and whiskey.

-What's that, Sam turned.

-Gitchigumi, another round, please?

He fumbled the glass as he was drawing the beer and it shattered atwinkle on the floor. I smiled at Blondie and winked.

-Fuck, I said. My glass eye.

July

Doppler

That I cannot blame
or forgive them,
these people, for their

loneliness, their faces
swimming and spent on sheets
of glass. *Gonna buy me back*

that Washburn 12-string
from down at the pawn
once I get me up the money.

Skin the place that lives
between scars when the earth
suddenly is too much below.

And whose scream moves
toward you, and far
must it go to arrive?

Soundtrack

The Maytals, *Pressure Drop*
Bob Dylan, *Lenny Bruce*
Leadbelly, *Linin' Track*
The Pogues, *Body of an American*
Smog, *Held*
Led Zeppelin, *Kashmir*

Nothing much happened for a while at July's outset. Patman was back, and in and out of Squirrel Haus, at random intervals, unpredictably and without augury or call. He reaffirmed he didn't know anything about the squirrel in the freezer. Afternoons, I would find him on Big Red drinking Icehouse as usual, after my day spent angled over things material, everything ridden with dirt. Days were work and run with repetition from sidewalk block to sidewalk block. Suitors came and went from Michelle's, but things had quieted there. No more caterwauling junkies crept by night. Wim was back, and had been learning a new method for making methamphetamines, and we sampled his wares as he regaled us with tales of the process and driving the many counties and country roads, small town to small town, to procure enough cold medicine and remain untraced. He and Patman had teamed up and were making ample amounts of money. Patman even paid me back fifty dollars I'd loaned him. Pickle was sick, so Griffin drove him to his cousin's place to dry out and mend. Olateju still came by, noiseless in the dark of Griffin's room, and usually gone in the mornings. I bought the $150 stationwagon I'd seen with Noel and Brom, and spraypainted it with several cans of silver primer, christening it The Silver Bullet over a bottle of rum. We put the bottle's contents to human use then broke the glass on the hood. Zeke and Isis were fine, as was my family, and Griffin's. Kell would be leaving toward the end of the month, and went on random screeds after too much beer about the EPA and the forest service and land-rape policies. I was donating plasma three times a week for folding money, after work before the clinic closed, driving lightheadedly home in the rarified summer air trembling with all its heat and chance.

Zeke took a Thursday off so he could take Isis for a check-up. I took it off too. I talked Wim into letting me see his meth operation, since he seemed to be doing very well for himself. He consented after a few hours of badgering, and we went one Saturday to a stark-faced farmhouse out among the loll and roll of the summery hills and the wide farmlands full of corn and the weeds in ditches, undulate among the winds. He explained along the way that it wasn't exactly his operation, but that it was run by a guy named Laurence, Wim being a sort of manager. Wim flipped through the radio stations, and fidgeted with his police scanner. Mostly static on the radio, and he shut it off. We pulled up in a driveway off the gravel road, the waft of road dust that trailed us now catching up. We stood outside in the yard, a tire swing twirled from a tall rope in a tall tree, and a vacant polebarn rose red past the farmhouse, aslant a little as if the sky sat directly on its gable peak. We walked there. Inside, its hayloft empty, and a few pieces of tack and other equine fare hung from railroad spikes driven into the great timbers that rose out of the well-trod and dry ground. Wim stamped the hard dirt floor and sat on the hood of a seatless Ford Taurus, saying Laurence would be out in a while. He pointed out the tiny cameras all around the barn while we waited. A voice came through a speaker.

-Who the hell is that with you?

-It's cool, Wim said. He's a friend.

-What the fuck were you thinking, Wim?

-Laurence, he's cool. I've known him my whole life.

-Oh, so now you're using my name?

Then silence. Wim shrugged, saying in a low voice that Laurence was always paranoid at first until he got high.

-He's a chatty Cathy after that, Wim said.

-You realize that this is distribution, right? As in, the feds. As in DEA.

-Yes, but I try to focus on the positive. That's your problem. Always a pessimist.

-Whatever, Wim, I said and lit a smoke. How do you even know this guy?

-Friends of friends. He was some chemistry major in college.

-Well, I have to hand it to him, I said. He's actually doing something with his degree.

-He plays up the farmer bit, too.

-Why? I asked.

-Social camouflage, Wim said. Who knows? Maybe he just likes the fashion.

Ten minutes passed and the backdoor of the farmhouse opened. Laurence walked slowly to the barn. He looked the part of a farmer. Overalls, John Deere hat, big hands, toe-caps of his Red Wings worn through to the steel. Cliched, but accurate. Laurence took Wim aside to an empty stall for a long chat and I sat on the hood of the car and smoked. They came back from their powwow. He approached me, a foot from me and lifted my shirt.

-You a cop? he asked.

-No, I'm not, I said.

-Better not be. Smoke this.

He fished a length of tin foil from the front bib pocket, a thick dark residue running its length, like a tar-patched canoe. He handed me a hollowed pen and butane lighter. I smoked some, and then some more, and handed the apparatus back to him. Laurence walked to the barn door and slid it shut, and asked Wim to do the same to the rear door. He then brought out a baggie full of crystal from the large center-pocket of his overalls. He shoveled in the prow a heap of crumbly yellow flakes and powder that boiled brown and then black with the bright blue gas from his butane lighter burning underneath.

-Had to be sure, he said.

-He's cool, Laurence, Wim replied.

The foil carouseled around many times and with each silver revolution, Laurence became more and more friendly, smile broadening incrementally, teeth showing. Finally, he lit a cigarette and said we could do the same and clapped me on the shoulder. Wim lit a joint and passed it around. I declined.

Laurence went inside the house to check on something.

-I told you he'd warm up after he got high.

-And I thought it was just part of my charm.

A helicopter buzzed faintly a few miles away. Laurence came back out to the barn.

-Fucking DEA, he said.

I panned the horizon too.

-DEA, I said. Are you serious?

Wim shaded his eyes, looking after the sound.

-Are they going to raid the place? he asked.

-I told you the other day. They've got nothing on me.

He hooked his fingers in his bibs. I kicked at some of the hay in the dirt. The logic seemed considerably off. The helicopter flew by a mile off, blades in choppy whir synched with our speed-gilled neurons boiling in their vat of grey matter. I was sweating badly. Laurence was hopped up and suggested that we go inside. We were consigned to the first floor only. A litany of women in various states of physical decline sat around in their underwear in the kitchen, skin mushed and drooping, eyes vacant and all of them set to certain small tasks, rotate splotches on their skin like a TV screen going bad. A few in the bare kitchen at a table sorting myriad pills. A few other were stripping the heads off kitchen matches into neat little piles and the sticks of wood were swept into a waiting receptacle under the table. Another was peeling lithium batteries with pairs of needlenose and normal pliers. There were bags of cat litter and rock salt, cans of starting fluid, acetone, sterno, toluene, all stacked and lined along the shelves of the broad kitchen. It was a beautiful house, a homesteader, and I commented on the quality of the thick oak baseboards and crown molding. None of the women spoke, but looked up momentarily with eyes the color of nothing. The place was devoid of dirt or dust, sparsely furnished. A lone man sat in the corner, almost a shadow, with a shotgun on his lap, staring idly ahead at nothing and everything.

Others of the nearly denuded women poured the less toxic liquids into labeled beakers and jars to be used later, meting out specific doses like apothecaries of old, brake fluid, acetone, charcoal fluid. The fatal stuff lay below us, in the sealed basement, Laurence told me, the anhydrous ammonia and the various acids and cutting agents, the toxic phosphine gas byproduct from the cooking which would render us dead in seconds. None wore ventilators upstairs, and there was no smell of ammonia or chemicals in the house, except the innocuous stuff upstairs. The lab was airtight in the basement with no chance of leaking, Laurence explained with a reassuring nod. He looked outside again and again, and motioned us out there. He walked along a line in the grass slightly greener than the lawn, stopped at a larger pass of mismatched sod and stamped his foot.

-Main filter, he said in a low voice.

He walked us back toward the silo, an old brick affair two stories tall, and opened a small hatch on the side. Laurence ran his finger along the property, explaining the fumes from the basement lab came along a buried pipe, was filtered, and vented underneath the silo into a concrete bunker where the gases diffused into the soil without odor.

-What about the well water? I asked. Isn't it poisoned?

Laurence pointed to a large water tank near the corner of the house.

-We get all of our water there, he said.

-Impressive, I said, and it was.

Trembled again with crank, Wim and I left an hour later, and he drove me home. He now jabbered on about taking over Laurence's niche with his own side business. Business was picking up and he and Patman could barely find enough cough and cold medicine to maintain stock. We went back to Squirrel Haus and gobbled some Percocet and cheap scotch to wean off the meth. By five, Wim was on his sailor legs and rubbing his whiskey mittens together. He asked me whether I wanted to go downtown, but I said no. He asked me whether I wanted to get in on the meth with him, and no again. He nodded and gave me a rough hug and left. No need at all to get caught up in the rotten, actual business of drugs, I thought. I took another Percocet to balance the crank. I was happy to find a spate of silence that evening, and painted, with the occasional moment at the typewriter, working in the sweaty light till it sputtered and dark fell flat across the firmament's gorge.

Patman slammed the kitchen door around 8:00 and stood at the fridge looking for a beer. I walked out to join him.

-How's tricks? I said. You throw any piss in anyone's face lately?

-Tricks and treats, man. You guys are almost out of beer.

-I met Laurence today, I said. He's an interesting sort.

-Wim's never let me meet him, man.

-Why not?

-I don't know, man, I think it's because of the side lab me and Wim have. Conflict of interest, man. Fuck staying here tonight. Let's go downtown, man. I think Griffin said he's going to be down there. Kell too.

-I'll follow your lead, Patman.

He swilled the remainder from his can and tossed it in the sink.

-You know what you need to do, man? Have a block party. There's just not enough civic cohesion around here, man.

-That's not a bad idea, Pat. Not at all.

-I'm full of good ideas, man.

-Like making meth and potentially pissing off your competition, for whom Wim is working?

-Wim's got it all under control, man. He's smart like that.

On the way downtown, we hashed out plans for the block party. We would get the proper permits, invite the neighbors, and have a pleasant evening like a normal neighborhood. We sat down in the Deadwood, and started making a list of preparations. We had the name: *Block and Awe.* I went to the bar to grab another beer, and I bumped into Greg. I hadn't seen him in years. Greg was still snapping pictures and writing for the newspaper, he said, and would I be interested in buying some ethyl ether. He had a surplus that he'd stolen from a photography studio where he worked part time, and didn't want it to go to waste. I said most certainly, and handed him a cigarette, and told him he'd drink for free at *Block and Awe* in return. He was still living in Gaslight Village, he said and we shook hands. Griffin and Kell showed up, and we all drank late, and slept late. The next day was a day of benighted freedom. Independence Day.

July 4th was a blur of hedonism laced with personal danger in the worst possible ways that ended with a brawl in the Kittyhawk down the street from Squirrel Haus, a lower-end half biker, half loadie drinkhole, where you could buy a gram of shitty blow from the bartender, gummy and reeking of cutting agents for fifty bucks. Kell had bought a number of American flags, and he and I and Griffin and Wim and Patman marched down and into the bar, waving Old Glory about, telling everyone we were veterans and ain't America the best damned place in the world, and then we put sparklers into our bandanas and the guys around the bar thought that was funny. Someone bought us a round of drinks, and we posted high the glasses with deep bows in the patron's direction, saluting his American Legion mesh-backed ball cap. Kell made himself a crown of sparklers and flags and Griffin lit it. Patman stuck some bottlerockets into it, which flared forth and the guys around the bar thought that was less funny, and when Kell's crown of sparklers and flags caught on fire and he threw it on the floor, stomping at the red, white and blackened plastic, the guys in the bar surged toward us in an angry mass of skull-rings and leather. A heavy hand with several pointed rings caught me jagged across the temple and ripped open my scalp. We pushed across the room toward the door and Patman throwing pool balls, and Griffin lighting sparklers and tossing them into the crowd. We were just about free from the riling throng, wobbling and pushing and punching, chopping and swinging liberally.

The donnybrook spilled into the parking lot, and where we had more room there was no chance of being surrounded. We stood and the patrons stood in the parking lot, fifteen feet apart. We stood laughing. One of them pulled out a gun, but he didn't raise it. Just held it there near his waist. The old bikers and hoodlums grew tired. Their beers warming, a few dismissively waved at us, and walked back inside. The guy with the gun holstered it back under his vest. We strode to Squirrel Haus and partook of solids, liquids and vapors, free and American and for the moment broad of shoulder, heart and promise. My heart felt wild and terrible, deathless and akimbo. We laughed and smiled and saluted one another well into the night, general private sergeant major, and we felt emperors all.

Saturday morning found Kell and I outside, bruised and groggy, nursing slow beers in stunted air. We were debating the evening's activities. I worked my jaw around with the bottle held to my head, the throb a dull rejoinder of messy pain, and me picking pieces of dry-black blood from my hair. Michelle's friends in the red Gangsta Mobile swung onto the street, the hill of bass from their stereo, and the car's panels rattled loudly with each peal of the subwoofer. The whole car seemed about to dissociate and fall piecemeal in the street. There was a new guy with the others as they got out of the car in the driveway. Two of them walked back to Michelle's. The third limped his way over to us on the stoop, the left leg of his blue sweatpants was rolled up to his knee.

-Yo, whassup.

-How's it going?

He limped over toward us.

-Yall know who own that silver car over there?

-That's mine, I said. It's the Silver Bullett. Pretty sweet ride, eh?

-You wan sell it?

-How much you offering? I asked.

-Whabout fo hunned?

Scratching my chin in a pensive fashion, I paused.

-Okay. Four hundred, I said. Sold, my man. No checks.

- Why, you ain't got no bank account?

-They won't give me one, I said.

-Who need a bank? All those mufuckers do is steal yo money. You got the papers and shit for it?

-Everything's legit.

-Cool, he said.

-Where you from? Kell asked.

-Chicago, he said. Livin here now.

-What brought you here?

-You know, tryin to get by. That car's gon look dope. I got some friends who do that shit, fixin cars. Get some rims, some paint, new stereo.

- What do you guys do in town?

-Little of this, little of that. You know, hustlin and shit. I'll bring the cash by in an hour. Say, dawg, what's with the deer head there?

-That's Diomedes the Godslayer. He brings us good luck.

-Bring you niggas any luck?

-Well, I just sold a car to you.

-Say, man, what if I said three hunned?

-Well, you said four first, Kell said.

-Yeah, no shit, he said and smiled. Aight, I'll be back in an hour or so.

-Sounds good. Nice doing business with you. See you in an hour.

-Aight. Peace.

He loped in his angular gait around the side of the house

toward Michelle's, and I went inside. I was giddy. I'd make a profit of two hundred and fifty dollars on the car and I had barely ever used it. The randomness seemed too well-placed. Kell took a seat on Big Red.

-Did you ever even drive that thing? he asked.

-Only once after Griffin drove me out there to buy it. It runs like shit.

-Why'd you buy it then? Kell asked.

-I have no clue, I said.

The guy was back within the hour with a wad of fives and tens and twenties, ratty and damp paper scrip, pulled from a money clip with a winking pit bull on it. He handed the money over to me, and we stood in the kitchen as I counted the bills out onto the counter.

-You're forty short here, I said.

-Yeah, I know. That's all the cash I had on me. How bout this. You come over to my boy's crib. He live right across the tracks there. You can see it from here. You come by tomorrow, and I'll have yo money there. He my dawg.

-What's the address?

-Those green apartments there. Number 309.

-What's your friend's name? I asked.

-Ask for Dre. Tell him Warrantt sent you.

-I can trust you on this, right?

-Shit, white man never trust a nigga.

We laughed and we signed the papers, and it was done. Warrantt was evidently his legal name. He wrote it out on the title transfer, two Rs, two Ts. The Silver Bullett was another man's burden now. He started the Bullett and puttered away, head bobbing to the speakers yet to be installed. Kell and I hopped in the White Elephant and drove to the supermarket and loaded up on necessities. I could also use the extra money to pay for the city permit for *Block and Awe*. I had some more coffee, and started my rounds down the street, asking the neighbors about a block party. Everyone sounded interested and nodded thoughtfully at the idea. I told them I'd take care of the permits. I had friends in high places, I explained. I then biked over to Greg's, and Kell went downtown to copy some fliers for the fiesta that we'd drawn that morning. We'd have it at the end of the month. Plenty of time to go through the official channels.

I'd been pounding on Greg's door for the better part of five minutes, alternating fistfalls with toeing at the ratty carpet in the musty hallway of his apartment building. Finally Greg greeted me in a bathrobe with a deep bow. His room looked as if someone had loaded a catapult with clothes and records and pieces of paper and empty cigarette packs and launched the assemblage into his apartment.

-Jesus, Greg, has someone laid siege to you?

-Just the Bush administration and my editor, he said, and God and my ex-wife and fuckall everyone else. IRS probably next. You want anything to drink? I've got milk or whiskey. Or both if that's your poison.

-I'm good on both fronts, but thanks. How's slinging corporate media jargon treating you?

-It's a living, he said. Fuck, let me find that ether.

-Be sure to drop by the block party, I said.

-Sounds rad. I'll be there. Here it is.

He came up from under a pile of cardboard and shoes. I took the bottle, sepia-colored glass and liquid sploshing inside.

-You sure you don't want any money for this? I asked.

-Nah. Easy come, he said. You gave me those hits of acid back in the day.

-Thanks. No good deed. So, what happened to this place?

-Nah, got divorced about six months ago. You're observing the proverbial aftermath.

-I live in a world of aftermath, my friend. Self-destruction hath no fury.

-It's why they only name hurricanes after women, he said.

-I think I will take you up on that whiskey, I said.

He rummaged around some more amid the boxes and empties and rolling glass bottles.

-Coming right up.

He paused for a moment.

-You seeing anyone? he asked.

-Not right now, I said.

-A little peace and quiet from the womanflesh never hurt anyone.

-True, I said. Though I wouldn't exactly pass up a chance.

We traded pleasantries over a couple of smokes. I had to meet Kell downtown to post fliers at three, so I excused myself and we shook hands. I reminded him about the block party. He said he'd be there with bells and bullets on, and judging from his toothy, high-wire smile, I believed it. I put the bottle in my bag and biked back downtown.

Kell was waiting in the Pedmall, smiling toward the restaurant we'd burned the month before. I was out of breath by the time I got there. I wasn't sure whether the city would issue the permit for the block party, but we would advertise anyway. The flier depicted Squirrel Haus at page bottom, Diomedes swollen up epically over the rest of the page, his antlers spelling out date and time and place. I had to light a cigarette to catch my breath, and nodded to Kell.

-Why did you quit smoking? I asked. You get enough carcinogens standing in the middle of forest fires?

-I only smoke when I'm fighting fires, he said. I've got a special bandana with a hole cut to fit.

We handed out a few more fliers, but it was boring work. I put the rest of them on top of a nearby car to let the wind do the work. I told Kell I had an errand to run so he went back to Squirrel Haus. I biked over and donated plasma, and bought beer and cigarettes with the proceeds. I kept the ether secret in case

Patman would have designs on it. Thieves and honor.

The next day was Sunday, the Sabbath, and to keep it holy we got the brothers and friends together and held The Ether Olympics, in honor of our proud nation's birthday, a few days late. The only event we had was drinking beer and soaking some bandanas in ether, tying them to our faces, then running as far as we could. The heat was stifling, and the sun swam like a slow loom in the high cirrus and cumulus threading the blue, a tapestry of drifting destinations and endings, far toward the horizon.

We assembled the tribe in the park, everyone laughing, the sun and beer washing out the pall of Monday looming. We painted a starting line in pink marking paint across the lushy, thick green grass, and Zeke brought a hundred-foot tape measure for pinpoint accuracy to measure exactly. He wouldn't be partaking of the games, and nursed his one beer.

We all lined up on the pink. I doused each contestant's bandana with a healthy amount of ether. The fumes filled the air, the wind unable to blow away the tinny, hospital smell.

-Nobody get antsy. This must be a fair and balanced competition. When I give the go, you have to tie the bandana around your mouth and run as far as you can. Any infractions will be dealt with swiftly and painfully. Zeke will personally beat your kidneys with Diomedes until you piss blood.

I had used nearly a quarter of the bottle readying the line, and doused my own bandana. I took my place in the line, and gave the ready.

-And, go!

I pulled the cloth to my face, holding my breath. No use falling over at the starting line, I thought. I glanced to my left. Kermit had been breathing the fumes prior to my announcement, and he fell backwards from the line, giggling, rooted on his posterior with his hand over his bandana and mouth. I lurched forward, and after a few broad steps I inhaled. Griffin had broken out in front of the pack, but was hunched over now, running in a lurched gait, his arms oaring for balance. The wave of stupefaction that rolled over me was brilliant, a blast of nerve-melting euphoria mixed with gas-huffing nausea, the hum of a celestial aether in the ears. I took a deeper breath as we sailed down the green. My feet felt like glass. Griffin jakeleggedly fell over, face first, into the grass and lay there. Noel's giant frame careened sideways in front of me, nearly knocking me down, and sped to my right beyond my periphery, cursing and laughing wildly with a whoop, and then loomed again into view. I couldn't feel my arms, though they were pumping at my sides, back and forth. My eyes glossed and vision glazed. Noel tripped over Wim, stumbled, regained his balance and chugged along another seven feet before his feet tangled and he fell over. My right leg then gave out, and I was crossed over myself, dizzily reeling, a mental, slow-motion tumble down into the green lawn. I tried to wheel my body to gain an extra foot or two, but I fell in the wrong direction.

I pulled the bandana from my mouth, head fuzzed and thick. Everyone lay scattered around the field, breathing heavily. Zeke was laughing at the whole mess. Woozy, I stood up. Zeke took charge of the officiating. First place went to Noel, second to Wim. Their lines were longest, but by no means straightest, so that had to be taken into account. The prizes were a six pack of Guinness and Pacifico respectively, but the two champions, in fitting spirit and magnanimity, shared their spoils with the rest of us, and we huffed a little more ether with the beer chasers to keep our keels even.

Toward and before the crepuscular stretch of purple evening where we sat in the backyard at Squirrel Haus I saw a long strand of spider silk catch the light and wave in undulant bands, passing the glint like a visible telegraph signal from ground to the gable where it was affixed, a word on the tongue of the wind, harmony and tension. That harmony of tensions. World diaphanous for a moment, and then the moment passed. Patman came by a few hours later when other friends drifted their particular ways, and after the fudge-headedness wore off, we went over to collect my forty dollars from Warrantt's compadre. He lived in a generic chockablock housing complex, doors aligned externally like a motor hotel's, five flights total, stacked one on the other. I took the stairs up and found 309. Three fistheel pounds were greeted almost instantly by a towering set of puff-chested fellows in dark glasses, one guy black and the other white. Both enormous. They walked us back until we were against the banister with a full thirty feet below me. The darker gent spoke.

-What do you want?

-Warrantt sent me to talk to Dre. He owes me forty bucks.

-No one here owe you shit.

-We're just here for business. Easy now, man, Patman said, his hands balling.

-No, yes, no one here owes me money, I said, but Warrantt does. He said Dre would cover it.

-Who told you there a Dre here, the lighter gent asked.

-Warrantt, I said. Two r's, two t's. He bought a car from me the other day. The Silver Bullett. Two t's.

They looked at each other for a moment, soundless and big, then back to us. I noticed a bulge at the beltline under the white guy's button up. They turned and opened the door, the lighter gent went in. The darker gent stood, head up a little, looking down at me and then Patman. I sat on the banister and lit a cigarette and loaned one to Patman, my eyes steadily on the man whose eyes were steadily on me. I pretended I was looking elsewhere out in the parking lot thirty-five feet below, calm, arms stretched out along the railing, but behind my cheap aviators I tried to brace for whatever weirdness this episode might portend. I would push Patman at him, then run. I knew he'd do the same.

From the door emerged a much smaller guy, a black albino,

five inches shorter than me, and a full foot shorter than the bruisers that flanked him. He was well-dressed, and all manner of gold trinkets hung loose from his neck and pale wrists. The bodyguards stepped aside and he came closer. Behind them I saw the place, dark and smoky, children playing with scattered toys and a menagerie of shapes lay on couches with animated flames burning under tinfoil, straws extended from faces in the gloom. The blue hissing of butane lighters serrating the illusory calm of the dim apartment. Other shapes lay prone or slumped against the walls. I guessed it a shooting gallery or meth den, or both. A kid sat on the floor banging two aspirin bottles together, making car noises. The albino shut the door and thick chains of gold swung on his hand. He took off his sunglasses. He had a large scar over his left eye, ropy and splitting the eyebrow and spilling onto his cheek, a raised fleck of it on his eyelid, like a dried worm partitioned and glued in three pink pieces to his face. That eye a dull grey, sightless and the color of his skin. The other eye a bright red in its lack of pigment. He put the sunglasses back on his face and pointed to the neighboring apartment.

-Can talk in there, he said. Not outside.

The neighboring place was spare and uninhabited. Lawn furniture leaned against a wall, and he unfolded one chair and set it down, then motioned toward the other chairs with his chin. He whispered to one of the men at his flank, who then left. He spoke as he sat, facing us.

-How you know Warrantt? he said.

I unfolded a chair and sat, too, and the large shape took position behind us.

-He bought my car, I said.

-How come you sayin I owe you money? He owe you, not me.

-Well, I said.

-Where you live?

-Nearby, I said. Why?

-Cause you know where I be, and now I wanna know where

you be.

The large man standing behind us shifted and popped his neck.

-I live in an apartment over on Daniel Street, Michelle's neighbor.

-And who Michelle?

-A neighbor, I said. I assumed you knew her.

-She black?

-Yes, she's black, I said.

-You think all black folk know each other?

-That's not what he meant, man, Patman said.

Dre smiled at us.

-And how much Warrantt owe you? he asked.

-Forty bucks is all, I said. He bought my car recently and was short forty bucks and said you'd cover him.

Dre thought for a moment and then started laughing.

-Forty dollars, he said, shaking his head. You mufuckas get bothered by forty bucks?

-A deal's a deal, man, Patman said, hitting his knee.

Dre stopped laughing.

-So this nigga told you I'd pay his shit, like I'm his bank.

Patman leaned forward in his chair.

-Hey, man, we just wanted to get the money. We're not here to hassle you, man.

Dre took off his glasses, his red eye studying Patman for several long seconds, taking in the tattoos.

-Where you do time?

-Time? Nevada, man, Patman said.

-How long?

-Two years. Got paroled, man.

-What you in for?

-They got me on distribution, but it was bullshit, man. It was entrapment.

Dre nodded and looked behind us.

-Yo, Hun, do I got ATM tattooed on my face? It say ATM on my face?

-Nope, the big man said.

-Then why these mufuckas here asking me for money?

-No idea, the big man replied.

-Look, I said, trying to rise, we can go. I'm not trying to piss anyone off. You're right. Forty dollars isn't that big a deal.

-No, Dre said. You came over here and we gonna settle this. Have a seat.

A hand forced me back into the chair.

-See, Dre continued, you a dabbler. You got all these wrong convictions about how the world work. I can see it with my eye. You come over here, and you think you gon get paid. That's a white man's thinkin. Your boy there, he at least got conviction. Look in his eyes. He your boy, right? Take a look.

I turned slightly toward Patman, but didn't take my eyes from Dre.

-Problem with you, Dre said, you ain't never *been* convicted. My boy Moon, he got conviction. My boy Hun here, he got conviction. Lots of convictions. And this odd mufuckin friend of yours here, he got it. You, you don't. You ain't never had to fight cause you ain't had the option. You chose that shit, and that's why.

-I didn't come over here to start trouble, I said. Warrantt vouched and said that—

Dre stood up and flipped the chair behind him his voice a full bellow now.

-That nigga ain't vouched for shit. I don't need niggas vouching for me. I don't need my crew giving out my address to white boys they just meet like we all friends. What, you wanna bring over some fucking food and have a cookout? Be all neighborly and shit? Start some fuckin Oprah's book club?

The door opened and shut. Two now stood behind us.

-Everything okay over there? Dre asked him. I looked back.

The man nodded in consent.

-If it's a problem, we can just leave. Forty dollars isn't a big deal, I said.

Dre smiled and a ray of light through the curtain made his red eye flash.

-No, no. You here now, he said. We settle this shit now.

I turned and smiled weakly at the form behind me.

-Say, you're into commodities, right, man, Patman started in. I can supply you with meth. One hand feeds the other, man.

Dre laughed.

-Now I got Stupid Mufucka written on my forehead? Moon, check these mufuckas for a wire.

A hand roughed its way across our chests.

-Wants me to go in bizness with some white boys I ain't even know.

The giants behind us laughed. I gave Patman a look, which he roundly ignored.

-I got a friend, man, we got a friend who's a cook. We don't have distribution, man. We could go into business together.

Dre laughed again and shook his head. He righted the chair and sat down.

-You a binnessman, now, Dre said. Now you here to talk binness? Shit, Moon, look like I forgot my briefcase and binness cards.

I kept silent. This was far out of my depth, and the vibe was too weird and serious.

-Yeah, businessman, man. Expansion. My buddy makes some good shit, man.

Dre laughed again, and his minions laughed in accord. Patman laughed too.

-Aight. I respect initiative. You crazy, maybe, but got conviction and shit. You bring something tonight to Moon and Hun, they sample it, then they let me know, and I let you know. Just you. You leave this one behind.

He pointed at me.

-We haven't talked prices yet, man.

-Oh, Dre said, we talk prices if your shit is any good. Say, what's your name?

-Patman.

-Why they call you Patman?

-I don't know why they call me Patman, man. They just always have.

Dre stood and we stood, and Hun and Moon parted like goliath gates, and before we left, Dre pulled out a large fold of cash bound by a thick red rubber band. He handed me a fifty and said keep the change. I thanked him and walked out. We were halfway home before I spoke.

-Jesus, Pat. Shit just got X-rated, real quick in there.

-I know, man. That was awesome.

-What the fuck were you thinking? I said.

-What do you mean, man?

-Don't you think you should have consulted Wim before volunteering him to cook meth for a bunch of Chicago gangstas?

-You need to work on your networking skills, man. Like he said, conviction, man. It's like the block party.

-Do not bring that nonsense to Squirrel Haus, I said. We've got enough to worry about as it is. I don't need an actual conviction for drug trafficking.

-Don't worry. I know everything there is about binness and pleasure, man. He laughed and said binness again.

I walked the humidity to the convenience store and bought some beer and smokes, and returned to Squirrel Haus where Griffin and Olateju were sitting on the couch, fused with a thin sweat of inactivity, watching a movie she'd brought. Patman was in my room on the phone. I handed around cans and told them the story. Griffin and I agreed to have nothing to do with Wim's or Patman's drug doings, and Griffin smiled at Olateju who looked at him with her big dark eyes. We said nothing more about it, and Sunday evening passed, indolent and calm in contrast to an hour prior. I watched the movie without watching it and talked without saying anything, and went to bed early at 1:00.

I took Monday afternoon off to run the permit papers and money to the appropriate offices for *Block and Awe*, saying to the receptionist on the third floor that I was also working a city contract in the hopes of further legitimization of my request. Her eyes stared directly through me, not registering anything but what was on the form. I filled out the eleven parts of name and address. Other answers were more esoteric. Event name: *Block and Awe*. Event location: *Squirrel Haus*. The last read, State the number and type of any animals to be used. I wrote, *One. Pickle*. I handed her the form.

-A pickle is not an animal. Could you clarify what you mean?

-He's our dog, ma'am.

-Will he be performing?

-Performing? No, ma'am. Unless you count slobbering for food a performance.

She didn't smile, but merely applied a liberal amount of whiteout to the space.

-How much will this permit cost? I asked.

-They're free.

-Free?

-Yes, she said. What is a squirrel house?

-It's an art gallery.

-It's a commercial property?

-No, no. Informal. I live there.

-In a place called Squirrel Haus?

She spelled it out. H, a, u, s.

-It's a family tradition, I said. From the old country. You're sure there's no fee for the permit?

She stared at me for a moment, then nodded.

-I'm quite certain. What day exactly do you want to apply for? You've only written here Last Friday of the Month.

-Sorry about that I didn't have a calendar.

-Did you mean the twenty-fourth, she said, and pointed at the corner of the calendar.

-Exactly, I said. Thanks.

-It will take up to a week for a response.

-Ma'am, I cannot thank you enough for your help.

I left the building and arrived at the car just as the meter ran out. Like a poem, the day ticked by in meter and rhyme, and I could feel its pulse along the wind that gave flesh to the light. I felt good and drove home, and clacked out a draft of a poem on my Underwood, having to retype some of the words a few times. I needed a new ribbon.

Patman was excited that night, hugging himself with his hands tucked in his armpits. His meeting with Dre had gone well, somehow, and now he was off on any number of enterprises. He needed no plying that night to divulge a new plan. He had learned through, I assumed, some meth-battered crony of his, that a certain low-level drug dealer I knew would be out of town until the end of July, flyfishing and vacationing in Minnesota. Patman had the idea to break into the guy's house and rob him of a large stash of drugs. He said the mark's name again. Jay.

-Pat, I said, you're selling drugs with Wim, and now you want to go B&E? You're on parole. Also, I know Jay. He's not a bad guy.

-He's not my friend, man. He makes a ton of money, and I know where he keeps his shit. I wouldn't rip off a friend, man.

-He keeps his shit in a big safe. You learn how to pick locks as well as bungholes in jail?

-Fuck you, man. I know the combination.

-How do you know that?

-His ex-girlfriend told me. I was fucking her last week, and she told me all about this shit, man. The combination is her birthday. He cheated on her, so now she's getting her revenge, man.

-What if he changed it? I said.

-He didn't change it, man.

-You're a fucking mess, Patman, I said.

Patman sat back, indignant.

-Fine. I'll do it by myself and keep everything, man. It's not like he's your friend.

-No, but I know the guy, I said.

-Have it your way, man.

My eyes rolled.

-You get caught, don't ask me to help you out.

-You think Griffin would let me borrow his gun, man?

-Are you fucking nuts? I said.

-Just in case, man. What if I need it?

-If you need it, then it means you got caught, I said. In which case, a gun is the last of your problems.

-I won't get caught, man. This is the easy part. Do you have a ski mask?

-I'm not giving you a fucking thing to go and break into someone's house.

-Shit, he said, grabbing my wrist to see my watch. I have to call my PO, man. Is that date accurate?

-You talk to your parole officer?

-Every week, man. I bring in a fake dick full of clean piss, and I go in the bathroom in his office. Easy peasey. I use this realistic looking dildo, man.

-Patman, you, you are the white man's burden.

-Yeah, well, we all have to do our part, man.

Patman used the phone, and then scrambled out the door, possessed, his daemon at him full throttle. I sat on the couch, opened a beer, and shook my head. Pussy Versus Pussy Franco mewed and purred and I threw him to the floor. Griffin came home from his lady's around nine.

-Patman's going to break into Jay's house.

-What? Griffin said and looked at me.

-You heard me.

-What the fuck is that idiot thinking? Griffin asked.

-He wanted to borrow your gun, I said.

-Did you let him?

-I'm not an idiot, I said. He wanted me to come along. I loaned him five bucks to buy a ski mask.

-Where the fuck is he going to get a ski mask in July? That guy is whacked in the head. He'll probably buy pantyhose and there will be a story in the news about some lunatic running around Iowa City scaring children wearing women's panties on his head.

I laughed.

- Oh, I got all the paperwork in for the permit, I said.

-When will we know if we get it?

-No idea. It was free though.

-You're buying then, he said and smiled.

Early days now, and long. Breaking blocks of concrete, setting the forms, pouring cement forth from the hopper slough. Undoing the forms, moving street to street like peddlers of stone and blood. Zeke was tense, and had been for weeks. Finances and a kid, a company with one employee, a city contract he was obliged to finish by the end of August. I worked as ably as I could, griping little to lend him some mental space. On an afternoon I was shoveling a channel along the side of a stretch of sidewalk, a girl watching me from her porch. I was getting irritated with the heat and being observed. She stood up.

-Do you want some water?

-I've got some. Thanks. You in college?

-Why?

-You're not at work.

-I'm on medical leave.

-From what?

-I had cancer, she said.

-Maybe I will have that water.

I sat on her porch with her. She'd had non-Hodgkin's lymphoma, and lived. A one percent chance. She wasn't pretty, but her eyes were and were flecked in the iris-edges. I got her number and invited her to Squirrel Haus. I finished digging out the sidewalk and cut the three blocks free from the other slabs. I looked at firmament and air. Days. The sky was an alchemical blue. It was paper, it was burning, it was music.

That night Griffin called Pete and booked Horizontal Jesus for *Block and Awe*. Pete said sure, if they drank for free, and we called others, assigning tasks. Kell was back from his parents and said he would take care of the fire. I explained that we'd need no fire, but he was in charge of drinking a lot of beer. Patman had come back the night before, Wednesday, eyes burnt and red-rimmed. He had indeed made off with Jay's stash as well as several hundred dollars and been rollicking the past week, cavorting, and up at both ends of day. He even gave me back the five dollars I'd loaned him, though it required asking. After his binge, he still had three ounces of weed, two eightballs of coke, some glass and several eighths of mushrooms, and a few handfuls of pharmaceuticals that weren't identifiable. It was left undetermined how much he'd ingested. Jay hadn't kept much on hand, so Patman seemed disappointed, but he was king for a few days, high as a fiddler on a madhouse fence, his face a garland of acne and cracks of skin and high-voltage smiles. I bought half of his ill-gotten wares, he freely gave the rest, and deep we delved.

Ezekiel had put an ad in the paper for an extra worker, figuring that the wage he'd pay, low at that, would offset the slowish pace and accelerate the job. I couldn't do my end alone. The first guy he hired was a wiry-framed acting-school dropout named Andy who got out of his car with his tool belt on, backwards, pushing his rimless glasses up his bulbous nose, shaking his hands like a

Tourette's victim as if he were loosening up for a role in a play. Zeke drove off, leaving us to tasks. Andy tried to read my star signs. He said he was waiting to get hired at the carpenters' union. He had an uncle that worked there. After lunch he refused to help me lift the rented plate compactor out of the grade. It weighed two hundred pounds, basically a big steel plate with a vibrating motor strapped to the top. Andy said his back hurt, and waved his hand at my request. I dead-lifted it out, fully thirty heavier than me, threw it out into the grass, and burned my arm on the exhaust port grill. The pattern like a thunderbird. I told him he was fired. He nodded, got in his car and drove off to bigger and better things, like star charts and nepotism. Zeke was angry when he came back and spent half an hour on his phone, trying to line up someone else.

The new kid the next day was a non-descript all-American type whose clothes were clean. A beefy, stocky guy, cheeks red from shaving. He lasted two days of sledgehammering and hauling, lifting and bending. Playing high-school football and drinking protein shakes was not enough preparation for the doldrums of hard labor, as he learned. Another guy showed up the following day. He said he'd talked to Zeke the night before, and knew him from Tiffin. He appeared to be about 45, diminutive. His shaved head and shrunken face gave him a constant Gollum expression, and he was slightly hunched. He introduced himself as Ropey, a nickname given him as a child, by his grandpa, because as a child he'd liked rope. He was scratching over and again behind his ear and on his forearms. I'd set him to a task and he would hunker in and ratchet down, rapacious and unceasing, jabbering like a muted monkey at me or at his tools. He'd sneak off to the tool trailer once in a while and leave the place reeking of meth. I learned later that he was only twenty-six.

I entered the house at four-thirty, gliding beneath the visage of the deer, and was greeted by the gentle brush of the fans. I set my keys in Duchamp. Griffin was in the Harem, cleaning his PPK. He nodded at me and went back to work with a stained toothbrush and oil on the disassembled slide. I grabbed coldbeers, set one by Griffin, and took a seat on the floor by the fan, cracked the can and took a long sup.

-How's tricks?

-Low and lazy, he said. This heat is fucking killing me. You have to oil these damn guns so often in the humidity.

-No kidding. I feel like I'm walking through a whale's intestine. You need help cleaning that?

-Nah. I'm almost done, he said. I think Patman's been shooting it when we're not around.

-Shooting it where?

-God, I don't want to fucking know, Griffin said. I'd lock it up if I had somewhere to. You going to call cancer girl?

-No. I don't think so. She's nice and all, but that's a little too intense for me.

-Afraid she might give you the big C?

-Crabs? Nah, I said. I'm taking a break from women. What's up with Olateju? I haven't seen her around lately.

-We're taking a break, too, he said.

-Why?

-Who knows? She called me the other day and told me she was worried about me and you. That she thought being apart would make me realize what's important.

-Maybe she's just racist, I said. You going to try and patch things up?

-I don't know, he said. I'm not quite sure what I would say.

-You should take lessons from Patman, I said. Prison made him a regular Casanova.

-All prison did was make him batshit crazy. I'd rather give a baglady a rimjob than take relationship advice from him.

-The Olde Baglady Rimjob, I said. That's a page out of his book anyway. The old hobo blossom. He practically invented the technique.

-Have you heard from Wim at all?

-Not a peep since the last time we saw him, I asked.

-Doesn't he have a phone?

I told Griffin about Ropey, and we sat outside as the evening accrued, laughing and telling stories. The clouds traipsed, corrugated, trouty pink and flame-slid. Kell and Patman were in and out of Squirrel Haus, hither and thither, that night, and the gossamer edges of dark's damask flapped loose at edges unseen and unheard, raveling and un, and life fell forward inexorable, like Herakleitos said. I went to bed and felt enormity, felt my feet a million leagues away, dangling feathery and cool amid the haze of the juniper-colored aether. There was no reason for the feeling, no grand moment, no liminal shift. All this becoming, becoming, I thought, lying there, but becoming what? It just was.

Patman was in the kitchen when I woke, talking to Griffin. I grabbed a cup of Folgers.

-What are you doing up so early on a Tuesday? I said between sips.

-I was talking to Griffin about a new business plan, man.

Griffin rolled his eyes behind Patman's back and shook his head sadly in a recapitulation of whatever Patman had concocted. He filled his thermos with the rest of the coffee.

-Well, I'll let him explain it to you, Griffin said. I've got to head to work.

-Okay, later, man.

-Hasta, he replied.

-Later, I said.

-So, man, you wanna hear about my plan?

-Some other time. I have to get ready for work. Someone has to bring home the schweinefleisch.

-I'll tell you later, man. It's no problem. You guys have any more coffee? I think you're running low, man.

I stopped by Monk's house after work that night and drank a few bottles of wine from earthenware cups with him in his air conditioning. Haley was coming back next week, he explained. He looked shrunken, filed down, plied. A car honked outside. I poured him another glass and lit a cigarette. He lit a joint, offering, which I turned down with a thanks. Struggling after a few hours to his feet, unpinioned and awobble, he went and laid down in his room, closing the door behind him. I basked a while in the cool air before descending the stairs to greet the wall of heat outside. I got home and sat up painting with Griffin on the plastic tarp in the kitchen. Outside, a hobbled drunken voice hollered in the night.

-It's midnight, and all is fine and fucking untroubled in the world.

Griffin dipped his brush in the can of odorless spirits and rinsed it.

-I hope he's right.

There was a week of rain, and the Heart of Darkness bled across the floor in rivulets and waves, a font of brackish water spilled through the rotten sheetboard, the plastic we'd tacked up molded black underneath and festooned with bright green patches of mold like lichen erupting on rockface. We sandbagged the closet again trying to drive the water to the Bilge. I drilled a relief hole through the rot-flimsied floorboards to alleviate the flow. I called Fat Bastard and left several messages, and wrote a four-page letter detailing all the repairs that needed to be done as soon as the rain stopped, and made up some noise about mold infestations and toxic air. I tacked it out in a half an hour on my typewriter and had Griffin read it.

-You should put something in here saying that we won't pay rent until he fixes it.

-I think that's legal, isn't it? I said.

-It is in California, he said. Where's the lease?

He rummaged under his desk for a while.

-Yeah, it says here that he's responsible for repairs, blah blah blah. I'll stop by Monk's and check the legal statutes on the internet.

-You want to know something?

-What's that? I asked.

-I've never used the internet before, he said. Not once.

-Never? Not even for porn?

-Not even.

-You're not missing a whole lot, I said.

-Yeah, he said, I've got enough problems already without knowing the world's.

With the rain there was only prep work to do for work for the city project, and Gollum and I dug the sodden edges of the sidewalks, cutting and sledgehammering out the chunks, setting forms, and the various exigencies of etcaeteras that bevel down the day. I returned home daily, soaked and muddied and would by morning slip my feet back into the everdamp boots and poncho, and sully myself with the earth's rebate of its dark, clodden, churned self. We had a number of sandbags left over from Heart of Darkness' levee-bursting, so Griffin and I moved my bed, set up sandbags and cushions in my room and fired arrows down the hallway.

I sold the White Elephant to Pete the next Friday, telling Zeke that I needed the day off. Pete wanted the van to haul around Horizontal Jesus' equipment. With the proceeds I bought an '84 Toyota pickup, 4x4, with a solid front axle that had been advertised in the paper. The engine ran smooth and tight, but the bed was rusting out. But I needed a truck for the concrete job, and it was the right price, and was decent enough on gas. I stopped by Michelle's when I got back to Squirrel Haus, though I didn't want to broach her confidence with any regularity, and bought a gross of Percocet. My body ached from the constant wet, and the pills brought dull, cottony peace as was their trick.

That Saturday the rain broke and we divined another project. Griffin had a set of small saddlebags, thick and well-oiled leather, stitched well. We put them on Pickle and had him run around the house as a test. The bags slipped immediately off. We punched two sets of holes in the leather, and ran nylon paracord through so that we could secure the bags across his brisket underneath, and in front spanning his chest. We tested the bags by loading them with a case of beer and set off on our bikes to visit Noel. Pickle needed exercise. He was smoking nearly four packs a day, between me and Griffin.

The harness worked perfectly. Pickle trotted along beside us, grinning and bounding, his claws tacking on the pavement. The pommel sat firm, resting across his massive shoulders, held at the blades from slipping too far forward. We took him up the street, and back. Then a bit further, and then loaded with beer, like a St. Bernard with flagon at collar, ready to help the wounded and thirsty alike. We were taking it slow on Pickle. We didn't want him to strain anything. He pranced beside us, quick feet and sudden giant excited bounds forth. We loaded in a full case of beer, and tested the weight on either side, adjusting the paracord to avoid him problem or discomfort. We called over to Noel's and said we'd be by in a while, and we coasted leisurely down the avenues. Ten minutes into Pickle's constitutional, a sleek black Mercedes pulled up alongside, slowing to our pace. Its tinted window slid down, the driver staring at us, and a woman in the passenger seat wearing a look of sheer disgust behind Gucci glasses that made her face look buggish.

-How could you do that to that poor dog? That's animal cruelty. You're sick, she said.

Griffin turned, grinning, to the car.

-Ma'am, we need to get him in shape, he said deadpan. How

else do you think he's going to win all the dogfights around this town? Do you want him to go in out of shape or something? He's in training.

I edged my bike toward the car.

-Have you ever seen such a happier dog? Right Pickle?

Pickle reared at his name and the cans plunked dully in the bags, and he panted heavy with thick slobber flying and barked.

-That's right, fucker, Griffin said. You're going to maul those other dogs.

The woman recoiled back into her seat at our words, shaking her head in little spasms, her mouth open. The driver leaned across her.

-You assholes should be in jail, he said.

-You assholes should mind your own yuppie business, Griffin continued. You don't want to get mixed up with the dog-fighting cartel around here. They're savages, the whole lot of them. They eat people like you then take a siesta.

Jaw unhinged, the woman stared straight forward, and the man's rancid sneer disappeared again behind the tinted glass as it flowed up with mutterings of police and savages issuing before the window snapped up and the car sped off. We slowed and stopped. Was it a crime to saddle a dog? Maybe in places like Boulder or Davis, but not here. Griffin leaned over and rubbed Pickle's head.

-I'd never let those rich fuckers stop you from having fun, he said. Do you want to have more fun?

Pickle sat on his haunches, the saddlebags shifting back, cans clanking in the leather pockets, and he barked loudly again. We had a beer, and then started off on our bikes again. Pickle watched us for a moment, then redoubled his pace to catch up, atrot and the click of his paws on the street kept a mirthful time as we crafted the afternoon into a device of our own making and creed.

Block and Awe arrived. We received a hearty dose of handshakes and not unfriendly smiles from the neighbors. Kegs arrived, and someone offered to order more. Cups were sold, and my pockets swelled with ones and fives. I explained that the profits would go to a charity, neglecting, of course, to inform them that Griffin and I were the charity. Groups assembled on lawn and asphalt, and the band was setting up. July air thick with plot, all sweat and smoking and laughing. At either end of the block, we'd set up Goldberg Bros. barricades. Zeke loaned them, but couldn't come. Drinks and talk, cool and shadowy, measured the evening. There was a longish set by the band, and an encore, the bugs ringing loudly in the silence that settled between songs and after. Neighbors who would normally not piss on us if we were on fire got soused and ribbed us with elbows about Diomedes, saying it was the funniest thing they'd ever seen, talking about hunting trips they'd taken in their youth with grandfathers and uncles. We had hidden a good keg of beer behind Squirrel Haus, our private vintage, and we'd regularly slip back for some lawn arrows in the lowlight. All manner of friend made concourse in hours seeped with the humid and toothy time.

Michelle was mingling in the crowd, a guy I'd never seen before, tall, spindly, following her with a lazy disinterest, the smoke trailing from his mouth incessant. Most of the assemblage didn't know her, but I noticed in the waning light that the ones who did cast their sidelong glances with furtive, low talk and movements of cups in hands. She saw me and waved. I traded her two Percocet for two plastic cups behind Squirrel Haus, and she introduced her consort. His name was Paul. He chain-smoked Camel studs, and had just had a liver transplant. He showed me the scar, staples removed, thick and red the vein of cured flesh that ran across his abdomen. He sounded intelligent. His story, combined with his association with Michelle didn't add up. I excused myself with a bow, and drifted back into the dusk. Olateju showed up out of nowhere, and gave me a hug, asking for Griffin. I gave approximate guesses, not knowing, and pointed along the street. I was happy she was back. She made him happy. That made me happy.

The kegs tapped early and the mélange furled, and drinks came from homestead and any intrepid explorer willing to walk two blocks to the store. Lawn chairs' aluminum legs rattling across the street and ringed around coolers of coldbeer, and blankets spread on lawns and some children sleeping or running, and a few tiki lamps lit along the block. Little tribes huddled around first flames, the block illumined and run with low din of chatter and peal of laughter at intervals. A police cruiser nudged against a barricade on Kirkwood Street, I saw, and I set my beer down and walked over. The cop looked at my proffered permit and said we had one more hour until we'd have to disassemble the carnival. I declined a polite interchange saying only thanks and waved, immune to authority for the night, with the paper in my hand.

Later, some rougher elements began in among the assemblage. I recognized one of Michelle's consorts, a lean guy, usually driving the red, thumping Monte Carlo, Warrantt's friend. He was talking to Griffin and Olateju down the block from where I stood, chatting with a divorcee about alimony and how stupid she was to ever marry such and such asshole. I heard some yelling, and then Griffin stood up and threw his beer aside. There was more yelling and Olateju was in the middle of them, with her finger stuck in the face of the guy, her head cocked to one side, and on a roll. By the time I got down there, the guy had pushed past the crowd. Inquiring, I learned that he'd asked Olateju what a fine sister was doing with a whiteboy, which set Griffin off, and her, but she'd managed to resolve it peacefully. I brought around some beers for us, and we retired to the backyard in the waning light in need of no more trouble than we could shape with hands. Warrantt came around and apologized for his friend, limping still, but the limp looked real and he had stitches on one cheek. I guessed that Dre had set him straight for making an ATM of him.

We took the barricades in an hour later and freed the streets. Wim was there now, and we snuck inside one by one to braff little bumps of his proffered gak which was pretty good, making sure the womenfolk would not see and rejoinder us with wilting words of reproach and health. Then we sat behind Squirrel Haus in the rear yard and watched Kell, lit from the firepit he'd mortared up on a bored day with river rocks and bags of cement, as he drew a mural across the back of the house with charcoal, the stalactite stars in strains of domed tranquility above us in the strange abyss that haunts the mind on nights of serenity or fear, his hands black and rowing against the house, shadow like a doppelganger moving with a volition its own borrowed from the flames and times dim in the human memory, the scene unfolding there, totemic and a story told long ago and long told, shapes and figures across the house, symbols of going and becoming, Kell's eyes wild in the heat and the beer and the speed, exchanging a kohl nub for a flaming branch from the firepit and rendering whole with scissoring elbows and incendiary end of the stylus an ushered history, and with every pass sparks issued like he the hobbled armorer over the fabled shield, his way and representation there lit all apiece, the assembled tribe behind him admiring and raising unseen beers to his ministry, faces emerging and disappearing in the flick of fire in the group and on the wall, and the world was only Griffin and Kell, Noel, my brother, and Wim and Haley and Monk, and Patman, Olateju, and all friends there and not there, and above our progenitors there in paleotime who brought us in, and their progeny shaped and bright now like a flintspark, and our progeny to come who will lay us in state on cold rock, the ashen etching of pictograms of names as across a granite gravestone held fast in dirt, boneclenched words, script and circular there on the illumined tablet of the house, everything Minoan and true beyond the words' telling, that none but the initiated could read, and we like a calcite edifice grew toward those shadows of stars, gleaming like wet new beings in the fiery drip of light, and we bent toward every single thing above and below, and the stars again as always like muzzleflash of longoff guns preceding report and ball, that spark barely visible behind the blindfold of void and dark that stood above our little human fire, and what do the living care of what has not yet arrived?

The next morning neighbors were out, stuffy-headed, cleaning up debris and bottles from along the street and curb. Bland pleasantries were employed, and no one seemed too interested in talking past a desultory wave or nod. Whatever pulse the night had held had ceased, falling mute, and neighbors slid away from one another in ritualized silence, that kind of urban warfare seen in the solemn edges of lawns trimmed, sidewalks shoveled, or leaves raked up only to exacting borders of property, borders and lines drawn up in the fragmentary, ephemeral, scoopable, cuttable, erasable dominions. I cleaned up in front of Squirrel Haus, as did Griffin and we sat out the rest of the day in the back shooting arrows with Kell, and slapping scant mosquitoes filled with our blood returning it in blotches to our skin and smoked. I was going to ask Wim about the deal with Dre, but I didn't.

Kell was leaving for Arizona the following day, and we hit the bricks that led downtown. I saw Jan at the Deadwood that night while we were out and rummaging the town, hoping to run across old flames or new sparks, and we sat down and had a few beers with her. I hadn't seen her since grad school. She stuck around after post-matriculation, like a lot of writers there, and hunkered down into a pantomime of employment so riven of soul and interest that all font of creativity shriveled in the aftermath of salaried wages which I silently envied and vocally derided. Despite her slim Asian build, her tolerance for cheap beer and lewd talk remained substantial. We had idly flirted in college, but nothing had ever come of it. She gestured across the table at me after we'd finished a few rounds, suggesting we go for a walk down to the river. I gave a caddish wink back to the table, and Kell stood and we hugged and I wished him a safe journey. I was never one for adieus. See you soon was all I ever said.

The night was warm and the breeze cut the humidity down tolerably. I stopped at a gas station and bought some beer, the brown sack crinkling with our steps. I was trying to rhapsodize and sound poetic, jabbering in broken French about Verlaine.

Jan grabbed my arm, and then my hand, and I couldn't figure that out. It was sudden, unexpected. I'd have likely imagined a hundred dollars to materialize suddenly in my wallet than for her to make any stab at amorous attention.

-Aren't you still dating Rob? I asked.

-We broke up.

-I'm sorry to hear that, I said. Was it long ago?

-Long enough, she said with eyes burning coolly.

-Allah, be merciful.

I was feeling good about things now. She had always sidestepped my advances. I had given up long ago, especially as she'd been dating another friend of mine, and most recently Rob. I liked Rob. I'd left Jan alone the whole time, relegated her to friend, because of Rob and all other interceding formulations. All was fair and game now, though, and the river scenic and trussed with vistas and dark corners for interlude and touch.

We got to the river, backlit by the Union. I thought of the deposed farmers and Barb the Chainsmoking Lesbian inside cleaning and wiping up scraps of food made from that which they for generations had once cultivated. I wished them all well in my mind, thankful, though, to be done janitoring, reminding myself to give Barb a call if I could find her phone number. We found a motorless johnboat locked and chained to the dock. The chain ran through a metal ring screwed into the pulpy wood. After a minute of kicking it, and nearly tipping into the water, I knocked the ring free from the slick, half-rotten deck. The chain fell into the water, and the boat started gliding. I pulled the boat back to the dock by its prow, and held it as she got in. The oars there in the boat. I got in and pushed off the deck, sending us out into the river with a silent plash. She rummaged for two beers and opened one, and lit a cigarette, exhaling loudly. She was staring at me, exhaling breathily and staring. I set the oars in the oarlocks and started us up the river.

-Something on your mind? I said.

She said nothing, and I hauled the boat out to the further bank, sluicing through with small soundless pulls, until we were away from the lights and potential trouble of onlooker or owner. I nursed a beer with quick occasional sips where it sat in the ribs. I rowed against the current, not wanting to drift down toward the spillway near the power plant. I rambled about struggle and work, the cancer girl and the flicker of money in hand. Jan smoked and drank, looking up. I leaned into the oars and we trawled up past the park and the floodplain houses, large willows tentacled across our heads as we drew underneath, and the specters of frogs spocked into the water's edge as we passed, and the boat in a gentle kilter, left to right.

I ran the boat around the long bend, and we neared Coralville's main street, the waterway turning right, running behind the row of restaurants lining the strip. Jan took her shirt off. To have been the wind that night, brushing up against her purple-olive skin, her tiny breasts and nipples erect and perfect, there, the ambient light of streetlamps illuminating, joining together, this exalted moment of serenity. The beers rolled on the wood, her face lit red with a long drag of her smoke, her eyes gauntlets of intent the color of a darker Jupiter and me the great red storm that sat swirling in its reflection. I found a branch hanging low into the water and grabbed it, holding the boat static and lapping against the drift of the flow. I stared at her and smiled, then laughed. I fished a beer and drank it, lit a smoke, all with my free hand. She lay back, her body, two arches on an arch, slim and beautiful aqueduct. I talked on.

I let go of the branch some several minutes later, and hauled for the dock, trying to not make obvious my rush. We rewound the river and I coasted to the landing. She put her shirt on. We docked, and I lodged the chain between the seams of the deckboards where we found the boat. It waved and knocked the dock with the current. We walked our measured steps back to her place. The stars wheeled like a whorled conch. I felt the world of measure and portent underfoot the way to hers, and up the stairs of her home. She didn't speak a word that night on, after the boat. We knew the commerce of silence and of speech. Our commerce now and always was stories, everyone's stories, vice and versa, verse and voice.

August

Loki

look, earth fills earth
imperfectly and leaves these:

a cipher miscued, a tree
shook with angels, a rotting

tooth and is how the dead
are carried, with chord, branch,

and a swallow's wing when
diving quick and then

breaking back up, the arc
and flight making with a body's

swiftness and appurtenance
an instance and a deception,

an aphasia of such grace
we thought it was our lives

Soundtrack

The Pogues, *I'm a Man You Don't Meet Everyday*
Led Zeppelin, *In the Evening*
Mississippi Fred McDowell, *Jesus on the Mainline*
David Allen Coe, *You Never Even Called Me by my Name*
Men at Work, *Dr. Heckell and Mr. Jive*
Bob Dylan, *Where Are You Tonight (Journey Through Dark Heat)*

The weather fussed and Heart of Darkness started in with its seep. The closet gangrenous, thick dark veins of rot that ran the whole space through. I drilled another hole in the floor, wearing Griffin's hazmat mask. I then lay out several fresh sheets of plastic over the old and another over the scissor doors inside and out, and repositioned the sandbag. Squirrel Haus' rooms ran with a musty accretion in the air, a pallor. Scent like an earthen basement full of canned foodstuffs long gone to spoil and mush. I finished my repair, and sat down to type out another letter to Fat Bastard, telling him that we would not be paying rent next month unless he fixed Heart of Darkness, referring to it by its Xtian name. I took a shower and when I stepped out from the curtain and wiped the smogged mirror, I was struck by the image of the many water droplets standing on my skin, like leprous sores risen up from once vital flesh, pustules and boils like a constellation of plague in a pattern of an unreadable glot. I toweled away the water and, like the patient of a vagrant miracle healer, I was healed.

Patman was skulking about town in his growing and wanton fanfaronade of dirty clothes and hempen trinkets and his ever-present bag of crank, looking like a pasty, torsional shaman. I came home from a day's labor to find him clacking slowly at my typewriter, sitting on Big Red, typing away on the charred remains of Hellraiser. Meth hung in the air, and a transvestite in desperate need of a shave sat on the floor, playing video games. Patman's head was shaved now.

-Want a hit from the foil, man?

I nodded and lit the silver canoe.

-Where exactly are you living these days, Pat?

-Here and there, man. Wim's got me busy driving all over the place for cold medicine.

-Do you even have a license? I asked.

The tranny whooped about something on the screen.

-No, he said as if the idea was dully ludicrous. I've been using Wim's license. That's why I shaved my head, man. Got his social security number memorized and everything.

-You guys look nothing alike, I said. He's taller than you by four inches.

He was concentrating on his typing and hadn't heard me. Bored by futility, I left the odd couple each clacking away on buttons and keys and went to the kitchen. I leaned over to Pickle and dropped him a piece of cheese.

-I think they're both just killer gorgeous, the tranny said without turning, loud enough for the house to hear.

I rubbed Pickle's head in the kitchen.

-Next time, just maul him, would you, I said. There's plenty more cheese in it for you. Hell, Pickle, I'll buy you a whole fucking wheel and get you laid.

Pickle nodded and glazed the floor in a loving drool, his eyes affectionate and darting back and forth between the fridge and the rat-a-tat-tit noise in the living room. I grabbed beers from the fridge.

-You guys stay out of my room, I said. Griffin's too.

-Who you calling a guy? the transvestite laughed through garish red lips, then turned back to the TV.

Patman paused his clacking, and took a rip from the foil.

-Yeah, man, can't you be more sensitive?

Monk called and broke the odd scene. I was sitting at the Foxhead an hour later with him, chatting about boxing, and about Haley. The crank was mostly gone, cut through with the demon rum and lukewarm PBR from the draught in plastic pitcher after plastic pitcher. Haley ran in and found us exactly as I brought up her health. Her eyes white and irked and hazed. She explained in breathless rush that there was a bat on Monk's porch. I assumed it was some withdrawal symptom. Monk had a huge porch, screened, which stretched the whole facade of the building on the second floor, and he said she'd been clean for a while. She wanted us to come and exorcise the darkling creature. We walked the few blocks back and upstairs, and I strode out onto the porch, seeing nothing. Haley peered in through the interior window and Monk stood by the door. I walked the length checking behind the bookcase and in a potted plant hanging from the ceiling, and up around the nooks and corners. I was about to give up when finally I saw the bat, brownish, about the size of a stunted, hairy banana, hanging in the potted plant at the end of the porch. I tossed a book at the plant and the bat shot out. Monk squeaked and slammed the door, and the bat flew long ovals like an elliptical, irregular planet around me where I stood in the center of the space, a full twenty feet long by six wide.

Its jerky flight ran several cycles past, counterclockwise, as if hung from a string held by an epileptic in full seizure. I put my arms out wide and flapped them a little, the bat passing close enough that I felt it disturb the air. On its fifth circuit I snaked out my left hand and caught the creature midflight, and I closed my other hand over it, holding its head between the first two fingers of my right hand. I held it up to the window for Haley to see and she wailed and ran off into the house. Monk eyed it with uncertain looks then locked the door. A little brown bat, and it gnashed its little incisors at my skin. Its long tongue dashed out between the teeth, and its eyes were the color of blood and ink lacquered and polished, the towering, beautiful ears like pink-ridged caverns that led back into echoes of time primordial, and it squirmed there in my palm, shivering. I instructed Monk to let me in so I could walk it through the house and let it go outside, but he wouldn't open the door. Pissed, I tried opening the window screen, but it wouldn't budge, so I kicked it loose from its moorings and it fell the story down with a tinny thud into some bushes. I let the little beastie go with an opening of my hands and it disappeared back into the black night. Monk yelled through the door.

-Thanks a lot, he said. What if it comes back? There's no screen now.

-Get a blunderbuss, I said. There's a war on, don't you know?

Haley laughed and we walked back to the Foxhead, our drinks were still sweating on the scarred and tattooed tabletop. No one the bar around had ever heard of a person catching a bat like that, and neither had I. Haley bought me a bottle of decent beer, and she leaned and pawed at Monk's arms and face and shoulders. Back in love, I thought, and good for them. I figured no one would believe me about catching a bat midflight, but it was true and if the truth is not oath enough itself, then let a lien be levied against the flesh the universe lays wagered in all things vast yet countable that sat naked and vulnerable to the eyes and ears and thought and hands and then erode and disappear. I caught that fucking bat. When I walked home that night, the stars were vocative, and they spoke only to me.

Home, there was a message on the machine from my socialist friend who'd be picketing suchandsuch church tomorrow. She'd taken my earlier idea, and my idea from the block party, to organize a rally. She wasn't inviting me along, but wanted to communicate a thanks. I made a note of the time and place and erased the message. I had no idea where Griffin was, but I patted Pickle and pulled his scruff and we watched a movie until the chloroform night and its soporific voice overtook me and I fell asleep where I sat.

I woke early. Patman had manifested and lay asleep, naked, in Griffin's abandoned bed with the tranny in the crook of his arm, and I crept around the house to avoid rousing them. I walked with Pickle over to the protest after a breakfast of coffee and cheese, which I shared with him. The picketers arrived en masse and suddenly, a full thirty strong, as the congregation was finishing and coming out from their prayers, shaking hands with the padre and kids in starched jackets and crinoline dresses cavorting on the lawn. The protestors stood in the street and on the sidewalk, and some on the cathedral lawn, picket signs bobbing. There was a faint hint of patchouli. The police were there within five minutes.

I saw my friend, Stella, hold up a piece of paper in a cop's face and it was torn away from her, read without a glance and tossed to the ground. She spun around and was in cuffs in the time it took me to exhale a plume of smoke. Signs among the milieu sawed up and down in the air as the parishioners and police alike took to them in atavistic harmony, no greater metaphor needed. A few protestors were punched by men in their Sunday finery, and the women screeched and the kids were crying, and another cop had a girl with dreadlocks face down, wrenching her arm, and she yelling out in a pain which cannot be rehearsed, except in a crash-course jiu-jitsu masters seminar. A few were maced where they stood or lay, and I smiled in dark sympathy. Pickle was perked by the melee and the odors and his tail went and he ruffled his haunch, but I grabbed his collar and sat him down with a stern dictum. Within ten minutes all rights to peaceably assemble were lain strewn among the silly signs and rumpled grass across the street where the churchgoers pointed fingers and some wept and others fumed and the priest sat on the stone steps shaking his head believing a little in disbelief. Seven police cars had converged, and those of the protesting throng still free had been sent scrabbled and mute back to their hookahs and compost piles and dogeared copies of Marx and posters of Che, or whatever. The rest sat cowed in squad cars, and very few looked like they'd ever been in one before. Rookies, I thought.

I walked home. Griffin had been out of town with Olateju, and they were standing in the kitchen toasting some bread, the coffee pot burbling and Griffin flipping pieces of bacon. I got a beer and sat on the edge of Big Red and leaned into the kitchen.

-Did Patman leave? I said.

-About an hour ago with that nasty transvestite? she said. Where'd you get off to?

-You missed a barnburner this morning, I said. A friend of mine tried to picket a church in response to that church picketing Planned Parenthood. You'd have loved it.

-What happened? he asked. Was it as good as that abortion riot we were in?

Olateju looked at him, eyes fixed as in warning.

-Some of them got arrested, I said. Some got maced. Some beaten. Some of the church folk were fighting with the hippies too.

-Well, like it says in the Bible, Don't fuck with God. He's a wrathful bastardo.

-He is great and vengeful, amen. How have you been Olateju?

-I've been okay, she said. You?

-How was your weekend? I asked.

-Great, Griffin said.

-So, what did you do?

-We went camping again, he said, and swam and slapped mosquitoes from each other's asses all night. It was good. How about you?

-I caught a bat.

-Huh, she said. Bullshit.

-No, I'm serious. Over at Monk's. Ask him or Haley. Boom. Right out of midair.

-Bullshit, Griffin said and laughed.

-No, true.

-You really caught a bat?

-I'm serious, I said. Left-handed.

There was work and then there wasn't, weekend's rising shape shaking loose the pall of prior days, and one could stride free with unslithered pockets out into the imbricated night that linked with aeons, with drink, with grins and palms clapping and hot weather. Friday night I wrote a sonnet, impromptu, on the back of a girl's hand at a bar in Sharpie like a letter of introduction from the muses themselves and later I held the hand that bore the words as she led me back to her apartment, the next morning proving me prophet when she went to the bathroom to wash. The last line read *There are some words you can't wash from your hands*, which she couldn't and I read her again from the faded but legible words on her dewy skin, massaging her palm with my thumb. We tussled again until noon, and we stacked our bodies each on each like dolmens across the pale plain of day.

I returned to Squirrel Haus. Wim's truck was there. I stood in the yard for a moment, square under Diomedes' aegis, and spat a thin, gruely blood on the sidewalk. My gums were bleeding. I checked them in the bathroom mirror. They'd receded quite a bit, as if my teeth were growing straight out my skull like a beaver's. Receding gums, I thought, no matter. I'll just comb them forward. I called Stella the socialista to find out any further details about spending a night in the hoosegow, and see if she was mending from the beating she took. She said there would be fanfare in the paper and possible lawsuits for police brutality. A smashing success for their crew. I told her to keep fighting the good fight and hung up. Griffin came home from the supermarket. I helped him ferry in the supplies. We'd been low on food for a few days, and we were starting to dip into the I's in the bathroom telephone book. I paid him half for the groceries. He rifled in the sacks and pulled out two beers.

-I had to grab food before we turned into the Donner party, he said. I was about to eat that squirrel in the freezer.

-To hell with the squirrel. We could live off Pickle for weeks, eating like kings, I said and ruffled the dog's head. Did you grab toilet paper, comrade?

-Fuck, he said. I totally forgot.

-Is Wim here?

-Nope, but check this out, he said. You're going to flip.

He motioned with his beer toward my room and I followed him into the basement. There was a steel drum the size of a large bucket of drywall mud set on the part of the floor not damp or mold-ridden. Griffin kicked it lightly with his boot and it responded with a dull twang.

-So I come down here to do some laundry, and what do I find but this little drum.

-So, Wim put it here? I asked.

-I have to assume that he did, he said. Take a guess what's inside.

-New Coke? I said. Ark of the Covenant?

-Guess again.

-Just tell me, I said. Some meth chemicals of Wim's?

-Sure, if you're running a biker meth lab, he said.

-Biker meth?

I lit an angry cigarette.

-What is it? I asked. What is it this time?

-P2P, he said. Check the label. Fucking P2P.

-Why the fuck is he bringing it here, I said.

Griffin lit an angrier smoke and cocked his eyebrows.

-More importantly, he said, where the hell did he get it? That drum alone must be worth twenty grand.

-What, is he going to start a lab here in Squirrel Haus?

-He must have stole it, Griffin said and flipped his smoke to the floor. We could do ten years just for having this stuff here. Having that stuff is like intent to distribute.

-Why the fuck leave it here in our place? I said.

Griffin laughed and picked at a cobweb above him.

-Hell if I know, he said. I think his brain is going to mush.

-Goddammit. Obviously.

Wordless, I walked upstairs and grabbed several beers, and walked back down in the moldy damp of the Bilge.

-Well, his truck's out front, I said. He should be by at some point.

- I can feel something in the air, something wicked this way comes, Griffin said. Strange things.

-Why don't we have normal friends who want to borrow cups of sugar or five bucks for gas? I said. I'm so sick of this. We should just move.

-Move where?

-Colorado. Tierra del Fuego. Become Laplanders. Anywhere, I said. This shit is getting out of hand.

-Let's just keep this under tabs, he said. I'm going to have a little chat with Wim the White Wizard about making us accomplices to manufacturing a class-one narcotic.

Griffin took as low an octave as his chords could muster, smiling, and kicked the drum again and it rang there.

-Drums, he intoned. Drums in the deep.

Ropey had quit or been arrested or killed or abducted by aliens or fallen into Mount Doom for all we knew the previous week, and I felt I'd never see his rotty brown teeth again. He'd stopped showing up, answered none of Zeke's calls, and was not at home when we drove by. Zeke hired a pinch-hit-employee he'd once worked with named Tim. He was lanky and of a young and hippied persuasion, but he was nice and worked hard, breaking only to roll cigarettes that dangled loosely from his lip in perpetual fixity. He was steady for two days, disappeared for one and returned again for another two, on a regular interval, and then disappeared without comment. He called a few days later from Arizona, apologizing, explaining that he'd had a dream telling him to go on a spirit quest. Walkabouts Tim gone walkabouts. Zeke then hired a guy who used to do carpentry for Little Paul named Joe who worked with us for one day and was hospitalized that same night during an argument with his wife over dinner which ended with him concussed and laid unconscious by a can of green beans she hurled at his head. She made the effort to call Zeke that morning and explain the situation. Jolly Joe, the Green Giant.

-Jesus, Zeke said as he closed his phone. Good work is harder and harder to find.

The Squirrel Haus vibe was growing weird. Wim's truck sat in front of the house unmoved. Michelle's coterie was still coming and going. I came home one afternoon to find Scuba Hank passed out in the yard, Brom standing over him holding his paramedic bag, ambulance lights winking in the street. I shrugged and offered Brom some coke, which he took. Later in the week while we were at work, Patman left a bag of weed for Griffin stuck to the Harem wall with a knife. I had a vague sense of something impending and insistent, as if the air and sky and the weathervane trees took on a posture that the right eyes could read, and I myopic. It was time to get out. I had put in applications to several community colleges all around the state, and even to the university itself, on a lark. I printed several copies of my resume at the library and typed up each cover letter on my typewriter, assuming they might like the vintage feel of the keys' strike marks on the paper. I applied for office jobs, a teaching gig at a Montessori school, any city jobs that were open, bank teller, insurance underwriter, office jobs with the city. Maybe I'd get lucky and fall into a sinecure, I reasoned. The worm has to turn every once in a while.

I worked solo most of the week, while Zeke sighted and scouted the upcoming sites, marking the sidewalks, and called in orders and paid his bills on time. He hired another guy he knew who was back from Colorado, Frank, a heavy pot smoker, which was their communal bond. Frank had been fired from his last carpentry job when his foreman found him sleeping in a bathtub on the construction site, a piece of cardboard pulled over himself for camouflage. He packed his things and drove back to Iowa to live with his parents, and spoke about moving soon to Florida to soak up the sun and drink coldbeer and hammer nails and hammer the girls alike.

We were out with Pickle on a constitutional that Thursday after respective labor, him loping alongside with the saddlebags swinging. A VW van puttered up in the opposing lane and stopped. A smiling blonde face leaned out of the window, addressing Griffin.

-Cool set up, guys. Can I ride him?

-Sure. Griffin said. Two bits.

-Say, we just got into town. You guys know where we can score some weed? We don't really know anyone around here.

Griffin said sure, and we walked to the van. Their license plates said Pennsylvania. I tossed my bike behind the van, and walked to the passenger window, calling Pickle over to keep him out of traffic. The van had a resinous smell to it, and was full of fast-food wrappers. A twenty-something with a broad smile and an electrified blonde beard sat in the driver's seat, and three girls occupied the remaining spaces. The girl in the passenger seat spoke to me, while the others leaned forward from the back.

-So, you guys live around here?

-Sure do, he said. What are you all doing? Road trip?

-Yeah, we're driving back to Boulder from Pennsylvania. We study there. What do you do?

-I write poems, I said. What do you study?

Griffin was taking a down payment from the guy, half, setting up a later rendezvous.

-We're art majors.

-Painting, drawing, sculpture?

-I design jewelry. They both paint.

-Cool. Griffin and I are painters, too. My name's Dunham.

She leaned into her smile.

-I'm Ingrid, and that's Jan and Frida. And no, not Kahlo.

-It's a pleasure to meet you all. So, we live three blocks over on Daniels Street. Swing by in a few hours.

I wrote the address down on a food wrapper and their van puttered with its rachitic muffler up the street. Griffin re-counted the money they'd given him.

-How much did they want? I asked.

-An ounce, he said. I don't have that much.

-Should we try Noel's?

-Sure, Griffin said. Did you give them the real address?

-Yeah.

-Okay. Noel's.

-What's the guy's name?

-He said it was Popeye, Griffin said with a sad nod.

-Popeye?

-Yup, he said. What's this world coming to?

We biked to Noel's and sat in his kitchen, divvying coldbeer from the saddlebags with cowboy whoops while he weighed out the ounce on digital scales. Griffin pointed to the scales.

-Don't be afraid to shave a little, he said. We don't know these people.

-What kind of dealer would I be if I ripped my customers off?

-Exactly like every drug dealer I've ever met, I said.

-Exactly. I, my friend, am a professional. I don't cheat people, Noel said.

-Suit yourself. What are you up to tonight?

-Nothing much, Griffin said. Might go downtown.

-Have you seen or heard from Wim or Patman? Griffin asked.

-Not for weeks, Noel said. Why?

-Stop by Squirrel Haus before you do, me and Dunham have something to show you.

We were home a long hour before the VW pulled to a stop in front. The heat like laths across the afternoon and a breeze barely fitting through them, and the midday bugs were rattling their afternoon exoskeletons in monotone pulse. I went outside and waved, as they were standing outside of the van, trepid. In they came, each passing a strange look upwards at Diomedes' throat where he hung in haunting judgment of all he surveyed below his fearful carriage and state. Something about the Godslayer seemed to bother the lot.

They pulled out the rest of the money, and Griffin tossed the baggie to Popeye. I had trouble calling him by his sobriquet, and reverted to dude. We traded stories and swapped jokes and emails and phone numbers. Griffin rolled a joint from his little sewing kit of goodies, and Popeye did the same, borrowing a paper. I walked and got two cases of beer, and by the time I was back, sweat-riddled and flagging, the house reeked of pot, detectable from fifty feet off, and the stereo was on, upbeat hippie shit. I cursed the hippie gods for the patchouli plagues and jam-band music they inflicted, and walked inside. Griffin had his PPK out, and was showing the girls how to hold it, release the clip and reload. Popeye was deep into his music, and sat staring at the stereo with its issuance of bongo and flute. But Diomedes forbade treating guests poorly, and I cursed the laws and gods of xenia too.

Noel stopped by a few hours later. The trustifarians had decided to kick back and stay the night. I left everyone inside in the kitchen painting on a giant roll of canvas that I'd tacked to the wall a few weeks ago, and motioned Noel outside. I led him to the backdoor, and down into the basement.

-Why are we taking the outside door? he asked.

-Just you wait.

Downstairs, I kicked the drum and it rang with a dull tremble.

-What's behind door number three? I asked.

He thought for a moment.

-A human head floating in honey?

-Close, but no cigarro.

-What is it? he asked. I'm not going to stand here and guess.

-P2P. Wim is stashing it here unbeknownst and unwelcome.

-Holy shit, Noel said. Where did he get that much of it?

-His meth mentor. I assume. He's the only logical explanation.

-That kingpin farmer guy you told me about? he said.

-I assume, I said. Where else is he going to get something like this? We came home the other day and here it was.

Noel kicked the drum and it tolled again. I rubbed my eyes.

-Friends like these, I said.

We ascended the stairs and rejoined the fiesta. Noel procured some coke from his camo backpack which the guests paid for, and he then threw a little more in out of Xtian kindness. We all took turns until our noses were spackled and we redoubled on the beer, dabbing the liquid into our desiccated noses. Joints were passed and I declined, as usual, and we had an archery tourney in the backyard by firelight. Frida broke the bow trying to launch an arrow from a sitting position, the bow on her feet, both arms rowing back, her back in arch against the draw. It snapped and the wild ends spun out from the soles of her Converse like tethered birds fleeing a gunshot. Laughter bounded forth.

We redoubled the fire and all sat admiring the fading remnants of Kell's masterpiece, still visible on the back of the house. Michelle's boarder, Paul, stopped outside and chainsmoked two Camel studs before he said hello, finally chatting and smoking more and nodding his head in approval of the mural through a haze of smoke before disappearing back upstairs. Popeye, of course, had a guitar and played hippie songs and Bob Marley and other dreck I didn't know. Olateju came by after work, and danced with Griffin, and we threw in more wood collected from a huge branch that had fallen in the backyard that we'd chopped up and lain in the sun to dry. We were inside and out at the pile of white powder and pulling heavily from my two bottles of Sailor Jack, and we finally retired to Squirrel Haus, and there was music at volume and some of them danced and we typed out bacchantic hymns and prayers to the seven heathen gods, and bodies soon were painted with watercolor and brush, flesh was out and reveled and quivering and quickly bedecked with color form and shape, and no mouth empty of lip or stupefacient or laugh, dervish in the major keys, and bodies with slick paint collided like flint striking more tinder we hadn't yet seen under our feet, and we rode atop the backbone of night and its tin-whistle frequencies, holding on like fools lashed to a fever-dream that slurred and roared and spun nameless in an abyss of discolored euphoria, consciousness meshed and unmeshed and crumpled, the body driven forth and leaning ever into minutes hung out like the carrots of Damocles, every hush a roar and everybody plied and overplied, a caloric heat drummed deep in the guts, body akimbo, body draped and body hung and slavering, and like those poor pilgrims fastened to the front of The Humungus warmachine, we rode and knew not in what Arcady or tartarus we might wake when our heads rolled out of the tumbling waters of sleep onto the shores of the day.

Alarum, alarum, alarum. My right hand flashed without my consent or knowledge, striking the floor desperately a few times until finally it thudded on the screeching clock's snooze. I pulled a pair of panties from over my eyes, and stared hard at the blurry phosphorescent red numerals. I knew I was late for work at Zeke's house. I looked left, my arm was wrapped around someone's leg, the calf covered in bristly blonde hair. I lifted the blanket and saw lady parts, and a slumbering, painted body, and another further over, naked, with the same set of equipment. I breathed a sigh of relief, but couldn't recall when the second girl had joined us. I slid my arm gently from under the slumbering form, rolled out and sat up off the side. I was painted blue, a Smurf with vitiligo. The sheets were coated with mottled patches of color where sweat and various accretions had plastered the sheets to our slumbering forms, and from where I rose there was a print of bluish purple, a Rorschach shroud of Turin. I left my Smurfy shadow in the bed. I stood, wobbled, body peeling from the bed like slick Velcro, with a head full of steel wool gauze, feeling like a taxidermist's botched apprentice work, rubbing dried flecks of blue paint from my forearms and face. I grabbed some clothes and veered toward the shower.

The water and steam, and alternate bouts of only cold did little to clear my head, and the agua pooled at my feet in a purply swirl. I flushed my nose with water, several times, till I could breathe through it. I leaned out and checked my face in the clouded mirror, still bluish, stained like a Bedouin. Soaped and resoaped and washed all over, I toweled the hue from my face and called my brother, luckily getting voice mail, and said that I'd be a little late. I noticed a message on the machine, from him, from last night, that had gone unheard in the din, saying he needed help at his house running new gutters and hanging some doors inside, too. I made coffee and smoked, and had a scalding cup, coughed heavily and spit some blood into the sink. My throat was raw, enflamed. I rinsed my mouth. I surveyed the room with unclear eyes. Popeye was asleep on the floor with his arm around Pickle and they snored and growled in harmony, and Frida slept on the couch, her face painted like an American flag and her feet the same. Griffin's door was open and I could make out Olateju's naked form, topless and chest swelling gently, covered at the waist, encircled by his arm. Where was Noel?

Ezekiel was out in his yard when I arrived in Tiffin and he rolled his eyes and shook his head in a not unkind manner, smiling as he tapped the imaginary watch at his wrist. I told him about the hippified chaos the night prior and then had some coffee and I had a handful of aspirin and then played peekaboo with Isis, and then we frisked about the house and worked. We hung the doors and ripped the old gutter troughs and affixed the new. The concrete project was nearly finished, he explained, and we'd be done, just a little past the city's allotted schedule, next week, so why not get some work done at his place in the meantime. Zeke said he didn't miss the vampirical nightlife and I could not but agree with him. He started laughing.

-You still have blue paint on your face, he said.

-Why didn't you tell me?

-Now where would the fun be in that?

I said goodbye to everyone, kissed Isis on her little forehead, Zeke cut me a check for helping, and with a little bonus for finishing the concrete project on time. I thanked him, drove down the road and merged onto the highway and made for the check-cashing place. Friday's end, and finally. The teller pushed forth the bills from behind the bulletproof glass in denominations of the lesser order. I went next door and grabbed some Nat Shermans and beer at the smoke shop, and drove home, brushing from my arms the sawdust glued in the dried sweat and dirt. I was going to take it easy this weekend, I thought. Rest. I needed respite. You can only push your body so much before something breaks. I had some painting to do, and I wanted to collate notes on some poems. There was no excuse to stop working.

I turned the corner on Daniels, greeted by six police cruisers and an ambulance in front of Squirrel Haus, their blue and red lights rotating in that peculiar fashion like tiny pulsars, crowding the street. Shock. Remorseless shock that ossified my tongue, splintered my bones. I stopped the truck at the turn and sat and closed my eyes and opened them, everything a slow blur of fettered mind and to-be-fettered body. I ground the gearbox into reverse, ready to back out and flee to a remote cave in Afghanistan where I would grow a beard, learn Arabic, convert to Islam and wait around for my seventy-two raisins. A cop pointed at me, palm up and fingers waving me toward him, fifteen paces off and coming right at me. Every curse and epithet that I could recall in all languages to the seven heathen gods to render unto Wim his due were muttered as I pushed in the clutch and engaged the gear, rolling my way forward, and back a million years, jail life springing so vividly to mind that I could taste the soap jammed in my mouth to hold my silence as some vicious gang raped me in the shower room. I tried to speak, but no words came out, my throat seized and gurgling, lungs working at ten percent, or maybe nine, and I gulped air and swallowed it.

-You live on this street, the cop asked.

-Uh, I said. Well.

-Do you live on this street?

-Just, uh. What, uh. Happened?

-There was an accident, the cop said. Do you live on this street? Otherwise, turn around.

A pale shroud fluttered on a cart being led from the rear of Squirrel Haus. It was hard to tell what was on it, or under the drawn sheet. I froze and was frozen, hands white on the steering wheel. The gurney turned toward me, and for all I knew it contained the drum of phenyl-2-propanone, enough to put the entire block away for twenty years with intent to distribute. Men in grey suits turned the gurney toward the street and it went oblong, as they skittered up to the ambulance, a form lying underneath the sheet floating as if in a strip-mall magic show act upon that unseen bier. This did not compute. I didn't see Griffin's truck. Just Wim's. No way the body was Griffin's.

-Is someone dead?

-An accident, the cop repeated. I can't say anything more except that you need to turn around in that driveway and find yourself another shortcut.

There were no hazmat teams on site, no drug dogs barking furiously at the house, and no FBI. No one wore a respirator or even gloves except the paramedics. Just local flatfoots. I relaxed a little, but my heart quivered and veered as if not my own. It felt like I'd taken an epipen of adrenaline straight into the eyeball. I did the calculus and took the risk.

-Well, I live there, I said.

-Where?

-That house, with the deer, I said. Downstairs.

-The place with the deer head?

-Yessir.

-The detective is going to need to ask you some questions, then, the cop said. Go ahead and park right here.

He looked at me through his cop glasses, and peered into my truck, my face reflected back in those mirrors, and his in mine. I did as asked and killed the engine. Right arm down and shading toward his gun, he stood near the truck. I suddenly remembered the hippies and scanned the area for their van, but it was gone. Were they some roving band of freaks who'd spared us, but killed Michelle and Scuba Hank and Paul? Who was under the body tarp? The idle rich are as unpredictable and thuggish as any street junkie, and ten times more dangerous with their lawyers. What had those kids done? I leaned against my vehicle. The cop asked for my license, registration, my etc.

I was reading his face, his demeanor, his hands. He was smiling, but a cop-smile, with a toilet-brush moustache, each end expertly manicured. After a series of questions and a radio interruption at his shoulder that was mostly static, he gave me back my identity and let me go inside. I smiled, and reached in the window for the beer. Were I in some sort of trouble, I'd have been cuffed and gagged and halfway to an interrogation cell by now. I feigned my comfort a little more. The cop just watched me lean in and grab the case of beer and smokes.

-Is it okay to go inside? I asked.

-You've got a dog in there? the cop asked. We heard barking.

-Uh, yeah, he's our guard dog.

-Guarding what? he asked.

-A man's castle is his own, I said.

-One of the detectives will talk to you shortly.

-No problem. Just tell him to knock loudly.

I thanked him and wished him a good day, and walked toward the house, trying very hard not to seize up in panic, keep the lungs' undulation slow and steady until inside. Michelle came outside crying and she looked up and met my eyes through her tears and I walked past and inside. The curtains were all drawn as usual, and the hippies had cleared out that morning. All the general household and electronic items were still where we left them, as well as a mess of bottles, cigarettes, roaches and a tie-dyed hat which I vaguely remembered belonging to one of the girls, a large fragment of blue glass from a mirror shattered months ago that held traces of a fine white powder sat on Hellraiser, a scorched lightbulb there too. A rampart of neatly stacked cans stacked on album covers stacked on cans. There were skulls painted on the wall of the Harem, some with throwing knives in them, and a number of knives sticking from a sheet of plywood we'd set up there too. A cornucopia of paraphernalia scattered about like a towhead drawing along the bark of the damned. I had somehow missed it all this morning in my stupor. My bed sheets were in the tub. I went downstairs.

The drum still sat where it had been left. I crouched near it in relief, an audible sigh issuing. I climbed back upstairs on wooden legs, rickety with the adrenaline dump, and I found some panties in the fridge when I got a beer. I walked each room with a bag, sweeping all the jailable materials in: pills, almost an eightball of coke, joints, more pills, some meth, and something that looked like a dried jalapeno but could have been a shroom for all I knew. All of it went into the toilet. I smashed the lightbulb there too, and tossed the metal part into the toilet tank. A year's worth of jail time floated on the water and with a flush, I felt slightly less apprehensive.

I stuffed Griffin's gun as well as several of his sentimental pipes inside several ziplock bags, sealing each. I poured some bleach in the outer bag to hopefully throw off any dogs, and crammed this weird package in a heating duct. I hustled again downstairs and stuck the P2P off into a corner and threw a lawnchair and a half-built birdhouse on it, and a tarp, some fake Xmas tree branches and whatever else I could find. I went back upstairs, swept the place again and found a test tube in the sink, black residue inside. I smashed it in the toilet and flushed, then watched through the front window, trying to figure out the details. Pickle, needing a better vantage, slipped his nose under the blinds, shifting his head back and forth to see. He growled in a low whisper and chopped his jaw at the activity in the yard as the police milled and talked and nodded into their radios. I listened at the window for a moment and heard talk of an accident and Michelle mentioned her boyfriend. She wasn't crying anymore.

Michelle had no boyfriend that I knew of. I ran through the list of her regulars. There were some semi-regulars, like Satan Claus with his pork and dreams. There was Doughboy, Scuba Hank, Bubba, some other guys we only knew by face or caterwaul, and there was Paul the Chimney, with his endless Camel studs. He had just had a liver transplant.

I frisked the house four more times in fifteen minutes when Griffin walked in. He looked gutshot. He shut the door and slid down it, visibly shaking. He looked around the house as if in an amnesiac stupor, his brain gone fugue and rogue, cigarette fluttering between his fingers. He stood as I gave him a beer, and sat heavily against the counter, rattling the dishes I'd stacked in the sink, and with the first slug of ichor seemed to compose himself, as a boxer brought back with smelling salts.

-What the fuck is going on? he asked.

-No fucking clue, I said. I think someone died. The cops said there was an accident.

-Where's that fucking drum? Griffin asked and lunged up.

-I hid it, I said. I didn't know what else to do. I swept the whole house, though. Flushed everything. Hid the gun. Pipes. Place should be clean.

-Holy shit, good job, Griffin exhaled.

-I thought we were going to jail when I pulled up, I said.

-Fuck, me too, he said. What if they want to search our place?

-Can they? I have no idea, I said. Can you call your cousin and ask him?

Griffin lit double cigarettes, handing one to me.

-But if they said it was an accident, why would they need to search our place? he said.

-But if it was an accident, why so many cops? Why is there a detective here?

-Maybe it was a bad accident, he said. Maybe they're bored. It is Iowa City.

I sucked the smoke down in three puffs and nubbed it in the sink. He called his cousin in Kansas City who said the cops would have to have reasonable cause to search our place. Or so he thought. How would he know, he said, and said some nastiness about family and hung up. Griffin double-checked the barrel in the Bilge and walked into the Harem with a coldbeer, looked at the pictogram skulls and the throwing knives in the wall and got a hammer and a nail and tacked it into the plaster and set a painting over the macabre congregation, pulling free the seven or so blades. I had been so keen on looking for drugs, I'd forgotten the knives. We sat by the window, chainsmoking and watching the cops come and go, listening to their footfalls and their muffled voices upstairs. Collectively we decided that Paul must have been on the lam from the authorities for something, and was hiding here until he healed and could get away, but he had tripped and fallen in the kitchen in his weakened state and wasted a perfectly good liver. You don't just get a liver transplant. How did this guy have the moxie and money for one? They had already taken the body, it seemed, but were still combing the place over. If it was an accident, why were there six cop cars? Where was Michelle during all of it? The questions even more vague than our conjectures.

A plainclothes detective came up and knocked on our door. We stepped outside on the stoop, explaining that we would invite him in, but Pickle was pretty nervous around strangers, so we would just talk outside. Another detective came over and relieved his understudy. He handed us each his card. He wanted to ask us a few questions. We consented, and was it okay if we smoked? He said of course. He took off his Oakleys, revealing close-set and slightly off-centered eyes. The left looked just a few degrees too far left, and the right eye swam the same. He had spiny hair like a shellacked hedgehog, and an overbite. His hair was amazing, like a werewolf's. We wouldn't mention the hippies who had stayed the night. It was just Griffin, Pickle and me, having some beers and smoking cigarettes until midnight-thirty when we went to bed.

He got out his notebook, and took our names and birthdays and driver's license numbers. He explained that Paul had been found dead at some point this morning by Michelle, who said she had been visiting friends elsewhere. We alternated in answering him.

-You guys were here last night?

-Yes, Griffin said, but we went to bed fairly early because we had to work today.

-So before you went to bed, did you hear anything out of the ordinary?

-No, I said. It's usually pretty quiet around here.

-No one else came in? No other visitors?

-We couldn't hear very well because we had our stereo on, Griffin said.

-Has there been any strange traffic to or from the house in recent months?

-Nothing out of the ordinary, I said.

-Some of the neighbors have reported a lot of noise coming from her door, late at night. People, mostly men, in and out of the place.

Griffin inhaled his cigarette deeply.

-We try to stay out of others' business, try to be neighborly, Griffin said.

-They also reported a red car, a Monte Carlo, with some guys wearing gang colors stopping by over the past couple of months.

-We met them once, I said. We're not here much during the day because of work, and we go out regularly.

-So you met these individuals?

-Just once, Griffin said.

-Can you describe them? How did they dress or act?

-Like guys, I said. I don't know. They didn't seem out of the ordinary.

-So you guys were here alone last night, and didn't hear anything?

-Nossir, Griffin said.

One of the other cops yelled something to him, and Detective Ziegler excused himself for a moment. Griffin read the card aloud, leaned over to me, chuckling nervously.

-Detective Tome Ziegler. The Ziggler, he said.

The Ziggler came back, looking over his notepad, crossing things out and writing things down.

-So you guys have lived here for how long?

-About four or five months, I said.

-Since when?

-Late January, Griffin said.

-And where do you work?

We explained in turn.

-Do you know a William Janson?

-Yes, I said.

The Ziggler flipped through his notes for a moment.

-His truck is parked out front.

-Did he do anything wrong? Griffin asked.

-No, the detective said, but I like to be thorough.

-He left us his truck in case we needed it, I said.

-Do you know where he is?

-We haven't seen Wim for a while, Griffin said.

-Had there ever been any domestic disputes that you heard?

-No. Nothing more than normal.

-Etc? Etc?

-Etc. and etc.

-Etc. Etc.

The Ziggler scribbled some more notes, and thanked us for our time.

-Sir, I said, may I ask why there's a detective here at an accident scene?

-A man in the apartment upstairs had an accident. I have to rule out foul play is all. That's why I'm here.

-Who was it? Griffin asked.

-Okay, thanks again for your time, the Ziggler said. If anything comes up, give me a call.

He pointed to his card in Griffin's hand.

-Of course, sir, we said in unison.

The Ziggler looked up at Diomedes with a weird smile.

-I won't even ask about that, he said.

He went back and talked to some of the other police. Griffin's part-time plumbing coworker, Angel, sauntered up to us in his uniform.

-What did you guys do this time? Angel said.

Griffin shook his head.

-Innocent this time around, Griffin said. Why are you working days?

-I'm alternating. Department's going to move me to days in a few months, so I'm getting a feel for it. Going to phase out the plumbing.

-Do you know what happened here? I asked.

-A guy fell down some stairs, he said. Seems pretty obvious. You know him at all?

I lit a smoke.

-No, Griffin said. Just some loadie who hung out upstairs a lot.

Angel took off, and we went inside, sitting in the Harem, chainsmoking and watching every movement, gesture and beck- like diviners reading the entrails of an eviscerated animal, plumbing for clues of the future in the warm gore of now. We listened at the window but heard little. Finally, the last squad car drifted away, and I went to the duct, retrieved the gun and gave it to Griffin.

We did another thorough sweep of the place with the cracked blinds drawn, combing the carpet and sills and cushions and crannies for anything I'd missed. After two hours at the task, we had fourteen more Percocet, several unidentifiable tablets that weren't vitamins, several that were, a cigarette wrapper with about half a gram of coke inside, an assortment of joints in various lengths, some bullets that didn't belong to Griffin's gun, twelve dollars in change, seven in cash, a pair of underwear I'd been missing since March and a pair of anonymous panties with little green ribbons, what looked to be a baby's tooth, an aspirin bottle with a few tablets left, a stem of marijuana with several salvageable buds, and a girl's makeup kit containing lip balm and a compact. I flipped it open and my eye caught itself there.

-Holy hell. I'm surprised we didn't find a rubber chicken and a Guatemalan refugee, I said.

-We should have done this months ago.

-How did we lose this much stuff in here? I said.

-I think the better question is, how did we not lose more?

Griffin paused for a long moment.

-Why in the hell was he asking questions about Wim?

We drank too much that night and talked too much and smoked too much and took too much from our new-found old trove. My nerves felt like a cicada's husk, brittle and emptied and harried in a maelstrom where it stuck, fastened to the skin of a tree. I took a number of pills and washed them down until it felt like my nervous system hung out of the ends of my fingers and each hair on my head felt electric and palpitating. Griffin went to bed early. My organs felt liquefied, a fustian mass in there, jumbled, swirling, wordly garble. I sat against the wall, and I had to sit down. The air felt like it was tasting me. I felt spit out. Everything felt jellied, my heart wasn't my own, my kidneys ached, my skull felt pupaefied. I caught my breath and walked toward my room, tasting the blood in my mouth. There was a message blinking on the answering machine and I pushed the button. It was Fat Bastard. *Yes, this is Dan O'Finn. What's this about a leak in the closet? I don't honestly know what you mean by a heart of darkness. I expect that you'll pay the rent next month. I'll be by this week to take a look at the closet. Thanks.*

Dead of night. Asleep. There was a rumble and a crash and Pickle barked and his heavy footfall raced back to my door and he scratched and butted at it. I shot up like a cobra out of a birthday cake, my mind on haunches. The crash was in the basement. I swung open my bedroom door where Pickle whinnied and pawed, and he strode into the room. I could see the basement light was on, a watery light emanating from the threshold, and a great din started below, things hurled and smashed in the recess, and a voice was arguing with itself in a junkie mumblese. I turned to Pickle.

-They always return to the scene of the crime. You ready to kill a killer, killer?

He panted, taut, and shook his shovel-head and flung his expectorants. I opened the door and Pickle raced downstairs, his claws scratching the wooden treads, him low in his frame for balance down the steep set of stairs. He'd had a great head start and I started down the stairs just as Griffin came in my room with a studded baseball bat, heading for the basement too. I rounded the corner expecting to see Pickle standing over a knocked-down, half-starved hooplehead, but he was busy licking Wim's hand. Wim turned to me, eyes big.

-Where the fuck is that goddamn drum?

September

Stylus

The simplest sun
falls into the grey water,
immolated and dancing,

of an ocean I have never seen
making an apogee of
what I would like my life

to have been. Cities are
constellations run through
with concrete, as they too fall,

fall amid the bleeding car alarms
from the empty lot of the Church
of the Time Before the Time

Before the Time. Let the living name
the price of clay. Too
easily the blood and dust

parables shed their skin.
Too easily night asserts itself
through the bare branches

scoring the sky like seiners'
nets, dragging this low over
the earth with no indication

of whom they are looking for,
or why, or for how long
this will go on.

Soundtrack:

Warren Zevon, *Detox Mansion*
Leadbelly, *Take this Hammer*
Rolling Stones, *Can't You Hear Me Knockin'*
Townes van Zandt, *Rex's Blues*
Wu Tang Clan, *Y'all Been Warned*
Led Zeppelin, *Bron-Y-Aur*

Explaining the death, the police, the detective and Michelle, I stood pointing at the drum and Wim looked where I pointed. He shook his head a little, then a lot, trying to get his brain in its addled state around what had happened that day. I gave him a cigarette, and his thumb fumbled four times on the lighter's child-protection safety device. Griffin sat in the ratty lawn chair, dropping the shillelagh's head on the concrete, the thing sawed to two feet, a piece of red leather on the handle with upholstery tacks studded throughout the top. He let it fall on the damp concrete, thudding dully, the cap and handle worn, frayed and scuffed. I asked Griffin for a smoke and squatted next to the P2P. Without the fear of the seven heathen gods in him, Wim might pull another stunt like this. I nodded at Griffin.

-I'd like to know why you dump a stolen drum of this stuff in our basement? Griffin said. Should I expect some hoodlums to burst in here with shotguns next?

-I'll get rid of it, Wim said. I needed to stash it till I got my new operation going.

-Where did you even get this stuff? I asked.

-Laurence had it sitting around. I figured he wouldn't miss it. No one cooks with this stuff anymore.

-What about Laurence? Griffin asked. Like he's not going to want it back?

-And you store it here, I said. I don't get it.

-He isn't going to miss that. Honestly. He doesn't care about it.

-Wim, Griffin said, Laurence isn't small time.

-I know. He's been at it for ten years, but it's a sinking ship. He's too busy with trying to evade the DEA. He's cracking. It's obvious.

-Let me get this straight, I said. You visit his place. In your truck. You then steal a drum of an illegal chemical from him worth twenty grand, store it in our basement, and then park your fucking truck in front of the place? All while there's a DEA investigation going on? And you say that he's cracking?

-How much meth have you been smoking? Griffin said.

-Look, I saw an opportunity and I took it, Wim countered. Laurence is going down at some point. I'll be there to fill the niche.

-How do you even know how to make meth from P2P? That's old school stuff, Griffin said.

-That's how I first learned, back at that commune, Wim explained. I'm partnered up with Dre. He's got muscle and distribution. I've got Patman, and the business has been good.

-Slow down there, Tony Mantegna, I said. You think Laurence isn't going to notice you running amok? You stole twenty grand of supplies from him. Do I have to remind you we had a street full of cops outside today? What if that detective ran your plates and you came up in some database associated with Laurence, or that shit back in Oregon. This is Homeland Security territory.

-Laurence didn't even remember he had that stuff, Wim repeated. He'll never know. He doesn't cook with it anymore. It was just sitting in the back of a truck bed.

Griffin tapped his cudgel a few more times on the floor. Wim looked at it. I looked up at Wim. He was inhaling a smoke breathlessly, and looked at me, eyes deadly serious now, the haze of adrenaline, fear and meth had been cut and he now stood tethered to reality in the grim basement with us, and he understood our bent. He shook his head again.

-Come on you guys, Wim said. It's not like I knew she'd up and kill someone. I just needed to stash it somewhere safe.

-Cops said it was an accident, Griffin said, the bat beating time with the words.

-You know what I mean, Wim said. How the fuck was I supposed to know?

-That's not the fucking point, Griffin continued. We've done some stupid shit. Quite often. But not 25-years-of-jail-time stupid. What if the cops had found some drugs in Michelle's, called a fucking canine unit to investigate and then it keels over when it gets a whiff of Squirrel Haus?

-That's circumstantial, Wim said. Besides, you couldn't do more than a few years for having the drum.

-What, did they teach you law at the commune, too? I asked.

-When have you ever known a cop to admit to circumstantial evidence? Griffin came back. Do you know how many pills and shit we found today? Just lying around in the couch and in the carpet? All that alone would be enough to put us away. I'm not taking the fall for anyone, for you, for him, for Pickle. No one.

-I'll get the drum out of here tonight, Wim said. That's why I came over.

-You think it's a good idea to break in like some junkie burglar? Like we don't have neighbors watching this place?

-But it's Friday, Wim said. The cops are gone.

I ran my fingers through my hair. Wim continued.

-You guys were sleeping, he said. I didn't want to wake you.

-You did fucking wake us, Griffin said rising. You were throwing shit around down here like some meth-addict squirrel. What if a neighbor saw you and thought you were breaking in? We'd have the fucking cops back here again.

-Guys. I'm sorry. I really am. I'll go. I'm sorry. I'll bring some of the new batch over when I'm done and make it up to you.

Wim left, out the back door, carrying the drum with an awkward waddle out to his truck. It was nearly five and there was no point going back to sleep, so I made coffee and Griffin and I sat in the kitchen in a pair of director's chairs I'd stolen from someone's patio, sipping java and ashing cigarette after cigarette into a Folger's coffee can between us, marveling at the palpable reality of the grotesquely abstract things in the world, Fate and Luck and Surprise and Horror and Fear. Griffin stood and made a centurion gesture, his hand balled at his heart and then the arm unfurled and his palm faced down.

-Those about to die salute you, he said with the smoke poking out from his thick fingers.

I repeated the gesture.

-Salve, salve. Go Hawks.

-What a fucking day, he said. Morning hasn't even started and this is what we have to deal with.

-Let's just hope there's a break from the shitstorm, I said.

-What do you want to do this weekend?

-Not think about today or yesterday, I said. We still have rent to pay.

-Has Fat Bastard fixed Heart of Darkness? he asked.

-No. You know he hasn't, I said.

-Then we don't pay. The air's too weird right now.

We went next door to Dorothy's at nine and offered to clean her gutters in advance of the coming leaf clot of autumn, hoping that an outward show of neighborly assistance might help distance us from Michelle in the neighborhood's eye. She smiled and offered us weak coffee the color of iodine. I leaned her dead husband's ladder against the pitch of the roof, and she came out and gestured us over to her door.

-What was all that commotion yesterday?

-All those police? Griffin asked.

-Yes, there was certainly a lot of them, she said. You boys aren't mixed up with her, are you?

-No, ma'am, Griffin said. We're just trying to get by like everyone else. Her business is her own.

-Just because I'm old doesn't make me stupid. She looks like trouble, and I had her pegged from the moment she moved in. I'm just not blind is all. Not yet anyway.

-No, ma'am, you certainly aren't, Griffin said.

We gutted the gutters and cleaned up last autumn's rotten leaves from the troughs and threw them to the ground, black patches around the yard. I had been hoping that any neighbors plying themselves at their windows would take notice of our civic engagement, and mentally distance us from Michelle. We took our time, making sure to stand on the peak when we smoked for full exposure in our panoramic philanthropy. When we were done, Dorothy offered us five dollars, and I folded back her creased and translucent fingers, thanking her.

Our good deed done, we waved to Dorothy at her bay window, and went back inside Squirrel Haus and took some speed balanced with Percocet we'd bought the week before when things were simpler. There were several people at Michelle's now, treading the floor heavily, voices muffled, obscured through the vents. I held my ear to the duct, but couldn't make anything out. There was a message from Greg on the machine. He said that there was a party near his place at the Gaslight that night, and that we should come. It would be full of writers, which is always a good time to drink heavily and yell at people.

-Writers are a skittish bunch, like gentle woodland creatures, Griffin said with a smile.

We were drunk by the time that we got to the party, comfortably, welcoming the change of venue. Not in reel-and-retch mode quite yet. Griffin was wearing Planana, a slick pleather affair the color of a radioactive Chiquita, a jacket that nearly always got him into a fight for some reason, as if the weird texture and color of the thing triggered deep primate impulses in all who bore witness to it. I warned him about it, but he waved me off saying he didn't believe in base superstitions, nor evolution, nor history, nor the Tooth Fairy, nor love. The air smelled antiseptic on our walk to the Gaslight, like a freshly bleached landscape that had been rinsed with silence and shade, and we walked the avenues in the breezy, chill air, steps paced by wind and the roundness of the earth below us, and we straddled it. We talked of hope that all the nastiness would subside, and of what we spoke we knew that we knew better.

Griffin and I reconnoitered the place by the people going in and out, and we walked up the flight of stairs. The house was an older sort, run down by human use. I hid our case of beer in a bush near the entryway and pocketed a few, just in case. Up to the second floor and throughout, on the landing and in the hallway was wood-paneling everywhere, inch-thick maple, and wooden stairs and floor that creaked with every step, each one a different tenor, like voices along. I saw Greg inside, and a couple of faces of people I knew from around town and a few peripherals from grad school. I slipped into the open kitchen, an island sat in the middle, loaded with bottles and a cooler of beer, as well as some offerings of the harder stuff. I knew the hostess, a poet, blonde, with sharp eyes and intelligent, but an Exeter and Wellesley Girl, and too good for the likes of me. I doffed an imaginary fedora her way as I grabbed two beers and slithered back among the mixture of bodies. I found Griffin talking about guns to Greg, and handed him a bottle which he poured into a plastic cup.

-Thanks, Griffin said. Let's not dip into our stash until we need to.

-Waste not, want not, I said.

Greg punched my shoulder.

-Hey, asshole, why didn't you get me one, then?

Griffin opened his beer with a lighter.

-Who's that? he asked, pointing to a blonde in a feather boa.

-Patroness, Greg said. She's from big mone. Even more than Wim. Spoiled rich kid turned writer.

-What a snack, Griffin said with a smile. She got a boyfriend?

-Hell if I know, Greg said. She's of the upper crust. I think her name is Sandy, or Sardine. Something like that.

-I am Griffin Buch, esquire, of the Manor de Squirrel, he said with a bow. A gentleman and purveyor of fine drink, connoisseur of cunnilingus. Friend of the homeless and scourge of the loadie.

He gave another sweeping bow, eyes impish.

-Well, go try and hang your shingle, if you dare, guv'nah, I said.

-Bully, suh. Right bully that will be, he replied, fingering in his cup and retrieving half of a pair of broken eyeglasses he'd found in the street the week before.

Griffin drew for her, and Greg introduced me around to some of his friends and pleasantries abounded. I walked the rooms, Griffin still making the hostess laugh, and I noticed a slim Asian girl, sitting by herself in a spare bedroom, looking through the *Maximus Poems*. I sat next her and pointed with my beer.

-In the face of sweetness piss, I said.

She looked up.

-Excuse me, she said.

-Line from a poem in there. Olson's great. I forget the name of the poem, but it's toward the front. *Letter Number Five*, or something like that. Maybe it's *Song Number Five*.

-I've only read his poem *The Kingfishers*.

-Another great one, I said. You read much poetry?

-I'm here in the grad program. For poetry.

-Congratulations, I said. That's great. I did my masters here a few years ago.

-In what?

-Poultry, just like you. I wrote a long poem in blank verse called *A Pullet's Progress*.

-Ha. Sounds fascinating.

She didn't seem fascinated, so I quoted some poems and made her laugh eventually. I got up to retrieve more drinks, and bowed deeply, as far as I could. I asked her name, and her eyes rhymed with light, she was so beautiful. She'd been raised Mormon, and grew up in Salt Lake City. I made a few jokes at the expense of the LDS, and she laughed again. I wrote my phone number on the page of the Olson poem I'd quoted, and tore it from the book. She looked horrified, but I ignored her ignominy and went to get a few more beers to line my pockets with. I offered her one, but she said she turned bright red if she drank too much because of a stomach enzyme deficiency. I called her a biological determinist.

Hours more or less later, the cooler was empty in the kitchen and the rooms were full of bodies pressed and some dancing. I moved sideways through the throng in my best Egyptian pose, and sidled finally up to the row of bottles, edging in with elbows and angles, and poured a glass of vodka, which bulged in a little dome at the rim. I bent over with lips pursed to suckle it, hands at the sides to prevent any of the bunch from spilling it. Bent over my little oasis, slurping in the little water. It tasted diluted, a half-fill, a ringer. I stood up and scanned the kitchen. Griffin was still talking to Sardine and she was laughing and holding his shoulder, leaning into his ear with smiles. I addressed her from across the kitchen island with the glass hoisted to share the mirth.

-What is this, I said, the Deadwood? All the booze is watered down. What gives?

Her face drained with a surprising rapidity. Full rage from go. I looked back at her quizzically, and put my hands up in a deferential pose, my eyebrows knitted in confusion combined with shock at her Jekylled transformation in a moment's notice. I looked to Griffin and he seemed pissed that I'd ruined her mood so effortlessly. I quaffed the glass's contents in one go, rubbing my stomach and smiling and nodding at her with an insistent grin, like a toothpaste commercial. I put up my thumb and mouthed thanks. This brought dread. She threw her highball glass at me, which I caught midair without thinking, and the contents splashed me and several innocent bystanders. I replaced the glass on the counter. Griffin tipped his beer toward me, eyes rolling and head rocking back and forth slowly as she pushed through the mass toward me. I mimed sorry to him as best I could and then Sardine was on me, shoving me back toward the door with considerable force from her small frame. Mention of the Deadwood had touched on some deep psychic scar tissue and the dam of ire flooded out and up through her larynx and directly at me.

-Get the fuck out. Get the fuck out, you cocksucker! You fucking lowlife asshole!

A number of the people I knew were looking at me, smiling their shiteating smiles. I grabbed the doorway where I'd been talking to the girl whose name rhymed with light, and she looked at me in shock. I resisted Sardine's shoving for a moment, holding telephone fingers to my head, looking at the girl and nodding. At the door, Sardine's efforts complete, I bowed, rolling my hand to the floor.

-I bid thee, afuckingdoo, madame, I said. Thank you for your hospitality, and fuck you very much.

Out the door, I stole an umbrella from her foyer and a cowboy hat, and I walked down the creaky stairs with plunder in arm, and there retrieved the case of beer from the bush. I lit a smoke and stood bestride the night, carcinogens spilling from lung to sky. Take that, nature, I thought. It was a good enough night to simply be.

I was languorous in finishing the cigarette, and was about to start treading home. I heard a voice from on high.

-Yo, D, wait up.

I looked up, and Griffin was starting out of one of the second-story windows. He threw his yellow jacket down, and mine which I'd forgotten amid the hysterics, and he tossed out a couple bottles of beer and half a fifth of gin. I caught one beer, and another, missing the third, its contents exploding in a bath of foam and shrapnel against my pants. I tied the arms of the Lumberjacket together and slung it on my shoulder in a hobo's hammock, cradling our remaining beers in their different recyclable casings, looking for an appropriate stick to complete the equipage and maybe some black greasepaint for a nice gaucho moustache and beard. Griffin broke most of the trellis slats as he descended, cursing at the wood as it cracked and flipped to the cement, his body pitching out for a moment until regaining grip with each dislodged swing down. Finally a large section of the trellis cracked and brought him down the remaining seven feet.

-Holy Christ, he said, tossing the large patch of wood into the bushes. That girl is nuts.

-What did she say? I asked. Why did she freak out?

-She was dating some bartender who worked at the Deadwood, and they broke up, and some other stuff about him. The Deadwood set her off. I forget what else she said. Bla bla bla. She was yelling at everyone, so I lit out, too. Oh, and I also found a flask of whiskey, he said, holding it up with a shake.

-Touché, I said. Look what I got.

I showed him the umbrella and hat. He unfurled the umbrella, popping it hard against its frame, then back, and twirled it Chaplinesque. It was a nice one, wooden handle and canvas canopy. He snapped it back and starting fencing with a tree, one hand behind his back. I let the cowboy hat dangle from my neck. It was too small for my head. On our way back we bought some lighter fluid from a convenience store, and when we got to Lucas Street we slowed and stopped. I doused the hat in lighter fluid and the umbrella. We sat and let the naphtha soak in, and had a few beers, talking of nothing in particular. We emptied the rest of the Ronsonol bottle's contents on the items, and slid our remaining beer cans into the hammock jackets hung like purses. I tied the hat to my head. It had little silver beads sewn into the brown leather. Griffin raised the umbrella and when ignited our respective charges whumped aflame. We ran down the street like escaped souls from hell, howling and laughing and wild and unfettered. Griffin whirled the thing around like Mjolnir until nothing but steel ribs remained, and I stomped out the hat, and then we cut left down another alley. We didn't want to risk being run down by the police for intended arson. We weren't idiots.

Back at Squirrel Haus, I stood on Griffin's shoulders at the door, wobbly but firm, and replaced Diomedes' bombardier hat with the little three-gallon Stetson, and hung the umbrella's bones from his hoof. We sat outside with Pickle and the night swam like history and the crest moon hung like a bloody lip on the dark's maw which we tended to with cold drink from my red and black hobo satchel, me like some antiquated sawbones working from little leather bags with glinting instruments. We talked about Wim and Patman, and Haley and Layna. I tried calling Brom, but again there was no answer. He'd been avoiding our calls for weeks. I threw the phone back inside.

-What an asshole, I said.

I was working again with Zeke at odd jobs, carpenting this and that, and hadn't received any requests for interviews from anywhere I'd applied, just a few form letters of rejection, saying the position had been filled, but they were grateful for my interest, etc. etc. Griffin and I dallied and played as the days shrunk. A hand of cold brushed across the treetops. I bought a brown, knee-length woolen coat from Goodwill that made me look like a Red October revolutionary. I tried sewing little holsters inside it to hold bottles, Molotov or not, but they fell out with every test. I could suture a wound, but not much else.

The Asian girl from the party, Dalia, called the next week, and I stopped by her place the next weekend. It was clean and tidy, and it smelled like things had been earnestly cooked there, and of rosewood, and of candles. I brought a few books for her to read, and she loaned me a few. I went home that night and wrote her a poem, and another, and she wrote me a few. I came over often, not pushing myself on her, and on one visit, she had put one poem of mine, titled *Homeostasis*, on her refrigerator.

She led me later to her room that night, and played some Otis Redding. I held her hand where we sat on the bed's edge, and I touched the downy skin of her elbow, finger running the back of her arm, and then I touched the rest of her and I saw her smile into mine. And later, more, and her, and more, clothes slipping, and then her nipples stood high, where she lay, off her little breasts like berries, purple and round above the dimpled aureoles. Stunning and sleek her frame, and she taut and flexing beneath my hands. She informed with whispers me that she hadn't been with many men, and I told her not to worry since I hadn't either. I woke up Sunday morning early, the room chilly and her recombinant and moving near me amid her dreams. I nestled at her nape and breathed in. Her skin smelled like a lifetime of frail autumns in which mortal people looked up through clear branches at the clear skies, where no one's minds clenched like teeth for want nor veered toward death or debt in those fallen moments of terrible sadness, and when I fell back asleep I knew no thought but then.

There was a highwire tension on the entire block from the neighbors that pulsed from Squirrel Haus. A police cruiser would swing onto the street and park right in front of the house, and I felt like I lived in a fishbowl. I came home to another yard of cops after work on a Tuesday. Maybe Wednesday. A man lay face down, cuffed, in the lawn, wriggling. Our front door was wide open. The scene had distracted me. Otherwise, I might have ducked my head down and drove past instead of stopping. I recognized two of the cops from the regular stakeout and they me. One pointed to me and waved me over. I gripped the steering wheel for a moment, grabbed my sack of beer, and walked toward the assemblage. There was a large cooler in the yard. One of the cops pointed to the guy on the ground.

-Do you know him? he asked.

-No, I said. Why is my door open?

-This guy kicked in your door. One of the neighbors saw and called it in.

I looked more closely at him. He looked like a loadie. I'd never seen him around.

-He says you know him? the cop said.

-I don't know him, I said.

-Come on, be a pal, the guy said and wriggled some more. I was stopping by like you told me to.

I looked at the cop and shook my head.

-Which brings me to a second point. When we found him, he was smoking meth.

-Okay, I said.

-He was also in your freezer, the cop said.

-I had some goddamn ice cream, said the wriggling man. It's hot today.

I said nothing.

-We found a dead squirrel, a gravestone and a blue jay in there, the cop said.

-In my freezer? Holy moly, I said.

-It was ice cream, the man said. Chocolate chip.

-I will be honest with you, the cop said, that's three pretty uncommon crimes right there in my experience. You've got a wildlife infraction, a dead songbird, and graverobbing.

He opened the large cooler. There was a quart of chocolate chip ice cream in there alongside the bodies and the gravestone.

-I didn't have those things in the house, I said. This lunatic must have put them there.

-Who you calling a lunatic?

-They were frozen pretty solid, the cop said. Like they'd been in a freezer for a while.

-So, I said, this methhead is running around with a bunch of thawing items, breaks into my house to get high and then sticks his stuff in my freezer. Somehow that's my fault?

-You're saying the items aren't yours.

-That's exactly what I'm saying, I said.

The cop informed me that he'd have to poke around in the house, and that I should wait in the yard with his partner. He came out ten minutes later, finding nothing else incriminating. I examined the door jamb. Shattered. They picked the man up by his elbows and loaded him and the cooler in the running squad car.

-Did the animals die of natural causes? I asked the cop.

He stared at me and rattled off some police codes into his radio and drove off. When Griffin got home, I explained the event to him.

-Good thing we cleaned the place out when we did, he said, and his face became pensive. Graverobbing would have looked pretty cool on a ticket.

Patman reappeared suddenly a few days later, haggard-faced and many days sleepless, with what seemed a bushel of mushrooms. He wouldn't give them away, but sold them at a reasonable friend discount. Pressed on the subject, he revealed that he'd robbed the transvestite I'd met a while back. Rob from the poor and give to the poor he explained. After trading some beer for a few bumps of crank, Patman slunk forth into the night.

I took a handful of the hallucinogens the following Thursday and went for a walk, the psilocybin working only on the lowest volume. It was a cold evening, breath massed in front of the face, an accreted, transparent metaphor for life. I was on campus without realizing it at first, and walked by the Van Allen physics building. I'd taken a Physics class there many years ago, realizing that my dream of becoming an astrophysicist would never be. I was terrible at math, and I had the bank account to prove it. There was a rustle from the tree near the entrance. No wind. The tree looked like it was being shaken, throttled. I stopped.

The tree was hung black, velvety and palpitating, as if covered by a living cape of shadow. A form rose and broke from the undulating, quivering body, spread its wings and flew overhead, four feet from tip to tip. The tree was full of ravens. Many murders of them, all silent and shivering in the tall sycamore. I'd never seen anything like it before. Not one cawed. That undulate mass jostling and all their dark eyes shining in the hangnail moon, and I stood rapt for half an hour until a car horn from the street caused the tree to explode upward, black wing against windless sky, and gravity upended, and I stared for a long time at the tree bones afterwards, and then the sky, and again at both for a while even after that.

-Eat your heart out, Poe, I said and walked home.

I turned onto Daniel Street from work the next day, and Wim's truck sat out front. He was inside watching some news about the war. I hadn't seen him for a few weeks, not since The Ides of August, the day of the accident and the police. His little business was running along, and he was dating a Japanese exchange student now who really liked anal he confided. I nodded and mmhmmed to much of what he said. I traded some of my ill-gotten mushrooms for some of his product, and he invited me by to see his operation. I declined. Wim handed me an envelope, saying it was payment for putting the P2P in our basement. I thanked him and tossed it on Hellraiser. We smoked some crank and took some pills and Wim departed. I checked the envelope. It had three thousand dollars in it. I put it inside a book, and stacked some poetry books on top of that. No one ever disturbed the poetry books.

Dalia had called in the meantime, inviting me over to play Scrabble with some friends of hers from the program. There was a knock on the rear door. I grabbed an extendable steel police baton from the kitchen drawer and stuffed it in my back pocket, stepping over the piles of clothes and books toward the rear entrance. It was Michelle, agitated, her queenly face framed by her brushed back and nervous hair. She nubbed out her Newport on the side of the house and lit another. Sweeping the area behind her with her eyes, she turned.

-Hey, baby. How are you?

-Okay. You?

-Still goin crazy over what happened to Paul, she said. Now I got these cops hasslin me, drivin up and down the street watchin me.

-It's not exactly pleasant for anyone, I said. What happened to him exactly?

I hadn't spoken to her since the incident. She'd been holed up the entire time.

-He fell down the stairs there, she said, pointing through the wall. Musta been dizzy or somethin.

-Hm. Yeah.

-Say, you wanna buy any pills? I'm real short on money right now and need some cash.

-There are cops around, I said.

-Come on, baby. I need the money.

-What do you have?

-What do you want?

-Whatever you've got? I said and exhaled.

She emptied her pockets of pills and scattered them around on the kitchen counter. Pickle eyed her from the Harem, and didn't come close. She tabulated the cost of each, and named them, and their effects. I color-coded them for future reference, and handed over a wad of mixed bills. She lit another cigarette.

-Thanks, baby. You're a life saver.

-Anything I can do to help, I said. What are neighbors for?

I swallowed a good number of them, swept the rest into the drawer, and set out for Dalia's. It was cold that night, so I put on the Trotskyite coat and bought two flask-sized bottles of Canadian Club. I walked the forty minutes, with pulls from the bottle, to Dalia's, and up the three flights of stairs. Laughter rang out from behind the door, and when she opened it, a slew of unfamiliar faces greeted me from the floor, arranged in a circle. Dalia kissed me on the cheek and I put my coat in her room, coaxing her in where I grabbed and whooshed her up in my arms, and smiled through kisses into her ear.

-You smell like booze, she complained.

-You smell like purty, I said.

-Put me down. I have to get back to my friends.

-We could make love real quick, I said.

-Are you serious?

-Sure. Serious as Squirrel Haus, I said. I rise, and fall, to the occasion.

-Put me down, she said.

-Yes, ma'am. Want some whiskey?

We settled in together, and played some board games with her assembled chums. There was an Irish guy there I knew who had designs on Dalia, like an obsessive leprechaun and Dalia the Blarney Stone itself. I kissed her cheek and looked him in the eye and he smiled at me, raising his beer. I raised the CC and drained the bottle.

We played Scrabble, and someone added an S to a word. Someone else tried arguing that spelling a word backwards still counted, citing Leonardo as proof. Another spelled something she claimed was Klingon, which due to Star Trek's cultural relevance was technically allowable, and pressed for her triple word score, full of X's and Q's. Everyone had their own little idiosyncratic rules. I let out a sigh.

-This isn't life, I said. You can't just make up rules as you go along.

The Leprechaun smiled at me, and a sarcastic twinge to his voice.

-You're a riot, he said.

-You want a riot, I asked and cocked my head.

He smiled again.

-Sure.

I got up and kicked the board at him, wooden tiles flew into his face and chest, the rest skittering across ceramic ones far into the next room. Dalia shot up and grabbed my shirt, dragging me to her room, slamming the door, fixed and heavy in its frame.

-What the hell are you doing?

-He's being an asshole, I said.

-You're being the asshole, she said.

-Fuck this noise.

-They're my friends.

-They're not my friends, I said.

-Then maybe you should leave.

-Maybe I was going to.

-Then do it.

-My pleasure.

She pushed away my amorous offering when I tried to kiss her. Coat yanked from the bed, I opened the door and drew a line for the outer portal, stepping through the circle of indignant faces, stopping briefly to bend down and smack the Leprechaun for good measure, full and with a cupped palm across his wee ear. He rolled over like a Buddha-shaped punching dummy and sat back up, legs still in full lotus. I smiled and walked out and slammed the door.

My adrenaline reserves were taxed and the combination of the pills and meth earlier and the whiskey and everything swam in my vision where the stairs reeled. I knocked on Dalia's door, with gentle knuckles, asking for a glass of water. My words were working fine, though my legs and eyes weren't. She opened it, and I leaned against the jam and spoke.

-The Council of the Revolution will concede that you are beautiful. May I have a glass of agua?

-Go home.

-Tell that fucker he'll get his, came the brogue from inside.

-Come on out, then, I said.

-What is wrong with you? Dalia said. Leave us alone. I can't believe you smacked Brian. What is wrong with you? Dunham, you hit my friend.

-Wee little Brian, I said. Dalia, come on. That guy's an ass.

-You're not funny, she said. I don't want to see you anymore. Go home.

- I'll apologize to him. Bring him a pot of gold and some Lucky Charms.

-Go home, she said.

-Dalia, I'm sorry. It was a joke. I'm leaving.

I was speaking some other choice words as she pushed me out and shut the door again, and low laughter was heard and some untoward remarks that I could only guess at, unable to discern them through the thick oak door. I knocked again and tried to explain something, but it was no use. I opted against kicking in the door. Calmer heads. I inhaled deeply and made sure I had my cigarettes, gripping the walls for the sake of my jimmylegs. I cursed the random pills I'd taken. I knew there would be stairs to deal with, that tight little stairwell and its horribly carpented, irregular rises and runs. My words worked fine, but my head was spinning from one or all of the pills I'd gobbled, and my legs were taking the side of my head, ignoring their noble purchase on terra firma. I walked down the hall at a forty-five degree angle, my shoulder sliding along the wall, bumping over the doors and trimwork. A wordless lament escaped my lips at the sight of the Escherian nightmare staircase. The whole flight down to the landing stuttered and whorled like bad TV reception, flickering there and then not, a grey film inbetween. I raised my leg and dangled my foot out over the abyss, and I leaned forward.

-The revolution will not be televised, I said.

I was rolling down the stairs before I knew that I was. A godawful racket on the way down the wooden treads, my head knocking one of the balustrades loose and then my boot catching between two others such that my left leg was wrenched above me on the stairs and my torso rested flat on the landing. A potted plant on the sill above my head, tiny African violets next to the windows. Could those really be blooming now, I thought. Were they fake? Lying there on my back, I heard a door open upstairs in the hall. I wiggled my boot free and got up and over to the next downhill trial. I decided to forego pretense and tucked and rolled expert as a gymnast down the next flight, and the next and next, stairs to landing, stairs to landing, until I was dizzily but safely at the bottom and quickly out the door and into the night. I somersaulted down the grassy hill in front of the house, and jogged and stumbled home. My head pulsed against the ministrations of the cool dark air. Griffin wasn't home. The house reeked of bleach and all the windows were open. The kitchen carpet was soggy and my eyes burned. There was a note, typed out, stuck to the fridge, from Patman saying he wanted to help clean the place so he dumped bleach all over the kitchen carpet. Pickle had been locked in the basement. I let him out and tied him up outside. I put on the hazmat mask, set some fans on the kitchen floor and sat in the Harem, cold, in a dreidel of dark, each wall with a name unpronounceable and in a script I could not read, all of it spinning.

I woke in the basement, next to Pickle, both nestled in sleeping bags and resting on pieces of Styrofoam to keep off the concrete. He licked me when I stirred. The house was cold, but the bleach smell had dissipated and the kitchen carpet looked jaundiced. There was an irate message from Dalia, about me smacking the guy and all the noise and all the blood in the stairwell and on the walls. The hullaballoo I understood. Her landlady, Dalia explained, had been listening to us arguing, but I couldn't understand the blood at all. I was a little sore, but I checked my head and back in the mirror as Dalia's voice issued from the phone, yelling and crying because her landlady had made her clean up the blood everywhere. I tried to explain that it couldn't have been me. I was unscathed. There was no evidence except circumstantial to link me to the blood. I told her I was like OJ, except innocent. She cried and then hung up, and answered none of my four subsequent calls.

I had a Sunday morning beer, for courage, mixed with coffee and eggs. I made some for Pickle. He lapped them up in a go, and we watched some news together. Fifty, a hundred, a hundred fifty Iraqis killed. I shut off the TV and had another beer. I tried to paint, but couldn't, and had another beer and walked Pickle to the park where I sat in a swing under the weak sun and threw sticks out in the grass for him to fetch for exercise. I walked home. I deleted Dalia's message and another message from Fat Bastard complaining that we hadn't paid our rent. I rubbed Pickle's shovel-shaped head and sipped my beer. I called Fat Bastard, standing outside, and recorded the conversation on the Dictaphone. I got him to admit the general condition of the place, the Heart of Darkness, his side of responsibility in maintenance. I rewound the tape several times after we hung up, listening to his wheezing, listening to him try and shirk responsibility. Yet, eventually he'd admitted on tape what I needed him to. I listened a last time, sat on Big Red and drank my beer slowly.

Griffin came home from a weekend with Olateju, where they'd lain in an Edenic bliss, taking mushrooms and fucking the weekend long down on his parents' land in a little cabin there. They came in and dumped their assortment of bags and poles and bric-a-brac in the kitchen. I explained the bleach and Patman, and I told him about the Leprechaun and Dalia, and Scrabble and the Escher Stairs, and played the tape of Fat Bastard's confessional. He laughed and we laughed, and Olateju shook her head. I got a call from a bakery, a nightshift job I'd applied to the week before, telling me to come in on Monday at eight sharp, at the big mall in Coralville, for an interview. It wasn't the work I wanted, but work it was.

Dalia called later that evening and told me that another tenant in the building was the bloody hallway culprit. The landlady found this out after seeing the other tenant's hand and head wrapped in a thick blanket of gauze. He had cut himself coming home after the bars on our Scrabble night, fell on a beer bottle and banged his head against a dumpster. He was the one who bled all over the hallway and floors. Anaemic and wan and whacked out of his mind he'd turned the apartment building into a set from a B-grade slasher flick, Dalia apologized to me despite the fact that the landlady never apologized for making Dalia clean up someone else's blood. I promised to make it all up to her, and brought her some late-blooming flowers from a garden along the walk to hers. I made her dinner of broiled salmon and rosemary potatoes, and I bit her nipples until she squealed and sprawled, laughing, and I tickled her asleep. I felt like we could at least maybe always be friends.

I left the next morning, jamming the flowers into a widemouth can from her recycling. She was still sleeping heavily. I idled on her couch for a few minutes, thinking of rousing her, but opted against it. Let those who can rest. I walked back to Squirrel Haus, and drove to the mall in Coralville amid the highway traffic for the bakery interview. It was a shitty chain store, but paid okay and I could eat for free. There was vague talk of 'The Mother of All Bread,' explained in a cultish way by the stern-lipped night manager. I'd be tested on the company's Mother Bread backstory after my first week. I gave appropriate answers and was hired, beginning next Monday. I then drove over to Zeke's, and we did some odd jobs around town, installing a chandelier and repairing some roof tiles. He had some trim work lined up the next week, he told me, but not enough for two people. Being a baker now, I wasn't concerned. I'd have work for the rest of the week if I wanted it he told me, which I did, and the weeks to come in front of a warm oven.

Griffin was home when I drove up that afternoon, talking to someone at the front door. He waved to me and the woman turned to look where I was parking. I grabbed my tools from the rusting pickup's bed, and carried them toward Squirrel Haus. I had to admit, the scorched cowboy hat looked pretty good on Diomedes' head, nestled between the antlers.

I was introduced to Vera, Paul's daughter, mid-thirties, mother of two, accountant. She was asking Griffin a lot of questions about Michelle and what he knew of Paul before his death. I invited her in, for privacy, since Michelle was probably listening upstairs. Pickle startled her at first, with his size, but he dropped a thick rubber gasket, slimy with spit, at her feet as a sign of friendship, and sat back on his haunches, reveling in his magnanimity.

Vera told us, with a few tears, about her father, and his problems, which included heavy drinking, as I'd suspected, and idle drug use at first, which snowballed eventually, him winding up living with a drug-slinging prostitute not long after a major operation, liver wrecked by Hep B and the same chemical and liquid solace he'd sought after the procedure to patch him up. He'd been a lawyer, too, as I'd suspected, and stood a poster child for all those born or positioned or destined to lose. We were very polite with her, though, and offered what we could about him, that he seemed very intelligent, and polite, given the circumstances, and that we were sorry. She told us she was opening an investigation, maybe a civil suit. The coroner's report said that the body had been found at the bottom of the stairs, evidently an accident, but there was more trauma to the brain and head that was consistent with a trip down some carpeted steps. It explained the police presence.

She cried a little, but we had no tissue to offer, and I didn't want to offer her a page from the bathroom phone book, well into the P's now. Somehow, of course, there was a substantial amount of money involved, and Michelle had access to part of it or all of Paul's bank account, or something. Details became hazed and circumspect, and for good reason. For all she really knew, we pushed her father down the stairs and were in on the whole thing. We repeated what we told the cops, and tried to sound helpful, but we wanted no part in another family's problems. She gave us each a card, and said that if we remembered anything to call her. We told her we would, and shook her soft hands, and wished her well and said that we were sorry for her loss, which we kind of were. I shut the door after her, and watched her walk toward her Mercedes, looking back and up for a moment, but I wasn't sure if she was looking at Diomedes or at Michelle's. I turned toward Griffin.

-Holy fucking hell, I said. This is getting out of hand.

-Do you think she killed him? Griffin asked.

-She's capable of it.

-Or maybe she had those Chicago guys do it, he said.

-For a little money, why not? He's just some loadie to them.

-Wouldn't we have heard that? I asked.

-What? Him getting stomped in the stairway?

-Yeah.

-Not that night, Griffin replied. Not with those hippies here.

-So there's going to be more cops around here than there already are?

-Did she say it was a private investigation?

-Either way, I said, it's too much traffic for our habits.

Night flopped and a light snow fell, spare and cold flakes that hung in their slow arcs and traceries, as if all slipped down guy wires each and each and each. Griffin was reading a book on Big Red, and the news on the TV mute. I called Wim, and then Noel, and then Dalia, but no one answered. A car pulled into the driveway, and gravel churned beneath the tires like grinding teeth. The door shook beneath the heel of a hand. I opened it to find Dre and his two large compadres at his flanks. Dre looked pinker than usual, flushed and excited where he stood on the stoop. I nodded at them.

-What's up?

-We come in? he said.

-What's the occasion?

Pickle squared off in the kitchen, tense. I saw Griffin slip something into his pocket in the Harem before entering the kitchen, kneeling next to Pickle to calm him down. The bodyguards wouldn't take their eyes off of the 140-pound canine that struggled bodily where Griffin held him. Dre lit a cigarillo. I lit a cigarette.

-How's business?

-Aight.

-How's Wim? I asked. We don't see much of him these days.

-He aight, Dre said. Makes his money, same as me. You know why I'm here?

-Nope.

-You know who show up at my crib? Some detective, name start with a Z.

-The Ziggler, Griffin said.

-Yeah, that Zig-zag-ziggalon muhfuckuh shows up, aksin questions and shit bout some Michelle, like I know the bitch.

-Why don't you talk to her? I said. She's right upstairs. We had nothing to do with this nonsense.

-I bout to talk to her, Dre said. You two ain't mention me to the police?

-Why would we? We've got our own problems. Maybe it was Warrantt. He's been in and out of here.

He stared at us both, and then turned to leave.

-We cool?

-We cool, Dre said. For now.

-If you see Wim, tell him to give me a call, I said.

-Yeah. Aight, whatever. Peace.

Pickle grunted as they left and circled to the back of the house. We watched from Griffin's darkened room through the broken slats, then we heard them stomp up the stairs, and voices were raised and suddenly there was a lot of quiet. Griffin went to a box on his desk and fished around in the dark.

-Where's my gun?

-It's not there, I said. I thought that's what you stuffed in your pants.

-No, just some brass knuckles, he said. This shit is getting way too serious.

-I think it is high time to hightail it out of here, I said.

-Maybe. Where the hell is my gun? Griffin said, still rummaging.

-You think Patman took it?

-I hope not, he said. It's registered in my name.

That weekend, after wary nights spent looking out the windows, waiting for a hail of bullets to rip through the walls, and the labor of days, we went out to blow off some steam. I had another grip of pills bought on discount from Michelle, who looked somehow terrified and composed, with a black eye and her cheek cut and swollen. Eyes inscrutable, like a succubus. I called Monk to see if he was up for some drinks, but he, like everyone else, wasn't home. Dalia had stopped answering my calls, too. Maybe the Leprechaun had her under his spell.

We ambled through the night downtown and took a tablet of this and of that. I opted only for Percocet and some speed, washed down with gintonics, and beer. It was a calm night, and not many people were out. It felt drained, downtown, dry in the season and self-conscious, like the city was listening at itself, aware of the strange silence that issued no issue but a resolute and stark nothingness. We got drunk and started home around midnight-thirty.

Griffin eyed a number of pumpkins sitting on the roof of a porch, candles burning lazily inside of them, and no lights on inside the house. Halloween's long reach extending back into September. Fuck it, he said and scrambled up on the banister, one hand holding the white pillar, and the other securing a grip on the roof's lip. He let go of the pillar and swung his body around, getting his other hand firmly on the roof's edge, then pulled himself halfway up, looped his right leg onto the roof, and rolled up. The three pumpkins sailed through the air one after the other. Two lost their lids and landed crumpled and unceremoniously in the lawn. The third was a beauty, though, thrown like a knuckleball or shot put, and had no rotation. Griffin laughed from on high.

-Like the Headless Horseman, he yelled. Watch out Ichabodmotherfuckingcrane.

The pumpkin came down in a long arc toward me, face-first for a moment, spinning and glowing, and the stem-cap coming loose during the fall. I sidestepped it, and it hit the sidewalk path leading up to the house, exploding with a gratifying ceremony of orange shrapnel and a pulpy crack. Griffin was yelling something about the finer virtues of the hessians, of their equestrian skills and penchant for cruelty. Someone yelled out from the darkness.

-What the fuck are you assholes doing? the voice said. You motherfuckers.

Three shapes came running out of the adjoining park across the street, emerging from the darkness. They looked down at their fallen jack-o-lanterns and then up at the grinning menace on their porch, arms up, a vanquisher of the lesser vegetable kingdom. Griffin was busy cackling at the gods with his head back. The largest of the three stepped toward the porch and pointed up. His two friends eyed me where I stood. The guy pointed at the ground.

-You cocksucker, one of them said. Get down here. I'll beat your fucking ass!

Griffin didn't say a word. He jumped down, his arms still raised and laughing. He hit the ground, rolled in the grass, and stood suddenly in one motion nose to nose with the pumpkins' caretaker.

-Beat my ass, Griffin said. Go ahead. I'll give you the first shot.

Griffin held out his hand, with a little bow, as if about to ask a debutante to her first waltz and seduction. I said nothing, standing there with arms crossed, enjoying the show, smiling serenely at them all. Griffin waited for a swing and then pushed the guy a little, then grabbed his shirt, and pumped him in the gut a few times. Hard shots. The guy pushed back and sank to the ground, his friend circling in around Griffin's flank, deciding to test his mettle. I moved closer. I looked at the guy Griffin had knocked down and spoke to him.

-Queensbury Rules, guys.

-Huh, he said.

Griffin pushed one of the others, grinning.

-I suppose you hate the Jews, too, don't you?

-Huh, the other one said.

The gut-punched guy stood up, holding his liver. Griffin was walking up to each and pushing them, but he threw no more punches. Neither did they. A police car pulled up, and two officers stepped out. Guy number three turned to me, his eyes wide, and leaned in and whispered to me he had a couple grams of pot in his pocket and had two priors already. I told him to relax. Everything was under control. The police are here to protect and serve, I assured him. Griffin sung out.

-Hola, Angel. What's going on, officers?

-I was going to ask you that, Griffin. You two fucking up again?

-Nope, Griffin said. Just horsing around some new friends. We were just heading home. They have class tomorrow, and we've got work.

-Tomorrow's Saturday, Angel said, surveying with his flash-light.

-We're doing a side project. A remodel, Griffin said.

Angel swiveled the light at the three guys, to Griffin, to me, the pumpkins in the yard. His partner turned to the one Griffin had punched in the stomach. Angel's partner had cop eyes, like a dimwit owl. Where his eyes moved, so went the rest of his head. His nightstick was out, and he jiggled its end at the guy. He gestured his stick toward Griffin and me.

-You guys know these two, he said.

With labored breath the first guy said we had met downtown, and had all walked back together. We were fast friends already, and bla bla bla. Angel knew it was bullshit, as did his partner. Griffin's eyes were shiny with adrenaline and rum. Angel turned to the three.

-You three live here?

-Yes, sir, the one said, holding his stomach.

-Go inside, Angel said.

The three walked in, the third guy looking at me with a sense of wonderment, face a mask of puzzled perplexity. Angel turned to me and Griffin and sternly admonished us, jabbing his night-stick into each of our chests.

-You two, go home. I'm not in the mood for any shit tonight, he said. This is my last nightshift before I go to days.

-Thanks, Angel, Griffin said. I owe you a cup of coffee. The good kind.

-You owe it to yourself to stop fucking up. The only reason I don't bust you is because my father-in-law needs decent workers. You work hard, but you're just constantly fucking up.

He poked us each again with the nightstick. The three guys watched from their bay window.

-Yessir, we'll go home, I said.

-Yessir, Griffin added. Thank you.

-God, I'd love to pistolwhip both of you, Angel said. I can't wait till I'm on dayshift permanently.

We thanked him, and as we were walking away, Angel spoke again.

-Seriously, guys. How many times have I let you idiots go? Next time I will do my job and take you in. Scare you straight before the other officers do.

We nodded and waved as the two uniforms reentered their squad car and flipped off the spinning lights. It was true. He had let us go on any number of fineable trespasses.

We were only three blocks away from the Pumpkin Day Massacre as we passed one of the common rental housing units that littered the area of town between campus and the further-flung professional residents. Not inexpensive three bedroom places usually rented out by students whose parents could foot the bill. We passed the front yard where five large Neanderthals stood around a cooler under the lone floodlight that illuminated the scene. A squadron of insects dove in and corkscrewed at the humming lamp. Giant types of guys, with meathook hands. Two were tossing a pigskin back and forth. One of them bounded toward us as we were passing, with his hand pushed out to Griffin.

-Hey, there, man, he said. Nice to fucking meet you.

He grabbed Griffin's hand and immediately pulled him in for a headbutt, but in his inebriate state, he jerked Griffin's arm too hard and butted his own fat face into Griffin's cranium, instantly bloodying his thick nose. Griffin was now circling the guy, hands up. I sidled over toward the others, who stood there, half-wit smiles on each simian pate. At the sight of further blood these four might be sent into a frenetic berserker rage, ready to toss down the dregs of Keystone Light and join the fray. These were the types of hooligans who would write out their names on your chest in their own feces. Frat types. The future business leaders, city council members, investment bankers.

These thoughts raced through my head. Hell, hadn't we been asking for exactly this for months? We had just evaded a night in jail a few minutes ago. Karma's vicious little noose tightened quickly. They would pound us bloody, then go inside and watch gangbang porn together and high five each other. The sound of bone on flesh brought me back. Griffin had socked the guy in the stomach to little effect.

I turned to the nearest brute. He had a massive forehead, exacerbated by his thinning blonde coiffe. His eyes dim with cheap beer. He was smiling at the spectacle, largely ignoring me.

The potbellied brute was still tussling with Griffin.

-Look at my gut! I'm fat, asshole, he yelled. You can't hurt me.

Griffin kicked him in the shin, and he toppled over, his hands cupped to his leg. I turned to the brute who seemed to have the brighter eyes amid the dim sets.

-Nice night, huh.

The blonde brute looked at me again, and then back at his friend lying on the ground. He was a few inches taller than me. He didn't reply. I leaned my head in, just out of range of a sucker punch if it came.

-Look, let's get down to brass taxes here, I said. My name is James Constance. I'm a lawyer, interning right now for the DA down in Keokuk. I've got connections here in Iowa City, too. It's where I went to law school. I can get your friend booked on aggravated assault. He'll spend the month in jail. Maybe more. If he's got any priors he'll be totally fucked unless you guys can afford to fly Johnny Cochrane out here. He attacked my friend there. You saw it, and I saw it. You can say there were no witnesses, but I've got the DA on my side, and I swear I'll ruin your friend's life. He'll never get a job with the kind of record I'll lay on him. My boss is the fucking DA. He gets pulled over here in town all the time when he visits. He drives drunk, gets caught with whores, and they never arrest him. We've got friends on the police force too. You want to be marked men in this town?

It was an idiot-savant torrent of words, a bumrush of retard strength conjured from the dregs of adrenaline whose sheer improbability and webwork of interrelations would cause his brain to hopefully seize in a nexus of futility. I had thrown down every last card from my misfiring synapses, and waited, hands down and balled with knuckles white. Luckily, I was wearing my glasses which gave me a slightly eggheaded air. Would just enough cerebral activity take place in that prematurely balding blonde dome that he would fall for this ruse, to discern basic cause and effect relationships? Could I argue aetiology with him?

He looked again at me, then back at the ruckus. The larger guy was shaking his belly at Griffin again, yelling.

-I'm a fat motherfucker, he yelled. Fat! Take your best shot, motherfucker.

The other two giants started in, yelling at their friend to kill, go for the kill. He hit Griffin with a clubbing right on the neck and Griffin went down.

-You guys would be accessories to his charges, too, I said. Material witnesses, guilty by association.

The blonde guy looked at me and then at his friend. Griffin had him in a tight choke hold now, ratcheting down on the guy's thick neck.

-Yo, Jer-dawg. Leave him alone.

The fat guy relaxed almost instantly at the command, obedient to the tone of voice and its brevity and insistence. Griffin let him go, warily stepping back a few paces. Jer-dawg started laughing between his deep inhalations, rubbing his belly. Griffin circled back out, toward the sidewalk, and I moved toward him, circling the wagons. The blonde flipped his head back, his thick chin pushing out, extending two fingers from his can of beer at us. I cursed myself for leaving my brass knuckles at home.

We walked away, relieved to be walking away and not limping or crawling, spitting shards of teeth from shreds of tongue. We were a few blocks away by now, nearing the bridge. As I was congratulating myself for pulling off the ruse with a head full of Percocet and rum and nerve-frying doses of adrenaline, Griffin wheeled around in an angry flash, suddenly, after a long bout of silence during our perambulation. Stooping he picked up a rock and hurled it down the block. A second passed and then we heard a loud whump as the rock hit the side of a house off away in the dark.

-I'll kill those motherfuckers, he said. Come on, this is bullshit. They think they own the streets, that they can jump a law-abiding member of the fucking human community? We've got friends in high places.

-I know. I'll call the D.A, I said.

-No, I'm fucking serious, he said. We should go curb stomp those assholes.

-I know, but not now.

-We can't let them get away with this shit.

The rising indignation was something I would have to contend with, and I was in no mood. I grabbed his arm, pulling him back, leaning against his furtive jerking as he began walking back to the scene of our escape. He dragged me a few steps as I tried to gain footing. Griffin was muttering and cursing, with alternate bouts of laughter. I yanked his arm again.

-I barely got us away from those bastards, I said. Fuck them. Come on, let it go. Live and let die. Let's get a few beers and watch *Red Dawn*. Let those pigs rot.

His straining slacked.

-Do we still have that movie at the house?

-I am pretty sure it's there, I said. Let's go get some coldbeer and see.

The struggle ceased. He seemed becalmed. We were both heading back now. Then he spun again, yelling, his fist raised in comic salute to absurdity and the stars' witness.

-Wolverines!! You goddamned pinko fratboys and all your kind should be exterminated, he yelled down the street again. Come on, D, let's go find a radiator to piss in.

Another roar died dully in the still air. He turned giggling and cartwheeled through someone's lawn. We were both laughing now. It was a fine night to be alive, and free, and walking on our own two legs, like trained wolverines caught only in the traps of breath and step and the iron maws of every impending morning's workaday week promise, but we were wolverines and would never stop gnawing gnawing gnawing.

October

Baedeker

denial and light
a holding pattern's lisp
lodestar cobalt leaf

now insert the delicate
the grass and orange peel
patois of bloom

or a phantom pain which
proved this was all enough
this appetite or thing

this transaction lit from within
the skewer the vertigo the evenings
until the fallout east of body

As my friend (botany student, Congan refugee) just this morning clapped my back as we stood on the sidewalk outside the bakery after our shift, and he pointed to the sparrows pecking their solitary breakfast out of someone's vomit from last night, *Doonam, regardez ce-la,* as in, Blood of my blood, my friend, this place is enough, however much blears in the slant and flight of the reasons and the cold light and the rain to come.

Soundtrack:

Merle Haggard, *Are the Good Times Really Over*
Rage Against the Machine, *Calm Like a Bomb*
Ray Charles, *Hard Times*
Rage Against the Machine, *The Ghost of Tom Joad (live)*
Dwight Yoakam, *A Thousand Miles from Nowhere*
Jedi Mind Tricks, *The Wolf*

Griffin and I had nearly the same birthday, and nearly the same attitude toward them. I wanted to spend it in absolute ignorance and denial. Griffin preferred repudiation and oblivion. Noel, however, would not accept our collective desire to be left the hell alone and to our own devices and suggested we all go to a strip club, out in Coralville, just off the highway. Nothing better to commemorate the day of your birth, he rejoined us, than naked women. He waved his hand dismissively at our pleas, and I tried bribing him with girls' phone numbers and booze. Nothing would work. We would have to go. Besides, most of our stuff was gone. I called and invited Monk along too. I'd never been to a strip club. But Friday night we were shanghaied and hadn't a choice. Noel paused for a moment, walked the house, and asked Griffin what was wrong with the place.

-We cleaned it, he said.

-Why?

-Ask Dunham.

I informed Noel about the weekend prior. Griffin and I had separately driven respectively to our respective parents, jumping the hoops and eating the cake and opening the packages of socks, which, in stark contrast to childhood, were actually very useful now. I was hugged and kissed and shaken and my father quoted some Bible verses about forgiveness, and then I left.

I had pulled up in front of Squirrel Haus in the dusk and ground the gear into park, lugging beer and supplies from the truckbed to the door. It took me about ten minutes to notice that anything was wrong inside until I saw that Heart of Darkness was standing open, the plastic sheets ripped out and lying on the floor next to the bathroom. I had assumed it was the shower curtain at first and had paid it no mind. The general condition of the place was just above a tsunami-savaged Quonset anyway, but something was off. I flipped on the light in the Harem. Our TV and VCR were smashed, the stereo mauled, and the CDs were scattered all around. I looked in Griffin's room. All his boxes had been overturned and emptied on his mattress. Some of my books had been torn apart, the rest kicked from their precarious stacks.

The basement had been upended, and all the junk thrown into the bilgewater. The furnace was dented and a panel pulled loose. Washer and drier sat face down. Luckily, the gas line to the drier hadn't pulled loose. I righted the appliances and was bending the furnace's panels back into their flanges when I heard the door open and shut and footsteps. Walking back upstairs, I saw the window on the rear door had been smashed. Pickle was sniffing at the carpet furiously, and Griffin dropped his duffel bag, looking into the Harem.

-What the fuck happened here?

-Happy fucking birthday, I said. I've only been back for an hour or so. They wrecked the whole place. It's all trashed. Even the basement.

Griffin walked into the Harem, surveying the damage. He pulled a small pocketknife from the wall with a single word written on it. Wim. He handed it to me.

-Well, I'm guessing Wim wasn't autographing his handiwork here, he said.

-This had to be Laurence, right? I said.

-Looking for that P2P, he said. Holy shit, this has gone way past X-rated.

I walked toward Heart of Darkness, its recess black with mold and it breathed a fungal humidity.

-They ripped this thing open too, I said. I hope they get lung cancer.

-We will, if anything, Griffin said. Fuck, I can't believe they smashed my TV. That thing actually worked.

I got a stapler and replaced some of the sheets of plastic, tacking them back into place. Griffin came into the kitchen with his wooden box. The perps had missed the drug stash at least. He pulled the blinds and cut out a few lines on a CD case, and whooshed two up his nose and held out the hollowed pen. The message machine still worked. There was a message from Fat Bastard saying he'd be by tomorrow, with apologies for not getting back sooner. I called him, thankfully got his voicemail, and told him we had everything under control and that the rent was in the mail.

-If I had the money, Griffin said, I'd move out of here tonight.

Noel laughed as I recounted the story, and said he had a TV we could have as a collective birthday present, and a DVD player too. I gathered up as many dollar bills as I could find, and a pocketful of loose change. We had any number of beers at Squirrel Haus and a handful of blow, drove over to Monk's, and Noel chauffeured the four of us out to the strip joint, a nondescript building like a warehouse, set back in a nameless road near the highway. Coralville had been trying to change its zoning laws to get rid of the joint, but hadn't yet managed, so there it sat, parking lot full of cars, with no sign to announce what lay inside except what everyone already knew. We snuck in two flasks of scotch inside our jackets.

Inside was everything I'd imagined. Noel licked his lips and smiled broadly. Griffin went for beers and Monk and I found a high table next to the wall, stealing a few chairs from adjoining patrons. Noel was already flipping bills onto the walkway, and the girl strode over and waggled her breasts at him and picked up the money. We tried to talk, but the music swelled, so screaming was the only currency of exchange we could muster through the driving techno rendition of various eighties songs. Topless girls walked around and flirted with the crowd, announced with their stage names, etc. etc. We smiled at them politely as they made the rounds to our table, but I wasn't interested in ponying up my hard-earned money for the fantasy, one dollar or a hundred, and so they left me alone.

Noel came over to the table, slamming a beer, and grabbed me, plunking me down near the stage and walkway, the brass pole just above. He threw down a large number of bills on the stage and the girl slunk over, smiling. She was Midwesternly pretty, with a nice body, but I kept trying to look at her face. She squatted in front of me, leaning in, breathily speaking into my ear.

-Why won't you look at my pussy? she asked.

-Because I'd rather look at your eyes, I said.

-What?

-You have nice eyes, I said again, louder.

She recoiled for a moment and stood up as though bee stung, and though I couldn't tell in the pulsing lights. Within a moment there was a large bouncer with his hand on my shoulder, addressing the girl.

-Any problems here?

-No. He's a sweetheart is all, she said. He's okay.

-You okay, bud? Don't give her any trouble, bud.

-Obviously I'm not, so get your hand off me, please.

She danced away, but came back, bending and twirling, glitter on her skin catching the strobes and lights. She twisted her torso and turned back to me, pausing for a moment, then leaned down again very close to my face.

-Do you like my ass?

-Sure, I said.

-It doesn't look too small?

-It's perfect, I said. Why?

-I think it's too small.

-Would you prefer a huge ass, I asked.

-No.

-Don't worry. You're lovely, ass and all. I'm sure your vagina is lovely too.

She smiled, and did some more moves, unfurling her arms to the music. I got up and left Noel's money, gave her a wink and went back to the table. Monk looked uncomfortable. Two very attractive girls came by the table. One white and the other black.

The darker one had a regal profile, like a pharaoh, and looked kind of like an Ethiopian ex of mine. They sashayed to the music, and leaned on Griffin when I told them it was his birthday, asking him if he wanted a private dance. Noel said he did, and gave them the cash. The white one led Griffin away. I turned to the other.

-Are you Ethiopian? I yelled.

-What? she mouthed.

-I'm curious, I said. You look Ethiopian. Where are your parents from?

She looked back somewhere toward the bar and communicated something in stripper code and one of the large bouncers joined us, appearing as if from a trapdoor in the flooring.

-I'm gonna warn you once. You got a problem or something, bud?

-I was asking about her family is all, I said.

-It's none of your fucking business, he said and poked me. She works here. You're just a guest.

-I didn't see a sign outside that said no questions allowed, I said.

-You wanna get smart with me, bud?

-He's sorry, Noel said. Won't happen again.

-Last warning, bud, the bouncer said. Next time I'll throw you out on your fucking ass.

-Don't worry, I said. There won't be a next time. Buddy.

He moved away from us, but stood near the door, giving us the shiteye. Monk finished a beer and got three more, setting them in front of us. Griffin wasn't back yet, and Monk took a long draw from his bottle.

-You're pretty suave tonight, he said.

-Christ, it's a fucking strip club, I said. Why is everyone so sensitive?

-It's a strip club, like you just said, Monk yelled and gulped at his beer.

-Well, if that's all it is, then I'll oblige, I said. You got any change?

I took the heavy load of coins from my pocket and started surreptitiously flipping them toward the stage. The coins barely visible in their arc through the strobelights where they landed about the strippers' thoroughfare. I lobbed a number of them, and pretty soon we all were. Griffin got back with a silly grin on his face and his face aglitter, and pulled out some more change when he saw what we were up to. We flicked out dime and nickel mortars, hands low in laps, thumbs springing, the specie arcing, sometimes falling short on someone's table, and other times veering left or right and out of view. Collateral damage. I hit one guy in the head and he started like a frightened doe, turning in our direction. After a few minutes, the catwalk was slick with coins, and the stripper with the nice ass was sashaying down the way. She hit a patch of them with her left foot and careened bodily off the side of the stage. Some guys helped her up, and she was bleeding from her nose. Someone pointed in our direction and the bouncer and another stormed our way with his hands up. Monk dropped his beer.

-How did they know? he said.

I scooped the remaining change into my hand and hurled it in the first guy's face, then grabbed his denim vest and kneed him squarely in the groin and pushed him at his partner, who stumbled and fell over a chair, knocking over another man who spilled his beer, and so on went the dominos. The general crowd helped to corral the bouncers, stymying them, rendering their size advantage moot. I jumped over some other forms and pushed for the door, our escape blocked by a large Pacific islander, who shook his head at us. Noel and Griffin and I rushed him in tandem, knocking him back through the door, his huge fallen frame rattling the wooden porch as we sailed over his carriage and out to the parking lot. Monk was running ahead of us for the car, a low run like a sprinter. We jogged and laughed, looking back, half expecting a shotgun full of rocksalt or birdshot to come booming our way. Griffin was laughing, but Noel was pissed when he started the car and spun out in the gravel.

-Dammit, he said. I didn't get a lap dance.

-I'll give you one later, Griffin said from the backseat. Don't worry. Your birthday is coming up.

-They know my face now, Noel said. I can't go back there.

-Just get a girlfriend, I said.

-You're missing the point.

-I want to go home, Monk said. That was too much.

-Monk, no one goes home tonight, Noel said. It's everyone's birthday. Has anyone seen Brom lately? Let's give him a call too.

I used Noel's cell phone to call Brom, and he told me flatly that he couldn't come to Squirrel Haus anymore. Contact with us was wrecking him. I called him a pussy and hung up. We went next to Gabe's, the shithole bar where we'd seen the Nazis months prior. The skinheads weren't there. A band was playing upstairs, and the bar was crowded with the misfits gathered. There was the usual reek of piss, the strong ammonia kind, and everyone had piercings all over their faces. We drank heavily inside and out, preferring the chilly, mostly deserted patio to the noisy din. Noel sat up very straight for a moment, risen from his slump at the picnic table where he'd been braffing a few lines of blow off the edge of a credit card. He looked at Griffin.

-Where's Olateju been? he asked.

I nodded at the question.

-Yeah, I said. Where is she?

-Don't know, Griffin said. Don't care. She stopped answering my calls. Won't answer her door. Hasn't been at work in a while.

-Since when? Noel said.

-I'd rather not think about it, Griffin said, so drop it.

We made nice with a group of girls inside and invited them to come back to Squirrel Haus with us, bribing them with joints we rolled at the table and pills dregged up from inside our cigarette packs. They'd actually heard of the house, and Griffin and I looked at each other across the table, waggling eyebrows in mockery of our hard-won fame. Celebrities. I nearly got in a fight before we left when I asked a particularly pierced girl if I could borrow her face to scrape the ice off my windshield. Her boyfriend took offense, as was his right, but I told him I'd rip his septum ring out, and he backed down.

Monk went home, and said that Haley would be around in a week or two, and he drifted away into the dark on wobbled legs. The girls came back to Squirrel Haus with us, and Noel dumped out some fine white powder, and we crushed some other pills and gummed our noses with the medicine. At four, I'd had enough, and opted for bed. Griffin was in a haze, his eyes glassy, no one at home, but his body still functioning on instinct, buoyed by heavy doses of coke and meth and speed and by any number of pills. I pulled a girl from the floor and led her by the hand toward the boudoir.

Half an hour later there was a commotion and things were being broken in the living room. I put on some shorts and went to investigate. Noel was passed out on Big Red, with his arm around one of the girls. Griffin sat by a stack of CDs, mine, and was throwing them, one by one, against the wall, a pile of plastic half circles lying on the floor beneath. The other girl was following suit, laughing wildly, as I stood in the doorway.

-What the fuck are you doing? I said.

Griffin looked at me, but he wasn't there. His eyes were open, dimmed and they fixed on me. He garbled something and set down the CD he held. Finger pointed at them, I turned to go back to bed.

-Next person that throws anything is in fucking trouble, I said.

The moment my back was to them a CD whizzed past my head, crashing in the kitchen followed by another one that broke on the wall by the door. I spun around and Griffin was already up, laughing, crouched, but it wasn't him that stalked toward me. I put my hands out and low, in case of a bumrush, trying to calm him down. I had never fought him before, and didn't feel like letting Squirrel Haus bear witness to the first instance. I looked at Griffin.

-Look, I said. Calm down. I'm not going to fight you.

He sprang a jab into my face and I could taste my nose, feeling the cartilage crinkle. I countered with my left, uppercutting him under the jaw, and circled right, ducking under a wild left-handed haymaker that he threw in a lunging fury. I grabbed his arm, hoping to get a lock on his elbow or wrist, but he spun and burrowed under my left arm, getting the back of his neck under my armpit and grabbed my wrist and threw me down with his hip. I wobbled back up and hit him with a right cross that stumbled him and he ran straight through the next punch, knocking me into the wall where the plaster buckled and cracked, and I stepped on the girl's hand, her screaming. I landed several good hooks to his jaw, his chin taking each, and then he hit me with a straight right I didn't see coming which snapped my head back, tasting my teeth now, and I grabbed him, trying to pin his arms down. Looking over his shoulder where we jostled, I saw the girl from my room standing with mouth agape at the kitchen door, wrapped in my blanket, and her flesh like a clarion call, sirenic like a mirage, breasts and breast heaving with panic at the warfare in the Harem. I struggled with Griffin and looked at her for a moment, wishing I had stayed in bed. I hit him again flush and hard and still he came. He kneed me in the balls. It took two or three seconds for the rush of nerve-bending nausea to sweep up from pit to temple and down I went. He grabbed me around the neck, securing a headlock, and I stood back up, hunched forward to pick him off his feet, holding his forearm with my left hand to free some air, pumping my right elbow into his ribs behind me, over and again. He was beyond pain and sense, though, and I drove them sharply as best I could into where I guessed his liver to be, glancing my funnybone off his hip which dropped me again to a knee and gave him a moment. He slid his forearm around, the bone flat on my windpipe. I turned my chin into his forearm to get some room to breathe, and brought a cupped palm around behind my head against his ear, which caused him to release me. We stood, panting dumb brutes, each leaning forward in violent anticipation, all bonds dissolved and intentions of redrum played in our eyes.

The girls moved between us in the interregnum, each with fearful looks and soft words, and they led us each to our respective rooms as we cast furtive looks over our shoulders. Noel had never budged on the couch, and lay sawing logs with his arm around the girl who slept as soundly as him.

I woke the next morning, throat swollen next to closing, the peacemaking girl next to me, idle in her dreams. I kissed her cheek and got up and drank a few glasses of water, each swallow more painful, and everything tasting coppery. I blew black from my nose in a clump of scabrous, clotted lumps, and ran a piece of paper deep in, feeling the cuts and abrasions in the tissue. I worked the nose back and forth. It wasn't broken, but was a little more crooked. I went back in and lay down next to the sleeping form in my bed.

She woke me later with movement, a stretch, and I stirred and rolled my arm onto her. She withdrew underneath it, and slid out of bed, dressing in haste, and blew me a kiss as she left. I got up. The house was empty, and Griffin's truck was gone. I worked my jaw, and it popped several times in the socket. I took a few aspirin and a Percocet and sat out on the cold stoop and smoked while my jaw ticked and my body dopplered back and forth with pain.

A week passed, me working as a baker at night, cuts on my lips and head and in my mouth all healing. I'd gotten a strange look from the manager when I showed up my first evening for work, eye blacked and red patches of skin, knuckles scraped, lip swabbed with Vaseline. Griffin and I didn't speak that week. I couldn't speak except in a croak for several days, anyway, my throat healing. We'd pass each other without a glance in the mornings as I came from work and he about to leave, and I'd spend the evenings before work over at Monk's or Noel's or with the girl I met at the baking job, Jessica. We hit it off my first night and she invited me out for breakfast the morning after our shift. She was a philosophy major, in love with Hume, so we'd sit around or fuck or talk about the Scottish Enlightenment, getting drunk on cheap table wine at five in the morning as our break ended, and racing each other back to her place through the sleeping streets. It was an excellent first week of work. Besides, at any point, Patman could show up back at Squirrel Haus and wreak his havoc, or Wim, or we'd be gunned down in a hail of bullets by some albino gangsta's henchmen because of Michelle, or maybe a gang of wronged transvestites would show up, looking to extract vengeance for their stolen goods. Good grief, I thought, isn't this Iowa City, the Great Pillow of the Midwest?

After days of avoiding one another, Griffin finally broke the silence Friday morning.

-That was like white-on-white crime, he said.

-It was something.

-Look, I'm really sorry, D. I don't know what happened. I can buy you the CDs and replace them.

-I'm not pissed about some CDs, I said.

-I know. I'm sorry.

-I know. I'm sorry too, I said.

We shook hands with a rough hug, slapping backs. He handed me a Nat Sherman cigarette, a confetti varietal, red.

-You hit like a fucking mule, he said. And I think you cracked one of my ribs, I think. I can barely breathe. I can't lift my arms above my head.

-I still can't swallow right, I said. I think you realigned my throat and my nose.

-That which doesn't kill me will be replaced by something that will, he said. Maybe we should calm down the drinking and the drugs. I'm sorry. I was out of control.

-I don't think that would be a bad idea to cut back, I said. Holy hell, I totally forgot.

-Forgot about what? he said.

I went to my room and retrieved the envelope that Wim had given me from under the pile of poetry books.

-I didn't know what to do with this, I said. Then I forgot I had it.

-What is it?

-Money. A lot of money. From Wim, as an apology for the P2P. I didn't spend any of it.

-How much?

-About three thousand bucks, I said.

That afternoon when he got home from work, Griffin and I tallied our average daily consumption for the past many months: 2 packs of cigarettes, 20 beers apiece, half a bottle of liquor between us, between 4 and 7 pills in variety, sometimes 2 to 3 foils of meth each, the odd bump of coke, two to three joints for Griffin, four aspirin, and into the miscellaneous category went the odd ingestions of heroin, salvia, shrooms, acid and various whatnots. How we were even relatively functional remained a mystery. The fight was forgotten. We leaned that night into the future on four bottles of three-dollar wine, and within a few weeks, our faces filled back out. There were no more break-ins and we hadn't heard from Patman or Wim or Dre or anyone in weeks. Things seemed to be calming down.

I started inviting Jessica over to stay in the mornings and we'd pass Griffin in the weak autumn light, and he'd bid us adoo and shuffle off to work. I was still scouring the want ads, looking for pretty much any job, but the better-paying construction was slimming down for the coming winter, and most of the low-end jobs were gone too. Baking was okay, but it was tedious. I had imagined myself flipping bread and kneading the soft dough and learning a trade with a puff of flour on my cheeks, shoveling loaves and croissants in and out of brick ovens, but it was all prepackaged foodstuffs that came frozen on multilayered trays out of a freezer truck, and our only task was to stagger the baking times so that everything was cooked properly when the early-morning employees shuffled in with their pert uniforms and dozy eyes.

Most nights I worked alongside Jessica and we'd steal kisses or fool around in the freezer between punching buttons for the preprogrammed oven cycles. Some nights I worked with Lionel, a forty-year-old Congan refugee who was studying days at the community college so he could open his own restaurant. He'd studied botany back home. He was obsessed with owning a Lexus, and had a deep voice and laughed at nearly everything, the baritone chuckle resonating off the gleaming counters of metal and racks, a laugh like warm bread. We spoke French to one another, making fun of the boss. He was homesick. I was sick of home.

I called an ad for a limo service Friday morning when the Now Hiring appeared in the paper and they told me that they were still hiring for two positions, but I would have to drive north to Cedar Rapids and fill out an application. I drove north toward the airport, and I arrived at the main office around eleven. A plane was taking off from the nearby tarmac, and I watched its rumbling frame gain altitude and cleave the air and disappear into the azure. I hadn't been on a plane in years, and envied every soul on board their freedom to move, to move, to move. There were a number of black cars, and limos, and stretched vehicles, all penned behind a razor-wire fence. Another limo, presumably just back from a trip, was idling driverless near the office's door. I combed my hair in its beetly rear window, and tried to see through the reflective glass.

Passably groomed, I walked in and talked with the manager. The idling limo's driver sat in a chair, his belly large and his eyes as glazed as the donut he shoveled into his mouth. I filled out some forms and struck up conversation. The driver informed me it was a great job, and with the limos, business could be slow, but the tips were usually pretty solid. I'd work days for the first month or so, and I'd have to get my chauffeur's license, and pay all the fees myself, and pass the test at the DMV, and get some documents testifying to a clean driving and criminal record. I only had a few speeding tickets, I said, but was told that wouldn't be a problem. I knew my criminal record was miraculously free of legal detritus. I shook hands with Stu the manager, and offered the driver, Dewey, a napkin for his sugar-crusted hands.

I had the night off from the bakery and the day to myself. I drove home, fantasizing about the limo job, carting the idle rich hither and thither, in a little suit and shiny black hat, ferrying them wherever they wanted to go, and waiting outside the auto, sitting on the hood smoking, the meter running, while they shopped or fucked in the backseat, and I'd always be respectful and yessir this and no ma'am that, and there would be no shame in the job because there was no shame in being employed.

When I got home, there was a message from Fat Bastard, but I couldn't understand what he said, his wheezing enveloping the recording. I called Jessica but she wasn't home. Someone knocked on the door and Pickle turned his head and barked, low and dusky. I could see through the shadow cast on the blind that it wasn't Fat Bastard. I didn't even remember how much rent we likely owed him. I was greeted by a plain-looking guy, wearing a clip-on tie and razor bumps all over his mealy face. His right hand whipped out of his shiny Player's Club jacket with surprising rapidity and my left hand snaked at his, lizard brain response. What I found myself holding was in fact a letter, and not a snubnose Smith and Wesson .38. Just a piece of paper. He turned brusquely and motioned with his head over his shoulder.

-You've been served, he said.

Surprised that I hadn't been gutshot, I opened the envelope, and rather wished I had been shot. It was a court summons, scheduled next month. Plaintiff, Fat Bastard. Defendants, us. We were to vacate the premises by the end of the month, which gave us all of ten days. He was suing us for two/three months of back rent which we'd have gladly paid had he just done some goddamn repairs as was his job. There was no total listed on the form for what we owed. No matter, I thought. I went inside and found the lease, missing our initials, indicating that the house was not up to our snuff. We'd have our day in court and show the fat fucker the meaning of justice.

I went back inside and threw the letter on the counter, then checked the mailbox for any more bad noise. There was a letter there from Haley, Canadian postage stamp on the envelope. I opened it, looked at her looping cursive there on the page.

Dear Dunham,

I'm writing you here from Conrad's study, all the books stacked around me in double-decker shelves. You'd love it here. You need a ladder to ascend to retrieve the higher ones, and Conrad pushes me around on the ladders like amusement park rides. You'd really appreciate the woodwork here, though. It's so carefully wrought. And all these books in order, everything in order here. Except for me. I'm writing to apologize to you. I should be writing to Monk first, but I wanted to make sure I got this letter written and sent off to you, and I apologize in advance that it is so short. I've been a reprehensible ass these past months, but, you see my dear

Dunham, that I've had no mirror in which to figure myself, no real thing by which to measure who I was, and especially who I've become. This sounds stupid, I guess. I guess you're reading this and judging me, my actions, and now my words. You're always judging. I know you don't always mean to, but you do. When I chose to ruin my marriage, I chose to do so with you. That much was conscious, and that much was my fault. I need you to forgive me for that because Robert will never forgive me. I'm lonely here. You can't imagine how lonely it is with these people. I want something real, something beautifully simple. I want to get clean. I am coming back to Iowa soon. I, as you've noticed, haven't dropped any quotes into this letter. I am serious. I am tired of hiding behind other people's words, and pithy little retorts. That's all I do here. Then I get high. I am so fucking alone, Dunham. I mention nothing here so that I can mention everything when I return. When I get back, I need to know that you'll still be my friend. I am always yours.

All my love, yours,

H

I sat there and read the letter a few times, and thought. The phone rang. It was the limo company asking whether I had started my CDL license paperwork yet. I said that I had been studying the book since I left their office that morning, and would have it in a few days. He explained that I could start once I had it. They were shorthanded and needed the extra drivers as soon as possible. I said I would get right on it. I would work nights at the bakery, and my days would soon be filled with shlepping folks around. I'd save some money and leave Iowa. Since we were cutting back on our narcotics intake, it would be no problem. We'd need Wim's mea-culpa money for the eviction. Fat Bastard would keep the deposit, of course, considering the state of the place. That was fair.

Griffin came home. I showed him the subpoena. He laughed and got a beer.

-I've got a job lined up as a limo driver, I said.

-No way. Movin' on up? That's going to be sweet, he said.

-I hope so, I said. I can't take construction work anymore.

-Getting soft on me?

-No, I said. I'm going to live off of Wim's money. Where the fuck is he anyway?

-Hide nor hair for a long while now, Griffin said. He's off the reservation.

-I hope he's okay.

-You think Laurence found him? Griffin asked.

-Maybe, but I doubt it, I said. Wim's still crafty.

Griffin handed me a smoke, shaking one out of the pack with a flick of his wrist.

-I'll call his parents later tonight and see.

We decided to celebrate the limo gig and nothing and everything in particular, so we loaded into my truck and went downtown. It was chilly. I drove the heaterless pickup and parked it in the free lot a few blocks from the Pedmall. I'd called Brom and Monk and Wim and Jessica and tried Dalia, and Griffin tried Olateju, and I tried Kermit. Everyone was staying in.

We didn't drink much that night at the Foxhead, and then drove home. We stopped at the gas station along the way back, and Griffin grabbed a six pack of tallboys while I sat in the car revving the engine, trying to spread heat into the cab. My hands were fairly numb, but I was used to it from the construction trade, which I would gracefully be leaving once I passed the background check and licensing for the limo work. It was an easy two blocks back to Squirrel Haus, and finally a restful weekend spread out in my mind. Rest, and I'd spend the mornings at Jessica's. I pulled out of the lot, turning left, and straight through a green light, up the hill, past the porn shops, and left at the funeral home. I glanced in the mirror as I stopped in front of Squirrel Haus, just in time to see a squad car turning the corner. It's blue and red lights came on as it settled behind the Trojan Horse.

-Fuck Jesus, what the hell did I do?

-Did you signal? Griffin asked.

-Of course, I said. Where were those guys hiding this time?

-I didn't see them in the funeral parlor's lot, he said.

-Shit, I said. I've got a bag of pills and stuff in my coat.

I reached in my pocket and tossed it in Griffin's lap. Griffin took a baggie of weed from his coat pocket, careful not to incriminate himself by erratic movements. He drew his left leg up on the seat and stuffed the baggies into his boot. I needed something to mask the beer on my breath. I remembered an apocryphal trick, but I had to do it fast.

-Do you have any pennies?

-Shit, no, only quarters, he said.

-Does that trick even work?

-Hell if I know.

-I wish I hadn't thrown all my change at that stripper, I said.

I kept my posture very straight, knowing they could only see a dim outline of me through the thick plastic to the rear, and snaked my hand into the ashtray. There were some pennies stuck to the ashtray's bottom, gummed together with ash and some unctuous resin comprised of Moutain Dew. I'd ignited the ashtray when I stubbed a smoke out, lighting the mass of dried butts aflame while I was driving down the highway the month prior and doused the bonfire with Mountain Dew.

I managed to break a penny free and stuck it in my mouth, ashy cigarettes and charcoal taste. Griffin handed me his cigarette and lit another, trying to hotbox the car to mask any smell of alcohol. I puffed and dragged and could feel the filter wimple between my fingers from the heat of the inhalations. Griffin nubbed his Camel out in the ashtray only partially, its smoke winnowing up into the truck. He lit another.

Within sixty seconds of stopping in front of Squirrel Haus, we were joined by two other squad cars, making it a three on one hog-pile. I thought it odd. Why would they need more than one car for backup? Were that many cops casing Michelle's place? We had Angel as a character reference. By the time the officer arrived at my door, I had forgotten about the acrid taste in my mouth and was constructing my alibi.

I rolled down the window when the cop tapped on it with his flashlight, and was blinded a moment later by the bright bulb.

-Well, I thought I had arrested Cheech and Chong when you rolled that down, the voice said. What are you boys smoking in there?

-Cigarettes, I said.

-That sure is a lot of smoke, the voice said. I saw it coming out of the windows and thought you were on fire.

That voice, that voice. God, I knew that voice. His flashlight blinded me again.

-Just good old-fashioned legal cigarettes, sir, I said. May I ask why you stopped me, sir?

-Your tail-light is out.

-Which one? I checked them a day ago, I said.

-Doesn't matter. It's out. Now I'm curious, the voice said very dryly, you want to try and quote any more of the constitution to me?

Fuck. It was Welsh. Officer Welsh. The same weasel-eyed cocksucker whom I had brushed off with my pithy remarks about the Fourth Amendment those many moons ago. Can't the white man get any justice in this world?

-What exactly did I do wrong? I asked.

-You failed to use your left indicator when you made the turn onto Daniel Street, which led me to pull you over, and I observed a lot of smoke coming from your vehicle which was suspicious.

I knew my tail-light wasn't out. Griffin and I always did a spot check before driving home from the bars. No reason to give Johnny Law an easy, baited line to pull us over. Or, had we checked the lights that night? Was I imagining our diligence that night? No matter, I thought, the cops are real enough.

-Well, luckily I live right here.

-I know where you live, he said. I remember.

Griffin was looking down, completely immobile. I didn't blame him. He had an undisclosed amount of pot and pills wrapped in the baggies, stuffed between the tongue and laces of his workboot, and God knows what else. The other officer's flash-light seemed to pin him to his seat like an alien's tractor beam in an abduction movie. My mind raced. Griffin sat stock still, looking down, the cast of light made the whole car blue and sterile like an autopsy room.

-Please get out of the car, sir, Welsh said with a smile. I detect the presence of alcohol.

-I detect it too, his partner said from the other side of the car.

I could see a few of the neighbors at their windows. The whole street, normally dark and serene, was now lit up by the twirl of three cop cars' cherries and headlights. I did as asked, and stood, leaning against the hood.

-Don't you need to see my license and registration first?

-I know who you are, Welsh said. Would you please put out that cigarette?

-Can't I finish it? They're expensive these days.

-Put it out.

I dropped the smoke and stamped it out.

-You want a littering ticket, too? he said.

I picked up the butt. He told me to stay put, and leaned over and rolled up the car window, and shut the door, isolating us outside and Griffin inside. Some of the neighbors had turned their living room lights off, and I could see their silhouettes at the windows, watching us, like shades, from their dark spaces.

-License and registration, please.

I opened the door and Griffin fished out the paper. I handed the documents to Welsh. He scribbled some things in his notebook, and his partner brought over a breathalyzer unit. I had the choice not to take the field test, or I could go to the hospital and take a blood test, but I had no money to pay for it with me and no credit card, and not taking the breathalyzer, I knew, would automatically cost me my license for six months. I figured that I wasn't above the legal limit, and hopefully the coin in my mouth, carefully placed near my left wisdom tooth, would prove the stories true. I agreed to take the test, and Welsh told me to blow into the contraption's tube, in a humming fashion, informing me that if I blew incorrectly or tried to mess with the device in any way that he would arrest me on obstruction. I knew that was malarkey, grandstanding cop talk, but I followed suit, figuring that it might give me some time to figure a way out of the situation. Be polite, and be civil, like you were raised. Maybe justice will win the day. I hummed into the machine. He looked at the reading, and then at me. Obviously, it was not the reading he wanted.

He then ran me through the circus act of the field sobriety test, reciting the ABCs backwards, touching the nose, following the point of a pen with the eyes. He told me I would have to walk a straight line. He looked around, and with a grin told me that since there were no lines painted on the street we could use the sidewalk. His partner shut off the headlights to the squad car, and the other cops did the same. Now, the phantasmagoric scene ran epileptically, illuminated only by the wheeling red and blue lights, and his Maglite pointed down. We walked over to the sidewalk opposite Squirrel Haus, and he told me to walk down one edge of the cracked, uneven sidewalk, heel to toe, for ten paces, then spin around without lifting my feet, and proceed another ten paces.

It would have been a challenge during the day considering

the clumps of grass and dirt that overran the sidewalk's border, the sticks and debris, the jutting blocks. And hadn't I just spent months replacing blocks exactly as fucked up as these? He shone the light directly on my boots rather than the area in front of me so it was impossible to see. At step number seven, I hit my head on a low branch and waved it off, ducking under it on my return.

He told me when I had finished the fanfare that I had failed every test. I asked him how fair it was to make me walk in the dark, and he smiled again. I tried asking how I failed the ABC test. He told me straightforwardly that I had failed it. Failed everything. I started reciting the Greek alphabet backwards and he told me to shut up, then I started singing the ABC song *en espanol*. He grabbed me and spun me around and threw my hands on the hood of the car. He pushed me over the front of the Trojan Horse, and rifled through my pockets, patting my legs and boots. I looked at Griffin and tried to smile. Welsh's hand found my crotch.

-Is that you? Is that you?

-I donated one ball to a wounded veteran, sir. The rest is me, I said.

He leaned toward my ear, menacing, and I turned toward him and could see his chin jutting, all tooth and sneer.

-Don't get smart, or I'll have them strip search you downtown, he said.

-Downtown? For what?

-Contraband. Drugs. They'll run a flashlight up your ass if I tell them you're not cooperating.

-I was cooperating, I said. All the neighbors saw it. I've got witnesses.

-You've got what I write down. That's all you got, so shut the fuck up.

The time for decorum was over. He took my lighter and butterfly knife and the Dictaphone and my flask of decent scotch, and the cuffs went on, tight, digging into the wrists. It had all happened suddenly. There was no way for me to get my brain around it. A frantic unmooring of my senses, surreal, the whole thing slipping moment by moment by. I was having a few beers, going to straighten up, drive a limo, save some money, and now off to Sugarland, the hoosegow. The other cops just sat in their cars, watching.

I looked up again through the windshield at Griffin. He looked at me, his lips pursed, eyes glowing in the flashlight glare of Welsh's partner, alternatingly blue then red, then blue and red. Griffin rolled down his window and tried to engage the partner, but I couldn't hear what he said. The partner tapped the window with his nightstick, some words were spoken, and he rolled the window back up. The cop then told him to get out of the car and go inside. He gathered the sack of beer and sheepishly walked toward the house. Welsh was pushing me toward the squad car. Griffin turned.

-I'm sorry, brother, he said. I'll save you a beer.

-Avenge my death, I said.

Welsh pushed me.

-Let's go.

He shoved my head down, but not low enough and banged it against the doorframe as he thrust me through. The door swung shut on me, me there in the back, on the hard plastic seat. I ran through the whole scenario again and again. There was no possible way that he had seen me signal or not signal, since the closest car was over a block away. It was physically impossible, so he had been parked and lied about that, or he was outright lying about the taillight being out. He drove the car a bit past the speed limit, and I watched the lights of Squirrel Haus disappear as we turned the corner near the park.

-So you were driving and you saw me not signal? I asked. Behind me? How far were you?

-I saw you fail to use your indicator, like I said.

-Look, I just want to get this story straight. I think that's fair.

You've got your revenge.

-Revenge?

His voice was coy to the extent of cuteness. A smiling voice of personal triumph. I slumped back.

-Fuck it, I said.

-Did you just say fuck you?

-I said fuck it. I left you out of the equation.

-If you talk one more time and I'll have your truck towed, Welsh said. I'm doing you a favor not impounding it.

I sank further into the seat, resigned, trying to find a comfortable way to place my hands which were numb now from lack of blood. Dead. The police radio was bleating something, but I didn't hear it. It didn't matter that he hadn't followed any form of protocol and had bamboozled me. The neighbors couldn't be called to help. They had watched, had possibly seen the entire bullshit proceedings, but they were all sick of Michelle, and all the problems she had brought to the neighborhood, and we lived in the same house, so what did they care of me. We didn't belong in polite society as much as she didn't. Blight and pox. I was lost in thought, furious and beaten.

On the drive Welsh turned to his partner.

-You know, I think he did tell me to fuck off, he said.

-No, I didn't, I said.

-That a fact, the other cop asked. What was the alcohol reading?

-.93.

-I think he did tell you to fuck off, in fact.

I was watching this banter through the plexiglass divider, and when the cruiser took a side street and parked with lights off in a lightless alley, I began to worry, positioning myself in the center of the backseat. They both got out and opened either door. Welsh pulled at my coat, banging my head again on the frame and deposited me on the ground, then pulled out his nightstick, and stuck it into my chest where I lay. He prodded me again.

-Say it.

-Say what?

-Go ahead, tell me to fuck off again, he said.

I got up and he hit my thigh, then my knee and down again to the cold ground I tumbled. Again with the nightstick poking into my stomach.

-Get up.

I got up, and this time his partner's club around my neck, and Welsh opened my steel flask and sniffed at the contents. He smiled at me. The grip on my neck went very tight, jerking my head back, and Welsh grabbed my chin and stuck the flask into my mouth and plugged my nose. My teeth clanked on the steel rim and I gagged on scotch out of the gaps in his fingers and my nose, but the liquid continued to issue forth and I swallowed as much as I could, a struck panic along my back and felt like I was drowning in a river of whiskey, like an old bluesman's dream. The partner let me go and I fell on my face, gagging and retching. Welsh leaned down.

-You get any puke on my boots and I'll make you lick it up.

I coughed some more, snot and muck from my nose that I couldn't siphon back in or dislodge from where it coated my face. Welsh smiled at his partner, then at me as he grabbed my collar.

-Get in the fucking car.

At the station I was led in, limping and reeking of booze and vomit now, and I took another breathalyzer. .12. Over the limit. The clock read 12:43. I was led back outside after signing a few documents, and put into a transport with a few other guys, all blitzed out of their minds, obvious casualties of public intox infractions. At the jailhouse I traded in my clothes for county orange, had my picture taken. All my belongings were arrayed on a little shelf behind which stood a guard with a butt-chin and very dark skin, and the guard went through them. My flask was missing, and my knife too. The Dictaphone was still there. The guard riffled my wallet, laying out all the various IDs I'd been printing the past few months through Greg's professional lamination hook-up at the newspaper. The guard laid them out on the shelf between us, flipping each down with a slap from his large, dark thumb: My White Male Privilege Card, lifelong membership. My Mexican Lucha Libre/Hat Dancing/Home Depot League Platinum Card. My African Dirt Punchers Sport League and Team Affiliation (Congalese Division). My Styx Diner's Club Card (Two Pennies for the Old Guy). My Snake Plissken International Press Card (eye patch photoshopped in). When he got to my Old Timey Pickin' and Grinnin' Negro Minstrel and Spiritual Revival Membership Card he looked at me coldly, then back to where Greg's friend had altered the photo, with me in blackface. Olateju had thought it funny.

-Inside joke. Some of my best friends are black.

He glared, silent, and flipped through a few more, then threw it all into a large envelope, and I signed another piece of paper, and was led to a cell where a few shapes lay about in the half-light. The guard uncuffed me. Steel shut on steel, and I put my hands on the bars. So this was jail. Most of my friends had spent at least a night or two in jail, but I never had. Griffin had been arrested in San Diego for public intox, he'd told me, and spent thirty-six hours in the general holding cell with SDs finest street thugs, trannies, pimps and gang bangers, wearing only his flip-flops and a pair of board shorts until they gave him his phone call and his girlfriend bailed him out.

There was one cot open in the place, a lower bunk, so I lay down on the rubber mat, unable to close my eyes. The drunk above me snored violently, chortled bursts like choking on a tongue. I sat up and punched the underside of his berth. No change. I got up and paced the cell, listening to the cacophony, pacing back and forth. I walked back in the still cell, sat down on the lower bunk, scooted back against the wall, and punched the cot above me with short, tight blows to pass the time. He never stirred, gargling his tongue. Pop, pop, pop, my fist on the rubber, like a giant target mitt. Pop, pop. I got up and washed my face, blew my nose, taste of the vomit tinged with scotch still there.

At 4:30 in the morning, the cell lights came on, and a guard came down the hall, rattling the cage bars with a truncheon. We were given cereal and milk, with a bottle of water, and sat in the area adjoining the cells, seated along the floor. I drank the water and left the food. We were led back into our cells and waited until seven, then carted to another room and a judge came on the TV, and we were called individually to stand in front of the box, where charges were read and verdicts doled out. The bailiff called five people ahead of me, one guy getting 20 years from the TV for his third count of forgery and fraud. I was as eloquent as I could be with her. I was about to start in about Welsh when the Telejudge cut me off. I was fined five hundred dollars, would lose my license, and then released of my own recognizance, and the next case called. After I was given back my clothes I saw that my flask and butterfly knife were still missing. I checked the Dictaphone. The tape with Fat Bastard's confession was gone too. I asked the bailiff to check and see whether any of my things were somewhere in back, but he waved me off and said I'd have to talk to the arresting officer, since he was the one who turned in any items. I walked home and got some money from Wim's envelope. Griffin wasn't home. I slammed a beer and drove downtown to find a lawyer.

He said it would cost a thousand dollars to try and get me exonerated. I explained the story, the assault and the frame, but he said that the cop's story was the official version, and stuck to this even after I'd explained that Welsh had done it all simply because I'd invoked my constitutional rights. I paid him three hundred, and he scheduled a substance-abuse screening at MECCA, the Mid-Eastern Council on Chemical Abuse, the following Monday. They would evaluate my substance abuse and recommend treatment. I still owed the lawyer another seven hundred, and he didn't seem too sure he could do anything but get a deferred judgment, which I could do on my own. I stopped by Jessica's and told her the story, and feel asleep on her frilly bed for an hour.

Griffin was back by the time I got home, and I told him about getting assaulted by the cops, and the missing cassette tape, and the lawyer and everything else. I took a long quaff of a beer he gave me.

-There's nothing I can do, I said. Nothing I can prove.

-After they took you away, one of the cops broke your tail light. I tried to take a photo, but it was too dark.

-Do we have a camera? I asked.

-That was also a problem, he said.

-Thanks. I also have to do drug counseling.

-Just lie to them. Do not admit to doing a single drug. Ever, he warned.

-Why not?

-I had to do it once. They'll get real chatty with you, try to draw you out, friendly like. I had to do it after my DUI in California, and I lied and told them that I smoked a joint, once, just one, on my birthday when I was sixteen because my friends pressured me into it.

-What happened?

-The guy said I was a drug addict, he said, and I had to go to fifteen sessions about drug abuse. They cost a hundred and fifty for each visit.

-Holy shit.

-Just straight-faced lie. It's a fucking racket they've got running. I still can't believe they beat you up.

-King Fucking Minus, I said and finished my beer.

-That fucking sucks about the tape, he said. At least you got to finish your scotch.

I was in The Books now, officially registered as criminal abuser of substances, a menace to myself and the greater community, condemned by my own blood. .12. Never mind the cops assaulting me. I drove out Monday morning from Jessica's house to see the substance-abuse counselor to assess the severity of my court-appointed substance-abuse problem. The lawyer had given me a sheet of paper which listed all the various fees and fines, and the fee for my assessment alone was $50, scheduled at 9:30 in the morning, payable there in cash or cashier's check. No personal checks, just personal problems accepted. When I arrived I applied a fresh layer of deodorant, making sure to rub down my shirt, too, with some Jovan musk I'd found in Griffin's room. I got out and tucked everything into my pants, smoothing out the shirt front, popping in a few pieces of gum. I left my cigarettes in the car.

I was directed inside to fill out several forms, with a whole host of boxes to check, and places to initial, with boxes at the bottom of each page for my autograph. After twenty minutes of this and that box, marking *Other* for my ethnicity, I was called into a man's office. It was cluttered with folders and files, a small window with the blinds drawn behind his desk. I sat down next to a stack of boxes crammed and bulging with case files, my knees just touching the front of his desk. While the office was in disarray, the case-working doctor was not. He had a shirt that was painful to look at, it was so white, glowing like an incandescent beacon. He had a little gold cross hanging from the reading lamp on his desk, and a St. Christopher pendant too.

-Hello there. I'm Dr. James Cafri, but you can call me Jim.

-Hello, Jim. Dunham.

-Well, sorry, Dr. Jim, please. I assume you know why you're here.

-Yeah, I'm sure you do too, Dr. Jim, sir.

-Well, basically my job is to assess your level of addiction, or addictions, and to suggest ways that you can cope with and beat them. Was this your first arrest for drunken driving?

-Yes, first and last, I said. Most certainly.

He scribbled.

-Okay, let's begin at the beginning. Do you consider yourself a heavy drinker? Have you had any history of substance use or abuse? Or perhaps in your family?

-No, sir. That night was my first real drinking experience in a long time. It was my friend's birthday. He was in the car with me and had hurt his leg falling out of a tree, and that's why I drove. He couldn't work the pedal.

-A tree? What happened?

-You see, he's a lover of nature. We call him Nature Boy. He wanted to be a biologist, but he can't spell. He's dyslexic and his teachers in college thought he was slow. He dropped out, but he never lost his passion. He was climbing a tree, to get a look at some squirrels, and it had been raining and he fell.

He looked at my arrest sheet.

-He was climbing a tree at night? That night?

-He was after squirrels, I guess. Yes, that night.

-Squirrels, he said flatly.

-Something about research on nesting habits. You'd have to ask him.

-So he's okay now?

-It's a sprain. Nothing was broken. He'll be more careful, though. That's for sure. I was just giving him a ride and we'd had a few beers for the pain.

-And for his birthday?

-Yes, I said. To celebrate.

A youngish woman interrupted this, telling Dr. Jim that something something something.

-Okay, he said. Well, we've got to move through this. So, when was the last time you consumed alcohol?

-You mean prior to my incarceration?

-Yes.

-Maybe when I was an undergrad, and a few times as a

graduate student, I said. When I was accepted and once when I graduated. I was a double major as an undergrad in English and Philosophy with a Spanish minor, so I was way too busy to do much drinking. Sometimes I would have a glass of wine at dinner with my girlfriend. Why is this place called MECCA anyway?

- So you never drink alone? How much wine did you consume on average per month? Where did you go graduate school?

-Alone? Never, I said. Who has time? As for how much wine, I would say a glass or so. It was a long time ago. Do you like wine?

- Oh, well, once in a while, when I have Italian food. So you prefer beer?

-I don't have a preference. I missed church the next day, after I was arrested.

-You mean you don't care what you drink?

-No, no, I mean that it's all the same to me because I rarely have time to drink.

-So you've been around drugs, you say.

-Did I say that?

-You've never tried pot, even? Not once?

-No, sir.

-Come on. Really? If it's just once you can tell me. It's not the worst thing in the world.

-I think I must have been around 14, maybe 15. Some friends of mine tried it, and I was hanging out with them and there was a lot of smoke in the car. They had some of it, and I really didn't want to try it. Even the smell of it actually made me vomit. I didn't like it. I was a long-distance runner. I almost made state.

-And you inhaled, he said with a flat tone.

-No, it was all second-hand. I coughed a lot and then I threw up. It made me feel awful. I was in cross-country, and didn't want to ruin my lungs.

-Do you smoke now?

-Smoke what? What are we talking about?

-Cigarettes, anything else, stuff like that.

-No, well, I do smoke cigarettes sometimes. There's a chemical correlative between nicotine and caffeine. I drink coffee every morning. They complement each other. I don't smoke too much, though, since I still run quite a bit, and I'd like to get back in to boxing.

-A boxing writer who knows chemistry? This sounds like you're quite the character.

I stayed silent. He looked at the clock on the wall, and scribbled loudly.

-Well, Dunham, I have another appointment coming in soon. In fact, it looks like he's finishing up the paperwork now. I am going to recommend to the court that you undergo the weekend counseling session, in two weeks. It takes two days, a Saturday and a Sunday. We'll send you your reservation and the information packet, which should arrive next week. It costs four hundred dollars, and you can pay now or at the hotel reception when you get there. Cash, cashier's check or credit card are all fine. You seem like a good, well-intentioned person, with a bright future. Just be sure to make better decisions in that future if you want to keep it bright.

-Oh, I will, Doctor Cafri. You can count on it.

-Okay, Dunham, take care, and God bless, and good luck with your writing. I hope to see you at St. Mary's in the future.

-Yes, thank you, and good luck with your counseling. Go east, young man. Praise be to Allah, and Muhammad is his prophet.

I stomped the bright hallways to the exit, glowering. I drove toward Squirrel Haus. The substance-abusing weekends had turned into the substance-abuse-intervention weekend, and would cost another four hundred dollars. I had luckily escaped the additional counseling sessions. I stopped and got some beer, and decided to drive over to Noel's for some coke if he had it. Just a tiny taste. I needed a little pick up. When I explained the story, he gave me a gram for free. Consolation. Griffin had called him and told him about the police brutality earlier. We nattered for a few hours and I went home.

Griffin's truck was gone when I pulled up in front in front of the house. There was a car parked in the driveway, probably for Michelle. I didn't recognize it. She wouldn't have to worry about being evicted. She was on Section 8 housing and got her rent comped. We'd soon be rid of her and Fat Bastard and the Heart of Darkness, I thought, and walked inside. Pickle didn't greet me, and I assumed Griffin had taken him for a constitutional. I checked the machine in the kitchen and there was another message from the limo company, and one from Wim telling me to call him but he neglected to leave the number. I deleted it and put the beer in the fridge, and opened a can. I heard a sound behind me.

-What were you waiting for, Pickle, a goddamned invitation to the kitchen?

I turned and saw the image of a large revolver, held sideways, grow in slow motion very large in front of my face, nickel plated, its oddly long cylinder moving toward me. Just before it slammed into my nose, I thought, What an oddly long cylinder. Oh, that would be a Taurus Judge. Then my vision went red as my head bucked back and a shock splintered my nose.

I was knocked down, tasting the salt and copper in the blood that ran down the back of my throat and out across my lips. Blinking my eyes for a moment until I could see through the haze, I looked up and there was Dre and his two cronies, and the revolver pointed at me. I checked my nose, and it didn't seem to be broken. My teeth felt intact. I still had the can in my hand, and ran the back of my hand across my lips to clear the red. I put my hands up, shoulder height from where I crouched, took a drink from the can to clear my mouth and spit the mixture to the floor.

-What the fuck are you assholes doing?

-We the assholes now, Dre said?

-What the hell, Dre? I told you I didn't talk to the cops about you.

-That was your boy Wim on the machine. Where he at?

I touched my nose and wiped a thin trail of blood.

-I don't know. I haven't seen him for weeks.

-What about the other one?

-They don't live here, I said.

-Yeah, well, yo boy fucked up.

-Who?

-You know who.

-Who?

-That hippy muhfuckuh.

-Patman?

I got up, my hands still raised, and had to lean against the counter. My equilibrium was out of whack, and I was spitting blood. The revolver tracked me and Moon cocked the hammer when I reached into and fumbled a smoke out of my shirt pocket. The walls reeling and vertiginous. I worked my jaw around trying to ease the ache that had spread in concentric circles to the rest of my head and shoulders, a throb reaching from the ears outward. I tried to remain calm and find out what warranted me taking a pistolwhipping in Patman's stead. Dre shrugged his shoulders a little, and jutted his chin out.

-So where's your boy?

-Dammit, Dre, what did he do? I think you cracked one of my fillings. It's not like I can afford to fix anything.

-You tellin me you don't know? Now, I know you and your other boy ain't got the balls go robbing shit, but I gotta ask. You tellin me you don't know?

The gun leveled at me.

-Know about what? Christ, I'm lucky I don't have a fucking hematoma right now or a concussion.

-I can make that happen, muhfucka. It's gon get worse for you,

you don't tell me what you know and what you don't know.

-How can I tell you what I don't know? What did he do?

Dre set in, his good eye flashing red in the light. Patman had evidently convinced Warrantt to flip on Dre, and they'd robbed Dre's little drug den together.

-How the fuck I ain't gon know it was one of my boys? he said. That mufucka dumb. Always been.

Hun nodded.

-Where's Warrantt? I asked.

-He ain't none of yo concern. No one's concern no more.

-So how do you know it was Patman?

-Caught up with Warrantt and he fessed everything. We aksed him real nice.

Hun nodded again, with a smile.

-Now, Dre continued, I wan find out if yo boy had anything to do with this shit.

-Who, Wim?

-Who the fuck else I talkin about? Yo hippie friend a dead mufucka when I catch him. He robs my place, and who else got cock and puss tattooed on they hands? Mufucka had a James Bond gun and everything. Didn't even bother to wear gloves or nothin.

I took a step back and fished out another smoke. This would have all been hard to process on a clear sunny day over a cup of chamomile tea, but with a cracked tooth, bleeding nose and gun, impossible. Dre turned to his compatriots.

-Moon.

The big man moved at me and grabbed my shirt. The gun tilted at my head.

-Where they at? Dre asked calmly.

-I don't know, Dre. I really don't.

-Where they at?

Moon cocked the hammer.

-Could you please take that gun off me?

-Moon.

The hammer was lowered, and came down on my head again, but more politely this time. I fell against the counter and he let go of my shirt.

-Look, I haven't seen Patman in weeks, I said. He disappeared. Someone broke in our house a week or so ago. Then some methhead broke in. Wim's missing. I just got out of jail a couple of days ago. I don't know anything.

-What was you in jail for?

-OWI.

They all laughed. Moon laughed so hard he doubled over, the pistol shaking in his grip.

-Imma find that mufucka. Mark my words. Imma skullfuck that motherfucker, nomesane, when I get him.

-I believe I do know, I said.

-Aight, let's bounce.

The pale gangsta and his posse left, cold air rushing in the open door, and I sat against the counter, nursing the beer and holding the can against my nose, inhaling and exhaling through it slowly, wiping the dribbled blood. Too many weird angles. There was a bill from the phone company on the counter. Our *National Geographic* ruse-account had finally run out. We'd be out of Squirrel Haus, and not a moment too soon. I heard a whimper in the other room, raspy. I walked into the Harem, and found Pickle in a pool of blood in Griffin's room, stabbed in the side of his chest with a screwdriver. The wound bubbled and sucked with his short breaths through dark fur. His eye fixed on me. I ran to him, crouching by his side, my hand in the warm blood. I touched his head and he whined again.

-Pickle Pickle Pickle.

I ran to the phone and called Brom and told him I needed his help and to bring his med bag. I called Noel. Hands bloody and shaking, I ran over to the funeral home, but the lot was full and I ran back. I didn't know where to go. Brom was over ten minutes later and found me cradling Pickle's massive head on my lap. He muttered Jesus over and over, and Noel said nothing when he arrived. Brom said he'd been stabbed in the lung and there was nothing to do. He'd choke on his own blood. I rubbed his fur under his jaw and for a moment his tongue lolled and the blood dripping still. His big eye fixed on mine, shone there a moment, shone there a few more moments, and went dull. I rubbed his ears and put my mouth there, saying his name over and over, and we all cried.

Griffin came home, drunk, an hour later, bellowing as he opened the door.

-D, things just got X-rated, he said. You won't fucking believe this.

He came into the living room and saw us, still sitting around Pickle, wiping the tears from our noses. He stared a long minute, the sight registering. He managed to ask what had happened, and then he broke at the explanation. We three had to hold him as he raged and screamed, spit flying from his teeth, and he swore to kill Dre and Hun and Moon. We calmed him as we could, and after a few more heaves against us, he settled into a low, rolling weep, shuddering and heaving quietly. He sat down, holding the dog's head in his arm and beating the floor with his fist. We left him and gathered in the kitchen.

He joined us half an hour later, clearing his throat with half a can of beer, and wiped his eyes.

-He needs a funeral..

November

Mythos

That day that X called me about his wife.
Called and said she'd gone missing.
Obviously didn't know about her affair

with me three months prior. When she came back,
she said she spent the whole day looking at pearl-
handled straight razors, *just to look*.

Now she's disappeared within the confines
of a map no one owns. So tell me what's exempt.
I've admitted to the human form.

I've allowed for the dubious prayers,
and allotted tragedies like fingernail clippings.
I have rubbed the dull crown-metals clean.

This is the way Mars and Jupiter and Venus
don't even shine unbeholden in their bric-a-brac
dark. Theirs is a steady passion and combinant

failure to be more than gauzed bodies on an autopsy
table, failing like that gravity that each body draws and gives
in echoic traceries, attempting to attract even simplest words,
like

the failure of the shadows across drawn draperies,
the failure of the payphone that rings and rings on the corner, the failure
of the moans and yelling from the anterior room of the rental house,

these persistent and nearer instances pulsing like the thin nervous
blue of the waning winterlight falling elliptic, helpless, on these houses
lining the street on my walk home, full of a light of their own.

Soundtrack:

Rage Against the Machine, *Bulls on Parade*

George Jones, *Still Doing Time*

Tom Waits, *Come on Up to the House*

Richard Hugo, *Degrees of Gray in Philipsburg*

The Kossoy Sisters, *I'll Fly Away*

Warren Zevon, *Keep Me in Your Heart*

Griffin, Noel and I hauled Pickle's frame with a tarp into Griffin's truck the next day, our eyes red-rimmed and heads gauzy. We drove south to Griffin's parents' land. We spent the morning felling trees, chainsaws braying in the still air, and the slow split and crack of the frozen trees as they swung to earth. We cut them to length and hauled them with a small tractor his father kept in a shed up to the top of a hill, overlooking the pond. A dock floated out in the middle, water reflecting the white sky, dock a tiny iris therein. We set to notching the ends, and stacked the pyre, filling it with smaller branches. We poured kerosene and motor oil on the stack, laying Pickle's massive frame there, wrapped in a sheet. Griffin leaned over the shroud, said a few quiet words, and lit the bottom of the mass. Flame built slowly and we passed a bottle of whiskey between us, tears slow and quiet down our faces that dried in the gnawing heat of the fire.

-It would kind of be nice if it was raining, Griffin said. Maybe some bagpipes or something, too.

He forced a laugh, and Noel then I laughed and hugged his shoulders. We stood, wiping our noses and eyes, and the fire grew larger and we had to take a step back, and another. The fire swelled and lurched and did its thing until the heap collapsed into a spray of spark and ash an hour and a half later. Later still only a mound of smoking char. Griffin kicked a smoking log-end with his boot and tossed in the bottle and the remainders therein. He turned and nodded and walked back to the truck. We drove back to Iowa City wordless. Griffin walked inside Squirrel Haus and scrubbed the dried blood from his wooden floor with a chunk of steel wool and a shirt. The paint on the floor came off, but the blood had sunk into the grain, indelible.

We had five days left at Squirrel Haus, and I had the counseling weekend coming up, and we had court as well, and a drug dealer who wanted to murder a friend, another drug dealer nearly murdered by a friend. And Pickle. And the phone bill. Griffin came into the kitchen and brought a round of beers to me and Noel. We braffed a few lines off the counter for courage, went downtown to a bar, talked for several hours, and started home, Noel to his and we to ours, walking through the evening, in the haze of cold and wind, the scape stripped of any poetry and its etcaetera, bones of trees along the avenues and their voices full of etcaetera, and the lidless headlights that rolled dully along the etcaetera, and the bleary grey Midwestern skies fettered with clouds a dull dirty orange etcaetera, wrapping the night in a cocoon of gauzy etcaetera. We hustled through the streets for the cold. We came down Johnson Street, trailing two guys ambling ahead of us. They paused outside an apartment building, lighting their cigarettes under the big-watted florescent lamp. One of them turned to look at us passing in the dimness. We passed by and I grabbed Griffin.

-That's them.

-Who? he said.

-Remember, that fat fuck and his friends who started that fight? The fat guy? Those frat assholes.

-The frassholes?

-That's him. And the tall blonde guy too.

Griffin squinted their way.

-What do you want to do? he asked.

-Serve a little justice.

-Squirrel Haus Justice. For Pickle.

We slid off to the side of the building and they finished their cigarettes and went inside. We followed at a discreet remove, and scurried after them, coming in the opposite set of doors in the rear of the building, and watching from the stairwell as the two plodded inside and up to the second floor. We pinpointed the room and set our coats in the nearer stairwell. We wrapped our scarves around our faces, and removed our belts and wound them around our right hands, buckles hanging with a solid seven or eight inches of play. I listened at the door. There were two sets of voices, amid the din of a sporting event on the television, moving around the apartment. Only two people home. Jer-Dawg and his giant, Swedish mongoloid friend on whom I'd managed the ruse. I knocked on the door, giving Griffin a nod, and stuck my thumb over the peephole, my arm extended from where I stood by the hinges on the right.

-Yo, Jer-Dawg, it's Chet. Open up, dude, I said.

There was some rustling inside and footfalls, and a voice intoned something. The bolt shunted and the knob turned, and as the door opened Griffin wound up and kicked at it, snapping the chain and delivering the steel door full into the pudgy face, knocking Jer-Dawg's fat frame down and in we stormed. Griffin swept the door shut and was raining fists and the buckle onto the prostrate body that curled doubly over into a little wigwam, and I hurdled a couch straight at the blongoloid who was eating a bowl of cereal in the kitchen, Captain Crunch with Crunchberries, the box open, next to a gallon of milk on the counter. He stood there in a sleeveless wife-beater with spoon nearly in his mouth, in full shock at the sudden apparition of two strangers in his tidy abode flying in like a dervish of rabid howler monkeys and bearing down on him and his roommate with very obvious bad intention.

I slapped the metal buckle across the bridge of his nose, and brought it back against his jaw. I was splashed by some milk and bits of food as the bowl dropped and he with a whimper dropped, holding his broken and blood-battered face. I kicked him in the stomach and punched at his nose repeatedly with the fist-wrapped leather.

Fighting, in its undistilled and raw form, was an ugly thing to be a part of, regardless, and few that are regularly involved in it would admit, but no one really wins a fight. The next day, full of sore hands, sore heads, loose teeth, swollen eyes, limps from the kicks to shins, blood in the nose for a week, swollen testicles, aching knees, and often a hitch in the back from wrenching and wrestling on the ground. There were no winners. Fate, or the seven mad gods, or we, had stripped the world back to the color of chaos. We stomped the fear of Pickle and Squirrel Haus and Diomedes into the crumpled pair.

What we did to those two was not fighting. It was violence. Furied movement through space occupied by someone else, and it was not fair and it might not even have been deserved. I lashed the blonde several times across the back and face and shoulders with the buckle, and wherever he rolled exposed a new spot of flesh and the belt swung and he writhed and screamed in high-pitched peals. Griffin had clubbed Jer-Dawg unconscious and stood panting over where he lay, his mouth gaped, thick blood like slathered plaster on his face. I lifted my boot and brought it fully into the blongoloid's stomach again. He rolled on his side, his arms and face a mottled mess of crimson and welts that rose from his pale skin in sickening red splotches of burst blood vessels beneath the flesh, like a lily's petal, speckled and dappled and grained with flecks of red. He put up an arm, sobbing, his face turned to the floor, and his other hand coiled in his yellow hair, slick now with bates of blood. I stopped, and Griffin grabbed my arm and pulled me out of the apartment. No one was in the hall. No one had heard. We retrieved our coats and ran through an alley behind the complex toward Squirrel Haus. Home, we had a few more beers and never spoke of The Frassacre again. When we checked the papers the next day, no mention was made in the police reports. We washed our clothes and belts several times, and ourselves, bleaching all the while.

Whenever home for those remaining few days, the nerves were high. Hammers or brickbats or blunderbusses at the ready. Griffin's gun was gone, so we spent a lot of time looking cautiously out the window through the edge of the blinds holding hammers or Griffin's club. Out of everyone, Noel stuck with us, regardless, coming over once in a while to help with repairs or surveillance. I quit the bakery job after securing a third-shift copy-editing gig through a temp agency, but was still snuggling with Jessica regularly. Griffin and I fixed and cleaned the house as best we could on our last day there, knowing that Fat Bastard would regardless keep the deposit, meaning we only owed him two months of rent, which seemed like a ridiculous amount to sue someone over. We left unceremoniously, at night, and Griffin stood on my shoulders to unmount Diomedes from above the door, brushing the thin dusting of snow from his nappy and peeling fur. We threw the few boxes of our stuff in the trucks, and left our mattresses in each room, Waterworld and the Dais, leaning against the walls. The bathroom phonebook was ripped into the V's, sitting on the toilet tank. We walked Big Red down to the park and left it in the middle of the wide, white grass that crunched dryly underfoot, sky glowing its low-watt orange above us. I'd spent most of the day patching the numerous holes in the walls and respackled them with equipment and supplies borrowed from Ezekiel, painting and repainting the mismatched replacement drywall and the walls, covering up the skulls and rubbing spackle into the knife marks with my thumb, touching up the paint again with some extra primer I'd found in a rusty can in the basement. The mottled kitchen carpet flopped pale, patches of color and less color spread across from Patman's failed bleaching attempt. I took a knee to scrub at the bloodstains in the kitchen and the bathroom and the Harem. The ceiling repainted where soot and smoke had discolored it. Bleach poured on the entire bathroom, the liquid dumped raw from the bottle and my eyes aflame from it. The deadbolt replaced that Griffin kicked in. The sandbags emptied in my room and the errant holes there from misfired arrows patched. Griffin had borrowed a vacuum from Noel and was busy on the floors, great rattling from the tube as it sucked up countless pot seeds and rocks and God knows what in the Harem. Some of the thick shag carpet was singed and mottled and black so he took scissors to it, trimming the damage away, but in all, in the end, the place didn't look much different than how we'd found it. Griffin shut the machine off in the kitchen.

-Hey, what ever happened to Pussy Versus Pussy Franco?

-Holy hell, I said. I completely forgot about that cat, I said.

-When's the last time you saw it?

-No idea, I said. Two months? Three? It gave Pickle fleas and cut out.

At the mention of the name, Griffin stiffened and turned the vacuum back on. We moved the paintings last, and Hellraiser was put into Griffin's truck. He'd stay with Noel for a week or so, and I'd stay with Jessica. Figworth von Esquire was long dead, his dry leaves still clung to him like time-worn armor gone patina, foliage as dry as bay leaves, and so we gave him a hero's funeral in the backyard, setting him in the firepit and lighting him ablaze. I threw in a handful of pennies and then walked to my truck.

I looked back at Squirrel Haus as we drove in our different directions. Michelle's lights were on, and the downstairs was dark and empty, and small fire in the backyard. It looked strange, not seeing Diomedes atop the door. I drove over to Jessica's, made her dinner, and then went to work that night at a new job, copy-editing for a printing company. It was mindnumbing, but it was indoor work, and away from the cold and not as hectic as the bakery. I measured and ruled ads against proofs all night, making sure the margins were correct, I'd look for misspellings, circling those in blue pencil, and margin troubles with red, then initial it, and file it away for someone else to proof my proof, re-proof their proof of my proof, and then send it back to be reprinted. Since it was a night job, I was left mostly alone, and sat in a big office full of desks that belonged to other people, their little pictures and lives smiling up at me, anonymously, they all adrift in wide constellations. We'd be safe at Noel's and Jessica's. No interested parties knew where they lived, except Patman, and we figured he was in Old Mexico by now.

I bought some Altoids from a bartender downtown a couple of days later. I took a few one night an hour before my shift ended. He said it was ecstasy, LSD and cocaine, but it felt like strychnine, PCP and speed. I was bug-eyed by the time I left work and was hallucinating badly when I got to Jessica's. She had thrown a party the night before, taking the day off from work. I walked into the dim room full of sleeping forms that lay about in deathlike poses, them shuddering and rolling on the floor as if full of newly hatched spiders' eggs, the tiny creatures burrowing out of their flesh, and all the people they were not people, and I couldn't find Jessica. In a state of panic I maced the room of sleeping revelers and lit the posters on her apartment door on fire to prevent anyone from following me. Jessica found me in the hallway downstairs, smoking and knocking and jabbering at someone else's door, muttering bloody talk at a wall. There was a lot of bad noise between us, and she kicked me out. I'd kept most of my stuff under tarps in my truck, and nothing at Jessica's, so when I drove off in the night with the people coughing and cursing and gasping and some putting out the smoldering door, I lost nothing except everything and her.

Noel was up when I arrived at his place and offered me a rum and coke, and some coke, which helped calm me down. He listened patiently as I jabbered about vampires lying wrapped in cocoons full of spider hatchlings, and he smiled his reassuring, knowing smile. I apologized about trying to kill him when he was a zombie. I drank too much absinthe that night from a bottle Noel kept on his refrigerator, and then ended up pulling a knife on him, which he smiled at and took from me without breaking my arm, politely. I was chain-vomiting the next morning. I slept in Noel's shower, running cold water over my head, drinking liberally from its font, trying to stay hydrated, to keep water in my stomach as long as possible because I'd throw it up a minute after ingesting it. When I finally stopped hurling up the agua, and could drink without losing it, I'd never thought water could taste so good, and ran handful after handful from the shower's spigot into my mouth.

Griffin came back from work, and I was sitting on the bathtub's edge in my wet clothes. He handed me several envelopes he'd retrieved from Squirrel Haus' mailbox.

-We've got another problem, he said.

-What now?

-Angel's looking for you.

-About what? and my eyes bugged.

-Cops found the Silver Bullet.

-So?

-You might want to sit down for this.

-I am sitting down, I said.

-Okay. Get ready for this. Laurence is in the hospital. Critical condition. A few other people.

-From what, I asked. Meth lab blow up?

-No. Poisoned. And guess with what?

-I don't know, I said. Anhydrous fumes.

-That pesticide you gave to Wim. They found that bottle in the car.

-Poisoned how?

-Someone dumped that stuff in that farmhouse cistern, he said. Poisoned the whole group.

My brain was still very fuzzy from the day in Noel's vomitorium.

-Wait, I said. So why me?

-Angel said they've got a whole toxicology thing on Laurence, the bottle, the cistern.

-And how do you know all this? I asked.

-I spent four hours at the station today with Angel, Griffin said. He pulled me out of work and grilled me on just about everything. Seems the police know more than we thought.

I rolled my head in a wave of nausea, sipped from the faucet and threw it up.

-What does this have to do with me or you?

-The car had been in your name, and I might have told Angel about the squirrels you poisoned.

-When? Jesus. Why?

-It was a long time ago, you know, just workday stuff. Passing time. It was funny at the time.

-So now what?

Griffin tried to sound reassuring. Noel came in.

-Angel is just covering bases. You're not a suspect, he said.

-Suspect for what? Noel asked.

-Who is the suspect? I asked.

-Patman, Griffin said.

-So Angel knows about Patman?

I lit a nervous cigarette.

-So they think he tried to kill Laurence? I said.

Griffin shook his head.

-He wouldn't say. I got all of that out of him, and he couldn't say anything further since they're calling it an attempted murder. But my best guess is that Patman's the main suspect. I was as vague as possible, since I wanted to talk with you first.

-We need to find Wim, I said.

-If he's still in the state, I'm pretty sure he's hiding in some underground bunker somewhere.

-We've got court next week too, I said. Fat Bastard.

-I'm thinking we just skip town, Griffin said with a nod.

-I would, I said, but I've got to do that fucking counseling lockdown this weekend. If I miss it, they'll put out a warrant for me. I won't have a license anyway.

We called everyone with a remote connection to Wim or Patman, trying to gather clues. We might have been looking for a chupacabra, since there were only rumors and sightings at odd hours of the night. Some associates had heard about the poisoning, others wanted to place orders for meth, others who had placed orders wanted their product. No one had a clue where anyone was.

-Oh, and if that wasn't enough, Griffin said and handed me another envelope. I found this in the mailbox at Squirrel Haus.

I looked at the sheets. Fat Bastard was suing us for five thousand dollars for a heap of damages to the house, pinning every possible problem the house had ever had on our chests like diseased leeches. He was even suing us for building the firepit, saying it would cost three hundred dollars to remove.

The next day, I sold the Trojan Horse at a loss to some Guatemalans who wanted to drive it all the way home, saying they needed something with a solid front axle to navigate the pit-strewn roads of their homeland, but it all sounded like bullshit. I asked them if they knew Milario, holding my hands low to indicate his height, but they didn't. I bought a white Geo Tracker ragtop for a hundred bucks, with no heat, no radio, and a leaking power-steering pump. I budgeted the remainder of Wim's money to pay for the Rehab Mountain Weekend Extravaganza.

I borrowed Noel's phone and called Haley. She said she would be back in a few weeks and asked about her letter. I said I got it, and thanked her. She sounded cheery and talked of finishing her PhD. She was trying to patch things up with Monk, and her words rose with hope. I told her about Patman and Laurence, the court case. She said we'd do fine. Bootstraps, she said. I told her I would see her soon and she said she loved me before we hung up.

Angel found me the following morning after my overnight shift. I went with him to the police station. Did I know where Patman was, and why did I sell the car, and where did I get it, and did I know anything about any pesticides, and what was Wim's involvement? I rattled answers in line with instinct, vague and cagey and thin. He didn't believe me and said I would go to jail if I forgot to tell him anything, but I didn't know anything and told him as much.

-Angel, I honestly don't know where Pat is. He's obviously skipped town, and if he hasn't, he's a fucking idiot.

-I've got one more question for you. You're educated, right? Griffin told me you taught in Utah, taught college even, went to grad school here and everything. What the hell are you doing with these guys? Why are you fucking up your life like this?

-That was more than one question, I said.

He shook his head and smiled.

-Okay. Have it your way, tough guy. I'll be in touch.

-Okay, I said. Have a good day, sir.

Patman showed up at Noel's that Friday, climbing up the fire escape and in through a back window, startling everyone when he emerged from the bedroom. At the sight of him, Griffin rushed and tackled him, punching Patman in the face with every word. Patman dead-lifted Griffin and threw him down.

-They killed Pickle, you fucking piece of garbage, Griffin said, rising.

We held Griffin back, and he flailed. Patman sat up and licked the blood from his lips.

-I'm sorry, man. I didn't know.

-Let's let him explain, Noel said. What is happening here, Pat?

Patman told us the stories. Him robbing Dre, with Warrantt as getaway driver. The poisoning of Laurence. The whole bottle poured in the cistern one night. Cooking meth with Wim. The capture of Warrantt, while Patman had gotten away. Strange and tattooed nexus around which this wild-winged albatross was tethered. He grabbed an Icehouse from his coat pocket.

-Oh yeah. Wim got arrested, man.

Griffin slammed his beer on the couch, several impolite epithets ensued.

-What? Noel asked. When?

As if talking of a dialogue he'd overheard, Patman began. He'd been helping Wim cook meth, doing little chores and learning the trade. Dre had found out where they were cooking and reported the lab to the cops, who raided the place when Patman had been off buying cold medicine for a new batch, since Wim was experimenting with the P2P and couldn't quite get it right. Patman had been driving zigzags up and down, town to city to gas station and supermarket, along the Iowa-Illinois border, a two-day adventure. Back in Iowa City, he had stopped by for a bj and to do some drugs with the tranny he'd burglarized, which made Patman even later getting back to Wim, and had saved him from going to jail. He told us that he'd left in the morning and when he got back, there was police tape everywhere and a hazmat team with floodlights in the yard. Wim would do anywhere from one to five years, probably, Patman said.

-Dre did all that just to get back at me, man. It seems pretty unfair to Wim.

-How do you know it was Dre? Noel asked.

-Who else would it be, man?

Griffin stood up and left.

-I'm going to fucking kill him if he stays here any longer, he said.

I flung an empty can at Patman.

-Do you have any idea how fucking far gone you are? I said. That psycho killed Pickle, held a gun in my face and beat the shit out of me. The cops are looking for you.

Patman nodded.

-Well, you didn't do anything wrong, man. What can they do to you? It's me they're looking for, man. You've got nothing to worry about.

An hour later, Patman lit out, taking the fire escape, and Noel, Griffin, and I trekked to the Foxhead to try and triangulate Patman's tale. We drew out the series of events on a sheet of paper, arrows and roman numerals and rough dates. Pesticide to me, to Wim, to Patman, to Laurence's stomach. Plus, I had to go to the Substance Abuse Session the next morning. No amount of swill beer could loose the pall that hung over the table, until, like a dumbstruck miracle, a girl bought me a drink. The first time any girl ever had. It came on the bartop and the barkeep pointed at a cute blonde in a booth. I went over to her. She recognized me from a party a few years ago in grad school. I had no recollection of her, but lied, Of course Of course and How had she been, trying to coax out her name in a roundabout way as if I had that kind of memory. She was in a booth with a friend, an incomprehensible Scotsman who owned a vegan restaurant in town. He was always getting drunk and trying to steal people's coats, and I remembered him from my grad school days. He seemed upset that she'd bought someone else a drink. I chatted her up, hoping I didn't look strung or stressed out past the point of decent human erections. He got up to avail himself of the bathroom, and I leaned across the table to the girl, Mira, the bartender had told me. She brushed her blonde hair back behind her ear.

-We can go back to my place, if you want? she said. Say, leave in ten minutes?

-This is really not a good time for me, I said. I'm sorry. Really. I'm wanted by a criminal syndicate. Also, I have to do a weekend rehab thing this weekend.

-Rehab for what, she asked.

-DUI, I said. Nothing major.

I got her number, and she said we could meet after Happy Funtime Rehab Weekend. I went back to Noel and Griffin and gave them a shrug. We decided to leave and convene at Noel's. I put my coat on and walked outside. The Scottish guy followed us and grabbed me by the sleeve.

-Thamon koh.

-This isn't your coat. It's mine. I've had it for years. Get your hand off me.

-Whaggunnuhdoo?

-Do? Leave your drunk ass here, I said.

-Thamme koh, marfookah.

-It's not your goddamned coat.

-Yah doono um. Ahl tayme koh an arn dahm thin ah wahn.

I rolled my eyes. Griffin and Noel watched on.

-What? Speak English, I said. You immigrants are all the same. Speaking your gibberish and stealing the white man's jobs.

MacBoor grabbed my coat again, and jabbered with his brick-tongue, and I looked at Noel and Griffin. I rolled my eyes at them and knocked his hand loose.

-Seriously, I said. Don't fucking touch me again.

-Yah gwoon fuhk yar treg hud.

MacBoor came at me again. I hit him square in the nose with a right, my toes skidding a bit on the sidewalk ice. His eyes went wide and his body stiff, falling backwards like a rake into the snow. The girl ran outside, and yelled at me from her crouch, cradling his head.

-Get out of here, you animals, she said.

-I'll call you, I said. We have fun time.

-Go to hell, jerk, she said, helping the fallen man sit up.

I shrugged, and we walked back to Noel's. I woke the next day at six-thirty, made coffee and roused Noel to give me a ride to the Substance Abuse Seminar. Not saying much, we drove out to a Best Western, just off the highway and he dropped me off, waved and rolled away. I bought a couple packs of cigarettes and prepared myself for the lockdown. There were a large number of people gathered outside the main doors, smoking and talking in the thin grey light. I joined them.

-Rehab Mountain Weekend Adventure, I asked.

A thin-haired guy nodded with a smoke dangling from a lip.

-Yup. You got a light? Gonna be a long weekend. This is my second one.

We were motioned inside by a tall man with puffy white hair, registered at the desk and filled out some forms that said if we were caught drinking for the next two days we'd have to redo the weekend again, and pay for it again, too. Some people had suitcases and bags, and we took our belongings to the conference hall and sat down at long desks. A bored-looking cop with a watery smile and no service firearm greeted us and P.A.'d us until noon, when we were given loose scrambled eggs, bacon, and toast like spongy leather.

So went Rehab Happy Funtime Weekend. We were in lock down. The Gala Event Reception Room's doors remained closed, except for random and frequent smoke breaks, and we listened to a cop tell us until eight that night that we would be quizzed on everything he said at random intervals tomorrow, and that if we didn't pass three out of five quizzes that we would then be required to retake the course. Someone asked him if they'd have to pay again, and he looked at her as if he'd never heard a stupider question. The officer was trying to be friendly, trying to play Good Cop with us throughout. His talk was interspersed with a group circle. We had to move the desks to the sides of the room and talk about the times we got drunk or high, and what it all meant, and how it hurt our families, and how we were ruining the lives of those we cared most about. It was Chicken Shit for the Soul, although some people cried, head in hands, and appeared to be serious. And on the cop talked, and the counselor talked about his former addictions, and on the sophistry went.

We ate dinner at seven. Flimsy portions of roast beef and mixed vegetables that had been boiled as flavorless as the Styrofoam trays that held the grub. Room assignments and keys were read off and we trudged to our respective cells, each person quiet and begrudged. My roommate's name was Mike, an inveterate drunk, sixty I guessed, with a splotchy nose, who stripped down to his big white underwear within minutes of opening the door, his cigarette never leaving his mouth except to light another. He lifted a bottle of vodka from his suitcase and winked at me, flipping on the TV.

-Ain't safe yet to drink. They'll come round midnight and do that breath thing.

-Christ. This is like jail, I said. Will they tuck us in too?

-Hell. Ain't nuthin like jail. I been to this thing two times already.

Mike scratched unceremoniously at his off-white whiteys.

-And, he continued, I done ten months once.

-For what, I asked.

-Possession. Got myself into a little trouble with the meth.

I nodded.

-That shit is trouble. Capital T, I said.

-Trouble ain't even start to describe that shit. Take me now to drinking. Mostly.

-Me too. I'm health conscious. How'd you end up here? Traffic stop?

-Wrecked my truck driving back to my farm. Wrecked out in a field.

-How'd anyone know you wrecked if it was in a field?

-They was a house sittin in the field where I wrecked. Woke up sittin in my truck, plowed into this porch and them people just yellin and screamin.

-Heh. Jesus. You kill anyone?

-Jest a porch. Killt a porch and my truck.

-Killed your license too, I said.

-License? Hell, ain't had one of them fer years.

We weren't allowed to move around in the halls once we were in our rooms, and so we sat inside and Mike watched TV and I read the Gideon's Bible, both of us smoking heavily, the room thick with the ropy swirls that tracked like miniature galaxies and then disappeared. There was a knock at 11:34, and I opened the door. The mealymouthed cop was there with the counselor, and we each had to blow into the little machine, and so this pair went down the hall, their knocking growing fainter and then louder through our door as they went the length of rooms on one side and returned down the other. By the time the knocks got louder Mike was well into his bottle. I declined it mostly because he mouthed the whole rim when he drank, and a thin bridge of spittle connected it to his lip. More for him, he nodded, and more he had.

He fell asleep after draining half and I stood at the window and looked at the parking lot, and the cars moving by on the highway beyond, lights upon lights, in their freefalls of movement and escape. The next day, before breakfast, we were breathalyzed again. Mike stood behind me in line, fuming, and goddamning the tricky sunsabitches, stamping his feet on the cream-colored tiles, and when it was his turn, he failed and started waving his hands at the cop.

-You ain't done this last time I was here.

-Now just calm down, the cop said. We have the right to test you any time we want.

-I ain't read that in the papers I signed.

-It's all there.

-Well, damn your papers.

He grabbed the counselor's clipboard, threw it down and stormed off in order to, he said to everyone with a whoop, get fucking shitpile drunk. The survivors made it through the day, a few not passing their self-evaluation quizzes, and I called Noel for a ride from the payphone at six that evening. I stood in the cold for half an hour. He handed me a roadbeer when I got in his car and wedged my feet up into the floorboards to warm my frozen toes, the pain of thawing like the vestige of spring among the earth. Noel spun his tires in a patch of ice for effect as we drove away.

-Did you learn anything?

-Yeah, I said. Don't get caught.

-You're not going to like what's waiting for you at home.

He was right. Investigating the poisoning, and using Griffin's story of my massacre of the squirrels, Angel had ordered a hazmat test on Squirrel Haus, which of course turned up more than a trace of the chlordecone. Fat Bastard had been given a bill of fifteen grand by the EPA to cover the cost of the toxic cleanup. It was all in a tightly-written two-page letter on embossed stationary, sitting on Noel's coffee table. Fifteen grand. Just like that. Fat Bastard had a brother on the force and had caught wind of our association with the entire mess.

-How did they find us at Noel's?

-Fat Bastard's brother called my boss, who gave Fat Bastard my brother's number, since he was one of my emergency contacts, and he called my parents, who called Wim's parents, who got Noel's number from Wim.

-What? I said. Wim?

-Wim is out, Griffin said. His family bailed him out yesterday. He has to wear an ankle collar though and he's under house arrest. He's staying with them right now, I guess. No visitors allowed at Janson Mansion.

I took a beer.

-So what about Fat Bastard? I asked.

-He said he's going to pin the EPA charges on us.

-Can this get any fucking worse? I said with a long exhale.

-Probably, Noel said with a small nod.

We had court coming that Thursday, and I worked the nights away at the part-time copy-editing and proofing job. Mindcrippling. Files and the plastic bags and rulers, and red pencils and blue. I took frequent smoke breaks, sneaking past the night manager's office toward the warehouse where the huge printers whirred and people scurried around in hardhats and goggles with reams of paper and tubs of ink, and the giant presses hummed. No one noticed me coming and going, and I took no notice of them.

Wednesday afternoon, Griffin and I went to Goodwill to buy some appropriate clothes for court. The only shirt I could find that didn't have armpits stained the color of tea was too big for me, but I bought it anyway, and selected a flag tie with a shiny 'Merican flag print. Griffin located a yellow paisley shirt with buttoned loops on the shoulders like rolled epaulettes, and a square linen tie. Pants were almost impossible, and at best mine were four sizes too big, and Griffin's much the same, in brown and black respectively, a pair of pleated Dockers and some Haggar slacks. Total, fifteen dollars and eighty-seven cents.

Back at Noel's we went over our strategy for court. Griffin had called his cousin on Noel's cell phone, and we listened to his points about the courtroom on speakerphone. I had been slowly memorizing the Iowa Residential Landlord and Tenant Law the previous few weeks, twenty or so pages of legal hoopla, stocked with words that would hopefully allow us to wriggle free. The key terms his cousin told us were Good Faith, which we entered into the rental contract with, thinking Fat Bastard would fix the house as was his duty. Unconscionability was next, allowing us to put forth evidence that he willfully ignored his duties as the renter. Lastly, was Notice. Had we given him reasonable notice for Heart of Darkness and thus stopped paying rent for two or three months? The legalese was tricky. We hadn't sent any letters through certified mail, nor had we hand delivered our complaints, as per the law, but there was also the Uniform Residential Landlord and Tenant Law which defined Notice differently. He said we shouldn't have to worry about the EPA fine. That was circumstantial.

§ 1.304. [Notice] (a) A person has notice of a fact if (1) he has actual knowledge of it, (2) he has received a notice or notification of it, or (3) from all the facts and circumstances known to him at the time in question he has reason to know that it exists. A person "knows" or "has knowledge" of a fact if he has actual knowledge of it. (b) A person "notifies" or "gives" a notice or notification to another person by taking steps reasonably calculated to inform the other in ordinary course whether or not the other actually comes to know of it. A person "receives" a notice or notification when (1) it comes to his attention; or (2) in the case of the landlord, it is delivered at the place of business of the landlord through which the rental agreement was made or at any place held out by him as the place for receipt of the communication; or (3) in the case of the tenant, it is delivered in hand to the tenant or mailed by registered or certified mail to him at the place held out by him as the place for receipt of the communication, or in the absence of such designation, to his last known place of residence. (c) "Notice," knowledge of a notice or notification received by an organization is effective for a particular transaction from the time it is brought to the attention of the individual conducting that transaction, and in any event from the time it would have been brought to his attention if the organization had exercised reasonable diligence.

It all seemed pretty clear cut. Fat Bastard had full knowledge of the problem when we'd tried to repair Heart of Darkness in the first month of living there. We could use this fact to derail his accusations about the damage to the house and thus his whole case would be shot down. If I had the cassette tape, our case would be even stronger. We'd simply have to ride out the EPS part of things. Griffin called his boss and took the next day off. I tried calling Misha to see whether she knew anyone from law school who could help us, but she didn't answer her phone. I went out that night alone, walking the paths slick with ice and footprints. I stopped in the Airliner, hoping to see Jessica. The place, jammed with bodies, offered no view, so I left. I took the alley and a voice rang behind me. I turned to see the Nazi gang, six strong, shiny leather jackets backlit. Mullethawk ran forward with a sneer, the others in tow.

-I thought that was you, he said.

-What are the fucking odds? I muttered and leaned forward, bracing for the inevitable.

In a diaphanous morning light we dressed and duded up. My

face was a puffed mess of splotchy reds, all gash and bruise. Griffin put butterfly bandaids on the cuts, saying it might help us win sympathy points. I put on my new old clothes, and Noel did my tie, and I threw on my Dance Dance Russian Revolution coat, and went outside and had a cigarette. Noel wished us luck and we drove downtown toward the courthouse, the world white with snow, and shining in a sun that felt new. My cigarette froze to the gash in my lip and pulled free a chunk of skin when I took it from my mouth.

We parked and shoveled a handful of nickels into the meter, the early traffic still weak, listless drivers idling by down the uncrowded streets. Walking to the courthouse we got coffee at the Java Casa, and Olateju was working. She listened, her eyes sympathetic and worried when she looked at my busted face, as Griffin explained our predicament, and told him to call her later once we'd won. They hadn't spoken in a long time now, he told me as we walked out.

We saw Fat Bastard parking at the courthouse when we arrived, taking his place in a handicapped spot, slipping the placard onto his rearview mirror. He waved us over to his truck and rolled down his window.

-I'm sorry it had to come to this, boys. Wheeze wheeze. You get that hazmat report? What the hell were you thinking?

-You're not sorry. You made up all that damage, I said. We repaired everything in that house, even all the broken shit that was there when we moved in. That hazmat thing wasn't us.

-Looks someone already worked you over pretty well. Wheeze wheeze. You get in a fight?

-No worse than what you're trying to do, Griffin said.

-I guess we'll see what the judge says. Wheeze.

-We've got pictures and everything else, Griffin told him.

-You've got your proof, and I've got mine. Wheeze.

-What proof could you have? It's bullshit, I said.

-You guys look like clowns. Wheeze.

-Why wouldn't we? Griffin said. This whole case is a circus. We're just dressing the part.

-Let's see how the judge likes that, Fat Bastard said and rolled up his window.

Heels of hard leather clacked and echoed around the courthouse entryway and halls, as clerks and others shuffled around, preparing the day's doings. We had to fill out some forms since we were representing ourselves. The secretary handed us a pen, but we had our own. I signed mine Dunham Outis Goldberg, and my place of residence 123 Cockaigne Place. The secretary asked where the street was located, and I explained that my family was from the old country. She looked puzzled, and took the papers and told us we'd be in courtroom number two, with mediation at nine.

We sat down in an adjoining room with a lawyer. Fat Bastard on one side, and we on the other of a series of connected tables. He presented a laundry list of bullshit, saying that we had ruined the house, not paid our rent, flooded the basement, drilled holes in the floor, had allowed animals to take refuge inside against his orders, wrecked a closet due to maltreatment of the living space, and etc. It was only somewhat true. We showed the mediating lawyer a series of pictures we'd taken after we moved in, water pouring in through Heart of Darkness like a spigot, the rotten basement, the exterior, the squirrel hole. How, we posited, could all this damage have possibly happened in so little time? I retrieved our coup-de-grace and laid it in front of the barrister, our uninitialed lease, the original, the only interpretation of which was that we'd taken issue with the condition of the house at signing, which in a legal definition, I argued, would constitute Prior Notice of the problems he was blaming us for, rendering his argument invalid as well as the trumped-up damages Fat Bastard was levying against us. I quoted liberally from the Iowa Rental Code, and the lawyer nodded quietly when I spoke, which made me feel more confident.

Fat Bastard tried to counter that we had signed the lease, but the lawyer stopped him and said that the lack of our initials in the box meant he bore the burden of proof. He mentioned the EPA report, but it was a different case, the lawyer said, which gave me some more confidence. The lawyer, trying to save the court our squabble, asked what we thought would be fair to pay, to which Griffin replied nothing. We had paid our rent and in good conscience until Fat Bastard had broken the Good Faith agreement by refusing to fix anything, bla bla bla civil disobedience. The lawyer agreed that there was sufficient evidence to proceed to trial bla bla, and we adjourned and went outside for a cigarette until our case would be heard. Smiles abounded outside as we puffed away, the day grown warm and redolent. We thought maybe we'd countersue him for something. We'd get out from under this and be done with this long and weird chapter. Though the house was worse for wear, it certainly wasn't in any worse shape than when we moved in, we reasoned. A little more toxic, perhaps, but we would worry about that later. We had a few hours until court and went for a late breakfast and Bloody Mary's, looked over our case a few more times, and then strode back in the clear cold toward the courthouse, and into courtroom number two.

The judge gave us an odd look as we were called, trying to interpret our clothing and my lasagna-like face, but she addressed Fat Bastard by his first name, asking about his children and he hers. Griffin punched me under the desk where we sat before the judge's high desk. She was birdfaced and hawkish, round glasses and a grey mushroom shaped coiffe. We all palmed the Bible and right hands were raised. I introduced into evidence twenty-three photographs, the lease, and I tried to introduce two affidavits, notarized and signed by my brother attesting to the house's sorry state, and another from the previous tenants, testifying on paper to Fat Bastard's foul treatment of them and his unwillingness to fix anything in the house. He objected and was sustained on the letters, saying that he had no prior knowledge of them. The judge said we should have subpoenaed our witnesses and wouldn't allow their testimony.

Fat Bastard introduced a Xeroxed copy of the lease, magically including our initials, in direct contradiction of our original document. He introduced a copy of a letter I'd typed him once in a semi-drunk state when he'd been pressing us for the rent back in August. It was blurry and almost entirely illegible except the part that said, "We'll get you're your money, etc. etc." Fat Bastard said he'd lost the original. I looked it over and complained that he hadn't brought these documents up in mediation, and cited my letter from Zeke, and then tried to cite my evidence. She informed me that he doesn't have to present anything in mediation since the evidence is not sworn. The only part that was visible was a paragraph toward the end in which I'd promised to pay him the remaining rent. My name was clear on the document, which was enough to enter it. I tried objecting to this, saying that the letter was out of context and had been written because of the house's condition. She rejected my plea, and overruled me. El Fatto then brought out a thirteen-page spreadsheet printout of the various damages to the house, and then the EPA report. It read like an autopsy of the house as we'd inherited it on day one, blaming us for everything from trash in the yard to holes in the exterior wall, to aggravating structural damage, and ruining the carpet in the kitchen.

-I object, Griffin said. Is he going to blame us for 9/11 and AIDS and childhood obesity and the jimmyleg now?

The judge warned him with contempt. Fat Bastard continued, testifying that we had overcharged him for repairs. False testimony. No bill of sale, no receipt. The judge asked us whether we could prove the amount of time and money we had spent repairing the house. We said no. He produced from his swollen, liver-colored folder a copy of the receipt he had given us, calling us liars and charlatans.

The next part happened very swiftly. The judge looked at the two piles of evidence, sifting them and simply said that given Fat Bastard's status in the community and the professionalism of his proffered documents, she found in his favor. $5000, $2500 each. Her gavel came down and it was over. The EPA case, though she said with a sick benevolence, would be waived, since it was too circumstantial for small claims and would have to be pursued in a different court. I asked her how his documents were admissible and ours weren't. We had originals and he had forged copies. She said judgment had been rendered. Stunned, we rose. Stunned, we left. Fat Bastard remained seated. He had another case after ours, against another tenant, and pulled out another sheaf of printed bullshit. We passed the incoming defendant. He'd just watched our well-reasoned and well-argued and well-documented case go to shit by the power of the spreadsheet. Beaten by Microsoft Excel.

-Fuck you, Bill Gates, Griffin muttered.

I swept outside in a rush and threw my folder and the printout of the Rental Laws into the snow next to the courthouse, the pages scrabbling in the wind across the tundraed space. A law student trailed us, asking whether she could interview us for a class she was taking. Griffin spat on the ground and yelled her away. It was one o'clock, and we took a booth at Joe's Tavern, ordering tacos and several shots of mescal with as many beer backs as the bartender would supply, telling him we'd just lost a court case. He looked at our clothes as if to say of course, and we walked our drinks to a table. Griffin looked at the various wounds on the table, notes of lovers and fighters gouged into the surface.

-What just happened? he said.

-I have no fucking idea.

-She completely ignored the pictures, he said. The fucking

lease.

-The law doesn't mean shit, I said.

-Not here.

-It's like they knew each other, I said.

-He's probably in there every week, suing poor schmucks like us.

-Think about it. He runs and owns two hundred rental properties. That's how much in property tax?

-Yeah. And property tax pays whose salary. Fucking bitch judge.

Noel couldn't believe we'd lost to the tune of the total sum, and offered some consolation cocaine. Griffin called Olateju and went to see her after her shift ended. Dre and his hooligans knocked on Noel's door that afternoon. They'd tracked Patman, learning that he'd been there recently. I called my brother and asked him if I could stay with him for a week or two, and he sounded iffy on the phone, and I offered to stay out of sight in the basement. He consented and I hung up. That night at work I was told that they didn't need me anymore, the manager's dry and crinkly voice very matter of fact. I saw Misha later that night, walking around downtown, bundled and wrapped in woolen things for the cold. I waved to her and came closer. I hadn't seen her in months.

-What happened to your face, Dunham?

-A misunderstanding, I said. Some bigots had a problem. How have you been?

-Good. Busy with classes. I'm writing another paper for a law review. You?

-You wouldn't believe me. You have time for a drink?

-Like I said, I've got that paper. What happened?

-I was arrested and framed by the police after a murder in the house, then a friend started a drug war, attempting to kill one of the dealers, which spilled over onto me and Griffin. There's more. What's your article about?

-Philately, she said.

-I never knew you were in to stamps.

-It's about my grandfather.

-The mailman that used to work for Dutch Schultz, I asked.

-Yes. It's about his stamp collection.

-So it's a memoir?

-Sort of, she said. Why didn't you call me when you were arrested?

-I tried to. I didn't think you'd help.

-I might have, had I known, she said.

-Doesn't matter now. You dating anyone?

-Yes.

-May I ask whom, I asked.

-Someone. You wouldn't know her.

-Rejoined the Sapphic Sisterhood, eh?

-Don't be rude, she said. Just this once can you not be an asshole?

-No, I'm kidding, I said. You know I'm just jealous. I'm happy for you.

-Then stop being rude.

-Sorry. Are you happy? I asked.

-Yes.

-I'm sorry, I said.

-What?

-That's good, I said. Someone deserves to be.

-Take care of yourself, please, she said, and touched at the bruises on my forehead.

Her feet and shoulders then moved askance, indicating a desire to leave, and what else was there to say? I gave her a hug, and she me. She put her earplugs back in each, left then right, the same order she put in her contact lenses every morning, and pushed play on the device, the screen's light shining there in her coat pocket through the fabric on her left breast, and she looked at me and tried to smile, and the little light faded there above her heart, and she walked away.

I went feral. I stayed underground, living in my brother's basement, far from Iowa City, down in the cold earth. I emerged only to walk to buy beer and slices of pizza from Casey's. I never went upstairs. News filtered in from above me for weeks, and I rarely went out. Wim showed up one night, knocking on the basement door. He told me that Laurence was in critical condition and that they were trying to pin conspiracy and first-degree murder on Patman. He was pulling up stakes and fleeing the state, heading for parts unknown. I didn't bother asking whether I could borrow any money. He talked fast, and we hugged and he was gone. Griffin called a few days later and told me that Wim had been arrested. He'd cut off his ankle tracker and driven off with a bunch of camping supplies, hoping to make it out to Redwood National Forest and disappear in another commune somewhere, but he was caught by a park ranger in Nebraska while swimming illegally after hours in a state park lake. He'd tried to deflect and buy time, saying he didn't have his identification, but the ranger had already gone through his pants on the shore. He'd be shipped back to face all the charges, and now as a captured fugitive. It was a federal crime to cross state lines.

My brother called down into the basement a few days later, saying I had a message from a guy named Monk. When I called him back, he said he'd been trying to track me down, but I'd disappeared. Haley had died in Toronto of a heroin overdose. The trustifarian, Conrad, had found her pale and lifeless body, choked with vomit, a few mornings before and that the cops had come to Monk's house, her last known residence, to tell him. It was too clean, all of it, my life like an accountant's ledger, lined and ruled and dictated, and all red scrawls that ran the columns down. I told Monk I would come by soon, hung up, and went back downstairs.

That night, thick in a bottle of cheap whiskey, I sat staring at the whitewashed cinderblocks of my borrowed hole. Nothing. No thoughts, no memories, no emotions. I could see my breath at each exhalation, and watched it fade into the color of air. I got up. I opened the door. I went outside. It was cold. The snow was half-shin deep, the moon bluing everything. The lights in my brother's house were on, in all the houses up and down the block. Through the window I could see Kate sitting on the couch, holding Isis, watching the television. My brother was in the kitchen washing some dishes. I walked through the backyard and the trees scourging the wind, the wind sharpening the branches keen and bare. I walked into the pristine field behind his house. A white expanse of snow bordered by the acres of woodlots and trees, black.

I made it halfway through the field and I dropped to my knees, whiskey spilling into the snow, and put my face into the hardpack white. For a moment nothing came. Nothing. I couldn't see Haley's face at all. Couldn't draw her to mind except a body, except a mouth, full of bile and maggots and just that, a mouth. Then a tremor started in my feet, and a deep guttural sobless and speechless moan in my throat, my lungs, my stomach. I couldn't breathe. I balled my fists. I couldn't sit up. I beat the bottle against my temples. It felt like the back of my throat was being scraped out by the hoarse and inveterate sound in me, like barbed wire being pulled out of my stomach, across my tongue and mouth and breath, like a fakir drawing out yards of swallowed gauze. My hands and head and knees and feet were numb in the snow. An illumined contrail hung in the sky, a ghost of other people's motion forward.

My eyes felt like napalm, my lungs like dirt. I wanted to be set on fire. Stars tearing at my teeth. Their gravity palpable. My jaw would not unclench. She was dead. Her smile was dead. Her brain was dead. Her electricity dead. I beat my fists and the bottle against my skull. This body was words, spit out over the tongue of the earth and what we say has no definition or meaning and what is spoken dies filterless in the snow. The bottle rang dully off my head where I beat it, hoping it would break, but the bottle held and bludgeoned my cranium until blood ran into my mouth, and the taste of it like a coin.

A few minutes later I could finally sit up, but I couldn't breathe, my stomach was clenched and splayed, chest heaving, only cold cracks of wintered air seeping in the lungs. The snot and tears and blood and spit and snow dribbled. I sat there for I don't know how long. There was just the wind moving across a ragged ball of rock, and gravity holding against it, the cold wind speaking me like a name, and speaking my cold dead friend no more.

I sat there a long time, until there was no more room to sit, and I got up, knees aching and pinpricked by cold, and I walked back into the basement. Zeke was there.

-What happened?

-Haley's dead.

Quiet for a while.

-I'm sorry, he said. Jesus, Dunham, I'm sorry. Do you need anything?

I wiped my mouth.

-You got any money? he said. Need anything? A job? You got money?

-Some.

-Okay, and he said, put a hand on my shoulder, and went upstairs.

Ezekiel gave me a job spraying varnish on some redwood siding for an upcoming project. I stood in his garage, the fine and toxic mist jetting from the nozzle in the cold, the compressor's motor winding up and down and noisy. Zeke came out to check the progress and offered me work on the siding project if I wanted. I told him I did. He said maybe the next summer we could go out and frame up the cabin in Colorado. I told him that would be good. He said he was sorry about everything. I thanked him, set the sprayer down and went into the basement. I lay down on the sleeping bag with no thought of anything. A scratching near the wall where black ants moved in their line, the murmur there of them. Their procession ran the entire wall, little vessels, the murmur of them there.

A clear afternoon a few days later, I was smoking and staring out the little window in the basement set above the washer and dryer, blowing the smoke out the aperture because I didn't want to hurt the baby, and because it was too cold outside. It was Thursday maybe. I saw a figure walking out in the white field behind the house, a dark form which stopped in the middle of the bright snow and glint. I knew him. He was Zeke's neighbor, an old farmer who'd gotten rich by selling his land to a corporation and retired to the small quiet of Tiffin. He had Alzheimer's, my brother had told me.

I walked outside, threw my cigarette into the snow. I trudged up to him through the ankle-deep crust. He watched me walk up, and when I got close to him, I could see that he had been crying, his bright blue eyes foggy with tears and senility. He had no boots on. He wiped his tears away in the biting air. I put my hand on his shoulder.

-Hello, there, sir. You need any help?

-Well, it's the goddamndest thing, the man said. I know I live around here, but I can't quite tell where.

-I know where you live. I'll take you back to your wife.

-Yes, I know, he said. I grew up around here. I know that much.

-She'll take care of you. Let me help you back inside. It's cold out here. Come on, sir. Mr. Freer, sir, I'll get you home. Come with me, it's right there.

I pointed at his house, two away from my brother's, down the hill. I looked at the snow. His tracks were all over the place. He'd been out here a while, wandering in his overalls and spring jacket. I felt like maybe I should carry him back. She had diabetes, a bad case that worsened in the past year, which made her legs useless, Zeke had said. She sat indoors all day, and could no longer take care of Joe like she had, and now as he fell further down into the mixture of memory and delusion, it was nearly impossible to help.

-That's not my house.

-Sure it is. I know for a fact, I said. You're my brother's neighbor. You live right there.

-I did not grow up in that house, he said. My house burned years ago. My dad bought the farm after that. It's not my house.

His voice was rising, stained with cold and terror, a small tremor in his hands. I tried to calm him as best I could.

-You live right next to my brother, Ezekiel, and he shovels your sidewalk every time it snows. He brought his baby by your house three days ago. Do you remember?

-Yes, yes. Beautiful baby she is, he said.

-Yes, Isis. You know her. And her father, my brother, lives right next to you. Just two houses over. Come on, keep walking.

It took five minutes of coaxing him along through the hardscrabble snow to get him to the door, but he refused to go inside. His back stoop was icy in patches, and I didn't want him slipping. His toes were bright red.

-That's not where I lived. It's not, he said.

-Can we just go inside? Your feet are going to get frostbite if they haven't already. Come on, sir, right inside. Let's just warm up a bit.

I opened the screen door, and beat loudly against the old, solid wood door. I opened it, and called inside.

-Ma'am? Ms. Freer? I'm Ezekiel's brother. I found Joe out walking around.

I peered back into the warm house. It smelled of bread and

knitting, the yellow odors of a house long lived in, quietly and warmly, that weird comfort in the homes of old Midwesterners. His wife, Jan, was asleep on the couch, a shawl and blanket over her shoulders and lap. I led Joe inside, him protesting and holding at the doorjamb.

-Ma'am, I said. Excuse me?

She sat up, startled, and pulling her glasses on from the tether around her neck.

-What's that? Joe?

-Ma'am, I'm sorry to scare you. I'm Ezekiel's brother. We met a few months ago, remember? I found Joe out walking in the snow. I'm not sure how long he was out there.

-Joe, she said. Joseph?

He looked at her.

-That's not my wife, he said. I don't live here.

He was crying again, and I led him into the living room, to the seat next to Jan.

-Of course you live here, Joseph. I'm Jan, your wife. Sit down, sit down.

I eased him into the chair. He seemed terrified, but compliant.

-Could you get his socks, please, dear? My old legs are useless, and I can't get around much anymore. They're just right there on that shelf behind you.

I slipped the wet socks off of Joe's red, cracked feet. I put his slippers on him, and turned him toward the kerosene space heater with its feeble heat.

-Ma'am, is there anyone you want me to call? Maybe have someone come over?

-Yes, yes, she said. Our son's number is there on the board, near the phone in the kitchen. His name is Joe Junior, listed there as Junior. Oh, it's such a thing to get old and nothing works anymore.

She shook her head, bemused at everything in the world and she smiled at Joe and spoke quietly to him. I put a blanket around Joe's shoulders and a towel around his feet, and went to the kitchen. There was an old rotary phone and a wooden placard next to it, with God Bless this House engraved into it, and a yellowed list of numbers. Pictures of them all on the fridge, old Xmas cards and some drawings. I called their son, and explained what had happened. He thanked me, and I hung up the phone. I went back and told Jan that they were on their way, and she thanked me, and said that I didn't have to wait around. She could take care of Joe, and she had just dozed off earlier and forgot to lock the door, and would I mind locking it on the way out.

I twisted the lock on the handle, and waved back at them. Jan waved. Joe sat there. I shut the door and went out into the gangly cold, drooping and high and white in all the air. I walked through the other neighbor's backyard, and down the stairs and into the earth again, and lay down on my sleeping bag on the hard concrete floor. We love and we die and we love.

Years before when Zeke had bought the house from the shut-in Korean War vet, the basement had been full of dirt, rock hard, permafrosted from years of neglect and deep winters. It was like mining, chipping away with pickaxes swung sideways because of the low ceiling. Like excavating a buried city. Toward the back of the basement there was barely two feet from the dirt to the joists, the whole room flooded with muck that had washed in through the paneless windows every spring, and then frozen in the later months, a thick integument of imbricated soil the consistency of granite. I felt like Schliemann unearthing Troy.

Over a month of work, we'd uncovered a small couch, animal bones, old toys the color of age, a deep freeze that held dried shapes of things long underground. Day by day we'd worked, chipping away, hauling the clumps of dirt out with a rope pulley and wheelbarrow up and out the drop door to a growing pile in the yard. As the job wore on, eventually, nearing the back wall we found a number of mason jars, most broken, that held dark viscous liquids and shapes of unidentifiable vegetable matter. Some we recovered and discarded, and others were shattered by the earth, and others by our tools. Digging further in one day, alone, I broke open an unseen jar with the pick. The jar had been on the bottom shelf of a mangled metal frame. I bent over to look in the jar-shaped cavity and saw a snake. A two-headed snake, preserved in yellowed alcohol, body a whitegrey tube of loose flesh. The jar had been on its side, and bits of skin and scale floated and swirled in the recessed pocket, resembling a footprint filled with water. I picked the fragile mutant up with a stick and placed it in a coffee can filled with mineral spirits by the door. Ezekiel came down later from where he'd been working upstairs to talk and dropped a cigarette into the can which cuncussed with a whumping boom, the contents aflame and immolating. Zeke jumped and immediately put a chunk of wood over the can, killing the oxygen.

-What are you trying to do, burn my house down before I even move in?

-Goddammit, I found a two-headed snake buried in the dirt here. I put it in that can to keep it until I got some formaldehyde or something.

He looked inside the smoldering can.

-A two-headed snake? he said. Bullshit.

Days bore days that did not move, stunted and grey and washed with cold in every minute. Working in the garage, I looped songs on the CD player, sprayed vaporized particles of red stain on the salmon-colored redwood while my feet went numb. Expensive and lovely the redwood. Bleareyed and sleepless, I would stand there in the cold garage, inhaling fumes in the small place, spraying the long boards with two thin layers of weather-resistant varnish. Then flip each board on its rack, and spray the back side. I did this in days of noon, and went to the basement, sitting on the hard cold floor. I didn't want to go upstairs unless it was really necessary. I didn't want to see the baby, her eyes bright and smiling. I lay on my sleeping bag and the little camping mat, towels hung over the two windows to block the light, with my hands behind my head and no thoughts would come, nauseous with the fumes from the garage, head drained of words. I would then go to the garage. The spray gun's pump would whistle, and the spray would issue, and what color was anything anyway?

I saw Griffin a few days after Thanksgiving, over at Noel's. Dre's goons had caught Patman at his tranny friend's and beat him well into brain damage. He was in a coma in the hospital. If he recovered, he'd face trial for murder. Dre and his crew had disappeared. There was nothing much left for us in Iowa City except debts and death. Noel and Griffin and I signed a bloodpact, promising to visit Asia within five years. We started a bank account in Noel's name, Griffin and I contributing five each to the minimum fifty. Griffin said he'd visited Patman in the hospital, but there was nothing left of him except some basic motor function. Wim was awaiting transfer to a federal pen. Griffin had managed to repair things in California with Layna, and would be heading west after visiting his parents. He'd sojourn in Arizona with Kell, too. I had plans to go see Treble and his wife in Colorado, crash there for a few weeks and try to find work there with a college or construction crew. My license would expire soon because of the deferred judgment. I still hadn't paid the lawyer. Go West, young men, we concluded.

Noel wasn't home, so Griffin and I drove out into the country, weeds and dead willow stalks upcrept from the snow. Grey skies bright with refraction, pale and long, a dumb smeariness to them, and the dark trees stood along the hillocks like withering columns that couldn't bear the weight of so much nothing any longer. We drove in silence mostly, radio off, cigarettes a final currency and vocabulary. We wound down the gravel roads and the half-melt snow, ice. Arriving at an area outside of town designated for shooting, Griffin pulled a Sig Sauer and Nazibear from under his seat, and shook them both with a smile. We walked around the range. No one else was there, and piles of junk lay about, riddled with holes. Fridges, microwaves, TVs, signs, a car door. A child's rocking horse. Innumerable cans and bottles punctured and shattered. The river wended its marshy way and was the color of the sky, sliding along fifty feet behind the berm that rose to block the bullets from skipping off into the woods. A .22 can carry for a mile. I loaded the gun, .40. He set the grinning bear on a post.

-Where'd you get this? I asked. The Sig.

-It's Kell's, he said. It was at my parents'. I took it after Thanksgiving.

We took turns shooting at Nazibear. Griffin nicked an ear and got the left arm, parts of the grinning bear chipping, and more striking only air. There were three shots left, I missed the first two. Griffin took the gun and walked to Nazibear, took aim. Its head poofed a little blast of white powder, the gaily-colored forehead gone, Nazibear reeled slow and toppled from the stump. Griffin walked back and slapped me on the shoulder.

-Sun-ripened Jesus, he said. That motherfucker's finally gone.

- Well, we couldn't let him outlive us.

-It looks like your face is healing up okay, he said, rubbing his neck.

-I wish I could say the same for my liver and soul. And my life. Boohoo, right?

Griffin nodded, silent for a moment, and took a solemn tone.

-I'm sorry about Haley, D. I don't think I really told you yet. I didn't know how.

-I know, Griff. Thanks. I appreciate it. I'm sorry too. Sorry about Pickle and every other fucking thing.

-You doing okay?

-Yeah. You?

-Once we're clear of this place. How's Monk?

-Same as me, I said. I went into town the other day and we got shitpile drunk, during the sleetstorm, and drank and slipped and cried all over the ice. He's not taking it very well.

-Are you taking it okay? he asked.

-I honestly can't process anything anymore. It's too much. It's ridiculous.

Griffin lit a smoke, and his eyes were solemn.

-Tell him I'm sorry.

-I will. Thanks, I said. Back to California, huh.

-Looks that way, he said. I've got to get out of here. Time to flee. Try to make things work out with Layna. How long will you be in Colorado?

-No idea, I said. Treble said I could crash on their couch as long as I want, but I don't want to wear out my welcome. I might just go and live on the land. Go rogue. Off the grid. Maybe live there till summer when Zeke comes out and we build the cabin.

-What? Griffin asked. Just camp out in the Colorado wilderness in the middle of winter? Why not come visit me in California where it's warm?

Palm down, I spread my arms and smiled.

-Why not be a mountain man? I'll be like Jeremiah Johnson and fight Injuns. We've got a tool shed out there on the land. I'll clear it out and live in it.

- The offer still stands, he said. Give me a few months to sort things out and then come out and visit. Oh, I drove by Squirrel Haus the other day and you won't believe it. The whole place is sided. Vinyl siding, and I think they're putting on a new roof. Looks brand new.

-What about the EPA thing?

-Your tax dollars hard at work, but not mine, he smiled.

I lit another cigarette, nodding.

-You tell your parents you're leaving? I asked.

-Yeah. What could they say? Jesus loves the little children, and all that baloney parade.

-He sure doesn't love us, I said. I think I might spend a little time down there with my folks before Colorado. They're getting up there in age.

-Prodigal son style?

-Nah, I said. I just feel like I should. Was Michelle still at Squirrel Haus?

Griffin sniffled a bit.

-No idea, he said. I don't think so. There was a sign in the front that said For Rent.

-The Fat Bastard that Could. You're not going to pay him either?

-Let it go to a collection agency. I'll still never pay. Nothing from nothing.

There was a long silence and Griffin fiddled with the pistol.

-Can you believe it all, I said. Haley. Pickle. Wim and Patman. The fucking court case. Drug wars. Everything.

-Well, we're both heading west, D. Things have to get better, right? Just like in the movies.

-Giddyup, young man, I said. Straight into the cliché.

-Yeah, he said. Roll the credits and cue the tumbleweeds.

I smiled.

-Weird angles, he said and punched my arm. You know, it's not like I expect karma to give me a reacharound, but after this year, I think we're due.

-Lives in the lower case. By the Musk of Jovan, we are cursed, I said.

-Pork and dreams, he said, rubbing his stomach.

We laughed and I started coughing and spat a dark constellation of blood into the thin dusting of snow, copper taste in my mouth. The air was clear and our breath stood in it opaque and unmoving, diaphanous second selves. I looked down at the ground.

-Jesus, I have to quit smoking, I said. These things will kill you.

-Come on, Dunham, do you really want to live forever?

He smiled and I looked at him.

Yes, I said. Yes.

Acknowledgments

My sincere thanks to my friends and family in America and Korea. You know who you are. My thanks to the following journals where some of these poems have appeared: Gut Cult, Past Simple, 2 Rivers. Thanks to Sora Mayberg, Matt Beckman, Nina Gunnell and Lee Da Yung for their feedback. Thanks and sincere apologies to Kim Lina. My thanks to Lily Adu for her kindness many years ago. And especial thanks to Diane, without whom nothing is possible.

About the author

Dustin Hellberg is an assistant professor with Yonsei University. He graduated from the Iowa Writer's Workshop in poetry at the age of 24. He is a PhD candidate with EGS in Switzerland, working with the philosophy of Charles Peirce. He currently lives in Seoul, South Korea and is working on a novel and novella.